This is Sharon Ellery's third book published by Austin Macauley Publishers. She still resides in London.

I was inspired by the ITV program *Long Lost Family!* Those families had been ripped apart due to their circumstances.

So I would like to dedicate this book to the families that have been affected by stories like this.

Sharon Ellery

SECRETS OR LIES

AUSTIN MACAULEY PUBLISHERS™
LONDON * CAMBRIDGE * NEW YORK * SHARJAH

Copyright © Sharon Ellery 2024

The right of Sharon Ellery to be identified as author of this work has been asserted by the author in accordance with sections 77 and 78 of the Copyright, Designs and Patents Act 1988.

All rights reserved. No part of this publication may be reproduced, stored in a retrieval system, or transmitted in any form or by any means, electronic, mechanical, photocopying, recording, or otherwise, without the prior permission of the publishers.

Any person who commits any unauthorised act in relation to this publication may be liable to criminal prosecution and civil claims for damages.

This is a work of fiction. Names, characters, businesses, places, events, locales, and incidents are either the products of the author's imagination or used in a fictitious manner. Any resemblance to actual persons, living or dead, or actual events is purely coincidental.

A CIP catalogue record for this title is available from the British Library.

ISBN 9781035863754 (Paperback)
ISBN 9781035863761 (ePub e-book)

www.austinmacauley.com

First Published 2024
Austin Macauley Publishers Ltd®
1 Canada Square
Canary Wharf
London
E14 5AA

I would like to thank Alison for her help with the Colorado side of my book, also Glynis, who has encouraged me every step of the way.

Other books by Sharon Ellery

Siblings
Shadows in the Rainbow

Chapter 1

"Boom, boom, boom, boom, congratulations and celebrations when I tell everyone that you're in love with me. Congratulations and jubilations! I want the world to know I'm happy as can be," sang out Cliff Richard on the record player. David was swirling Chrissy around the dance floor, which was really inside her mum's sitting room. It was the happiest day of her life; she had married David that lunchtime, the wedding was in the local registry office, and the reception after photos was back at her mum and dad's house for a cold buffet. That's how it was in those days. Get married, have your reception at home, and then off on your honeymoon. David hadn't told her where they were going yet; it was a surprise. The fondant fancies had all gone now; she liked them but didn't really get a look in with all of the kids, but never mind, everyone was enjoying themselves.

The music was booming out of the record player; Chrissy's dad, Phil, was the DJ, and he was loving it. He had put his tie around his head; he thought it looked cool, but Pam thought he looked ridiculous. He was happy; his youngest daughter had just gotten married, and they still had her elder sister, Diane, living at home with no intention of moving out. Chrissy had worn a lovely straight, long white dress to the floor, her hair down, and a white floral Alice band on her head. She had a short veil, but it all looked lovely, and she looked stunning. At 18, she looked just like a child bride, but she was a married lady now. David, on the other hand, wore his favourite suit—well, his only suit—it was navy blue. He wore a white shirt, a blue tie, and black shiny brogue shoes. Definitely a gentleman.

With his dark hair slicked back, he looked rather handsome. David was a bit older than Chrissy; he was 22. Her parents weren't too happy about it at first, but they slowly came around. The wedding was supposed to be the following summer, but it was brought forward as Chrissy was in the family way and didn't want anyone to really know at the time they thought they could get away with having a honeymoon baby. Everyone was up dancing; it had been a great day, but it was getting nearly to six o'clock. If they wanted to get on their honeymoon, Chrissy had better change so they could leave. Her mum went up to her bedroom with her so she could help her out of her wedding dress. She had a pale blue suit that she could still get into; once they left the reception and were out of sight of the guests, she could undo the button so she could breathe again.

Her mum kissed her goodbye, as did her dad. Diane was starting to cry; she was only older than Chrissy by two years, so she felt a little sad but delighted because she had the bedroom to herself. Well, at least for two weeks, she would have to move into the box room as Chrissy and David were coming back home to live until they could get themselves sorted out. David's mum, dad, and nan all came out to say goodbye to him and Chrissy; they only lived around the corner, so they would still see him when they got back. The cab was getting a little impatient. David's dad put their cases in the boot of the car; they all had their hugs, and they then got into the car. The cab driver drove off, and they were all waving to them, and they waved back at the crowd that had assembled there.

"Where to, mate?" asked the driver.

"The station, please," David replied.

Chrissy looked at her husband lovingly.

"Where are we going, David?" she asked him.

"It's a surprise; you will know soon enough." He smiled at his new bride.

They had had a busy few weeks, and the wedding had been arranged rather quickly in the circumstances. They pulled up outside the station; the driver opened up the boot and took out their luggage. David found a porter who was willing to help; he paid the cab, and they went inside to the ticket office and bought their tickets.

"Two return tickets to Devon, please?" asked David. "Oh, Devon, I have always wanted to go to Devon, David. Thank you," said Chrissy.

He picked up the tickets, read the monitors, then made their way to the platform. Thankfully, it was where they were; there were no stairs to go up and down, but there would be a way back.

They were on the platform for only about ten or fifteen minutes before their train pulled in. Once they got seated, Chrissy unbuttoned her skirt again. Thank goodness, when they get there, she can take it off. It was so hot; it was nearly the middle of August, and she was starting to swell a little. She was only a few months pregnant, but she had already put on half a stone. She was quite a slim young lady, so this was a bit of a shock to her. They were on the train for about two and a half hours. They pulled into Devon Station just after 9 pm, David got the luggage from the train, got a trolley, and left the station. The minicabs were already outside, waiting for people who would have come in from town before going to nightclubs.

David gave the driver the address of the bed and breakfast they were staying at. He had already called them earlier to say that they would be there about nineish. "Could they have something to eat that's not sandwiches?" he added. The lady on the other end of the phone said that would be all right; she would make them something and keep it on low heat, but she would only cook it at 8 pm, so it wouldn't get baked up. David took the case, and they went inside. The man was at reception to greet them; David signed in for them both, and the guy took them up to their room. It was on the second floor; they had a lift; they knew they were a honeymoon couple, so gave them a nice big room.

The man called Terry opened the door and gave David the key. "My missus, Jane, has cooked your meal for you; would you like to have it up here rather than go down to the dining room?" asked Terry.

"Yes, that would be lovely, and could you bring up some juice, orange juice or something, and a couple of beers?" asked David.

"Yes, that's no problem; see you in a few minutes," replied Terry. Terry returned with a tray and their food, and Jane was behind him with a wine cooler and a bottle of champagne for them to celebrate their wedding.

"Congratulations to you both," said Jane.

"Thank you," said Chrissy, smiling at both of them. She had just done up her button again, and they left the tray of food on the side.

"I know it's not romantic, but when you have had a cold buffet, the last thing you want in the evening is a sandwich," remarked David.

"It's okay, I understand," said Jane.

"Oh, thank you for making this especially for us, Mrs?" said Chrissy.

"Please call me Jane, and I know there's a lot going on your wedding day; it was a pleasure to make it honestly," replied Jane.

"Night to you both; breakfast is between 8.30–10 am. The dining room is downstairs, just past the bar in reception," Terry said, closing the door behind the two of them. David put the food on the table and put the tray on the floor. Chrissy was just delighted that she could now undo her skirt.

"Chris, just take it off and put on your night things so you are more comfortable," he told her. She did as she was told; she didn't mind; she knew David had her best interests at heart, and they both sat down at the table and ate their meal. "Shall we keep the champagne for tomorrow or something, David?" she asked him.

"Yes, why not? It's not like we are going to be drinking too late. I don't know about you, Chrissy, but I am bushed. You don't mind if we go to sleep, do you? I know it's not traditional, but we are both knackered," David suggested.

"No, that's fine, love. I am pretty tired, more than normal, but it has been an exciting day, and now, nearly three months have gone by, it's starting to get to me a bit, this pregnancy lark," replied Chrissy.

Once David was undressed, they both got into bed, and David hit the bedside lamp above the bed. "Night, love. Happy honeymoon," said David.

"Mmmm," replied Chrissy, fast asleep.

The next day, they both woke up early, and the sun was beaming into their room.

"Good morning, Mrs Crawford; did you sleep well, then?" asked David attentively, stroking his wife's hair as he said this. David looked at the clock; it was gone nine.

"We should really get up for breakfast, you know. Do you think you can face it, Chrissy?" he asked her.

"Well, I thought about maybe having boiled eggs and toast instead of a fry-up; then I should be able to keep it down," she told David. They got up, got washed and dressed, and then headed towards the dining room, which was on the ground floor. It would have been a sitting room and dining room combined if it were a normal house rather than a bed and breakfast. In the kitchen at the back, Terry came over and asked if they had a good night's sleep and what they would like for breakfast.

Chrissy put in her order. Terry told her that was fine, and yes, she would make the eggs slightly hard-boiled. Terry left them to put in their order and returned with a big pot of tea; their orange juice was already on the table. Chrissy didn't want any cereal, just her boiled eggs and toast. David opted for a full fry-up.

"What do you want to do today, Chrissy? I was thinking of having a look around town; see what's about?" David suggested. She nodded; she wasn't too worried about what they did; they were on their own for the first time in a little while with so much to do for the wedding. They had eaten, went back up to their room to freshen up, said goodbye to Terry and Jane, and then left. They walked out of the door and just followed their noses. "That way, towards the sea!" said Chrissy. David agreed, and off they went hand in hand towards the seafront.

They were out all day and came back exhausted from all of the sightseeing. When they returned, Chrissy had a lie-down and fell asleep for a couple of hours. They went downstairs for the evening meal and then went out afterwards. They knew they should stay in bed and breakfast for some quiet time, but they knew they could have that when they got back home; they had their own room, thankfully big enough for the three of them. Every day, they went out, explored Paignton, went down to the beach, looked at the shops, and before they knew it, it was time to go back home and get back to normality and reality. The holiday, or rather, honeymoon, was over. They were soon back, opening the front door with Chrissy's key. David was trying to lift her up to walk her over the threshold; well, that's what the newlyweds did, but Chrissy was worried David would drop her.

"Hi, everyone, we're home!" called out Chrissy and David.

"Well, look at you two; you look really well and rested; did you have a good time?" asked Pam, Chrissy's mum.

"Yes, Mum, it was great—beautiful weather, fresh air, seagulls trying to nick our food—but yes, Mum, we had a lovely time!" replied Chrissy.

"Mum, we had a great time," said David.

Pam was a little taken aback; she knew that they had gotten married and that she had gained a son-in-law but forgot he might call her mum. *Oh well, it could be worse,* she thought. Phil came in from the garden and said, "Eh, what's all the noise…" He stopped dead in his tracks.

"Well, hello, you two. Come on, my turn for a hug," Phil said, wanting to hug his daughter, then shook David's hand.

"Welcome home, lad," said David while shaking David's hand. Men didn't hug in those days; it was the seventies, and they just didn't do that.

Pam put the kettle on; she told Chrissy and David to sit down. She was making tea and a few sandwiches. "No, you stay there, Chrissy, love; your mum's fine, isn't that right, Pam?" said Phil rather loudly.

"What, Phil? Sorry, I can't hear you in here. Be out in a minute," Pam told him. Once the pleasantries were over, Phil took their luggage with David up to their bedroom. Pam had aired it and put some flowers in a vase in the window.

The place was spotless, and David knew they had made the right choice by living with his in-laws. He loved his family, but they were a bit more over the top. He put the suitcase on the bed and unzipped it, ready for when Chrissy came up. Even though it had been her bedroom, he wanted her to sort it out how she wanted it until they were able to find their own place. There was room for a crib and later on a cot, and for now that would do.

Chrissy did just that when she finally got upstairs; she knew she had tomorrow off but would be back at work on Monday. She worked at the local ABC Bakery; the work wasn't too taxing, so she should be able to stay there for as long as she could, but being on her feet all day wasn't going to be great. Chrissy and David settled in well at home. Well, Pam and Phil's. Pam's sister, Edie, lived around the corner; she was lovely but a bit of a busy body. Her husband, Arnold, who always knew when to be quiet, especially if Edie was talking, was a content man. Well, he was until he married Edie. The term henpecked comes to mind. Edie was four years older than Pam, and Joan, her younger sister, was four years younger than Pam.

Phil had a sister called Cherry, and she was married to Jim. The family all got on, and they all liked David. Edie used to frequent Pam and Phil's house practically every day; she seemed to have her nose in everyone's business, so if they wanted to keep something quiet, they always talked about it when they weren't there. Edie kept looking at Chrissy funny.

"Pam, are you sure that our Chrissy isn't in the family way; she seems to be putting on some weight around the middle?" quizzed Edie, who was eyeing up Chrissy quite closely.

"No, Edie, she's just been eating a lot on their honeymoon; that sea air makes you hungry; she said they tried lots of things they hadn't eaten before," said Pam, hoping that would shut Edie up. But not for long. David and Chrissy had gotten into quite a routine, both back at work. They had decided to give Pam five pounds a week for housekeeping, bed and board, and would also put a couple of quid extras towards their food. Pam went to the launderette twice a week. Diane would give her a hand on her day off. Chrissy could help loading and unloading the washing and folding it but not lifting it. She was nearly four months now and starting to show, and yes, Edie had finally guessed. Chrissy had gone to the loo to be sick when Edie was there, and she was listening at the door, so they called everyone together that evening and told them, but not how far along she was.

It wasn't anyone's business, not even Edie's, but at least it shut her up. Chrissy, David, Pam, and Phil sat down one evening. Diane had gone out to see her friend, Maxine, who lived up the road. Pam and Phil knew that the baby was due just after Christmas, so they wanted to get some stuff for the baby and Chrissy as well. In those days, scans weren't really done, so they had to wait until the baby came. Chrissy had been to her hospital and doctor appointments; men rarely went, so Pam went with her; she was getting big pretty quickly. The doctor put that weird-looking thing on Chrissy's tummy to hear the baby's heartbeat. He said that the baby had a great heartbeat—very strong. Everyone helped as much as they could. David was putting away money for them once he paid Pam, but it still wasn't enough to get a place.

So, they would have to stay longer than he had hoped for; he really wanted to be there only for a year or so, but he would have to wait and see. Christmas came, and it was a house full. Edie and Arnold came. Joan and Albert, Phil's sister Cherry, and Jim came over for Christmas with Chrissy, David, and Diane. It was a bit of a squeeze, but thankfully, they all only lived down the road or around the corner. Chrissy was getting really big now and struggling to get up and down the stairs; she would have to come down slowly on her bum and take her time going up them. Sometimes it would take her at least fifteen minutes. Once the New Year was over, Chrissy's appointments were getting more and more frequent; every couple of weeks, Pam was with her every step of the way.

One cold early February morning, Chrissy screamed out. David fell out of bed with the shock of the scream. Pam and Phil came running in, and Diane was still in her bed, fast asleep.

"Chrissy, what's wrong?" asked Pam.

"Mum, I think the baby's coming. I am getting really sharp pains," said Chrissy, trying to breathe.

"Go next door to Gladys and ask her to call for an ambulance. I know she won't want to be woken up. Mind you, Chrissy. You did scream, so go on, Phil, hurry up, your daughter's in labour; I wouldn't wonder."

Pam shouted at him. Phil did as he was told and ran next door to Gladys, who was most certainly awake when she heard Chrissy scream. Phil rushed back in and nearly fell over Chrissy's suitcase. He told Pam the ambulance was on its way. By now, Pam had quickly gotten dressed, threw a maternity dress over Chrissy, and David was dressed and ready to go.

Phil quickly got some clothes on, and then the ambulance turned up, checked on Chrissy, and yes, she was in labour. They helped her downstairs, the ambulance men trying not to fall over her suitcase; David went into the ambulance with her; Pam and Phil went in the car; a little mini followed the ambulance. When they got there, the ambulance crew got a trolley to put Chrissy on it and then wheeled her into reception, where she gave them her information. David looked uncomfortable. Pam and Phil had then run into reception. David and Phil went upstairs in the lift. Pam went with Chrissy to the delivery room, and the men stayed outside. That wasn't the done thing then; the men used to be in the room; it was women's work as it always had been. Chrissy was being hooked up to whatever machines were there, just to check on everything.

Pam was nervous but excited too; her little girl was having her own baby—not yet, but hopefully in a few hours. Phil went and got him and David a cup of tea; mind you, coffee would have been better. Help them stay awake. Chrissy was in lots of pain; she had been given gas and air for pain relief. She was trying to breathe steadily while this was happening. The nurse and midwife had been bobbing in and out, checking Chrissy. How dilated was she? A little longer, they felt. They both left, and then Chrissy screamed. They came running back in, checked her again, and she was ready to push.

"Chrissy, hold onto my hand; when it really hurts, squeeze it," said Pam, looking at her girl. Even though she was 18 and a married woman, she must have been terrified.

Chrissy let out a big scream, then a gasp from the midwife. "Now, Chrissy, the head is crowning, which means we can see it, but the next time you get a contraction, please push as hard as you can," said the midwife. "Do you understand?" she double-checked. Chrissy nodded, and an almighty pain came from nowhere. Chrissy screamed again and pushed as hard as she could, and a little pink thing flew out, then screamed. "It's a girl!" exclaimed the midwife.

She had cut the cord, and the nurse took her away to make sure there was no yucky stuff inside the baby. She weighed her.

"5 lbs, 4 oz; that's a good weight, Chrissy," said the nurse.

"Oh, hold on, there's something else coming," said Chrissy.

"Oh, that will be the afterbirth, Chrissy; not to worry," said the midwife again.

"No, I don't think so, nurse," Chrissy told her. With that, Chrissy gave another almighty push again, and another little pink thing flew out of her and just about stayed on the bed.

"Twins!" shouted Pam.

The midwife cut the cord, the nurse hadn't expected another one, as there was only one crib. She cleaned this baby up and tried to get the yucky stuff out of this little one. "What are you going to call them, Chrissy?" asked Pam, trying to ignore what the nurse and midwife were trying to do.

"Well, I liked Katie, and David like Kim, so Katie and Kim, I suppose. I wasn't expecting two, Mum," said Chrissy.

"Well, yes, you were, Chrissy, love, but nobody knew that," said Pam.

"Mum, what's going on? What are they doing with the baby, and why hasn't she cried yet?" asked Chrissy. Pam left her daughter to go and see what was going on. By then, the midwife pressed the red button; two doctors flew into the room; the midwife was explaining what was happening, and the nurse came over to Chrissy to help her with the afterbirth that was still inside her, which also came out. It was huge.

"Nurse, what's going on with my baby? Why hasn't she cried yet?" asked Chrissy, starting to cry now. Pam came back, tears welling in her eyes. The doctor came over and cleared his throat. "Mrs Crawford, I'm really sorry to have to break this to you, but your second daughter didn't make it; she was really small, only just over three pounds in weight. There is a condition where one twin can transfer all of the goodness to the other twin, while they seem to sacrifice themselves so the other twin can survive," he told her. Chrissy couldn't take it in. By this time, David and Phil were in the room; they saw all of the kerfuffle, and Pam went out and grabbed them both, so they only caught the back end of the conversation.

"So, you're telling us that our daughter has died, but I heard Mum shout out twins," said David. Who was now holding on tightly to Chrissy, who was silently crying.

"Mr Crawford, I am truly sorry, but sometimes this happens with twins, the one whose strength takes more of the goodness of the mother, and the other one sacrifices itself for its twin. I am truly sorry," he added and left the room. He beckoned the midwife to follow him, which she did. Also in tears, the midwife came back into the room. She went over to the crib, picked up Kim, whom the nurse had cleaned and put in a clean towel, and brought her over to Chrissy and

David. While she was sorting out Katie, she had already cleaned and weighed her, but now she didn't know what to do; she was biding her time. Meanwhile, Pam and Phil had left them to it for a few minutes; they knew they needed this little bit of time with their youngest daughter.

The midwife had come back out.

"Excuse me, nurse, sorry, midwife, did the younger baby, well, did she take a breath?" asked Pam.

"Yes, she did, but just the one, so yes, she can be registered for birth, and sadly, death, but that can be done later on. I will be back in a minute. Would you like to go back inside to be with your family? You can do so," she said.

Pam and Phil reluctantly opened the door to Chrissy holding the baby and David holding onto both of them.

"Oh, my loves, I am so sorry," said Pam, coming over to hug David, and then Chrissy, while looking at the baby. Phil went over to David and hugged him; he needed it; his baby had just died after being born. Pam then went over to the crib and saw the older one, just lying there, all content and quiet. Pam picked her up in her towel and cradled her. She brought her over to her family; at least she could be there with them for one time.

Pam handed Katie over to David. He held his daughter while her mum held her sister.

"Look, I know this probably isn't the right time for you two, but I do have my camera with me. Can I take a photo of all four of you, not just for you but for Katie when she gets older?" Both Chrissy and David nodded.

Phil stood at the end of the bed and took a couple of pictures, then Pam took Katie so they could get a couple with Kim. They could tell them apart because of their size. Kim was much smaller than Katie. Then Phil pulled away the camera.

The midwife came back in and said, "Chrissy and David, would you like a hand and foot stamp of Kim's hands and feet? That way there is proof that she was here; it's something for you both and for Katie later on," said the midwife. Again, they both nodded.

"I have blue ink. I will do it later on for you. Don't worry, it won't hurt her. But I am afraid that I have to take her away now; I will be back," she said, as she put her arms out to take Kim from Chrissy. Chrissy gave Kim a kiss on her forehead, and then so did David, Pam, and Phil, who were trying so hard to hold it together.

The midwife left the delivery room. Pam had a hold of Katie, and she handed her over to her mum and dad. Then they left the room. The midwife returned empty-handed and came to check on Chrissy to make sure she stopped bleeding; Chrissy had given Katie to David, who then put her back into her crib so the midwife could do her job. David returned to Pam and Phil, explained what was happening, and Pam left them to go back to Chrissy. David and Phil couldn't help it, but both started to cry for the daughter they had and the daughter they had lost. Pam held onto Chrissy's hand, and while the midwife did her checks, everything was fine. Even though Chrissy had had two babies, she didn't need stitches at all, but she was rather sore. The midwife left the room and then popped her head back in.

"Chrissy, are you breastfeeding or bottle-feeding?" she asked.

"Er, bottle, I think?" Chrissy replied.

"What brand?" she asked her.

"Oh, Cow and Gate, please, if you have it?" Chrissy told her. When the midwife returned with a bottle for Katie, Chrissy was then handed her daughter again so she could feed her.

Thankfully, she now has a nappy on, so Chrissy won't get wet or soiled. Pam left her and told David to go in and help or just watch his daughter being fed her first bottle. He wiped his eyes, which were now red and puffy, then went back to see his wife and daughter. Chrissy gave David a big smile.

"She's taking it, David. She's having a real guzzle," Chrissy said to her husband. He came over and sat next to her on the bed, held her hand on top of the one holding Katie's head, leant over, and kissed them both. Chrissy and David both had tears in their eyes.

"I will ask the midwife if we can see Kim again before you know; even if she's in a small crib, at least we can say goodbye on our own. What do you think, love?" he asked Chrissy.

"I think that would be precious, and at least we can have a little bit of time on our own with her, even for a few minutes."

Chrissy gulped back the tears as she said it to David. They both felt lost, even though they didn't know she was there. She was still their daughter, even for a few moments, but she will always be their little angel who will look down on them and her sister. The midwife came back in to see how Katie and the new parents were doing with the feeding. David asked if he could have a word with her, and she agreed. She came over to Chrissy, who was still holding Katie, who had just finished her milk.

"What I can do is bring her over to you on the ward. Well, you will be in a private room now, but David put up his hand. I'm sorry, Sister, but we can't afford a private room," he said rather nervously.

"No, Mr Crawford, it's nothing like that. Your wife and you have had a shock as well as a pleasant surprise, but both Chrissy and Katie will need some peace, so they will be going into a private room for tonight and seeing how they get on. I will bring Kim over to you once Chrissy gets settled. Is that okay?" she asked.

"Sorry, Sister," David said.

"Please call me Wendy, Mr Crawford. It's all arranged for both of them, but Chrissy, you will be moved in a little while; that bed can't be very comfortable for you. So, give me ten minutes and I will be back; also, your visitors have to go soon as well," Wendy told them both.

Both of them nodded to Wendy. It was lovely; Pam and Phil were still there, but they needed to get home and get some rest. David could make his own way home once he had his girls settled. Pam and Phil came back into the room to check on them all. They had already had a word with Wendy about feeling bits of spare parts, and they were going to head home.

Pam kissed Chrissy and Katie, then turned to David and kissed him on the cheek. "Pam, I will be along soon; I just want to get the girls settled on the ward or the room, sorry, then leave them for the night," he said.

"David, you do what's best for you; see you later, love," said Pam. Phil kissed both of the girls, shook, and then hugged David again.

"See you," he said to Chrissy and baby Katie. Then it was just the three of them. Wendy popped her head in again.

"Chrissy, we are going to move you now, so do you have your bag or suitcase with you?" she asked.

"Er, yes, it's over there in the corner," she said, as David picked it up and carried it with him. Chrissy was put into a wheelchair, which the porter had brought in. Wendy took Katie until Chrissy was comfortable, then handed her back to her mum.

As they left the delivery room, Chrissy, for some reason, had a good look around, then turned her head, and that same evening, they had some joy and sadness at the same time. She didn't ever want to be in that room, ever again. They got to the lift, with David walking behind her and the porter. They only had to go up one floor. The lift door opened, and the porter came out of the lift and turned left. Wendy was with them. She had climbed the stairs; she had Chrissy's notes with her and spoke to the lady on reception on that floor, where she then showed Chrissy her room, the first on their left. Wendy went with them; she held Katie for Chrissy so she could get into bed. Katie had a hospital gown on and a nappy, but Chrissy was too tired to put anything on her. Wendy had said she could do that in the morning, once she had some sleep.

Wendy also suggested that Katie go into the crib.

"It's lovely cuddling them, but you don't want her too used to the arms just yet. She will be fine. She has a good blanket and something on, so she won't be too hot." So, Wendy left them alone for a few minutes. David had put Chrissy's case down in the corner, out of the way, so she wouldn't trip over it.

"Oh, there's a bathroom here; that's handy, Chris," said David.

Wendy opened the door, and with a Moses basket in her hands, she put it down on the bed. David was a little shocked to see Kim there, as if she were asleep. Chrissy gasped, and she hadn't expected her to come dressed in a little pink Babygro; she looked so tiny against the huge feeling of the Moses basket.

"Can I hold her again, please?" asked Chrissy. Wendy thought for a moment. "I know you want to hold her and be a mummy to her, but it's too late—she saw Chrissy tear up again. Look, it's regulations; you're not supposed to, but it can't hurt. I will have to stay at the door. If my boss comes in, I am for it," Wendy told them.

Wendy picked up Kim and handed her to her mum. "Two minutes, okay?" whispered Wendy. Chrissy nodded, and David teared up again. They both kissed their daughter, who was slightly cold. Chrissy held her tightly but without squeezing her, then put her back into the Moses basket, took one long look, then had to look away. Wendy came and collected Kim.

"I will be back in a minute," she added.

She took the Moses basket away. Chrissy looked at Katie, who was now fast asleep, and Wendy came back.

"Now, David, when you come back tomorrow, I will have to give you the information you need, so when you go to register the births—the births, Kim as well as Katie?" David had interrupted. "Yes, both of the girls have to be registered for birth, but then you will have to register Kim's death, I am afraid. Once you have done that and gotten the relevant paperwork, you will have to decide about a funeral, not quickly but as soon as you can, Chrissy, because you don't want her lying in, well, you know what. Once we receive the necessary information and paperwork, the undertakers will sort out what you want and take Kim there for you to see her there if you want to know before, well, you know," said Wendy, wishing she didn't have to do this, but it is necessary and has to be done.

"Wendy, thank you for everything," said Chrissy.

"Yes, thank you. You have been a great help. Well, you know what I mean?" said David, tearing up again.

"I know, David. Now I suggest you kiss your wife and let her sleep; you know where she will be tomorrow. If you like this room and want to stay here, Chrissy, I'm sure we can sort something out. Well, night, both of you. Chrissy, I will see you sometime tomorrow; I'm not really up here, but will pop up when I can to see how you're doing here and little Katie," Wendy told them both.

"She's right, love. I had better make a move, but I will be back in the morning. Give her a kiss for me; I don't want to lean over her or you, for that matter," David said. He kissed his wife, and he left her for the night.

Chrissy looked over at her daughter. Slowly, the tears trickled down her face; she couldn't hold it in any longer. She let them come. She needed them to come, and they did for a good half hour. A nurse came to check on them both. She looked at Chrissy and asked, "Tea, Chrissy?" Chrissy nodded in reply.

She wiped her tears away. "There's no need for that, my love. If you want to cry, then you do so. Your little one is fast asleep, and she doesn't understand, but if you want to sob, you do so." All of the staff on that floor knew what had happened that evening; they were a great group of people, but Chrissy had only just met this nurse who was called Charlotte; she was so comforting. Once Chrissy had completely finished, Charlotte handed her tea, which wasn't as hot, but she wasn't bothered.

She had released a lot of emotion with those needed tears. Charlotte sat down with her for a little while. The ward was quiet. It was important to be there for the other patients, but tonight, it was for Chrissy.

"Chrissy, this may sound a bit nuts, but would you like to go and have a bath or something? Katie will be fine. It might just relax you," suggested Charlotte.

"Is it okay for me to have a bath, though? I have just had a baby?" she said, realising what she had just said.

"Did you have any stitches?" asked Charlotte.

"No, erm," replied Chrissy.

"Well, what about a warm bath? Not for long, though. That might help a bit. I will go and run one for you, and don't worry, I will check on Katie for you. You need this for you. Little miss is out like a light," Charlotte said as she was looking in on her in the crib. Charlotte didn't put too much water in.

"Chrissy, do you have other nightwear to put on?" she asked her.

"Yes, I have it in my suitcase. I think it's in the corner," said Chrissy. Charlotte put the case on its back and opened it; there on top were clean underwear, clean nightwear, and some stuff for the baby in white. Charlotte closed it again.

"Chrissy, I will bring your clean things into you here, then you can get straight into them. Oh, I forgot, do you have any pads?" she asked her.

"Oh, yes, I think there is a full pack in the case," said Chrissy.

"Don't worry, I will have a look if that's okay?" Charlotte asked her.

"Yes, of course," she said, so Charlotte went back to the case and saw the pack of pads on the top in the corner; she hadn't noticed them before. She took them to Chrissy, who had now lowered herself into the bath.

"Ahhhh, that does feel good," Chrissy moaned.

"Would you like these to go into the laundry? I tell you what, I will find you a carrier bag and put them in. I am sure your family will take them back with them tomorrow," suggested Charlotte. Chrissy wasn't listening. She was enjoying this warm feeling all over her body.

After about fifteen minutes, Chrissy thought she had better get out; she hadn't eaten anything for hours and was starting to feel peckish. She called for Charlotte, just so she would be steady getting out of the bath. Charlotte helped her, and then Chrissy dried herself off and put on her clean clothes. She mentioned to Charlotte that she hadn't eaten since earlier in the day. "Tea and toast?" Charlotte suggested.

"Mmmmm, yes, please," she replied.

"Back in a mo," replied Charlotte. She was back in a mo with her tea and toast. Chrissy sat on the bed; she felt a bit better than she had all day, her new baby in her crib next to her fast asleep and her other baby forever asleep downstairs somewhere.

Meanwhile, David had gotten home. Pam and Phil had been waiting for him to see how he was. When a baby is born, it's all focused on the mother; the father seems to get left out, but in this case, they were all at a loss.

"Tea, David?" asked Pam.

"Oh yes, please, thank you," he added.

"How are you feeling? I know that's a stupid question, David, but how are you?" asked Phil.

"I don't really know, Dad. It all seems a bit of a blur now. The midwife took Chrissy and Katie up to their ward. Well, they are in a room. I think it's better than being on a ward full of mums talking about their babies. How do you tell someone that we had two babies, but now we only have one? Anyway, Chrissy is settled. Katie had her first bottle. She guzzled the lot. Oh, you know that, you were still there. I have to collect some paperwork tomorrow for registering the births!" said David.

"Both girls' births?" asked Phil.

"Yes, both of them, because Kim had a breath; even though she didn't survive, she took a breath, so she was legally alive, but then I have to get her death registered as well, and then we have to make the arrangements. There's that funeral place in town, not far from the bakers where Chrissy works. Dad, is there another one in town? I can't let her walk past that place, even though she's finished working. Well, for now, it's not fair for her to go past it every time she's at work," said David, who had his head in his hands and started to cry, just like Chrissy did.

Once he started, he couldn't stop.

"It's just not fair, is it?" he said in between sobs. Pam went back into the kitchen; she started to cry too. He was right, it wasn't fair. She grabbed the brandy and brought it back into the living room.

"Here you are, David. I think we all need this tonight," she said, pouring it into each tea.

The door opened, and it was Diane. "Hello, what's everyone crying for?" she asked, a little puzzled. They told her, and she burst into tears also. This was some night, one they wouldn't ever forget.

Chapter 2

It was the morning of the funeral. While Chrissy was still in the hospital, David had gone and sorted out registering the girls' birth and Kim's death. He couldn't look at the certificate because he knew that it had made it final, but today was the day they were going to say goodbye to their little twin. Chrissy had been out of the hospital with Katie for a couple of days. She did what she could; she was still trying to get into a routine with her baby. They had been the day before to see Kim at the funeral directors; they had used 'Kent Funeral Service'. They were on the high street, not by the bakers but further along, near the men's tailor. But David had the idea the night before; he told Chrissy, but she was nearly asleep, so she wasn't really listening.

He had gone down to the jewellers; he wanted something for both girls; he had seen them the week before Chrissy had gone into labour, so he went back and got them both one. So when they went to see Kim, he took her one with him and showed it to Chrissy; she loved it. He asked the lady if she would put it on her for him; he didn't want to hurt her, not that he could, but she was still a delicate little thing. They left the room for a few minutes; they went over to have another look at their little girl; she looked beautiful in her white satin dress that Pam had picked out while Chrissy was still in the hospital. Kim was like Katie, nearly bald, no hair, so she put a ribbon on her head, one to match the dress, so now she looked like she was asleep in her pretty white satin dress, with a golden necklace with the letter 'K' on it. He had brought one for Katie too; she would wear hers when she was a little older, so she wouldn't strangle herself. Kim looked like a little doll, a little angel, fast asleep.

David and Chrissy had thanked the lady; they both kissed Kim on the forehead and then had to leave the room. Chrissy couldn't take it anymore; she had wanted both of her daughters to be okay, but it just wasn't meant to be. They hadn't told many people. Close family and a couple of friends, Edie and Arnold came, but Joan and Albert couldn't make it; Cherry and Jim came, but both were very subdued. The hearse pulled up outside the house, and Edie popped her head out. "Funeral cars are here, Pam, Phil."

Phil went to the front door. The undertaker tipped his hat to him. Phil closed the door again and went over to Chrissy and David. "Kids, the funeral cars are here. Are you both ready?" Phil asked David, who looked at his wife.

"Better do this for our Kim, then, David," said Chrissy.

She picked up Katie, who was crying. Chrissy held her tightly. Pam, Phil, and the other few people came. Chrissy, David, Pam, and Phil sat in the car behind the hearse. They didn't see the point of getting any other cars, so Edie and Arnold went with Cherry and Jim. Edie wanted to go into the main car; she always thought she should be in the middle of things, but this time, no way. This was for Chrissy and David; they chose Pam and Phil to be with them, and also, Pam could take hold of Katie if she was getting a little fussy or upset. Babies always knew when something different was happening, and as this baby was her twin, it's like she understood. The cars went slowly; there were lots of flowers practically covering the tiny white coffin that had a very small baby in it.

As they were going down the high street, people stopped, and men took off their hats as a mark of respect, but when they saw the small coffin, you could see the shock on their faces. They would look at the car behind, and then look at Chrissy and David. David took no notice; men rarely did, but women notice everything. Thankfully, they were away from the high street. Chrissy and David didn't want a full service at the church, so they asked if they could have a graveside service instead. They wanted to have Kim buried, as they could go there to visit throughout their lives. It would give them all some comfort to be able to go and talk to her and lay flowers for her. David had to sort out a plot for her; they didn't have one already, so he sorted that out so he and Chrissy could go together, but he wanted Kim to go there first, so once the grave had been sorted out, she would be put at the bottom of it, like at the feet, so she wouldn't be disturbed when he or Chrissy would be there.

The undertaker handed Kim to David, who took her and put her to the ground. It would be the last thing he could do for his youngest daughter. He wiped away a tear or two from his cheek. While Chrissy was full on crying, Pam was holding Katie, who was also crying so hard. It was as if she knew her sister was in the ground. They said their prayers, threw some dirt in, and put flowers in too. Chrissy had got a single pink rose; from today, pink roses resembled her girls; Pam had put one in also; then Phil and Edie threw some dirt in; then Arnold and Cherry had got a bunch of pink carnations that she put in; Jim put in dirt; he held his head low for a couple of moments, then he walked away, wiping tears from his eyes.

Once they had done what they had to, everyone had walked away from the grave. Chrissy couldn't leave. "Mum, it's like leaving one of my girls behind. I can't do it. Can't we just take her home again with us?" asked Chrissy.

"No, love, I am sorry, but this is the end of the road for Kim, but she will always be looking down on you and her dad, and most of all, Katie, her big sister. Come now, darling, we have to go. Katie needs feeding, and I expect changing, so let's go home," Pam encouraged.

But Chrissy wasn't budging. Pam handed Katie to her dad; she nodded.

"I won't be long, David," she told him.

"Mum, I can't leave her here; it's dark and depressing," said Chrissy.

"Chrissy, do you really think that your little girl is down in that box in the dirt? She's not, love. She's up there in the sky, in heaven with your uncle Jack and Grandad Grumps and Nanny Gladys. She's up there in the sunshine playing with the rabbits; they will be looking after her, my darling. What is in this hole and dirt is a shell, just the host of a body; her spirit and soul are already up in heaven, you see, you wait and see how many white feathers you see from now on, you see how many pennies you see or find, you see 'Pennies from Heaven'. She's up there, looking down on us, but Kim, she's making things lovely for us for when we go, like Uncle Jack, Grandad Grumps, and Nanny Gladys, so come on, let's take a last look at where we can come and visit on her birthday, at Christmas. Yes, I know you would her rather be here with us and Katie, but we will be, one day, eh, love?" said Pam.

Chrissy nodded. She knew what her mum was saying was right; it's just that she had never felt pain like this before. This made it real. All of a sudden, in the distance, Chrissy could hear her daughter crying, the one her husband was holding.

"Yeah, you're right, Mum, let's go," Chrissy said, as she turned around one last time, blew her daughter a kiss, then left to go and find her husband and daughter. When they got back home, everyone else was there, and Edie had taken it upon herself to open the buffet. Chrissy got out of the car, and on the wall, she saw the fattest white feather she had ever seen in her life. She looked up to the sky and blew another kiss.

"Thanks, Kim, love," said Chrissy.

She then went inside with her daughter and her husband; her daughter had thankfully stopped crying, and yes, she did want to be fed. Chrissy was in the kitchen getting Katie's bottle sorted out. Pam could hear a bit of raised voices, not arguing or shouting, but raised. It was Cherry and Edie. Edie was telling Cherry that Chrissy was still very young and she could still have more children if she wanted, but she wouldn't advise it.

Diane was in earshot, and she flew at Edie. "How dare you say that about my sister? You miserable old bat, she just buried one of her babies. How could anyone like you have any understanding of that? Now, I suggest you shut up before I make you, or you can leave; it's your choice," Diane confronted her.

"How dare you?" shouted Edie.

"No, Edie, I think you have said quite enough; Diane is right, so if you wouldn't mind," said Phil as he went to get Edie's coat. Arnold took it from him.

"Come on, Edie, they are right. They don't need you putting your oar in; come on home," said Arnold, looking at Phil as if to say, I am really sorry. Edie didn't want to move.

"Edie, home now!" shouted Arnold. Edie did as she was told; she was too shown up now to argue, but they knew it wasn't the end of it. As the oldest girl, she thought she should be involved in everything that was going on, the centre of attention, and always at the forefront of everything. Arnold apologised before he closed the door. Phil was behind him. Chrissy, thank goodness, was still in the kitchen. She didn't want to deal with Aunt Edie and her drama; she had had enough of that her whole life, but today, nothing was going to upset her more than she already was.

"Thanks, love, for that. I did want to say something, but you know it's your mum's sister, but you handled her well, love. I will say that," said Phil to Diane.

"Sorry, Dad, but she was just too much. I'm going to check on our Chrissy," Diane said, and she left the room.

Chrissy and David had managed to get through the day really without any problems, well—Auntie Edie—but they didn't deal with her; thankfully, Diane or Dad did. They were now up in their bedroom with Katie; she was drinking her bottle. They had already put away their funeral clothes; Katie was in a pink Babygro. Chrissy told David what her mum had said about Kim; she showed him the big, fat white feather; she had put it in her jewellery box; he was touched by that; it also gave him some comfort too. Now they just had to get on with their lives the best way they could anyway. Chrissy wanted to go to the cemetery on

Sunday, but just because Kim was no longer with them, it didn't mean they could take her some flowers. As sad as it was, it would help her and let Katie know what happened to her twin.

Chrissy didn't want to go all the time, just at main events like her birthday, Christmas, Mother's Day, and that sort of thing. David and Chrissy sat down a couple of weeks after the funeral. "Chrissy, love, I have had to look at the money we have; it looks like the funeral for Kim and the headstone we want to get her will practically clear out the rest of our savings. Now, I am not complaining at all, you know that, but it will mean we have to stay here for a while longer than we had anticipated. Is that all right with you? I mean, we have to still talk to Mum and Dad; I don't think it will be a problem, but are you okay with that?" David asked her.

"Of course, it's fine, David, as long as Mum and Dad agree, and I don't really think they would chuck us out after what we have been through, so yes, it's okay. It doesn't matter if our money has gone, it's for our beautiful girl, so we have to wait; that's okay too. Plus, we do have a roof over our heads, we have one beautiful girl, and we have food in our bellies, clothes on our backs, and shoes on our feet; what more could you need?" Chrissy added.

David leant over and gave her a kiss. He knew he did the right thing by marrying Chrissy; she and Katie were the best thing that had happened to him. They both went downstairs to talk to Pam and Phil about it.

"You do not need to go until you are all ready; we have plenty of room, and when Diane moves out, then Katie can have her room!" said Pam.

"I heard that, Mother," joked Diane.

"So, does that mean we are stuck with you longer than we thought?" added Diane. She loved having Chrissy, David, and Katie living there, even though she had no partner or children at the moment.

"I can be the drunken aunty bringing gifts to my nieces; sorry, niece," Diane said and quickly corrected herself. She had forgotten, but only for a second. Then she left the room and came back with a lovely pink soft teddy bear for Katie. "I hope you don't mind, Chrissy; I couldn't resist it, but I did get a second one, so if you want to put it up with Kim, then that's okay, but if not, in case it gets stolen, I got you a box, so you can put her little things in it; it's like a memory box. You can put your photos from the hospital and her little wristband thing that she had when she was born. Did I do right in getting it?" asked Diane, rather nervously.

Chrissy, David, Pam, and Phil all had tears in their eyes. "Of course, you did, you silly thing; it's a lovely gift. Thank you," said David. Chrissy couldn't talk, but she went over and hugged her big sister.

Phew, thought Diane. "I didn't want to get it wrong. Anyway, I have to go now. Oh, Auntie Edie is walking up the garden path. Do you want me to tell her to get stuffed when I leave? Oh, please let me; I liked that the other day. Please, please, please?" Diane was nearly begging.

"No, you leave your aunt Edie to me. Thank you, Diane," replied Pam.

Diane left the room, grabbed her jacket, and opened the front door, where Aunt Edie was standing. Pam was right on Diane's heels. "Er, and where do you think you are going?" asked Pam, who was holding onto the door, because Edie, who had ignored Diane, had her foot just inside the step.

"I don't think so," replied Pam.

"Pamela, I am your elder sister. I have come to visit you. Why won't you let me in?" asked Edie, a bit confused.

"After what you did the other day?" replied Pam.

"Why? What did I do the other day?" replied Edie, as if she had no idea she had done anything wrong at all.

"Well, Diane was rather rude to me, but I shall overlook that; you know she was upset; she can apologise to me next time I see her," said Edie, absolutely oblivious to what her actions and words did to her younger niece and her husband.

"Edie, you said some rather rude things about my daughter and her baby, who had just died. I don't think you're in a position to ask for an apology until you at least give one to her and her husband. Until you do that and not a throwaway one, a heartfelt one, you are not welcome to our home, so goodbye," said Pam, and she closed the front door just as Edie had swiftly moved her foot away.

"Hmm…" said Pam as she clapped her hands together. She went back inside, leaving Edie still on the doorstop, who then realised she wasn't going to get her way, and she turned and left. Chrissy, David, and Phil all clapped at Pam.

"About time, Pam!" said Phil.

"I'm sick of how she turned everything about herself. Diane apologises? I don't think so," Phil added.

They had a chuckle about that for a few days. They filled Diane in on what happened with Auntie Edie; she too chuckled.

"About time, Mum," said Diane.

"That's what Dad said," said Chrissy, who was now taking Katie up to their bedroom.

Katie was thriving; she was doing so well. "Mum, have you noticed how bright blue her eyes are? We didn't get to see Kim's, but I bet they were going to be the same," said Chrissy.

"Mmmm..." Mum replied. David was still working on his job, even though Chrissy said she would go back to work. Pam offered to have Katie, but David was having none of it. He wanted Chrissy to enjoy being at home, being a mum to their daughter; it would just mean the savings were going to take longer to get there, but he didn't mind; they were all happy. A few months down the line, maybe six, they had a call from the funeral home to say that now they could go and choose a headstone for Kim if they wanted the soil settled enough to put one on, so Chrissy and David took Katie to the undertakers. They weren't sure if it was a good thing to take Katie, but they felt she should be there.

They had a look at their books and decided on an open book, so they could put her up there. Then there would be space for both her and David as well.

"What words would you like, Mr and Mrs Crawford?" asked the lady there. They both had a thought, then Chrissy suggested.

"What about Kim Crawford? We blinked, and then you were gone. Born 18 February 1979—Died 18 February 1979. What do you think, David?" she asked him.

He had already teared up with the words, and so did the lady. "Yes, I think that's it. We don't need anything else, do we?" he offered.

"Now do you want a white book with gold letters or a black book with silver letters?" asked the lady, now wiping away her tears.

"I think white with gold would be better; she's only a little girl, and it will stand out. What do you think, Chrissy?" asked David.

"Perfect," she replied, saying she knew her husband was a big softy.

The lady told them how much it would be: £120. That will include your words and laying it down. It will be fine; it will take a couple of weeks.

"We will let you know when we have laid it down. Is that okay?" asked the lady; she had already composed herself again to her professionalism.

"Yes, that's fine. Can I come back today and pay you, as I didn't bring enough money with me? I am sorry, but I didn't know how much it would be, or can I leave with you what I have now, which is fifty pounds?" asked David a bit nervous because he was going to bring more with him, but he was all fingers and thumbs.

"Yes, Mr Crawford, that would be fine. I will write you out a receipt, then you can bring the balance, then we can put the order forward," the lady told him.

They left the building. "Chrissy, I will go back; there's no need for you and Katie to be there. Anyway, I will go straight back to work; that's all right, love?" he asked her.

"Yes, that's fine. Katie is due her feed now anyway. Thanks for that. I know it's eaten into our savings, but at least our girl has what she needs, and now it won't look like nobody loves her," Chrissy added.

When they got home, David rushed upstairs to get the money, then he left, giving Chrissy a kiss and one for Katie on the forehead.

"Where is David off to, Chrissy?" asked Pam.

"Oh, we didn't have enough for Kim's headstone, so he came back to collect the rest. I am just glad we had it," said Chrissy, and Pam just wished she hadn't put her foot in it.

"So, what did you choose for Kim, then?" asked Pam, wondering if she should have.

"We got a book, so we can put Kim at the top, then me and David can go underneath if there's room, or we can go on the other page," Chrissy told her.

"So, what words have you chosen, then?" asked Pam.

"Kim Crawford, We blinked, and then you were gone—born dah dah dah, died dah dah dah. That's okay, isn't it?" asked Chrissy, searching really for her mum's approval.

"You can't put dah dah dah on a headstone, Chrissy!" Pam told her.

"We haven't, Mum, but it's difficult to say the day," Chrissy told her mum, getting teary again.

"Well, let's wipe those tears away; we need to sort Katie out; she's hungry, I think," Pam said, drying away her tears.

"You know what day it is next Sunday, don't you, Chrissy?" Pam reminded Chrissy.

"It's your first wedding anniversary!" Pam told her.

"Blimey, I forgot with everything else going on. Well, we can't do anything. We won't want a party or anything; let's just have a nice meal at home. You know we can get steak or something," Chrissy told her.

"Well, then let me sort that out. Do you want to have a word with David to see if he wants to ask anyone over and make a night of it?" suggested Pam.

"I will have a word with him later on when he gets in; he has other things on his mind," Chrissy said.

Pam arranged everything for the anniversary night; Cherry and Jim were invited; Joan and Albert were invited; Sylvia and Fred, David's mum and dad, came; his brothers, Colin and Mark, didn't want to go; they were eighteen and sixteen; it wasn't cool to go to someone's house for dinner, so they both stayed at home. Phil did think that Sylvia was a trooper; she was the only woman in now a house of three men. It would have been four if David and Chrissy had chosen to live with them, but at least she would have had Chrissy, but they didn't really have the room either.

They had a lovely evening. Sylvia and Fred doted on Katie like Pam and Phil did. They didn't attend Kim's funeral. Sylvia said that she couldn't do it, but she knew Chrissy and David were very brave, and yes, they knew about what Edie had done. Sylvia would have probably lamped her one if she were there. They had a lovely evening, and Sylvia and Fred were invited over more often. The boys weren't really into babies, so they said thank you and visited more often than they had done in the past, which Pam and Phil were really grateful for, and Sylvia was delighted with the welcome and invites for the future. Time was going way too fast; they had already had Christmas upon them. They had brought Katie lots of things—toys, some new clothes, a piece of jewellery—that could be put away for when she's older. David chose a charm bracelet that she could have and keep, but he also brought a second one and put it away in Kim's box; he didn't tell Chrissy that he had done that; he didn't want to upset her.

He had brought Chrissy one as well; he had gotten a new charm that he would have brought for their wedding anniversary. He got a rose charm for Chrissy, symbolising love, sacrifice, and death. It would be a reminder that they lost a baby, but also the love for her too. He got the girls a wishbone, which could be added to the bracelet. They had a lovely day. Even Auntie Edie made an appearance; she had finally apologised to both Chrissy and David. Was it heartfelt? Well, it was all they were going to get, so hey ho. She and Arnold popped around later on in the day. Pam had asked them if they wanted to stay for dinner, but they had Arnold's sister Elsie coming over; they declined but were grateful for the offer. Sylvia and Fred had decided to stay home but invited everyone over for Boxing Day.

The holidays were now over, and David was back at work. They had decided to give Katie a party for her birthday, even though they would be at the cemetery in the morning. They wanted to give Katie a little something, so her birthday was also celebrated. So now, Katie was one year old, blossoming into a beautiful little tot; her bright blue eyes were definitely her redeeming feature; she had blonde hair like her mother; she was going to be a real heartbreaker.

David had gone out and got Katie another charm for her bracelet; he got her a four-leaf clover; he wanted to give his daughter as much good luck in her life as he could. That's what he wanted for his girls; he still felt that Kim was with them, even though that was physically impossible. When Chrissy was around, it was only one daughter, but his friends knew that he would talk as if he had two.

***

The years were slowly creeping up. David had managed to get more money saved; it took time and patience. His girls, Chrissy and Katie, had everything they needed; Diane had moved out the year before, so Katie had her room. Even though she was nearly four at the time, David and Chrissy thought it would be a good idea. Then she could have all of her things with her; she had grown into a lovely little girl; she had reached all of her milestones, which a tot should do: sitting up, crawling, holding her bottle. She was doing really well; she was now at nursery and loving it.

Chrissy had finally gone back to work when Katie went to the nursery to see if they could get their savings any higher, so when they do get their own place, it won't be such a shock to their systems with how much money they would need. Chrissy came home from work exhausted; she had only been back six months or so, but she hadn't felt so tired. Pam had collected Katie from the nursery, but Chrissy was still asleep. *It's not like my girl was asleep at the time*, Pam thought. She'd get Katie some dinner ready and get her nighttime things ready, because once she had her dinner, she would be in the bath.

Katie had a great appetite, thank goodness. When David came in from work, Chrissy was still asleep. Katie had had her bath and was in her pyjamas.

"Daddy," she called when he got in. She ran up to him, and he cuddled her.

"Mum, where's Chrissy?" David asked her.

"David, she's asleep up on your bed; she has been since she got in from work," Pam told him. He was confused, so he gave Katie to Pam.

"I will just check on her, Mum!" David told her. He went upstairs to their bedroom, and Chrissy was flat out. The curtains were drawn, so David opened them, hoping it would wake her up. Nothing. "Chrissy, Chrissy love, are you awake?" David practically sang to her.

"Mmm, yes, I am awake; why would you ask that, David?" Chrissy said with her eyes still shut.

"Chrissy, open your eyes, love," David suggested.

"Er, what? Oh, sorry, David," she replied.

"I didn't realise I had them shut still, you okay? Oh my god, where's Katie?" she said as she sat up all of a sudden.

"Katie is with your mum. She said that when you got back from work, you went for a lie-down, but you have been up here since then?" David told her.

"No, I can't have done, David. It's only four o'clock. Oh no, it's nearly seven. Why didn't anyone wake me? I have to feed Katie!" replied Chrissy. Getting off the bed, she nearly fell, but David managed to catch her.

"I think you need to see a doctor, Chrissy; this isn't like you, and you nearly landed on your face if I hadn't caught you!" David told her.

"So, I will call the doctor in the morning. No, actually, your mum had better do it. I am out too early, and when I remember, it will be too late for an appointment, so get an appointment with the doctor and let me know what he says, okay? Now, are you coming down for your dinner? I think it is shepherd's pie," David told her.

"Yes, I will be there in a minute!" said Chrissy.

"Not a chance; you might fall down the stairs. Now lean on me, and we can take it slowly," said David, reaching his arm out to put around Chrissy.

"I won't take no for an answer, Chrissy, love, so come on," he told her. She did as she was told; he supported her weight, and they slowly made it back downstairs.

"Hello, sleepyhead," said Pam when she saw Chrissy and David.

"Chrissy, what's wrong?" asked Pam, and Phil looked up. He was playing with Katie.

"Er, nothing," replied Chrissy.

"Yeah, right?" said David.

"Mum when she went to get off the bed, she nearly fell flat on her face if I hadn't caught her, so I had to bring her down; otherwise, she would still be upstairs fast asleep," David told his mother-in-law.

"Are you okay, Chrissy? Come on, tell me?" said Pam.

"Mum, I am just tired; I fell asleep and didn't realise the time," she answered.

"Chrissy, you were in here at 2 pm and you have slept for nearly five hours; that's not just tired. I think we need to get you to the doctor's, but he's closed now, so I will call in the morning. Good job you're not at work tomorrow. I will come with you. Katie won't have nursery, so we can all go. Don't worry, I will stay in the waiting room with Katie, so you can talk to the doctor privately."

The next morning, Pam, as agreed, made an appointment for her to see the doctor. "10 am, yes, that's fine, Janet. We will be there, thank you, for slotting her in," said Pam, hanging up the phone.

"Right, Chrissy, we will leave just after quarter to; you will be in time. It's only around the corner, so if you get ready, I will sort Katie out. Just leave her clothes out that you want her to wear. Come on now, we don't have all day," said Pam.

She knew her daughter wasn't well, but she didn't act as if she were ill. It was a bit of a mystery to her. They were ready and out the door in ten minutes; the doctor's were only a few minutes away. Pam opened the door so Chrissy could push Katie in her pram; she was getting so big, she wouldn't be using it for much longer. They sat down; they were only in there for a few minutes before Chrissy was called. She left her daughter with her mum and went into the doctor's room. "Now, Chrissy, what can I do for you?" he asked her.

"Well, I don't really know, doctor. I finished work yesterday, was home by 2 pm, and I went up for a laydown. Five hours later, I finally woke up when my husband called my name, but when I went to get up, I nearly fell over," she told him.

"So, you were dizzy, then?" asked the doctor.

"No, I just felt like my legs were like jelly, but I did feel a bit lightheaded," she said.

"Anything else?" he asked her.

"Well, I think I am going off my food, but where some foods I like but cannot eat, now I want to eat stuff I don't like, for example, I can't stand blue cheese, but that's all I want to eat, and mashed potato, on its own, though, with nothing else. Mum made shepherd's pie. I scraped off the mash and left the rest. It's weird, isn't it?" she suggested.

"Chrissy, did you bring a urine sample with you?" he asked her.

"Oh, no, sorry, I forgot. Do you want me to do one now?" she asked him.

"Yes, please. It would be better in the morning, but I think it will do just fine. So, he gave her a container for her to use. Don't forget to let the first bit go, then use the container until it's full, if that's possible," he told her.

She left his room and then went to the toilet, came back a few minutes later with a full container of yellow liquid.

"Ah, nice!" he said. Chrissy thought that was a bit odd, but he's a doctor.

"Yes, I will send this off to the lab, but I would like to take your blood pressure before you leave, is that okay?" he asked her.

He did what was necessary and then told her to call the surgery on Friday; he may have the results by then. He said goodbye to Chrissy, and she left his room. She went back out to the waiting room and found her mum and Katie.

"So, what did he say?" asked Pam.

"Well, I had to do a urine test, then he did my blood pressure, then told me to call on Friday for my results for my test!" replied Chrissy.

"Is that it?" Pam pressured for more information, but Chrissy didn't give any.

"Shall we go home?" asked Chrissy as Pam nodded, and they left the surgery. Friday came, and Chrissy called; she spoke to Janet again.

"Yes, of course. What time, Janet? Okay, at 2 pm, see you, then," said Chrissy, hanging up the phone.

"So, what did she say?" asked Pam.

"I have to go and see the doctor at 2 pm; my results have come back, and he wants to see me," Chrissy told her.

"Do you want me to come with you, Chrissy?" asked Pam.

"No, I think I will go on my own; will you watch Katie for me, though?" asked Chrissy.

"Of course, I will; you know you don't need to ask," Pam replied, looking at her only granddaughter.

It was nearly 1:45. Chrissy knew she could be there in minutes. "I'm off now, Mum; see you in a little bit," said Chrissy.

"Okay, love, don't worry, I am sure it will all be fine," Pam said encouragingly. Chrissy hoped she would have her mum's optimism and positive ideas.

Chrissy was soon at the surgery; she sat down until her name was called. "Ah, Chrissy, please sit down; I have some news for you," the doctor said.

Chrissy held her breath; she was now worried. "Okay, then let me have it," she said, but he held his hand up.

"It's good news, Chrissy," he said.

She sighed a sigh of relief.

"You are pregnant about eight weeks, I think. When was your last period? I forgot to ask you last time," he asked her.

Chrissy's mind was in a whirlwind. Pregnant, she couldn't be again; they were being so careful, she was thinking. "Chrissy, period, last one?" the doctor asked her again.

"Oh, now I didn't have one last month, but I thought that was because of the heatwave we had. I haven't had one since April, so, yes, about eight weeks," she told him.

"Well, congratulations, Mrs Crawford, Chrissy. It's great news," said the doctor.

"If you could make an appointment to come and see me again in a couple of weeks' time, then we can sort out what hospital you would like to go to," he said, but Chrissy wasn't listening; she couldn't take it in—not another baby, not yet; she had just had her girls. She said goodbye to the doctor and went to see Janet; she said she needed another appointment in a couple of weeks' time but couldn't remember why.

Janet sorted out her appointment, and she left the surgery, but instead of making her way home, she found herself heading towards the market where David worked. It was going around and around in her head; how could she be pregnant? They were being careful; she didn't know if she wanted any more children, not after last time. She was at the market. She went over to the stall where David was working. He took one look at his wife and asked her, "Chrissy, love, what's wrong? You're as white as a sheet, Chrissy?" he asked her, rather concerned.

"David, David, I'm, erm." She paused.

"Yes?" replied David.

"I'm pregnant!" she finally told him.

"Pregnant, Chrissy? Are you sure?" he asked, and she nodded.

"I have just come from the doctor's; I wanted to tell you first before anyone else. David, what are we going to do? What if it happens again? I don't think I could cope," she told him.

"Chrissy, we can't talk now, can we? I have to get back to work; you had better tell your mum and dad, though. It's not fair we live under their roof and they don't know about it. We can talk about it at home later on, that's all right?"

he asked her, and she nodded. He kissed her on the forehead, and she went back home.

She walked through the door, and her mum came running out. "Mum, where's Katie?" asked Chrissy.

"She's having a nap. I know you don't like her sleeping in the day, but she's worn out. Love her. So, come on, how did you get on? What did the doctor say?" Pam asked rather nervously.

Chrissy thought for a moment. "Mum, I'm pregnant."

Chapter 3

"Pregnant, are you sure, Chrissy?" squealed Pam.

"Yes, Mum, that's what the doctor wanted to see me about. I have been to see David; he said we would talk later on; he's busy. So now you know," said Chrissy quite sharply.

"Chrissy, why are you being like that?" asked Pam.

"Like what, Mum? Scared? I'm petrified. What if it happens again? What if I am going to have twins and one doesn't survive? How the hell am I going to cope? Once was hard enough," snapped Chrissy.

"Oh, Mum, I'm sorry. I don't mean to snap at you. I am so scared."

"Mum, how are we going to do this?" begged Chrissy, with a look of horror in her eyes. She was terrified.

"Look, Chrissy, I don't have all the answers; nobody does, but you and David talk; see what you both decide on," said Pam before she could say anymore.

"Decide on what? Whether to keep the baby, you mean, or just take our chances and wait and see, is that what you're saying, because that's the only option we have, have it or not, oh, and take our chances and see what happens when the baby or babies arrive; that's not a lot to go on, and yes, it's our options, but I just don't know what to do; all I know is that there is a life growing inside me, and I am terribly frightened," said Chrissy, coming up for air. She burst into tears at this stage, not knowing what to do.

She couldn't really make a decision on her own; there wasn't a decision. She had wanted another baby at some stage; she had just turned twenty-two. She knew she would wait for David to come in and talk about it, but she knew what she wanted, but did he want the same as her? She would have to wait and find out.

David came in as soon as he could, and Pam and Phil went into the kitchen to leave them to it. "So, Chrissy, do you want this baby? Because I do. I know we have been through the mill a lot over the last few years, but I think this baby would be a great addition to our family," David told her.

"I want the baby too. I have been thinking about it since I left the doctor's. We have overcome stuff before. David, I think I was in shock when the doctor told me, but I have been going through it, and yes, it has been tough. But if we don't have a baby now, well, when this little miracle has come into our lives, why not embrace it, and hopefully the medical team, knowing our history, will be more aware. What do you think?" asked Chrissy, a bit nervous.

Even though David said he wanted the baby, was he saying it for Chrissy's sake? "Chrissy, with time, technology comes along, and things change; they will be more equipped than last time, so yes, I think we should go ahead and yes, take our chances; we may be pleasantly surprised," David said, well, shouted, really.

Pam and Phil came back into the living room. "Well?" asked Phil.

"We are going to be a family of four, so now, Chrissy, you need to get back to the doctor's and see when and what your next appointment is for, yes?" quizzed David.

"Yes, of course, David; it will be closed now, but I will call in the morning. Thanks, love," she said, and she planted a kiss on his lips.

Pam and Phil looked away. "Now come on, you two; that's how this started," said Pam, laughing and pointing to Chrissy's tummy.

"I think we need to get this sorted out, Mum. Before we tell anyone, see how my first appointment goes. I don't want Edie starting to put her oar in again." Everyone laughed at that.

"Yes, that's fine, Janet. Thank you. I am a silly mare at times. Thank you again. Bye," said Chrissy as she put down the receiver.

"Well, when is the appointment?" asked Pam.

"It's next Tuesday at 10:30 am. I'm not working, but Katie isn't in nursery, so would you mind looking after her again? Mum, once September comes, she will be at school every day, so it will be easier. Oh, I hadn't thought, are we going to be able to afford another mouth to feed?" Chrissy said out loud.

"You will manage, Chrissy; most people do. They cut back where they need to, but you should be fine. Once you are safe over your three months, you should be, okay? Work up until you can't, if that's at all possible. Just see what happens," said Pam.

***

Chrissy's pregnancy was going very quickly. Once she had been to the doctor's and hospital appointments, she chose where she went before because they were top-notch and great with both babies. On her first hospital appointment, Pam went with her because David couldn't get the time off work, but Chrissy had a scan. She was a bit nervous. "Why are you scanning me? Is it because of what happened before?" asked Chrissy nervously.

"What happened before? Oh no, Chrissy, this is standard practice now. All new mothers have a scan done. They have two; one at eleven weeks and one at twenty now, because they want to check that the baby is growing and everything is working as it should be; that's all. I'm sorry for what happened last time, but this is now new technology," the scanographer told her.

Chrissy was convinced that it was because of before, and they didn't want to make the same mistake. "Anyway, Chrissy, can you hop on the bed for me and pull your trousers down a little bit, so I can put the gel on for you?"

"Ooohh, Mum! It's cold." Chrissy laughed.

When the lady put the tool on her tummy and pressed a bit, "Oh, it's not going to hurt the baby, this thing, is it?" asked Chrissy.

"No. Chrissy. It's for us to check. Oh yes, now I can see the little bubba," she said.

"Oh, Mum, come and have a look; it's my baby; well, our baby, look. Can we see where everything is? It looks like a bit of a big blob. I can't make anything out," said Chrissy.

"It is fine; it is too early to say if it's a boy or a girl," she said, then Chrissy interrupted her.

"Is it one or two, please?" asked Chrissy.

"It's one, just one," she told Chrissy. Chrissy was relieved, but she was still hoping there could be two.

"You will be able to see more at your twenty-week scan, so would you like the date roughly when your baby will be born, then?" the lady asked Chrissy.

Chrissy nodded. "Well, with the sizing and stuff and your date of your last period, the baby should be here on 20 January 1983. Give or take a day, depending on how impatient the baby is. That's me for today, so see you again in nine weeks. Have a great day, Chrissy!" said the lady.

"Oh, I forgot. Would you like a photo of your scan?" the lady asked. Chrissy said yes straight away.

"How many can I have?" asked Chrissy.

"Well, the first one is free for you, but if your mum wants one, it's a pound," she told them.

"Okay, can we have three altogether? Actually, better have made it four," said Chrissy. "Four?" asked Pam.

"Yes, one for me and David to put in his wallet, one for you and Dad, and one for Sylvia and Fred; they didn't have this last time, so I think they would like it now!" Chrissy said as a matter of fact.

"What about Aunt Edie?" asked Pam.

"Aunt Edie can whistle; she will have enough to say once she knows I'm pregnant, unless you have told her already, Mum?" said Chrissy, narrowing her eyes towards her mother.

"Not a chance; this was yours and David's call. You tell her, or if you tell her when you're ready, it's none of her business," said Pam.

"Here you go, Chrissy," said the lady, handing her all of the photographs.

Pam handed her the three-pound notes and said, "Thank you. Next time, the baby will be bigger, so you will be able to see more detail. Have a great day, lady, and see you soon, Chrissy," she said to her.

Chrissy was delighted with her picture; she couldn't stop looking at it. They got home, and Pam put the kettle on.

"Chrissy, put your feet up. I will put Katie down for a nap if you want. Happy, love?" asked Pam.

"Yes, of course. I might need a bath; that stuff is really sticky what they put on your tummy," replied Chrissy.

"Okay, love, why don't you go up now? I can settle Katie," said Pam again.

"Are you sure, Mum? Okay, thanks," Chrissy said.

She felt better after she had her bath. She had a snooze on the sofa while Pam got some stuff done. They then had lunch. Katie liked sitting down with her mum, eating her food; she would sit next to her on the sofa or next to her at the table. Katie loved her mum; she would look up at her and give her beautiful big smiles, and then Chrissy would do the same back.

"Mum, I wonder if the new baby will have the same bright blue eyes that Katie has," said Chrissy.

"You never know, Chrissy; you and Diane have the same eyes, the same as me, but Katie has her dad's eyes, but hers are a brighter blue than David's. His eyes are beautiful too, but hers are bluer. Oh, you know what I mean?" Pam laughed.

"Who has bluer eyes than me?" asked David as he walked in from the front door, catching the back end of the conversation. Chrissy showed him the scan photo, and he looked at it and asked what it was.

"David, that is our baby; you were right; the technology has come on so much in four years; they put this machine tool thing on my tummy, and you can see the picture of the baby!" Chrissy told him.

"What is it like?" he quizzed.

"No, silly, the baby is moving, but they take a still of the baby. The next time I go at twenty weeks, we can find out if it's a boy or girl, and it is one baby, by the way, so we don't have to worry about what happened before. So, are you pleased?" asked Chrissy.

"Chrissy, this is our baby; can I show it to Mum and Dad when I go around at the weekend?" asked David.

"No, because this is our photo; I had them do one for your mum and dad; my parents have one; I have another spare one for your wallet if you want it," said Chrissy.

"Of course, I want it, and yes, Mum and Dad will be chuffed. Can we go around at the weekend and show it to them? Well, give it to them," said David.

"Yes, we can, because don't forget there aren't many people who know about the baby," replied Chrissy.

"What about Aunt Edie?" asked David.

"What? She isn't getting a picture," said Chrissy.

"What did you say at the hospital, Chrissy, that she can whistle," Pam piped up.

"Can she whistle?" asked David, a bit confused.

"No, I meant she can whistle; she isn't having a photo that's just for us," she told David. David was pleased; he had had enough of her and her razor-sharp tongue.

He looked back down at his new baby. He went over to Katie, put her in his lap, and said, "Katie, look, this is your new baby brother or sister," David told her.

"Kim?" asked Katie.

"Oh, wow, where did that come from?" said Pam and Chrissy quietly.

"No, darling, that's not Kim, but we will know soon, if it's a brother or new sister," David replied.

"I don't want another sister; I want Kim," said Katie. David didn't know what to do; he put Katie back down on the floor with her toys.

"How on earth would she remember Kim? There are no photos of her, and we don't really talk about her in front of her, but we do go to the cemetery, so maybe she's remembering that; who knows? But let's not talk about the new baby for the moment; we don't want to upset Katie," said Chrissy.

The next couple of months flew by, and it was time for her twenty-week scan. She was so excited. This time, David came. Pam looked after Katie, and Chrissy had to give up work, but Katie managed to still go to nursery a couple of times a week.

"Mrs Crawford?" asked the scanographer.

Chrissy and David got up from their seats and followed the lady into the room. It was the same lady as before. This time, Chrissy got a look at her name; it was Joyce.

"Come in both of you. I'm glad you're wearing trousers again this time; I know it's a bit more uncomfortable, Chrissy." David helped her onto the couch bed thing. He helped her with her trousers. Thankfully, they had an elastic waistband. Joyce put the gel onto Chrissy's tummy. David was mesmerised by what she was doing; he hadn't even looked at the screen yet.

Joyce put the scanning tool onto Chrissy's tummy, and then David looked at the screen. He was flabbergasted. "Chrissy, look, it's our baby. Wow, talk about technology. This is great," he said, like a kid in a toyshop, smiling from ear to ear.

"There is still only one baby, isn't there, Joyce?" asked Chrissy a little nervous, but she had good right to be.

"Only one baby. Would you like to know what it is, then?" she asked them both, and they looked at each other and said yes.

"Well, you're going to have a little girl!" she told them. They both had huge grins on their faces.

"You already have a little girl; is this what you wanted?" Joyce asked them.

"Joyce, we weren't bothered if it was a boy or girl, as long as it was healthy," said David.

"But now we are going to have two girls," he said, winking at Chrissy as he said it. They were both delighted. Once Joyce had finished taking the baby's measurements, she asked if they would like a photo or four. She had remembered from last time.

"Can we have four again, please? She's getting so big. It's great to be able to see her features, but we will meet her properly in a few months' time, and now I can't wait; it's been a long time coming, to be honest," said Chrissy.

"Now you won't need to come back for another scan; the baby looks fine. Everything is how it should be, so good luck with everything, and hopefully, I will not see you for a few years at least." Joyce chuckled.

Chrissy cleaned herself up, and David helped her off the bed again. Joyce returned with the photos of the scan, and David paid her the money, same three pounds. You get your first one free, then pay after that, but they didn't mind; everyone would get another photo to see the bubb's progress. They were both beaming as they left the hospital. *At least it was just one,* thought Chrissy. David couldn't stop smiling the whole day. He dropped Chrissy home but went in with her and showed Pam the scan photo. He had put the last one in his wallet but was scared of losing them both now, so he left them on the bedside cabinet on his side of the bed. Katie never mentioned Kim again when she saw the last scan photo, and they didn't want to take a chance on it again, plus they didn't want to upset her.

Auntie Edie came around once in a while; she had been warned about how she chose her words; the family didn't want her to upset Chrissy or David, especially as it was unnecessary. She knew they were having a scan today, and she still made it her business to find out what was going on in the family. She had seen David leave the house, so she made her way around to Pam and thought she would have a look at the photo of the scan. Pam had only just put her one away; the other one she put in her handbag to give to Sylvia and Fred, and David had just put Chrissy's one in the bedroom by her side of the bed, so there weren't any for Miss Grubby Fingers to get her hands on.

"Mum, Auntie Edie is coming up the path; hide your photo of the scan," said Chrissy.

"Too late. It's in the kitchen drawer for now, but hush, don't let on," said Pam, who had all gotten wise of Edie and her antics.

The doorbell went off. "I'll get it, love. You put your feet up!" suggested Pam to Chrissy.

"Oh, hello, Edie, how are you? Come in," Pam offered. She moved out of the way and pulled the door open fully. Edie stepped inside. "How are you, Pam? Oh, hello, Chrissy, how are you, dear?" she asked in a condescending manner.

"Oh, I'm fine, Auntie Edie, just resting for the moment. Katie is at the nursery and not due back for a couple of hours, so how have you been?" asked Chrissy reluctantly.

"Oh, I'm fine, dear; nothing to complain about. Weren't you at the hospital today for one of those scan things? Did you get a photo this time?" asked Edie.

She didn't miss a trick. "Yes, we did go to the hospital, and yes, we did get a scan photo, but mine is upstairs, and I haven't got the energy to go up, sorry," said Chrissy. Aunt Edie wasn't going to take it lying down.

"Oh, Pam, do you have a photo of the baby that I can have a look at?" asked Edie.

Pam had just come out of the kitchen and into the living room. "What was that? Sorry, I didn't hear with the kettle boiling," said Pam, knowing full well what Edie wanted.

"I asked if you had a scan photo of the baby that I could have a look at," asked Edie, narrowing her eyes at Pam.

"Oh yes, let me get it for you," Pam said, knowing that Edie didn't miss a bloody thing.

Pam went to the kitchen, picked up her photo and took it back to an eager Edie. "Oh, look, you can really see the baby now—the eyes, the nose, and the mouth—and look how straight that spine is! That's great, Chrissy; are they sure that it's only one this time and not two?" asked Edie.

She couldn't help herself, could she? "No, Auntie Edie, it's only one, just one baby, a little girl," said Chrissy without realising it.

"Oh, another little girl; what are you going to call this one, then?" asked Edie.

"Oh, we haven't thought about it yet; there is plenty of time." Pam went to take the photo from Edie. But she was hanging onto it like a limpet. "Edie, can I have it back, please? I want to show it to Phil when he comes in from work. Thank you," said Pam. Edie knew she couldn't do anything with them watching, so she handed it back reluctantly, but at least she did hand it back.

Pam came back in with tea and some biscuits on a tray; she put them on the table. Chrissy looked like she was about to nod off. Edie had tea and took a couple of biscuits. She then sat back down again, but looking into the kitchen, she could see the photo of the scan on the side. She drank her tea, and Pam had left one for Chrissy on the table's nest. Pam excused herself and went upstairs to the toilet. Edie bolted like an athlete Into the kitchen, grabbed the scan photo, put it into her bag, and left her teacup and plate in the sink. She went back into the living room and then went to the hall.

"Pam, I'm going to be making tracks now, see you later," she said and bolted out the front door.

Pam came down and looked in the sitting room. "Chrissy love, did Edie just leave?" she asked.

"Sorry, Mum, no idea. I fell asleep," Chrissy replied.

She sat herself up so she could drink her tea. "That bloody woman. Next time we do something, we bloody well hide it. No wonder she was out of here as quick as Tessa Sanderson. That woman never misses a bloody thing," said Pam.

"Mum, what's up?" asked Chrissy, just pulling herself around from a quick nap.

"That bloody woman," said Pam.

"Aunt Edie?" Chrissy asked.

"Yes, bloody Edie, Chrissy. She has only taken my scan photo of the baby; it was left on the side while I went to spend a penny. She hotfooted it into the kitchen, probably poured her tea down the sink. Biscuits have gone, though, and she took the photo. What the bloody hell does she want of a baby that's not hers or a grandchild, but my grandchild? I know it's too late to get another from the hospital, but do you think the chemist around the corner will photocopy it for me, Chrissy? I didn't want to lose it, and I know you want to give the other one to David's mum and dad—that bloody woman—I could bloody kill her," said Pam.

"Finished, Mum?" asked Chrissy.

"Mum, it's a picture; she's probably jealous that we didn't get her one, but from now on, we don't leave her with Katie or anything to do with the baby, okay, because this behaviour isn't normal," said Chrissy.

"What do you mean normal? Edie has never been normal in her life. Wait until I tell your dad; he's going to go spare. What about David?" Pam asked.

"Look, as long as we don't leave stuff like that lying around, yes, it couldn't be helped; it was like she knew we were back from the hospital; she knew we were having a scan today. Mum, you don't think that Aunt Edie has our house bugged, do you? I mean, you never know; she's not psychic, but she always seems to know when we do stuff, which is why I think she bugged the house," said Chrissy.

"Oh well, it's time to get Katie. Do you want to come, and we can get your photocopied? Take the one in your bag, and then we can hide it," Chrissy suggested. They got back from collecting Katie, who was in a very chatty mood that afternoon. They had copied the photo on the way back. When they got in, Chrissy got Katie sorted out—something to eat, just a snack—and dinner wasn't going to be for a while. Pam took her photo upstairs to her bedroom to put it with the other photo, but it had gone.

She came back downstairs. "Chrissy, you know where the scan photo of the baby is?" She mouthed 'baby' so Katie wouldn't hear.

"Yes, the one we just did?"

Chrissy laughed. "No, the other one, the first one. Well, it's gone," said Pam.

"Mum, are you sure you haven't moved it yet?" asked Chrissy, then she had a funny look on her face. "Mum, you're not saying she has taken that one as well?" Chrissy quizzed her mum.

"Do you know what, Chrissy? I think she has. I looked in all of the drawers on my dressing table, thinking I had moved them, but they're gone. Completely gone. She must have gone through my stuff one day when I wasn't looking. What the hell does she want with these photos? Right, from now on, Edie cannot go upstairs unaccompanied; I can't trust her, Chrissy; she can't be trusted. What the bloody hell has she taken? I had better check in the shoeboxes your dad has put away with Katie's stuff in them," said Pam, really annoyed now.

She went back upstairs and came down with two shoeboxes, looking very puzzled. Katie was playing on the floor with her dollies, so she asked Chrissy to come over and have a look at them.

"Chrissy, have you put anything into these boxes that you think she may have taken?" asked Pam.

"No, why, Mum? Anyway, David has been putting the stuff in Katie's box; you know we have the one for KIM," she spelt out.

"Well, Chrissy, there's some weird stuff going on, take a look," suggested Pam. Chrissy opened Katie's box. There was her baby nametag from the hospital, her cord clip, a teddy bear, pink like Kim has, a gold chain with 'K' on it for when she's older, a charm bracelet with six charms on it, a wishbone, a K, a dove, a four-leaf clover, a dog and a cat, and room for more to come. "Mum, I think that's right," Chrissy told her.

"Now, have a look in the other box," said Pam. She opened Kim's box, which had her nametag, her card with her handprint and footprint that Wendy the midwife did for her, a pink teddy bear, a charm bracelet with a wishbone, a K, a dove, a four-leaf clover, a dog, and a cat.

"That's funny, Mum. I thought we only had one charm bracelet for Katie, not one for K.I.M." She again mouthed Kim's name.

"I have no idea what he was doing; maybe keeping it for the new baby," Pam suggested.

"But why? Until today, we didn't know we were having a girl. Maybe it was that he wanted to get a second one, even though it wouldn't be worn; maybe that is how he could deal with it, you know?" said Chrissy.

"Mum, could you put them back where you found them? I know we have a memory box for her, but I don't think we should let on about this at the moment, okay?"

Chrissy was a bit stern; she didn't want her husband to think they were spying on him for what he wanted to get his other daughter, who was no longer here. She would tackle it at a later date; at the moment, they had to get through this Edie situation. When both Phil and David came home from work, the women told them what Edie had done. Pam was going to go around to the chemist again in the morning and copy the other photo, but this time she was going to have to hide it, so she was also going to buy a couple of photo albums that would be hidden in her bedroom. If they disappeared again, she would know that Edie had gone through their home, and then she wouldn't be welcome ever again. As Pam had told the men, they had all agreed that Edie was not to be left alone in any room on her own again.

***

Chrissy was taking quick breaths. Her auntie Joan was staying with Katie while the others went to the hospital. Diane was on holiday; she had been skiing, the first time she had been abroad, but thought she would be back in time for the birth of the baby, but it was not meant to be. "Come on, you lot; I can't take anymore," said Chrissy.

"Now, please, Aunt Joan, DO NOT LET AUNT EDIE INTO THE HOUSE WHILE WE ARE GONE," said Chrissy through gritted teeth. She was having another contraction. David was now here; Pam had gone to grab Chrissy's bag, and Phil was in the car, waiting to take her to the hospital.

"Come on, you lot; I thought we were in a hurry!" shouted Phil from the car.

"Coming, love," said Pam, now helping Chrissy along. Pam couldn't help but look down towards Edie and Arnold's house; the lights were out, and hopefully, she was at Bingo at the local bingo hall, half a mile away. She would have no idea they were on their way to the hospital. Even once Phil pulled off, she had another quick look.

They got to the hospital in no time. Chrissy was rushed in, put in a wheelchair, just to get her to reception, then the labour ward. "How long are your contractions apart, Chrissy?" asked the receptionist.

"About every four minutes," she replied, then tried her quick breaths again. She was wheeled to the lift to take her upstairs; they all got in. Chrissy had hold of David's hand, and when she screamed, her grip on David's hand got tighter. He shuddered; then she loosened the grip. They were on the floor; there was a midwife and nurse to greet her. Pam took her case in with them, and both David and Phil waited outside the room like before.

The porter waited for the staff to put Chrissy onto the bed, then he left the room. They got Chrissy comfortable, and the midwife needed to examine her. "Not for a little while, but I will be keeping an eye on you, Chrissy; I will be back in a minute," said Fran, the midwife, to Chrissy, who was getting good at reading their name labels quickly.

She returned shortly after. "Your husband and dad look comfortable out in the hall, drinking tea, I think it was," said Fran.

"Oh, great for them; they don't have to do the hard work, cheeky sods," said Pam.

Chrissy was in a bit of pain. "Are you on gas and air, Chrissy, or are you having an epidural?" asked Fran.

"What's an epidural, Fran?" she inquired.

"It's what they put a needle in the back of the spine to help with pain relief, but once it takes effect, you won't be able to feel anything from the waist down; it's really effective," she told her.

"I'm not sure, really. Can I see how I get on with the gas and air first?" Chrissy asked.

"Yes, of course. Now, let me hook you up to this baby monitor. Then we can hear the baby's heartbeat," said Fran.

"Mum, it's a lot different from last time; they had that silver thing that looked like the bottom end of a trumpet and put that to my tummy to hear the baby's heartbeat. Funny how much change in a few years," said Chrissy.

Pam was looking at her a bit funny, then she realised that she was on the gas and air already. They checked the sheet printout on the monitor; everything looked fine. Fran checked again to see if Chrissy was dilated enough to give birth. Her contractions were getting stronger, but Fran didn't think Chrissy was feeling much at the moment.

Pam poked her head around the door, and yes, both the men were drinking tea. "Enjoying yourselves, are you both?" asked Pam. They were a little bit red when they replied that they were, even though that's not what they were there for.

"Pam, how is she doing?" asked Phil.

"She's okay at the moment; she's on the gas and air and feeling ever so good," Pam replied. She had a little chuckle to herself as she closed the door again.

Fran had her head and hands down at the bottom of the bed. "Now, Chrissy, are you feeling a lot of pain at the moment?" she asked.

"Fran, I don't think she's feeling anything at the moment; look at her face!" suggested Pam.

"Oh, right, I see what you mean; well, she is nearly ready to push, but I don't know if she's feeling anything, so you may have to help," Fran encouraged.

"How?" asked Pam, a bit scared now.

"Well, you have heard of bear down?" Fran asked.

"Yes, well, I think I need you to help her at the top of her shoulders, push her down, not off the bed obviously, but it might just encourage her to do it herself if she realises."

"Okay, I will do my best," said Pam nervously.

She got behind Chrissy and started to push her a bit, so she would realise that the nurse came over and did the same thing on the other side of her shoulders. It seemed to work, and all of a sudden, it was like Chrissy had woken up. "Hey, what are you doing?" she asked.

"Why are you pushing me? Oh, bloody hell, I can feel something coming," she screamed at them.

"We know; it's your baby. You needed some help, or rather a big push." Angela, the nurse, giggled.

"Well, it did the trick, Chrissy," said Pam. Chrissy was pushing and pushing, then gave an almighty push, and then this pink baby came out of her so quickly.

"Yes, it's a big girl; hang on, let me put her on the scales." The baby wailed.

"Good girl, get that stuff out of your lungs now," said Fran.

"Is she okay, Fran?" asked Chrissy, a bit nervous.

"She's fine, eight pounds, two ounces; oh my goodness, Chrissy, no wonder you were in a lot of pain; oh, hold on…"

"What?" asked Chrissy, desperate now.

"No, Chrissy, it's fine; the baby is fine. It's just that you have torn a little; you need some stitches. We can sort that out in a minute; you okay?" asked Fran.

"I am over the moon, Mum. Can you tell David that he will want to come in and see her," Chrissy asked.

"Of course, love, and you did good," Pam told her daughter, and she kissed her on the forehead before she left the room.

"Congratulations, David; that's fantastic. Eight pounds, wow," said Phil. Chrissy could hear the last bit of the conversation.

"Hi, love, how are you doing?" David asked her.

"I'm fine; waiting to meet our daughter," she replied, then Fran came over with her wrapped in a towel.

"I will be back in a minute to sort out those stitches," she said.

"Stitches? Who? The baby, Chrissy?" asked David.

"No, David, I, er, tore a little bit. I need a couple of stitches. It's nothing to worry about, honestly," she reassured her husband.

They were both looking at their new daughter. "So what are we going to call her, David? We haven't talked about names yet," said Chrissy.

"Why don't we have a think about it? We have a few days or so, then see what suits her," he said, then he kissed his wife.

"I love you, Chrissy," he told her.

"I know; I love you too," she replied.

Pam came back into the room. "Chrissy, the nurse gave me this for you, for the baby; you okay with this brand of milk for her?" Pam asked; she was nervous as if it were Chrissy's first baby, but with all things considered, she wanted to get it right.

"Yes, Mum, this one will be fine. Let me try it with her. Have you thought of any names yet, then?" asked Pam.

"Not yet; we want to wait and see what suits her." Fran came back in.

"Time for stitches now."

"I'm afraid," she said.

"That's my cue to go outside." Pam took the baby and fed her while Chrissy was being mended as such. David returned once Fran left the delivery room.

"Chrissy, I think me and your dad will make a move home; you three can have some time together, and then I can sort Katie out. Is that okay?" asked Pam.

"Yes, thanks, Mum, for everything," said David, kissing her on the cheek. Phil came in.

"Before we go, can I get a photo of the three of you? Or is that in poor taste?" asked Phil, a little unsure now if he had done the right thing.

"Of course, Dad, it's great; honestly, now we have one with Katie, Kim, and the new baby," said Chrissy.

Pam and Phil said goodbye to both of them and kissed the baby on the forehead. She wasn't bothered; she had been fed and had now fallen asleep. "Chrissy, we will be taking you up to the ward in a few minutes; do you have your case?" asked Fran. Then they heard a huge commotion in the hallway. They listened until they heard a very familiar voice.

"I know my niece had her baby here this evening; I would like to see her and my grand-niece if you don't mind," said Edie.

"Actually, mother and baby are doing well. Thank you for asking, but as far as seeing them, I'm afraid not; they are both very tired. I don't know who let you in here; you're not supposed to be in here; it's only for fathers to be and immediate family," said the big, bolshy receptionist.

"I am immediate family; Chrissy Crawford is my niece, my sister's daughter, so I would like to see her, please," Edie said, determined not to be left out of this joyous occasion.

"Now, as I said before, you're not supposed to be here, so if you do not leave, I will have to call security and have you—wait, you're not supposed to be down there," said the receptionist.

"Chrissy, Chrissy, where are you?" asked Edie. Just as she was about to open the door to the delivery room, where Chrissy, David, and the new baby were, security turned up and shoved her, moved her down the end of the hallway, and waited with her for the lift. She was trying to get away from them, but they were having none of it.

They were much bigger than her. "Just you wait until my sister hears about this; she will be furious that you treated me like this. I will report you!" she shouted.

"Do you think I should have gone out and sorted it out, Chrissy?" asked David.

"No chance; as soon as she would have seen you come out of the room, she would have barged in, so, no, we did the best thing and stayed quiet, and so did this little miss. Thank goodness. Anyway, the hospitals are geared up for this sort of thing," Chrissy told him.

When the security staff were sure that Edie was not going to return, they quickly moved Chrissy and the baby up onto the post-natal ward, so they could hopefully get some peace and rest. Fran came back in and helped Chrissy; she wanted to make sure those couple of stitches would still be intact.

"They will dissolve in a couple of weeks, so salt baths for now, Chrissy," she said. Chrissy nodded, and they were settled.

"Would you like me to change the baby? She may have had her first poo," said Fran.

"Well, that would have been because of Aunt Edie," said Chrissy.

"Oh, you heard the commotion, then?" asked Fran.

"Sorry, Fran, we couldn't ignore it; she's like a foghorn. I don't understand this entitlement to see the baby before anyone else," said Chrissy.

"Never mind; that's family for you. Would you like a cup of tea and something to eat? You haven't eaten in a while," she asked.

"Yes, please, tea and toast," replied Chrissy.

David could see that Chrissy was being very well looked after, so he said his goodbyes and asked his new daughter to return with a clean bottom, which she did, then he left to go home. Hopefully, he wouldn't bump into Edie now; she should be back at home, complaining to Arnold. David got home within about half an hour.

He filled Pam and Phil in with what happened at the hospital; they were horrified. "How could she do that? She was never bothered before when you had Katie. Actually, David, she changed after Kim had gone. She thought it was her right to put her oar in, and, to be honest, she hasn't stopped putting her oar in. What on earth are we going to do? It's like she's made it her life's mission to interfere with our lives and the kids," said Pam.

"Oh, wait until Diane hears about this, Mum," said David.

"Bear thinking about it; she will definitely go for her now," said Phil.

"Look, there's nothing she can do now," said Pam.

"Wanna bet, Pam, this is really not good, you know; it's like she's obsessed with us and the kids; we may have to get the police involved, you know," said Phil.

"Because you hear about these nutters and what they do—getting too involved in their families—they can really turn," said Phil.

Pam was looking down at Edie's house; the lights were off; maybe she was chewing off Arnold's ears. The next day, David took Katie to see Chrissy and the new baby. Thankfully, he checked that Edie wasn't outside; he didn't want a scene while he had Katie with him. They jumped in the car; car seats weren't really used in those days for children, so he made a sort of booster for her to sit on and then put on her seatbelt. He checked that it was tight enough if the car went forward but not too tight that it would hurt her; she was nearly four and becoming a big girl. They drove off and got to the hospital about ten minutes later. David got Katie out of the car, locked it up, and took her by the hand. They said hello in reception, and the staff were looking at Katie.

"What beautiful eyes she has," said one staff.

"Thank you," David replied. They took the lift to the third floor, then turned right once they got out. Chrissy was again on the side; they had space. So why not?

"Hello, darling, how did you sleep?" asked David.

"Fine, fine, how's my big girl, Katie? Have you got a kiss for Mummy?" asked Chrissy. David had picked her up, and she kissed her mum. Then she spotted the baby.

"Mummy, who is that?" she asked.

"That, Katie, is your new sister!" Chrissy replied.

"Not Kim, Mummy. Kim had no hair, so what's her name?" asked Katie. David and Chrissy were a little taken aback by Katie's words.

"Well, she doesn't have a name yet; do you have a name you want us to call her?" asked Chrissy; she thought it would be a good idea to include Katie in as much as she could so she didn't feel left out.

"Can we call her Jessica, Mummy?" asked Katie. She looked at David, and he nodded.

"Yes, I think Jessica is a beautiful name, like Katie is a beautiful name," said Chrissy.

"Hello, Jessica, I am your big sister Katie," she said, and with that, she leant over and kissed her on the cheek, and Jessica smiled.

Well, it might have been wind. Chrissy didn't know, but she was delighted that they had a name that Katie had chosen.

Chapter 4

Chrissy had been in the hospital for a few days after giving birth to Jessica. Phil and Pam had been up, and Sylvia and Fred had come as well, but they were on strict instructions not to let Aunt Edie in at all. Sadly, the security staff had had enough of her and were pretty glad when they found out that Chrissy and the baby were going to be discharged. David had left Katie with Pam and Phil; they had Joan also watching out for Edie to make sure she didn't come over as soon as they walked in the door. Pam had purchased some heavy net curtains with a great pattern, so it was very difficult to see inside, which they were all grateful for. Edie had been around the house to see and talk to Pam and Phil, but they all closed ranks on her and told her that the hospital suggested only immediate family and also Katie, no other children to visit, and in no uncertain terms, NO EXTENDED FAMILY WHATSOEVER.

They were glad they could tell her that, even though she was going to put in a complaint; all of the staff were going to back it up; she had been a real nuisance for all of them. When David arrived, Chrissy was all packed; she was still a bit sore but was having saltwater baths, and that was helping.

Jessica was all tucked up, ready to go home. Chrissy thanked the staff profusely for their help in keeping Edie away. "Actually, Chrissy, it was quite fun; it was like we were working for MI5 or something, radioing up to the ward and the security guard's office near the entrance, the things she was trying to do to get in to see you. Anyway, sadly, our security guards can't come home with you, so she's your problem now," said the nurse on duty.

"Thank you for everything, and I don't expect to be back for a few more years, if at all," she said, looking at David.

"Let's see, shall we?" He laughed.

They both left the room, waved at the staff at the nurses' station, then headed for the lift. They were out of the lift, and the reception staff and security staff came over and waved them off. They had a chuckle at the lengths they had to go to keep a family member out.

"Well, we won't forget them in a hurry!" said the receptionist.

David loaded Chrissy's suitcase into the boot, opened the back door, and let Chrissy get in. Then he handed her Jessica; they both liked that name, and it saved them time looking for another new name for a little girl when Katie named her, and why shouldn't she? She's part of the family too. David was very careful driving home; there weren't any potholes or anything; the roads were pretty good back then. He pulled up outside. Pam opened the door, and she came running over, looking both ways as she did. Joan was outside her door, keeping an eye on Edie's front door; nothing was going to spoil this moment for them.

Pam took hold of Jessica so Chrissy could get out of the car. David went to the boot for her case, and then Chrissy shut the car door. David slammed shut the boot, then locked it up and went inside. There was only a glimpse of the case, then the door shut. Edie was coming from the other direction and saw David's car and the back part of the suitcase, so she marched up the path and knocked on the door rather abruptly. They had shut the sitting room door before she had gotten there. Pam put her finger to her lips to say hush, then the baby started to cry. Oh no, it would be just now that she had knocked; they hadn't even had a chance to take their coats off and sit down.

She banged on the doorknocker again rather fiercely; Jessica was crying so loudly now that they couldn't ignore the door. Phil motioned for everyone to sit down and that he would get the door.

He took a deep breath, then opened the door. "Oh, hello, Edie; I didn't hear you there," he said. But she already had her foot in the door, trying to push her way through.

"Well, Phillip, aren't you going to let me in then to see my new grand-niece, because it seems that you're all trying to keep me from seeing her. Heavens know why!" she shouted. She did it, and she managed to get through Phil's arm.

"Well, this is all nice and cosy," said Edie.

"It's nice to see you home, Chrissy, and your new baby. Let me have a look at her," she said, practically snatching the baby from Chrissy's arms.

"Be careful, Edie; she's a new baby, not a piece of bloody meat for Sunday dinner," said Phil.

Pam was still trying to sort out the washing in the kitchen when she came back in. "I have to go and get Katie, Chrissy; I won't be long. Do you need anything at the shops?" she asked.

"Come on, Edie, you can come with me," suggested Pam quite roughly.

"But I have just gotten here," said Edie.

"Yes, and it's like we live in Timbuktu, so come on, you can see her when we get back," Pam said rather forcefully.

Pam pulled at her arm, opened the door, made sure Edie went first, and then followed her, pulling the door tightly shut so she couldn't double back.

Pam practically marched Edie down the road. "Pamela, what is the meaning of this? I only wanted to see Chrissy and the new baby," said Edie.

"Jessica, the new baby is called Jessica, and, yes, there will be time to see her later on. At the moment, I need to collect her big sister from nursery; she starts school soon; at Easter, really, once she's turned four," said Pam.

"Pamela, what is all of this about? You practically drag me out of the house, and now you're talking nonsense," said Edie, rather wrong-footed.

"Right now, let me tell you this, Mrs Big Sister, that is my daughter and granddaughter in that house, mine, not yours. You come over as if it's your daughter and granddaughter; you're so bloody caring; shame you didn't think about that when Chrissy and David lost their twin daughter, wasn't so bloody quiet then, was you? But now, now you think you can be in charge of my, yes, MY FAMILY, so before you get on your high horse, you will, and I mean WILL BACK OFF! DO YOU HEAR ME AND UNDERSTAND WHAT I AM SAYING? ALSO, YOU WILL NOT BE PUTTING A COMPLAINT INTO THE HOSPITAL OR ABOUT THE STAFF. THEY WERE ONLY DOING THEIR JOB. GOT IT? RIGHT, SO LET'S LEAVE IT THERE, SHALL WE, HUH?" shouted Pam, Edie had never heard Pam shout at her like that before.

They had already walked to the nursery; they picked Katie up and made their way back home. Edie was as quiet as a mouse all the way back, which confused Katie. Every time she saw Auntie Edie, she always had something to say. Pam opened the front door. Katie walked in, then Pam and Edie followed at the back. Katie walked straight up to Chrissy. "Mummy, you're back home, and you have Jessica. Hello, Jessica, this is our home and our family," said Katie, who then spun around and pointed her little finger at Edie and told her, "This is my sister Jessica, Auntie Edie. You will not hurt her or talk horrible to her," said Katie.

Everyone was rather stunned, including Edie, who made her excuses and left without saying a word back to anyone.

"What was all that about, Pam?" asked Phil.

"No idea, love," said Pam with a big smile on her face. "Now, Chrissy, I have sterilised some bottles for you. I knew you would be tired, but I haven't made up any feeds. I thought you would like to do that," said Pam.

"Isn't anyone going to ask about the elephant in the room?" asked Phil.

"What elephant, Grandad?" asked Katie.

"There isn't an elephant in the room; only the witch has gone!" said Katie.

"Oh, don't worry, they have been learning about witches," said Pam.

"That's what Katie's painting, but the teacher saw who was with me, so said she would give it to her tomorrow." Pam chuckled.

"We will talk later, Pam, about you know what," said Phil. David and Chrissy both nodded too.

Jessica was settling in well; Katie was loving being a big sister again, but she never mentioned Kim again; it was also coming up to Katie and Kim's birthday; Chrissy had tackled David about the bracelets for the girls; he was also going to get one for Jessica; he said he wanted to put one together for Kim, as if she were here. Chrissy understood that; she had wanted to do something also, but she had collected a few things for Kim, but it was okay. They had brought Katie a doll pram for her birthday. She had a baby doll that she now called Jessica, so when Chrissy was bathing Jessica, Katie would do it as well, feeding her and everything else.

"Well, it's giving her practice for when she's older, like babysitting, you know, when she wants to get a job." David laughed.

"A job? She's only four, David," replied Chrissy.

"Mummy, are we going to see Kim and take Jessica to meet her too?" asked Katie.

"Would you like us to take Jessica with us to see Kim?" asked Chrissy.

"Oh yes, I told Kim all about Jessica, and she very much wants to meet her, but not for Jessica to live with her because she lives with us at home. Kim is also looking after Jessica as well as me, Mummy," said Katie, as a matter of fact, as if she were talking about an older sister, not one the same age as her.

"Oh yes, Mummy, Kim told me to look after Jessica, not to let Aunt Edie come near her; she's not nice," said Katie. Chrissy was dumbfounded. Where on earth did all of this come from? Chrissy didn't think there were any clairvoyants or psychics in the family. One thing is for sure: Katie knew that Aunt Edie wasn't very nice to her mummy.

When Pam came in, Chrissy spoke very quietly about what Katie had said. "Mum, we don't have any clairvoyants or psychics in the family, do we, apart from a witch? Diane was right, you know; we should get Aunt Edie a broom for Christmas," joked Chrissy. Pam couldn't help herself either; she let out a chuckle or two.

A few weeks passed, and there was a lot going on. It was already March, so spring was in the air. Once in a while, David's boss would ask him to go to the market at the other end of town. Further on, there was a great place for all of their produce, and they started to get in certain flowers and bulbs to get started for the summer, so David was going on Monday. As it happened, Pam and Phil were going over to see Phil's nan, who was in a care home a couple of hours' drive away, so Chrissy was going to be home alone all day. Katie hadn't started school yet, even though she would be in a couple of weeks once Easter was over.

David left at about four in the morning, and he would be gone most of the day. Back at about four, there was always so much to do. On these days, he had worked for the boss for a number of years, and he trusted David. Pam and Phil left just after ten o'clock. Katie still had her pyjamas on. Jessica was having her elevenses when the doorbell went. Chrissy checked that Katie was okay, and she had Jessica in her arms. When she opened the door, she saw two women she hadn't seen before and a policeman.

"Yes, can I help you?" Chrissy asked.

"Chrissy Allen?" asked one of the ladies.

"No, Chrissy Crawford, actually. What can I do for you?" asked Chrissy, and the first lady budged past Chrissy.

"Er, excuse me, who do you think you are barging into my home? Who the bloody hell are you?" shouted Chrissy.

"Mrs Crawford, you say?" asked the second lady.

"What do you mean, I say? I am Mrs Crawford. What do you people want, and what does the police officer have to do here? What is going on?" asked Chrissy.

"When you have calmed down, Mrs Crawford, we will tell you," The second lady said.

"What do you mean, calm down? You barge into my home; you don't even get my name right. Who are you, and what do you want?" asked Chrissy again.

"It seems we have had some complaints!" said the first lady.

"Complaints about what?" asked Chrissy. "My girls are good girls; they haven't done anything. Yes, my baby cries, but what baby doesn't cry?" she added.

"Who are you?" asked Chrissy, as calm as she was going to get. Katie was standing by her mum now, getting scared; it wasn't long ago she had gotten up.

"Mummy, who are these people, and who is he?" Katie asked, pointing to the policeman.

"Mrs Crawford, may I sit down?" asked the first lady.

"No, you can't; you're not here for tea and cake, so who are you and what do you want? You said complaints; who has been complaining?" She then drew breath.

"That's better now, if we can get down to business!" said the second lady.

"What business are you talking about? You had better start at the beginning with these complaints."

"Right, I will start, but please don't start shouting again. There had been numerous complaints about your girls; they had not been kept well. Shall we say up to scratch as they should be?"

"Hold on, who are you?" asked Chrissy, getting a bit nervous as well as angry.

"I am Mrs Bundle, and this is my colleague, Miss Brownlee, and we are from social services!" said Mrs Bundle.

"Social services—what the hell do I want from social services? I haven't called you," said Chrissy.

"We know that, Mrs Crawford, as I said before you rudely interrupted me," said Mrs Bundle.

"As I was saying, we have had complaints that the children are, I would say, unkempt and neglected in their appearance, and we have been told that Katie has not got a good attendance record at nursery; she's due to start school soon, which we think is rather late, I'm afraid," said Mrs Bundle.

"Er, where have you heard all of this? Because if nursery had a problem with this, they would have surely told me, and about school, they told me when they had a place for Katie, so I don't know where you are going with this, so if you don't mind, I am asking you to leave; you're not welcome in my home," Chrissy finished as she was walking to the door to let them out.

"I'm afraid I can't let you do that, miss," said the policeman.

"And why not? You're in my home, not invited but barged past me," said Chrissy, without a chance to finish.

"Well, this isn't your home, is it really, Mrs Crawford? It's your parent's home, not yours; you don't own it or have your name on the tenancy," said Miss Brownlee.

"Well, actually, that's really none of your business, so I would like you to leave. I don't know why you're here. You can see our home; it's not a palace; it's a lived-in home, with two children under five, as you can both see with your own eyes," said Chrissy, getting pretty fed up with this now.

"But these weren't your only children, were they, Mrs Crawford? You already lost a little girl, didn't you?" said Mrs Bundle.

Now Chrissy was seeing red. "Get out, all of you! Get out of my house, before I get really mad and call your lot to remove these two nutters!" screamed Chrissy.

"We are not nutters, Mrs Crawford; it seems that you sound rather disturbed," said Miss Brownlee.

"Wouldn't you sound like a nutter? If someone was damaging your parenting skills, I am a good mum, no, a great mum, and I have overcome tragedy, but that's not your place to judge me, so if you would leave now, please. You have upset me and my girls, and I am not having it, so go," said Chrissy, on the verge of tears.

"We will go now, Mrs Crawford, but we will be taking the girls with us!" said Mrs Bundle.

"Oh no, you're not; these are my girls; they are happy, safe, clean, and not neglected, like you're trying to make out. HOW DARE YOU! GET OUT! GET OUT!" screamed Chrissy. Both girls were crying. Mrs Bundle went to take Jessica out of Chrissy's arms. Chrissy slapped her one. Miss Brownlee went to pick up Katie, and Katie bit her on her arm.

"I AM RIGHT. THESE CHILDREN ARE UNRULY. YOU DON'T DESERVE TO HAVE THEM. YOU SHOULD BE LOCKED UP!" shouted Mrs Bundle.

Both women struggled to get the children; Katie was holding onto her mother's leg and screaming; Chrissy was screaming; then there was a knock at the door. *If it's bloody Edie, I will swing for her*, thought Chrissy. But no, it was Joan.

"Auntie Joan, they are trying to take away my girls; they have some cock and bull story that I am neglecting my girls," said Chrissy.

Joan was standing in the way of the door. "Now I am going to say this only once. Get the hell out of my sister's home!" shouted Joan.

"So, we are right; this isn't your home, MRS CRAWFORD!" Mrs Bundle shouted, stressing on Mrs Crawford.

"This is my mother and father's home, and that has got nothing to do with it. Auntie Joan, they are saying all of these lies." While Chrissy was trying to talk Joan down about what was going on, both of the other ladies grabbed the girls, and the policeman let them walk out of the house, but he also stopped Chrissy from leaving the house. Joan was right behind her, and she was trying to grab his helmet to keep him from guarding the door.

But he was too tall. Once the ladies were out of sight, he then moved out of the way. Chrissy ran after the women, and so did Joan, but they couldn't find them. Chrissy was screaming for her girls, and Joan was trying to console her. "Chrissy, where did those women say they were from?" asked Joan, trying to calm Chrissy down.

"They said they were from social services; they said that Katie should already be at school." Chrissy was trying to remember, but she couldn't think of where they were going. She stood in the middle of the road and screamed her head off. There was only Joan there; her mum, dad, and David had all gone for the day. The neighbours were all coming out to see what was going on. Joan grabbed hold of Chrissy, who was crying uncontrollably; she didn't know what to do or where the girls had gone, and Jessica still hadn't finished her bottle when all of this had started.

"Chrissy, what was the policeman doing there?" asked Joan.

"I suppose to stop me from not letting the girls go. Why else would there be a policeman with two evil women?" said Chrissy rather hoarsely now.

A police car pulled up, and Chrissy banged on their bonnet to get their attention, which she did. They got out of the car and were ready to have a word with her, but they could see she was distressed, not angry. Once Chrissy and then Joan explained what happened, they were quite shocked. "Well, in instances like this, miss, we would send a WPC as a policewoman in case of any resistance from the mother, which we can see in this case is not the case. Have you seen these women before? Have you seen them at the hospital when you had your baby or your other daughter?" he asked calmly.

He knew this lady was genuine, but he had no idea this had happened. "I think you need to fill out a report about this at the station," said the police officer who seemed to be in charge.

"But I need to wait for my husband—"

The policeman interrupted, "Every minute you stand here is a minute wasted; please come down to the station; let's get the ball rolling on this and this lady here…?" said the policeman.

"My auntie Joan, my mum's younger sister."

"She can tell your mum or husband, but please come with us now," he said a bit firmly. Time was of the essence here.

Chrissy got in the back of the police car. Joan was going to wait outside for whoever turned up first, which was David. Some of the neighbours went down the market to get him, but he wasn't there, so they left a message. When Chrissy got to the station, they gave her a cup of tea and asked her to wait, just for a few minutes, while they found somewhere quiet where she could talk and remember. They needed as much information on all of these people, including the policeman. They found a room with enough space for a table and a couple of chairs, not like an interview room. A woman PC came in as well; they had a huge pad and pen so she could give enough information. They had covered lots of ground when they heard a huge commotion in the reception.

"But I was told my wife was here; someone has taken our daughters, and it's been a hell of a mess. I have just gotten back from work; once I was told what had happened, I was…"

"It's okay, John. I have his wife in here with me. Mr Crawford, please come in here. Your wife is giving us as much information as she can; we will get this sorted out," said the policeman.

"Yes, so Chrissy, what happened next?" he asked her, so she told him what she could remember, but then she kept remembering other stuff; thankfully, the policewoman was taking extra notes.

"Chrissy, you have given us very good descriptions of these women. Now what about the policeman?" asked the policeman.

"Oh, before I forget, Katie bit the other lady on the arm as she was trying to grab her, but they also brought up our baby that we lost; they were going on and on, and I was getting confused," she said.

"Chrissy, it's okay; well, it's not okay, but we need as much information. WPC Smith, did you get that down about the child biting the lady, who we don't know is actually from social services?" said the policeman.

"What's that about social services?" asked David.

"David, let me get all of this out while I can, and I will fill you in with it all," said Chrissy.

Then they heard another commotion outside, which was Pam and Phil with Joan. "So what's going on, then?" asked Joan.

"Mrs?"

"Mrs Dickson, officer. I was there when this was going on, but only when they were trying to get the girls, which, sadly, they did. Pam, I am so sorry I wasn't there before; they wouldn't have gotten them if Chrissy was on her own," Joan said to Pam, but when she turned to look at her, she felt awful.

"Okay, so Mrs Dickson, we need to get a statement from you too, just in case Chrissy hasn't given any information regarding their appearance," said the officer in reception.

There was a knock on the door, and the police officer said something to the one in charge. "Chrissy I will be back in a minute," he told her, and then he left the room.

"Oh, David, it was awful," said Chrissy.

David held his wife tightly. How on earth could this have happened? Though David and Chrissy were confident with the girls, she looked after them well, and they had everything they could want or need. The policeman returned, brought in a book, opened it, and asked if she could identify the policeman. She looked at the photos.

"Would it be worth your aunt having a look at these as well?" he asked her.

"I don't know; he had his back to her, and she did try and knock off his helmet just so she could move past him; she's not violent in any way shape or form," said Chrissy.

David nodded his head in agreement. They continued for another hour or so; they had given the book to Joan to have a look at, but she didn't know either. When they had finished, they let them go. "Chrissy, if you remember anything, anything at all, please let us know. Actually, if you can keep a pen and pad by you, you can write it down."

He told her, "Now go home and try and rest if that's at all possible." When they went back into the waiting room, Pam and Phil were there; they were asking lots of questions.

"Mum, can we wait until we get home?" asked David.

"Yes, of course," said Pam.

"Where's Joan, Mum?" asked Chrissy.

"Oh, she's still in with the policeman," said Pam.

"What time did you get here, and where is Auntie Edie? She's always in the thick of everything, but when something happens, she's nowhere to be seen. Excuse me, Mum," said Chrissy, then she went back into the room she had just left.

"I'm sorry to interrupt you, but I have just had a thought; this might not be anything, and I know you can't accuse folk until you have proof. I have an aunt who lives on our road, a few doors up. She's into everyone's business, but today, she's not around. As I said, you can't go around accusing innocent people, but if you could ask her where she was today, because some funny things have been happening over the last few months and before when my daughters were born and we lost one. Well, I am just saying, can you have a word with her, find out where she was today? I'm not telling you your job, but it is fishy her not being here; that's it really," Chrissy told them.

"Okay, Chrissy, we will have a word, and if you could try and remember what she has done over the last bit of time, it might be a coincidence, and that may be all. She may be seeing a sick relative, you never know; it could be harmless, but we will look into it. Now go home; you need rest," said the officer.

"I need a drink, that's what I need." Chrissy laughed.

She didn't mean to; it just sort of slipped out.

"Right, can we go home now, then?" asked David.

"Where's Edie?" asked Joan.

"Why did you say that, Joan?" asked Phil.

"Well, whenever stuff happens, she's the first one there. She's guilty of her absence," said Joan.

"Mum, the officer asked me to write down anything I remember in case I forgot some small detail. I know it sounds crazy, but I think this might have something to do with Auntie Edie; we need to go home and write down everything that she has done about Kim, the baby scan photo," said Chrissy.

"What scan photo?" asked David.

"Let's talk about it at home. Are you coming, Joan?" asked Pam.

"Yes, of course, I am just going to pop into Albert and get him over; is that all right?" asked Joan.

"Yes, of course," said Pam.

They drove home, and Joan went to get Albert.

"Fish and chips, okay for tea, if you're up to eating, that is?" asked Joan.

"Yes, please, I think we need to get our thinking caps on and write this all down, because pardon the pun, but there is definitely something fishy about this; it's too quick. On a day where nobody was in and Chrissy was on her own, Edie is out, which is unlike her, but we let the police talk to her, agreed?" said Phil.

"Agreed!" they said in unison.

***

"Well, that was a piece of cake, wasn't it?" said Mrs Bundle.

"Well, Patsy, actually," said Miss Brownlee.

"Yes, you, Miss Brownlee, Sandra, you played a blinder. I just hope Edie can get these kids to where they need to be soon," said Patsy.

"That woman put up a bloody fight; I don't know, I'm going to get a bruise on the back of my neck," said Trevor.

"What time are you in the office in the morning, Sandra? You have to put these ID things back, and you, Trevor, you had better not go outside for a while unless you shave off your beard, cut, and dye your hair," said Patsy.

"That little madam bit me on the arm. I will have to cover that up in the morning," said Sandra.

"Trevor, watch it, these kids will wake up otherwise," said Patsy.

They had already gotten out of town and were waiting for instructions from Edie; she had gone out for the day. I think she was sorting out the new couple; I think they are from America, but she had better get her skates on. They carried on driving for a little while, then stopped at a rundown building. They walked in through the front door and sat on the sofa, which was worse for wear. They had a crib for the baby, milk, and nappies; Edie had been buying stuff for months, they had a camp bed for Katie to sleep on.

Then the phone rang, and Sandra picked it up. "Hello, yes, yes, okay, Edie, yes, it went off, okay. Yes, they are here, both asleep; you're coming when? Oh, okay, well, see you then; yes, we know. Okay, see you tomorrow," said Sandra, putting the phone down.

"Well?" asked Trevor.

"All systems go," she replied. All three of them clapped their hands, and then Katie stirred. Jessica then woke up.

"Well, someone has to feed her. There are bottles made up in the fridge. I made them myself this morning," said Patsy, rather pleased with herself.

***

The next morning, the policeman knocked quite early. Chrissy wasn't asleep; she hadn't slept all night. She ran down the stairs, opened the front door, and they were all right behind her. "Yes, officer?" said Chrissy.

"Have you any news at all?" she added.

"No, Mrs Crawford, but I wanted to run something past you," said the police officer whom she saw last night.

Chrissy opened the front door and let the policeman and the lady police officer in; she directed them into the sitting room. "Now, Chrissy, it's Officer Milton, and this is WPC Prince. We had a call this morning from Mrs Bundle at social services; she had received a message on the office answering machine that they leave overnight in case of urgent cases. So, I was wondering if you would come along with us to identify Mrs Bundle to see if she was the lady who came here yesterday. Would you be up for that?" asked Officer Milton.

"Yes, yes, I would like you to give me a few minutes to get washed. As you can see, I am a bit of a mess; we haven't really slept, you see, with what…" Chrissy trailed off.

She left the room, and David came in also. "I'm coming; I want to see if this was the lady who stormed into our home and took our girls. I won't be taking no for an answer!" demanded David.

"I understand, sir, so if your mum and dad can stay here, just in case there is any news over the phone, will that be okay?" he asked. Pam and Phil, both nodded.

Chrissy returned a few minutes later, a bit fresher, washed, and in some clean clothes. She grabbed her handbag. "Ready?" asked Officer Milton.

"Ready as I will ever be," Chrissy replied. Both she and David followed the police to their cars. The social services offices were just past the high street, and they were there in no time.

"Yes, can we see Mr Brian Foster, please? He is expecting us," said Officer Milton. The lady at the reception left them and then returned with a tall, bald man but with a ginger moustache.

"Er, yes, officer?" asked Mr Foster.

"Yes, Officer Milton, and this is WPC Prince, and this is Mr and Mrs Crawford," said Officer Milton.

"Oh yes, please come this way," said Mr Foster. He led them away to an empty waiting room with various chairs inside. He motioned for them to be seated. "Now I understand from the message we received last night that these two members of my staff came to your home after a lot of waffle, sorry, lots of discrepancies. They then took your two girls; one is a little girl of four, and the other is a baby in arms, eight weeks old. Oh, Mrs Crawford, I am so sorry," he said.

He got up and called a lady, and she called another lady, and they both came into the room. They both looked at Chrissy and David, a little confused. "Let me introduce these ladies. He pointed to the one nearer the door; this is Mrs Bundle, and the other lady is Miss Brownlee. Now you say these are the ladies who came to your home yesterday?" asked Mr Foster. Both of the ladies had their mouths wide open.

"No, not these ladies; I have never seen them before," said Chrissy, eyeing them both up.

"You are sure, Mrs Crawford, because these are the ladies who you have said have been to your home?" asked Mr Foster again.

"No, no, it wasn't these ladies, but those are the names. I am sorry, ladies, but they are a bit unusual names, but no, it wasn't them; obviously, they used their names, which means it's connected with someone who works or worked here who would know their names," added Chrissy.

"I am sorry; I'm not accusing you, but they definitely used those names," Chrissy said again.

"That will be all, ladies, for now anyway!" said Officer Milton.

We don't want to be accusing innocent people, but Mrs Crawford is right; this doesn't mean it's an inside job; it could be anyone connected to these offices.

"Mr Foster, how long have the ladies been working here?" asked the WPC.

"Well, Mrs Bundle has only been here for about six months, but Miss Brownlee has been here for well over a year," he told them.

"Well, that could mean it's someone who has been here for a little time, maybe anyone. Do you do background checks on the staff? I don't mean your social workers, but what about the menial staff? Like cleaners and that?" asked Chrissy.

Mr Foster thought for a moment. "All of our social workers have to be checked because we are working with children, vulnerable children, but also vulnerable adults, but in this case, it's the children, so maybe we need to look at the list of staff who are not dealing directly with the cases but who could be around the office cleaning, the tea lady, or the post room department."

"This is a lot to think about, but it's necessary, so if you could give me a couple of hours for us to get a list together for these members of staff, they may be innocent, but they may know something," asked Mr Foster. This wasn't going to be an easy task, but it needed to be done.

"Mr and Mrs Crawford, we will do our best to get your girls back. We understand you have given the police plenty of information; if that can be shared with us, then that also may prove useful in finding the culprits. Thank you for now, and we shall be talking with you soon," said Mr Foster as he shook both Chrissy and David's hands.

They were both in shock. How can something like this happen? Officer Milton and WPC Prince took Chrissy and David home, where Pam and Phil were waiting patiently for news.

"We will be in touch with you as soon as we can, but we will need to get you a family liaison officer, who will be here with you this afternoon. Sorry, but it's been nuts trying to get everything sorted out; this has never happened here before, so we are still learning, I'm afraid. I will call later on with their name, so you have the right person dealing with you," said Officer Milton.

"Thank you for that, Officer Milton," said David, who shook his hand. David wasn't altogether so happy with the police, but on this occasion, he couldn't fault them.

Pam opened the door. "Guess who came around about ten minutes after you left with the police?" asked Pam.

"Oh, Auntie Edie? Where the bloody hell has she been since yesterday? For someone who is bloody nosey and gets her big oar in everyone's business, she definitely stayed away when she was actually bloody well needed," said Chrissy.

"So come on, where was she? What were her excuses, then?" Chrissy demanded.

"I think we need to get the police to talk to her. She's guilty of her absence; I shouldn't wonder," demanded Chrissy again.

"She said she had gone over to her friend in the next town over because her friend was sick; she didn't know anything about it until Joan saw her this morning and told her all about it," said Pam.

"So, she rushed over here, did she? Well, where is she now, then?" When Chrissy asked, David wasn't getting involved; when Chrissy was like this, he knew better, but this time he let rip.

"Actually, Pam, Phil, I think Chrissy is right on this one. I think that Edie could have something to do with this; she's been a pain since we lost Kim; she's always criticising our parenting. Look what happened when Chrissy was having Jessica; she had to have security remove her more than once; my money is on Edie. Sorry, Pam, I know she's your sister, but there is something not right about this," said David.

Glad to have let off some steam; thank goodness he didn't shout. Then he remembered that the baby wasn't upstairs. He sat down, put his head in his hands, and burst into tears. "Who could do this, Chrissy, love? These are our babies; haven't we been through enough already to lose all three of them now, not because they have died?" said David through tears.

The doorbell rang. Phil looked out of the window, and he mouthed Edie to Pam, who went straight to the door but closed the sitting room door first. She spoke to Edie on the doorstep, which Edie wasn't accustomed to.

She was trying to prise her foot inside, but Pam was having none of it. Then Chrissy cottoned on. She opened the door and saw her mum and Edie at the door. "Mum, let her in; I said, LET HER IN!" said Chrissy. Edie thought she had won over Chrissy. Pam moved out of the way, and Edie walked into the sitting room, where David lifted up his head.

"YOU! WHAT ARE YOU DOING HERE? COME TO GLOAT, HAVE YOU? WELL, YOU GOT WHAT YOU WANTED! US WITHOUT OUR GIRLS!" screamed David.

"David, let me handle this," said Chrissy rather calmly. Phil was nervous; he knew his girls were placid, but get their dander up and all hell breaks loose.

"So, Auntie Edie, you have finally turned up, funny that, because we thought you would stay away. The police would like to talk to you, you know, because you haven't been seen since early yesterday morning. Mum said you were with a sick friend since yesterday. Now I have known you all of my life, and I have never known you to do anything for anyone unless you will get something out of it, and how convenient you were away yesterday and some of today, not the day before. You NEVER DO ANYTHING FOR ANYONE, SO WHERE THE HELL HAVE YOU BEEN? AND HAVE YOU TAKEN OUR GIRLS? BECAUSE IF I FIND OUT YOU WERE BEHIND THIS OR HAD ANYTHING TO DO WITH THIS, I WILL NOT BE RESPONSIBLE FOR MY ACTIONS! DO YOU HEAR ME?" screamed Chrissy.

"WELL, DO YOU HEAR ME, AND DO YOU UNDERSTAND WHAT I AM SAYING?" Chrissy continued to scream, then she lost her voice.

The doorbell rang. Phil went to get it, and it was Diane. "What the hell is going on here, and why the bloody hell is there a police car outside?" asked Diane.

"There is a police car outside?" asked Chrissy.

"It looks like it's been there a while. What is—" Diane was interrupted by Pam. Chrissy was nearly purple in the face. Pam explained to her the events over the last twenty-four hours, and she looked straight at Edie.

"Well, come on, from what Chrissy has just screamed out, I am surprised the police or the neighbours haven't knocked down the front door," commanded Diane.

"I told your mum and dad that I have been on the other side of town, seeing a sick friend; she hasn't been well lately," said Edie, trying to sound convincing.

"Hang on a minute, where was Uncle Arnold? If you were there, where was he? Why didn't he come over instead and at least let you know? I take it your friend has a telephone?" asked Diane, not letting up with Edie.

The doorbell went again, but this time, it was the police, Officer Milton and WPC Prince, who came in with another lady. "Mrs Taylor, Mrs Elizabeth Taylor, Mr and Mrs Crawford," said Officer Milton.

"Oh, and who is this lady?" asked WPC Prince.

"Does it matter who I am?" asked Edie, thinking they wouldn't ask her anything else.

"Well, actually, yes, it does. Who are you?" asked WPC Prince.

"I am Edie, Pam's eldest sister," she said proudly.

"Oh, the elusive Edie Wilcox," said Chrissy.

"Oh, I get you now, the lady who you were screaming at a little while ago," said Officer Milton.

"We could hear you before we even got out of the panda car. Mrs Wilcox, we will need to speak to you, and I think now is a good time as any, as this is a double child abduction," said Officer Milton, showing Edie the door.

"If you could let Mrs Wilcox into the car, WPC Prince, I will be with you shortly," he told her. WPC Prince nodded her head and walked with Edie to the car.

"Now, Mrs Elizabeth Taylor will be with you most of the time, if there's any phone calls or anything," suggested Officer Milton.

"So, do you think this was an abduction or a kidnapping? Will someone be calling for a ransom, then?" asked Diane.

"At this point in time, miss, I'm afraid we don't really know, but as there has been no phone call, we have to assume it's an abduction. I have to go now, miss, so if there's anything, Mrs Taylor will be able to help you," he said, closing the door on the way out.

"Well, that's something, I suppose," said Chrissy.

"What?" they all asked. "Auntie Edie being taken away in a police car!" she replied. "Never thought I would see the day!" she added. The doorbell went again, and it was Joan asking how it went.

Pam introduced Joan to the family liaison officer. "Liz Taylor, oh, I have just thought, any relation at all?" asked Joan.

"No, afraid not." She laughed.

***

"So, Mrs Wilcox, where were you on Monday at around three o'clock?" asked WPC Prince.

"I was over on the other side of town with a friend who was sick," Edie told her.

"So, where was your husband, then?" Officer Milton asked.

"He went over to see his brother on the other side of town, in the opposite direction to where I was!" she told him.

"So, did he stay the night with his brothers, or did he return home?" he asked her.

"I don't know; he doesn't normally stay with his brother all night; he should have gone home," Edie said again.

"So, why didn't he contact you when he heard about the little girls being taken?" asked Officer Milton.

"Well, he doesn't really get involved like I do with the family; he stays in the background," she replied.

Yes, thought Officer Milton, *probably doesn't get a chance or a word in edgeways with this one.* He had to focus. They kept on at her for a couple of hours more, but they didn't get any further along. "So can I go now, then, please?" asked Edie, rather exhausted.

"Yes, you can go, but don't skip the country; we may need to speak to you again," they told her.

"Again? Why?" she asked, a bit dumb.

"Mrs Wilcox, there are still two little girls—well, a little girl and a baby—missing. We won't stop until we find them. Good day to you," Officer Milton said.

He opened the door for her, and she left the building. She walked down a few roads, left, then right, then left again, straight down, and then right at the top. She opened the door, picked up the receiver, put her money in, then dialled the number, and when it answered, she pushed her money into the slot where it was to be slotted in.

"Hello, Mr Steward. Yes, it's me, Mrs Carpenter. Yes, can we meet up tomorrow? Yes, that would be great over the, oh yes, the liquor shop. Okay, at four o'clock. I will see you then," Edie said, then put down the receiver.

She then picked it up again and called the house. "Yes, Sandra. Yes, it's me, Edie. I will be over tomorrow at three o'clock. Please have both of the girls ready; I will be taking them with me. Yes, see you then, bye!" said Edie, as if she were ordering a steak at the butcher's.

***

"So, Sandra, what the hell happened then when you were leaving?" asked Patsy.

"Well, I thought I was home and dry. I finished my shift, went down the back stairs, but had to sign out. Then I saw them: the coppers, the mum, and a man with her. I was so scared she would recognise me. I was out of there like a bullet out of a gun. I can't go back, Pat. That was such a close shave. I can't take any chances. Once these girls go, then I am out of here," said Sandra.

"So, where will you go then, Mrs Clever Cloggs?" asked Patsy.

"I have no idea, but anywhere that's not here. Once Edie pays us, I am gone, and I think you two both should as well. Trevor can't keep working on the market. If David doesn't recognise him, then Chrissy definitely will," said Sandra.

The phone rang. Patsy answered it. "Yes, okay, Edie, tomorrow at three," repeated Patsy.

"Right, that's it. Tomorrow we are out of here, got it?" said Patsy, also starting to get worried now.

This was getting really heavy now, and they all wanted out. *Edie and her bloody plans*, thought Patsy.

Chapter 5

"Mum, they aren't going to find the girls, are they?" asked Chrissy.

"Of course they will, Chrissy love; the police have great descriptions that you and Joanie gave them; they are looking for them; it's just this town, this part of the country. It's quite big, you know; they won't leave a stone unturned. You'll see; the girls will be back with us before you know it," said Pam, trying to convince herself as much as Chrissy.

They had been gone for a few days, and even Auntie Edie seemed to be trying her best to be a bit upbeat, but she was watching what she was saying; she was walking on eggshells more than anything else. Ding dong, there was a knock at the door.

"Is David there, please?" asked the man rather nervously.

Pam called David, and he rushed downstairs. "David, oh, I am glad I got you. Look, Teddy down the market said that he saw a lady with two kids, one a baby and the other a little girl. Now he's not sure if it's your nippers, but he told me to hotfoot it down here to you," said the young man, who worked at a stall a couple of stalls down from where David worked.

"Dad, will you come with me?" called David.

"Course, son," Phil replied.

He grabbed his jacket, and the three of them were out of the door. "We should really call the police, you know; let them know what Teddy saw!" said Pam.

"Oh, Mum, let's see first if it's the girls, then we can call the police before David and Dad kill whoever it is," said Chrissy, rather worried herself but feeling a bit of hope for the first time in days.

There was another knock at the door; it was Joan. "Hey, Pam, what's going on? I saw David, Phil, and another bloke legging it down towards the market," said Joan, a little shocked.

"Well, Teddy, who works up from David, saw a lady with two little girls, one a baby and the other a tot, so they have gone to have a look," encouraged Pam, because she didn't want to get Chrissy's hopes up.

Twenty minutes later, David, Phil, and the police knocked on the door.

"Mrs Crawford," said the policeman.

"Yes," replied Chrissy.

"You had better come in," she said, moving out of the way so they could come in. "Mrs Crawford, we do advise people NOT to take the law into their own hands. I saw your husband and your father, and a fair few people at the market literally jump on this lady who had her little girl and her baby in her pram; they frightened her half to death," said the police officer.

"But, sir, you are aware that our girls have been abducted?" asked Chrissy.

"Yes, Mrs Crawford, I do know that half the police force knows that, and we are doing our best at the moment trying to locate your daughters, but at the moment, we aren't finding any leads; we will get there; we are trying to find the imposters, but it looks like they have gone underground," he said.

"So, please, if you could refrain from your vigilante groups, I know the market is close-knit and you all look out for each other, but there will be utter chaos if we have to keep chasing people up the street with their prams and children because they are scared to go near the market," said the officer.

"It wasn't them; oh, it was the person Teddy saw, but it wasn't our girl, Chrissy, the little girl, yes, about our Katie's age, but the baby looked nearer to a year old," said David.

He went over to comfort his wife, who had started to cry. "I'm sorry, Mrs Crawford; I'm sorry," Officer Milton said, looking at Pam and Phil.

Phil showed him out and said something quietly to the policeman, who nodded his head in reply. As the officer opened the door, Edie was there, waiting to knock on the door. "What are the police doing here, Pam? Have they found the girls?" asked Edie, rather nervously excited.

Oh, bloody hell, she was really thinking. "No, it was a false alarm," Pam replied, nodding towards the kitchen. She explained what had happened.

"Oh, blimey, I bet the woman in the market had the fright of her life. Well, I will go. I don't want to be in the way, and you have a lot on your plate. See you later, Pam," said Edie.

Pam thought that Edie seemed to be mellowing; she doesn't seem so uptight. Edie slipped out of the door and made her way to the other end of the road, then left, then right, and at the bottom of that road, she went to a call box. She dialled the number, and one of them answered, "You haven't been out with those kids today, have you?" asked Edie.

"No, Edie, orders are orders; we have stayed in until you tell us different. Anyway, you said the girls had to be ready for three o'clock; that's only a couple of hours away; is that still the case?" asked the voice on the other end.

"Yes, and there is a bag on the side, a Mothercare bag with a lovely new outfit for them to wear, shoes for the big one, and a new blanket and bonnet for the baby. Please make sure they are ready for me to collect them," she said in her dulcet tones.

"Aye aye, Edie, see you later!" they replied. She put the phone down and smiled to herself. She headed back home. Arnold was already indoors, but he told Edie he was going back up to his allotment in a little while. His patch up there was a good size, and he wanted to turn over the soil so he could make a start on the veggies he wanted to plant. He wanted cabbages this year, but it was still a little early. He wanted to plant some spring onions, and they could be done now, so that was his task today. He would take a thermos of tea and a couple of sandwiches. They had a little hut or a shed, but it was big enough to put the tools he needed and a stool to sit on. He did have a blanket up there just in case it got cold, or rather, when Edie was doing his head in, he could escape.

Edie told Arnold that she was going to bed; she was getting a migraine. Maybe because of seeing the police at Pam and Phil's, it made her all nervous and anxious. She asked Arnold not to disturb her; she would probably be out for the count for hours like she has done in the past. She went upstairs, closed her curtains, and laid down on the bed until she heard the front door go. Ten minutes later, she looked out the window, and there he was, flask in hand, lunchbox, all set. She would give him ten minutes, just in case he came back. You never knew that Arnold, with an empty head, would forget everything, including his head if it wasn't screwed on.

Ten minutes had passed, and he hadn't come back. Edie went into her dresser and pulled open a drawer; there was a blue folder in it with everything of the girls she managed to get, even a photograph of them she took from Pam's photos, which Pam nearly caught her with, but she managed it, jumbled all of the photos up, and Pam didn't know whose photos she was looking at.

She had the girls' birth certificates, she had copies, and she had all the adoption paperwork. Thanks to Sandra, this had been a long time coming, but she had everything; all she had to do now was hand over the children.

She looked at her watch; she had to make a move now. She checked she had everything. She had been clever having none of the girls' stuff at her house or the stuff they had at the cottage. She put her gloves on. Edie wore gloves now and again, and thankfully for the cold weather, it was still okay for her to get away with wearing them. She ran out the back door, which would take her to the bus stop; her bus was due anytime now. She had also put two bottles of Calpol in her bag, which would be needed later on.

She hurried; she stuck her arm out for the bus; he stopped; she got on; it wasn't very busy for that time of day; people were collecting their children. It was only a few stops. She got off, went around this corner, straight down, then off sharply to the left. There was a cottage; it didn't look like anyone lived there; it wasn't quite derelict, but not far off it.

She knocked on the door. Sandra opened it. "Hello there—" She was about to say Edie, but Edie put her finger to her lips. She didn't want Katie to know it was her. She beckoned.

Sandra looked a bit shocked; she knew that she didn't want anyone to know she was there, but the kids would be going with her soon, but never mind. Edie stuck her head around the door. Katie was sitting on the sofa, and Jessica was in the pram, asleep. "Are they both ready? Did you put those clothes on them both like I asked you to?" asked Edie.

"Yes, Edie, as you said," Patsy told her.

"So, what have you done with the clothes they were wearing? You know the day?" demanded Edie.

"We put those back into the Mothercare bag, so when we leave, we can throw them far away," Sandra said, guessing that's what Edie wanted to hear, nowhere near where any of them had been.

"So, is there room for Katie to sit on the pram, away from Jessica's legs, so she can be pushed rather than walk?" asked Edie, a bit nervous now, only because of what had happened earlier that day.

"There is plenty of room for the bigger girl to sit and not sit on the baby, honest, Edie," said Patsy.

"Okay, then, let's get this show on the road. Now if you bring the pram out and you put the bigger one on the front, make sure she won't fall onto her sister if she falls asleep with the motion of the pram," said Edie.

"Edie, where are you going with these kids?" asked Sandra.

"It's better you don't know. Now you wait half an hour after I leave, then drive away. Where are you going anyway?" asked Edie.

She wanted to make sure they were going far away.

"We are getting out of the country; er, you haven't forgotten something, have you?" asked Trevor.

"Oh no, sorry, I forgot." She pulled out an envelope with a huge amount of money inside it. "Now you wait half an hour, do you hear? Also, if you could get rid of this baby and little girl stuff, I would appreciate it. Thank you, and hopefully, never see any of you again," Edie told them flatly.

Edie pushed the pram out of the cottage and headed down towards the other end of the road, away from the cottage. She couldn't go down any main roads, but there was an off-licence a little way down the road, a dry cleaner, a newsagent, and a Chinese takeaway. She walked past them all until she reached the off-licence; they were there already. *Great*, thought Edie. She walked up to them and asked them to walk with her around the corner; there was a shelter there, and they could talk there.

"Mrs Carpenter, this is rather out of the ordinary, isn't it? Handing these children over like this?" asked Mr Steward.

"Mr and Mrs Steward, would you still like to have these children? Otherwise, I can take them back to their foster family; it's just that I have to go to another family after I have met with you, so if you would like to continue?" she asked, slightly nervous.

"No, it's fine, Mrs Carpenter," said Mrs Steward. There was no way they were letting these girls go.

"Right, so here is the relevant paperwork for them: their birth certificates, their adoption paperwork, and all of the other relevant paperwork. If you could both sign the bottom, then you can take them with you. Are you living here in England or are you going abroad?" Edie asked, hoping they were taking them abroad, and then she would be in the clear.

"We are going back to America; the girls will have a wonderful life. We live on a ranch out in Colorado; they will have horses and a great outdoor life, so thank you, Mrs Carpenter. You have made all of our dreams come true," said Mrs Steward. Edie smiled.

She took back the paperwork, signed her signature on the bottom, handed them the original, and kept the copies, which she said she would file when she got back to the office.

"Oh, there's something else. Katie, the elder of the two, she keeps asking for her mum, but the poor mite may play up a bit for you on the airplane, so I have some Calpol here, all sealed. Nothing wrong with them; just in case she gets upset on the plane, it will help calm her down," said Edie, who then smiled at Mrs Steward.

"Okay, thank you, Mrs Carpenter. That's ever so kind of you," said Mrs Steward.

Edie smiled again and watched them go out of sight with the girls and the pram. She smiled to herself; she had done it. She just hoped those idiots had thrown away all of the clothes and stuff that was at the cottage.

***

"Right, you two, let's get a move on. Edie said after half an hour. It's been an hour; have you got your stuff ready? Are you all packed?" asked Trevor.

"Yes, Trev, don't worry, we are completely done. Do you have your passport? What about your money?" asked Patsy.

"Yeah, I have all of that; come on, let's get going; I don't want to be here any longer than we have to!" said Trevor.

He went outside to the car; they had parked it around the back of the cottage and put a tarpaulin over it, so nobody saw it. Now it was getting loaded up with their luggage. "Oh, don't forget that bag on the kitchen table, Trev!" said Sandra.

"I won't. I was going to pick it up last, you see, before I closed the door. We don't need the keys now, so they can go too," said Trevor.

He had another look around. They hadn't taken or gotten rid of the rest of the stuff; they wouldn't need to, especially as the keys would be gone too.

"That's it, all done, one last sweep. You both have everything, don't cha?" Trevor shouted.

"Yes, we do; we have already told you," said Patsy.

So, he slammed the door with the carrier bag in his hand, threw the keys inside it, and dumped it on Patsy's lap as she was sitting in the front.

"Off we go then," said Trevor.

He put the key in the ignition, turned on the engine, and then they were off. Once they got to the bottom, before they were getting ready to join the motorway, they spotted a bin. Patsy got out, threw it in the bin, jumped back into the car, laughing, and they headed off down the motorway towards the ferry, unaware that a policeman had seen them throw it away. He headed over the road towards the bin. He found a stick; he didn't know what was inside it. He prodded it, but it didn't move. He felt the keys, but thought, what the heck? So, he picked up the bag and took a look inside.

"Babies clothes and little girls' clothes, a set of keys—what on earth?" he said aloud. This was rather strange, he thought. He didn't know what to do with it, so he took it to the station; hopefully, someone there would know what to do. It wasn't like it was lost property, but why throw them in a bin? Why not give them to someone who needs them?

"Sarge, I didn't know what to do with them; who would throw something like that away?" said the policeman.

"Did you get a look at the person who threw it away—the bag, I mean?" asked his sergeant.

"A woman with gingerish-looking hair who looked like it had been dyed badly," he replied.

"Okay then, let's just book it in; surely someone will come forward for it," his sergeant replied. The policeman did as he was told; he made sure he put the date and time and where he found it.

"Well, hopefully, that's the last I see or hear about this," he said to himself. Then he went back out on his beat.

***

"You're not my mummy; where are those other people who were looking after me and Jessica?" asked Katie; even though she had only turned four, she was quite astute.

"Darling, you are with your mummy and daddy, and we are going on a trip, so as you're a little hot, I am going to give you some medicine to help get your temperature down, okay, sweetheart!" said Mrs Steward. They were nearly at the airport; they didn't want this little girl starting to kick off. Yes, they had their paperwork, but they didn't want to cause a scene.

Airport security can be quite tight; they didn't really want any questions. Katie took her medicine; she tried spitting it out, but she knew they were going to give her more, so she let them give it to her without any fuss. She turned around to check on Jessica; at least they were together.

"Nearly there, honey," said Robert, Marnie's husband.

"Okay, my love," she replied.

She looked at her two girls, even though they didn't have the girls on their passports. They had their adoption paperwork; they would have to show it at this end and then again at their end. They were both so happy; they had what they always wanted: a family and two little girls. They were so grateful that Mrs Carpenter could set this up for them so quickly. The car stopped. Robert got out of the car and helped his wife with their new daughters. Marnie was holding Jessica, and he took Katie out of her seat; she had a seatbelt on, and she had some sort of booster seat, which made her a bit higher up than normal.

They found their way to check-in; they didn't have much luggage; they had bought the girls some things that were in their luggage. Mr Steward, Robert, carried Katie, and Marnie Steward carried Jessica. They got through check-in quite quickly. Thankfully, they had a couple of bottles made up for Jessica; she hadn't really stirred, though. Marnie wanted to feed her on the plane when it took off, so it wouldn't hurt her ears, like having barley sugar was supposed to be good to suck on one to help. Jessica did need changing, though, so Marnie took her to the ladies', where she could be changed. There was a changing mat. She had brought nappies and wipes; she knew she had to really use cotton wool and water, but this wasn't normal; she would have to use wipes and then use toilet rolls to dry her off; hopefully, this wouldn't have happen to much before they took off.

Once she was sorted, they went through passport control, where Robert handed the guard the passports and the adoption papers. He looked through them thoroughly, then handed them back to Robert; they could go through. Now they were in duty-free; they didn't have to wait too long before they would board the plane, so Robert took Katie to the shops, while Marnie stayed with their hand luggage and, most importantly, Jessica. She was stirring a bit now, but not enough to need feeding yet. She had forgotten to ask Mrs Carpenter what time her last feed was, but Marnie thought they would soon know. Robert came back with a pink teddy bear for each of the girls, one a little larger than the other. Katie was holding onto that one, even though she was a bit drowsy. Thankfully, nobody really questioned it; they thought she was just tired.

Now, they were able to board. Robert continued to hold Katie, but he took the luggage, and Marnie held onto Jessica. They had dumped the pram before they got their car to take them to the airport. Robert and Marnie had both decided to leave it behind; they could get Jessie a new one once they got home. They had also made a decision to slightly change the girls' names, so Jessica was going to become Jessie and Katie was going to be just Kate. That way, they had a new start, without the horror of whatever happened to their parents; keeping their names would only make it harder on them.

They boarded their plane and took their seats. Robert had Kate on his lap, and Jessie was on Marnie's lap. "Excuse me, miss, is it possible to warm up the baby's milk so she can be fed? She's waking up now," said Marnie.

"Yes, of course, I will be back in a few minutes, ma'am," said the stewardess. They both sat back in their seats; they couldn't wait to be on home soil with their new family.

***

"Why wasn't I told about this? Where is it, then?" asked Officer Milton.

"Sorry, sir! We didn't make the connection straight away," said the policeman.

"You idiot, how come it wasn't uploaded to the system?" asked Officer Milton.

"This family has been going crazy out of their minds because their girls went missing," he said.

It had been two weeks since the policeman had seen the Mothercare carrier bag; it had been left in the evidence box at his station. It was only when Officer Milton was there on some other business that he spotted the bag.

"Now, we have to see the Crawfords and see if it was their children's clothes, but the keys—no idea what they are for," he said out loud.

"So, can I take this bag, then? You know this evidence bag?" Officer Milton asked.

"Oh yes, please do, sir, and I am really sorry for the cock-up, Officer Milton," said the policeman on duty. Officer Milton went back to his station. "WPC Prince, is she available?" asked the station officer.

"I will see, sir; I think she's in right now," he said.

"Yes, she is, sir; she's on her way. Is it important?" he asked him.

"Oh, yes, it could be," he replied. WPC Prince came into reception.

"Officer Milton, is everything all right?" she asked.

"Well, I don't know. This bag, this evidence bag, was picked up a couple of weeks ago, and instead of being uploaded onto our system, it was left in a storeroom with other evidence. They think these belonged to the Crawford children; well, I think it could belong to them really, so would you come over with me now and we can talk to them?" he asked.

"Of course, but you know, sir, it's not going to be easy," she told him.

"I know, because if it is their clothes, where on earth are they?" he scolded.

They got into their panda car and made their way over to Chrissy and David's place. Pam noticed them out of the window, getting out of the car. "Phil, Phil? Can you come here, please?" asked Pam.

"What's up, love?" he asked her, and then he saw the police car and them carrying something.

"I think you had better go and get David, Phil; this doesn't look too good!" she told him.

"Good thinking, back in a mo," said Phil. He grabbed his coat and was out of the door.

"Nothing we said, was it?" asked Officer Milton.

"No, but I think I need to get David here as quick as I can," he said, looking at the bag.

"Yes, I think you are right!" said the officer.

Phil hurried to the market as quickly as he could. David was serving. "David, mate, you have to come home," said Phil.

David took one look at Phil, and he knew something was wrong. He looked at Mark. "Go on, David; it looks important," Mark told him.

David took off his moneybag and handed it to Mark, and then he ran home as soon as Phil ran. Phil opened the door. David didn't have his key; he left it at work. "Yes, officer, have you found anything out about the girls?" David said rather fast, trying to catch his breath.

"I wanted to talk to both of you together, so thank you, Pam, for the tea. Now we can get down to business. This may be nothing, but I need to ask you something. A couple of weeks ago, a colleague of mine from another station saw a lady throw something in a bin outside of town; this was near the motorway.

Now he wasn't sure what it was." He then continued with the story. Once he finished, he handed both Chrissy and Phil gloves to put on, so if it were the girls' things, then he didn't want to get their fingerprints on the items, as they would have them tested for fingerprints by other people.

Once he opened the bag and pulled out Katie's dress and shoes and then the Babygro that Jessica was wearing, Chrissy burst into tears. "I take it these are their things, then?" said WPC Prince.

Officer Milton tried to look at her as if to say, shut up. "Mrs Crawford, we do need to take them back to the station with us, but we promise you that you can have them back when we have finished. Now, the keys?" said Officer Milton.

"What keys?" asked David.

"We didn't have any keys, just the girls. Oh, hang on, they could be where they hid the girls. Have you tried any doors to see if they fit?" asked David.

"Well, now if they aren't keys that you know of, we have to do just that. Thank you again, Mr and Mrs Crawford, and I am sorry, but you will have these items back," said WPC Prince.

"Can I ask you something—well, two things, really? Do you think we can get our girls back, and I know you have to take the items, but could I just smell them before you put chemicals on them? You see, they should still have their smells on them?" asked Chrissy.

"Yes, of course. But I will hold them, if that's okay?" replied WPC Prince.

Chrissy had them reach out to her; the Babygro that Jessica was wearing didn't smell like her anymore, just washing powder; the same was for Katie's dress. "Well, at least whoever had them looked after them," said Chrissy, her voice trailing off.

"Er, Officer Milton, sorry, can I ask you something else?" asked Chrissy.

"Yes, of course!" he replied.

"Is there going to be a file on our girls at social services now because of all of this?" she asked him rather quietly.

"I think, yes, there will be, Chrissy. As they were abducted, it will always be an open file until we know any different," said Officer Milton.

"We have to go now; time is of the essence. Thankfully, the items were sealed in a bag, so hopefully there won't really be any contamination."

Officer Milton and WPC Prince left Crawford's, and Joan came running over. She went into Pam and Phil, and Chrissy and David were hugging each other and crying. She took Joan into the kitchen and explained what had happened. She too started crying, which turned into sobbing. She started to blame herself for what happened that day; if she had been there earlier, she might have been able to stop them.

"Joanie, it's not your fault; you tried to stop them, but they were too quick, and that bloody copper," said Pam.

"But, Mum, he wasn't a real copper; Officer Milton told us that," said Chrissy, drying her eyes.

"David has to go back to work; he's going to take the rest of the day off; this has been a hard day," she said.

Mark told David to take the rest of the week off so his mind wouldn't be on the job; he would also pay him, and hopefully, he would be back to work on Monday as he had enough cover for the weekend and the busy days.

A couple of weeks later, Edie had been in and doing her duty so she looked like a concerned relative. She had stayed away from the cottage; she didn't want to be associated with it, but once she heard that the police had found the girl's clothes, apart from raging head to toe, she had to put on a brave face around her family, even her husband, who was the wiser. So, this one day, she decided to take a look for herself. She went out early, took the keys with her, still had her set, and made her way down there. She opened the door, poked her head inside, saw the kitchen was spotless, then went into the living room. There may not have been any rubbish, but all of the kids' stuff was there: the nappies, the baby milk cartons, their clothes. "Those three have left this place like pigsty; I don't have time, and to be honest, I shouldn't have to clean up their mess, bloody idiots," she said loudly.

She left the place, shut the door, but didn't lock it. She made her way home again. There were some kids playing outside, about twelve and thirteen years old. They saw Edie leave the building but not lock it. The door was left ajar, so they went inside. There wasn't anything to eat except babies' rusks, baby milk, alphabet spaghetti, and stuff like that. They saw the nappies, blankets, and stuff.

"Hey, Jimmy, your sister has a baby. I am sure she would like some new nappies," said Skip.

"Good thinking!" said Jimmy. They both grabbed a packet of nappies, then scarped straight into a policeman.

"Hey, you two, what have you got there, and how did you get into that house?" he asked them both quizzingly.

"Sorry, mister, we went into that house to see if there was any food inside, but all there was were rusks and baby milk; his sister had just had a baby; we thought she could use the nappies; that's all, sir," said Skip.

"You said there were loads of baby stuff in there, did you, sonny? I am sorry, matey, but I need to take those nappies off you. I think that could be a crime scene, you see," the policeman told them.

"Well, there's no blood in there or anything," said Skip.

"But I still need to take them back; actually, if you come with me, you could put them where you found them, and yes, I will need to take both of your fingerprints down the station!" said the policeman.

"Ah, why? We didn't do anything," said Jimmy.

"No, but we need to eliminate you from our inquiries; it's a good thing you have done here today, boys," said the policeman.

Both boys felt quite proud to have helped.

"Now, if you can stay with me outside, I need to call my boss to get down here sharpish. Is that okay? Oh, and do we need to tell your parents where you are? We don't want them to get worried," said the policeman.

But as he was saying, a tall man came over to speak to him; it was Jimmy's dad. "No, sir, they are not in trouble. I think they may have uncovered something very important today. You should be very proud of your son and his friend," said the policeman.

There were about six squad cars turning up, lots of red stripy tape put across the front of the cottage, and Jimmy and Skip were standing near the front. The other policemen were praising them, and once Officer Milton turned up, he also went over to the boys. He actually wanted to speak to Jimmy's dad. "Sir, do you live around here at all?" asked Officer Milton.

"Yes, I live over the road," he replied.

"Have you or your family seen anything suspicious for the last few weeks or so, hearing children crying or people coming and going?" he asked.

"No, officer, I am normally at work in the day; today is my day off; my wife is the best one to talk to; she's mostly at home with the children, you know, taking them to and from school like," Jimmy's dad told him.

"No, that's fine; it's just that we think this place has been hosting two little children, a baby in arms and a little tot of about four years old," said Officer Milton.

"Actually, my missus did say she could hear a baby crying at night, but I thought it was the cat next door. Apart from Jimmy's sister Maxine having a baby, youngster, you know what it's like, but she lives over on the other side of town, so it wasn't her little nipper. I will ask my wife when she gets back from shopping," he said.

Officer Milton thanked him and said he had to get back inside to check on something. They had found the other shoe that wasn't in the bag, so they all knew that this was where they had been hiding the girls. But where the hell were they now?

"I think we are going to have to see the Crawfords again; this time, we are going to bring them here," said Officer Milton.

"Er, excuse me, the man in charge," said Jimmy's dad.

Officer Milton came back out. "Yes, sir, sorry to bother you, but my boy has just told me something. Before they went into the building, a lady came out, and she didn't look too pleased he said. She slammed the door, but it didn't shut properly. That's why they went in; they said she looked like a miserable beggar," Jimmy's dad, Steve, told him.

"Jimmy, Jimmy, son, can you come over here and tell me what this lady looked like, please?" asked Officer Milton. So, they described her, and when they were asked if they would recognise her again if they saw her, they both said yes in unison.

"So, if you don't mind, boys, if we can take you to the police station, your dad can come too, but we need to let your parents know so that we can get our specialist drawer out, and they can draw her; is that okay?" asked Officer Milton.

"Can we go in a police car?" asked Skip.

"Yes, of course; let's let your parents know first; we don't want them to worry. If they see you in a police car, they may think you have done something wrong, and we know that's not the case," said another policeman.

Steve went over to Skip's house, which was two doors down from them. He explained to his dad, who was also on a day off, what was happening. He wanted to come too, just to make sure the boys behaved. So, off they all went. They were down there for a couple of hours; they were given treats, badges, pencils, colouring books; they were having a whale of a time, but most importantly, they gave a great description of Edie. Once they were done, they took the boys and their dads back home; they wanted to stay and see what else was happening. At the time, Officer Milton and WPC Prince had been to see the Crawfords, and they had brought them down.

"Is this where they had our girls?" asked Chrissy.

"Yes, Mrs Crawford, we have gone over the place with a fine-tooth comb, which I'm afraid is why we couldn't bring you down here before. You know the stuff we brought you? Well, when I got in here, I found Katie's other shoe, so I knew it was the place," he told them.

"So, how on earth did you find this place and know this was where they were being held?" asked David.

"Well, really, there were these two boys; they saw the door open ajar, and boys being boys, thought they would investigate. They found some food, but lots of other stuff, like nappies, talc, baby milk. They tried taking the nappies, but were found by one of my other colleagues. They told him what was inside, said they had to hand back the nappies, put them back where they found them, as they thought it could be a crime scene, which they thought was interesting," said Officer Milton.

"Hey, David, how are you, mate? What are you doing around here?" asked Steve.

"Steve, oh, mate, they think they found where they had my girls," said David.

"Oh no, it's your two nippers, David; it was Jimmy and Skip who found the place with the stuff inside. I am so sorry, mate," said Steve.

"What was that?" asked Chrissy.

"You two boys saw the stuff inside, and you told the police, what clever boys you are. Thank you, thank you," said Chrissy, planting a kiss on their heads.

They both grimaced, got off, but said nothing. "Yes, we have just come back from the police station!" said Steve. "The boys had to have their fingerprints taken so they could be eliminated, and they saw a lady come out of the building, but she didn't shut the door properly," said Steve, then shut his mouth.

"They saw a lady; oh my god, David, they saw a lady; I wonder if it's the lady who took the girls or one of them?" screamed Chrissy.

"Sorry, David," mouthed Steve.

"Don't worry," David mouthed back. "Officer Milton, is this right? These two clever boys saw a lady come out of the building. Was she a young lady, boy?" asked Chrissy.

"No, miss, she was old," said Skip.

"Now, that's not nice to say, old Skip," said his dad.

"Well, all people look old if they aren't kids," Jimmy said.

"You're not wrong there, son," said Officer Milton.

"Mrs Crawford, would you like to come in? You don't have to if you don't want to," asked WPC Prince.

"Yes, I think I need to; otherwise, I will never be able to sleep at night," answered Chrissy.

She went in with David; they could see the baby milk, rusks, and everything else they could see; they saw the girls' clothes. "Officer Milton, what are you doing with these clothes?" asked Chrissy.

"Well, once they are tested, you know, then we don't know. Are those the girls' things?" asked Officer Milton.

"No, they are not, but once they are washed, can you donate them to the social services foster care? I am sure they will be glad to have them. Also, the baby milk that isn't open, is there anyone who can take it?" asked Chrissy.

"Well, come to think of it, the only reason the boys were caught was because they were taking nappies for Jimmy's sister, who had not long had a baby," said WPC Prince.

"So, if she would like them, once you have finished with them and they haven't been tampered with, would you ask Jimmy's dad?" she asked.

"David, I can't stay in here, but you can if you want to," Chrissy suggested.

She left and went over to speak to Steve. She told him about the baby stuff, and he said he thought his daughter would be grateful for the stuff, but the police have to just check it first. He said that would be fine and that he was sorry for it being their children that were taken there by force. Chrissy had a tear, which she wiped away. She thanked the boys again and waited for David; he couldn't stand it in there either. They left and went home, spoke to Pam and Phil. They all cried together, Joan popped around, and they told her what had happened. David called his parents and offered for them to go over to them for a little while. They were out of the way of all of this hullabaloo.

They said yes, they would, but in a couple of days. Edie made an appearance once she heard what had happened. It was difficult for her to keep a straight face, but they were used to Edie, so they took no notice. Diane came over, and Edie left. She didn't like being around Diane; she made her nervous. A couple of days later, Chrissy went over to social services, where she had asked to see the two ladies she thought she had met who had taken away her girls.

Mrs Bundle and Miss Brownlee. "Thank you, Chrissy, for the clothes for the foster department; they were thrilled to have them; they are always running short. Now what can we do for you?" asked Mrs Bundle.

"I suppose there is going to be a file on my girls, yes?" she asked.

They both nodded their heads. "Okay, so what I would like to do if it's all right, I have a couple of photos here, one of me and my husband on our wedding day, and there are a few photos of us at Christmas, when Katie was born, when Jessica was born, and oh, I nearly forgot, I have written both of them a letter. If they are ever in touch, or you can find where they are, please don't think I have given up on them, because I haven't; it's just that it's so painful. I know it will get easier, but at the moment, no, it's not. So, if I can leave these things with you, will that be all right?" Chrissy asked them, and they both nodded.

"We are going away for a little while; this is killing us both, so thank you for your help, and hopefully, see you in the future with good news," Chrissy told them.

Chapter 6

Jessie had just started to stir, and Kate was still fast asleep; they were nearly there. "If you would all please put your seatbelts on, and we will be landing at Denver Colorado Airport in a little while; it's while we descend. Thank you very much," said the air stewardess.

She put down her tannoy phone and started to walk along the aisles so she could, with her colleagues, make sure everyone had their seatbelts on. It was different for children; they had a belt attached to them, even little Jessie.

"Wow, Robert, that felt like an awfully long flight, not like when we set off, but at least we will be home soon," said Marnie.

When the air stewardess asked if she would like another bottle warmed up for the baby, Marnie said that she had one left until she got home. Thankfully, Jessie had slept on a lot of the flight, considering she was nearly three months old.

The stewardess returned with the bottle. "We have to make some of these up as soon as we get in, Robert; thankfully, we have that big pot for now and sterilising tablets until we get everything we need for Jessie." Kate woke up fully now. Looking out of the window, she started to panic.

"Clouds, there are clouds out there; where are we?" shrieked Kate.

"It's okay, honey; we will be down soon, then we can go for a little drive. Robert, check on her honey; make sure she doesn't have a temperature; we may need to give her some more medicine," suggested Marnie.

"Okay, honey; where is it?" asked Robert.

"It's in the overhead baggage section, but we can't move from our seats now; we can ask the lady on her return back this way," she suggested again.

Robert asked the stewardess if she could get the bag down. "The brown one, please, honey, why thank you," said Robert.

The stewardess gave him the bag and started looking for the Calpol; thankfully, it had a syringe in it to administer medication rather than use a spoon.

He looked at the instructions and found only one 5 ml amount. "Yes, it says here, honey, just 5 ml; that's up to that point; that should be enough," he told her.

She had Jessie on her left-hand side so she could get the meds out of the bottle. She gave it to Kate, who didn't seem to want it. "But honey, you're getting a little hot; this will help, promise," said Marnie.

Kate did as she was told; she then turned her head away from Marnie and looked out at the other window. On the other side of the aisle, they didn't see clouds anymore, but there were lots and lots of green fields and lots of trees. They were at a distance, but that meant they were descending. When they had finished with the bag, Robert put it under the seat in front of him, so he still had legroom, but it wasn't in anyone's way. They sat tight; they could see out of the window, and they would be down soon. Robert was trying to show Kate, pointing outside, but she wasn't interested. She felt dozy again. She looked away. Poor Robert, he was trying, but it was early days; they only had the girls for just under twenty-four hours, and they were all tired. As soon as they got in, they could get the girls settled and then start making the necessary changes at home.

Thud and a whoosh speed that Kate had never known; they had landed. The seatbelt lights were still on, and they had to remain seated until they came to a complete stop.

"I need the toilet," said Kate.

"What, honey?" asked Marnie.

"Oh, she means she needs the john!" said Marnie.

"I should really take her, Robert, but we will have to wait until everyone gets up and off the plane," said Marnie.

"But will she be able to wait until then? I don't know. Miss, I am sorry to bother you again. My little girl wants to go to the john, but I am stuck here, and with all of the other passengers, would you be able to take her?" asked Marnie.

"Why, yes, of course; we have a john right here, if you could pass her over?" asked the nice lady. Robert handed her over, but he went with her to collect her once she was done. The lady was very kind and patient with Kate; she asked Kate her name and she told her, then they went inside, and Robert was standing outside, a little worried that Kate might say something about her name change or, worse, her mummy.

Then she came out a couple of minutes later. "All done; she's fine and completely dry considering it was a long flight," said the lady.

"I'm sorry, but I have to get back to my duties," she told them, waved to Kate, and then went about her things to do.

Once everyone had left the plane, Robert put Kate down, got the other carry-on bag down and put it on the floor. Then Marnie could hand him Jessie, who had slept rather well but was waking up. Thank goodness, they picked up a stroller for her before they got their plane, but that would do better for her when she's a bit older. Robert gave Jessie back. He picked up the luggage, and one of the male cabin crew helped him with the other one. As he carried Kate, they went down the staircase from the plane. Wow, it was hot. It was nearly April, but it was already hot. Once they had left the plane, they went over to the passport control, where Robert got out his paperwork. They showed it to the person in the booth; he looked at it and then let them go. They went to collect their luggage and then hopefully to collect their car, which should have still been waiting for them.

They got everything sorted out and made their way to their car. They had to get a car seat for both of the girls—a baby one for Jessie and a child one for Kate. Until now, Kate had been quite silent, but that was probably due to the Calpol she had been given. But now they were on their way home and the girls' new home. Robert and Marnie sat in the front and the girls in the back, strapped in. They were off to new horizons. Marnie and Robert were beaming; Kate was confused; and Jessie was wide awake, unaware of the new adventures that lay ahead for her. It was only a few miles away from the airport—well, about thirty-eight, really—and they will soon be home.

"Where's home?" asked Kate.

"We live just outside Evergreen, honey. It's on a ranch, with lots of land and room to run around, for letting off steam; you'll like it," said Robert. A little nervous now, they had the girls and were nearly home; at least they were on home turf now, and nobody was going to take their girls away from them.

Robert soon pulled into the driveway to their home. Kate looked around, but obviously she didn't know her new surroundings. Robert pulled the car to a stop, pulled up the handbrake, and turned off the engine. "Well, girls, we are home!" he said rather excitedly. Kate didn't seem too impressed, and Jessie was stirring.

"I think she's due some more formula. I hope Darlene picked up some for us. She should have been able to get everything for now until we can go to the store tomorrow," said Marnie.

"Tomorrow, Robert, me and the girls are probably too tired to go anywhere just now," she added, looking at him.

"I know, I know, I just wanted to show the girls off," Robert said to her.

"Robert, they are not trophies; they are our girls, new editions to our family, and there will soon be a time when they will be shown off, but not today, okay?" Marnie said, glaring at him this time. Robert knew she wasn't kidding; he picked up Kate, and Marnie got Jessie out of the car seat—well, baby car seat. She held her close, breathing in her smell—her baby smell. She then closed the car door.

Robert had only just opened the front door. "Hiya, honey," said a lovely high shrill. Kate jumped. She thought it was Auntie Edie again. She looked around and saw a small, rounded lady with chestnut brown-coloured hair.

"Hiya, Darlene, how are you?" asked Robert.

"Oh, honey, I am so pleased to see ya'll, especially these two little darlins," she told Robert. Marnie was coming to her now.

"Hiya, Darlene, how are you, honey?" asked Marnie.

"I'm all excited, that's what I am. Can I see the baby? How old is she?" asked Darlene.

"She's just turned twelve weeks now," said Marnie, trying to keep Darlene out of her face and out of the sun.

"Come in, Darlene!" shouted Robert. He had finally opened the door and got inside. Darlene didn't need to ask twice; she bolted in as quickly as she could. Kate was sitting on the sofa, rubbing her eyes.

Robert had brought the crib down for Jessie. "I got everything you both asked for. It's in the kitchen, and I put some up in the nursery. You know the diapers and that!" said Darlene, glad to have been of some help for a change.

Marnie took off some of the layers that Jessie had on; she was surprised she didn't have heatstroke. She took off her hat to show her little tuft of brown hair. Kate looked like her dad but had her mum's hair colour but her dad's bright blue eyes. Jessie looked like Chrissy but had David's hair colour.

"My, these girls are real pretty, Bob. They really are!" said Darlene.

"Well, you both look like you have your hands full. I will pop back later with Mitch and the kids, just to say hi and welcome the young ones," she added.

"Thank you, Darlene, for everything; see ya later," replied Marnie. She loved her sister-in-law, but sometimes she did go on.

Marnie put Jessie into the crib and went upstairs to see what Darlene had already picked up for them. She went into the nursery and saw she had indeed picked up about five packs of diapers, disposable ones—*That would be better,* thought Marnie. She had also picked up some cotton wool puffs. Marnie had already told her not to buy wipes just yet; the baby was too young, but she had gotten quite a lot of stuff. Kate had jumped off the sofa and gone over to the crib. Jessie was awake and looking around her new surroundings in her crib. She was only three months old, so she couldn't sit up at all yet. She was too little. Kate put her hand in the crib, and Jessie caught hold of her finger.

"Jessica, I have no idea where we are, who these people are, or where Mummy and Daddy are. Aunt Edie said they were dead, but I don't believe her; she's not a nice lady, taking us away from Mummy and Daddy. But I think we have to stay with these new people for now anyway until Mummy and Daddy come and find us," she said, giving her baby sister a big smile, which Jessie didn't understand.

Maybe Kate thought she was imagining it, but it looked like Jessie was smiling back at her, and then again, it might have been wind. Marnie returned with Robert; they wanted to show the girls the house. Well, it looked like a mansion; it was so big. Robert came over and took Kate's hand, and Marnie picked up Jessie. "Come on, darlin, let's show you your bedroom," said Robert. He held onto Kate's hand, not tightly; he didn't want to squash her. "Up, we go right up here," he told her. They went up the staircase, which had a lovely, thick oak handrail on both sides. It was a beautiful staircase.

Once they had reached the top, he headed towards the left. The first bedroom she saw was massive; it was decorated in cream with brown accessories. "That's Mummy and Daddy's room," said Robert. Kate snatched her hand away and ran inside, thinking she would find her mum and dad, but no, it was just an empty room except for furniture.

Robert followed her inside, and then he could see her confusion. "Honey, Kate, this is your mummy and daddy's room; that's me and Mummy there," he said, pointing towards Marnie. She looked so confused.

"But you're not my mummy and daddy; they are far away now. How come me and Jessica are coming to live here with you and not with Nanny Pam and Grandad Phil?" asked Kate, really not sure what was going on.

"Maybe she's more confused than we first thought, Marnie. I mean, look at her; she doesn't look happy to be here with us," said Robert, a little upset.

"Robert, it's going to take time; if Mrs Carpenter is right, these girls have just recently lost their parents. It's going to take some adjusting, so let's give it some time, eh?" suggested Marnie.

There was no way Marnie was giving these girls back to Nanny Pam or Grandad Phil anyway; who were these people? Kate would forget them; she would make sure of it.

"Now, come on, Robert, let's show Kate her and Jessie's room!" suggested Marnie again. So, Robert took hold of Kate's hand again; she took it reluctantly; she was confused; so much had happened since Jessica had come home from the hospital; then, those horrible ladies, she bit one of them; that felt good at the time. Thankfully, the lady didn't smack her. They had wandered onto the next bedroom, because between their new parents room, there was a bathroom, then Kate's room, which had been decorated in the softest pink colour. There was a big single bed with a brass bedstead; there were tonnes of teddy bears and lots and lots of dolls, every kind, baby dolls, skinny dolls; they had even got her a dollhouse. Kate's eyes were really wide; she couldn't take it in, then she spotted it, over in the corner—a big fluffy chestnut brown horse—a rocking horse, to be precise.

"Oooooh, is that for me?" asked Kate as she ran over to it; she couldn't get onto it. Robert helped her up. *We did it; she has seen something she likes.* He put her on and told her to be steady and to put her feet into the stirrups to help her hold onto the horse.

"Do you have a name for him, Kate?" asked Robert.

"Yes, Woody," stated Kate.

"Why Woody?" asked Robert, a little unsure.

"Well, he doesn't have feet that go on the floor, but this woody thing will help him stand up!" she said as a matter of fact.

He pushed her a little on it. "Actually, do you like horses?" asked Robert.

"Yes, I think so. I haven't seen many horses, why?" asked Kate.

"Well, we have stables and lots and lots of horses!" said Robert.

"Do you?" Kate replied, with her big, bright blue eyes as wide as saucers.

"All of this in here is for you: the teddies, dollies, and dollhouse. Do you think you would be happy here with Jess, Mummy, and me?" asked Robert, a little nervous; he had just asked the question, just in case she said no.

"Oh yes, Robert, I like it here a lot, and so will Jess," said Kate. Robert wasn't too worried; she called him Robert instead of Daddy; there was plenty of time for that later; she would be used to living there with him, Marnie and, of course, Jess.

"Where is Jessie going to sleep, then?" asked Kate, a bit inquisitive now. She took hold of Robert's hand and followed Marnie and Jessie a couple of doors down the hallway. There was another bathroom between Kate and Jessie's rooms. "Robert, how come there are two bathrooms?" asked Kate.

"Well, the first one, between Mummy and mine and your bedroom, is for Mummy and Daddy, and the one between yours and Jess's room is your bathroom to share," said Robert.

"Wow, that's a lot of bathrooms," said Kate, impressed.

"Well, we have another one on the other side of the staircase, as well as two more bedrooms," Robert told her.

"So, who else is living here, then?" asked Kate, getting a little confused.

"Or are we just guests as well?" she asked him.

"No, Kate, you and Jess live here with us; that's when we have visitors to stay. You know, I said that we have horses. Well, sometimes our family or friends come over for a few days in the holidays, so we all go horse riding together, sometimes down to the beach as well," Robert said. On hearing this, Kate couldn't believe what she was hearing.

"A beach near here?" said Kate, very surprised.

"Yes, Kate, we have horses, and we have cattle," said Robert. Now Kate was really confused.

"What's cattle?" asked Kate.

"You know cows and bulls!" replied Robert. Kate understood about cows; they had learnt about cows at nursery.

"It's where milk comes from," she stated.

"Yes, that's right, honey!" said Marnie, coming back out of Jess's room.

"Come on, you guys, don't you want to see Jess's room?" asked Marnie, a little annoyed.

"Coming, Marnie, I was just telling Kate about the horses," he told her.

"Yeah, I heard," Marnie replied.

"Well, Kate, this is where Jess is going to sleep. Do you like her room? It's a lovely lilac with clouds on the ceiling, and it gets darker the further down the walls it gets. Do you like it?" asked Marnie, beaming.

"Yes, it's lovely, but why aren't me and Jess together?" asked Kate.

"Don't you like your room, honey?" asked Marnie, a little crestfallen.

"Oh, it's lovely, Marnie; I just thought we would be together," said Kate, a little sad.

"When you lived at your other house, did you sleep in the same room as Jess?" asked Marnie a little nervous; she didn't want to start talking about her home before they got them, but she had to find out some things sometimes. This was going to happen.

"Oh no, Jess slept in her crib in Mummy and Daddy's room, and I had Diane's old bedroom when she moved out," Kate said, trying to sound a bit more grown up than she was.

"Okay, honey, but this is where Jess is going to sleep; this is her nursery until she gets bigger; then we can get a bed like yours if you like; you can come and help us choose it if you want?" encouraged Marnie.

Kate liked the idea that she was being included in things, like she used to be at home.

"Don't worry, Kate, we have a baby monitor; it's new. Like all of these things we got you both. So we put this one on in here, and then we take the other one and put that in our bedroom, and when Jess cries, we will hear her and then come and see what's wrong; you know if she needs feeding or her diaper changed," said Marnie.

"What's a diaper?" asked Kate.

"You know what babies wear when they wet themselves," said Marnie.

"Oh, you mean a nappy," said Kate.

"Nappy, diaper, yes, that's right, Kate. Now let's go back downstairs, unless you want to see the guest rooms, and I will take Jess back downstairs so I can get her formula on," said Marnie.

She felt exhausted; she didn't think a little girl would be so inquisitive or nosey. Robert took her to see the other rooms; she was enjoying it.

"So, when you get a bit more settled, we can take you down to the stables and see the horses, would you like that?" he asked.

"Oh yes, please," she said as she was skipping towards the staircase, but she stopped at the top.

Thank goodness for that, thought Robert. He thought she was going to skip down the stairs. Kate seemed to like the new house; she hadn't realised that she wasn't in England anymore, but she was starting to let herself go. Edie had told the stewards that the girls' parents were killed in a car crash because she wanted to get them settled with new parents as soon as possible, which both Marnie and

Robert were pleased with but thought it may be a bit too early. Maybe they should have stayed with foster parents, but then maybe Kate wouldn't want to leave them to go with both her and Robert, so she thought it would be better this way for all of them. Marnie fed Jess in her nursery; she had a rocking chair that would soothe Jess while she had her formula.

Kate seemed to spend more time with Robert, which he loved. He was happy that they were able to have two girls; even if there was no boy, that didn't matter. Both of them growing up on a ranch, they would get to learn lots of new things, and town was only a mile or so away, so they could go there every once in a while, but they would have them grow up near the land, fresh grass, the lake, stables—*What more could a little girl want?* he thought to himself.

Soon, it was time for the girls to go to bed. They had some night things, which Darlene had gotten. Once Marnie called her and gave her the girls' sizes, she had to convert them from English to American; the clothes sizes are different in both countries. Both Robert and Marnie put the girls to bed. Marnie had wanted to bathe Kate, but she didn't want to rush her. She wanted Kate to trust the two of them, but this was okay for all of them. Kate got into bed; even though it was a single bed, it was a bit high for her to climb into. Marnie tucked her into it; she had a big duvet with a lovely pink pattern on it.

"We are going to go shopping tomorrow, Kate, and get you some new things; would you like that?" asked Marnie.

"Oh yes, Marnie, thank you, and for Jessie as well?" asked Kate, a little nervous; she didn't know how things were going to work here, but only time would tell. She didn't think she would see her mum and dad again, but she could think of them. Thank goodness, she had her memories.

Auntie Edie was carrying Jessie and dragging Kate behind her. "Come on, lazy bones, we have to go and get this car; we are going home!" shouted Edie. They were running down this road. Auntie Edie had a hold of Kate's hand and was holding it quite tightly. "You two ain't getting away from me again, you naughty little brats!" screamed Edie.

"NO, NO, I'm not coming with you, Edie. No, Auntie Edie, let go of me. Please, Auntie Edie, let go of me. I don't want to go with you again. Leave me, and Jessie, we..." shouted Kate when Marnie and Robert bounded into her bedroom.

"Honey, you're having a nightmare," said Marnie, grabbing hold of Kate and holding her tight. Kate had huge tears running down her cheeks. Marnie kissed her forehead and wiped away her tears.

"Marnie, please don't let Auntie Edie take me and Jess away again!" demanded Kate.

"Nobody is taking you anywhere, honey; you're with us now, your new mummy and daddy; we won't let anyone hurt you; we promise!" said Marnie, actually looking rather terrified.

"Of course we won't, Kate; we both promise," added Robert.

Oh my goodness, what has happened to these girls, and who the hell was Auntie Edie? Though Robert didn't know what had happened to these girls, he knew that, come hell or high water, he wasn't letting anyone take them away. He took over from Marnie and hugged his new daughter, rocking her while holding her tight, so she felt secure and not scared. "You promise?" asked Kate.

"We promise, both of us," said Robert, looking around for Marnie, but she had gone to check on Jess.

"She's fast asleep, Robert; heard none of this; love her!" Marnie told him. Robert cradled his daughter until she fell asleep, which was about ten minutes later. She was dreaming that she and Jess were running through the meadow; even though she hadn't been there yet, she knew it was where she was living. Robert settled her back down onto her pillow. They left the night light on for her; they didn't think she was scared of the dark, but this might make her feel a bit more comforted.

"Do you know what, Marnie? I think this Edie woman has had an effect on Kate, not Jess, because she's a baby, but maybe the story we have been told isn't true?" said Robert.

"Now, Robert, whoever this Auntie Edie is, she won't come looking for the girls here; nobody knows we brought them to America except that Mrs Carpenter lady, so we and the girls will be fine. Let's see how Kate is; she may need therapy, but for now, let's just see if these nightmares continue. I'm going back to bed, and believe me, Robert, there is no reason on this earth that will make me give these girls back to anyone; they are ours now, end of," Marnie told him quite abruptly. He knew his wife was right, but something about this didn't feel right, and he also wanted to go back to sleep.

***

"Sarge, you will not believe what we have found at the airport," said the policeman.

"What is that, constable? Can you bring it in to the station?" asked Officer Milton.

"Er, yes, of course, but I would rather not touch it; you know, fingerprints and that," said the policeman.

"What is it, then, a bloody spacecraft?" asked Officer Milton.

"No, sir, it's a pram," he told him.

"A pram—who in the hell would leave a pram at the airport?" shouted Officer Milton.

"Oh, my word, I think you need to get a van over and they need to bring those ramp things, and for goodness' sake, please make sure you're wearing gloves; I don't want anyone's prints on these," he told him.

"Okay, Sarge!" said the policeman. He radioed in for a van with the ramp things so it could be wheeled onto the van.

"Someone will be with you soon, son. Thank you for this," he said to him.

The van turned up about half an hour later, and the driver, the mechanic, brought the ramp things so it could be wheeled up. "Have you got gloves with you, sir? The boss was very insistent, you see?" asked the mechanic.

"Yes, I have some; I have already put them on, see," he said, showing the guy his hands. They put up the ramp to the back of the van. The policeman wheeled it up slowly, and the mechanic put it in the back and put on the brake. He thought that would be enough to keep it stable.

"Are you coming back to the station, sir?" asked the mechanic.

"Oh yes, I will need to fill out a report and see the sarge, of course, so what if I sit in the back with it and then hopefully it won't move?" he told the mechanic. It was a transit van, so there was not really anywhere for the policeman to sit down except on the inside of the top of the wheels. The mechanic threw him a clean blanket.

"If you put that down there and then sit on it, it will keep you from getting your uniform dirty and mucky," said the mechanic.

The policeman did as he was told. The pram brake was on; it wasn't going anywhere, but if it did, the policeman could hopefully steady it. The mechanic shut the back doors and locked them, then went around the front, opened the door, and got inside. It was only a little way back to the station when they pulled up outside, where the vehicles were normally kept. Officer Milton was already outside waiting with WPC Prince, and they both looked a bit excited. The mechanic opened the back doors, pulled the ramp down, the policeman in the van took off the brake, and the mechanic wheeled the pram down. Officer Milton was practically clapping; he was nearly jumping for joy.

"Do you think this is the one, sir? Do you think this is the pram the two girls were taken in to the airport, I mean?" asked WPC Prince.

"I am hoping so; provided the elements haven't been against us, we can check for fingerprints, and hopefully, this will give us a new lead though!" he said to the few people around him.

"The only thing, sir. I am wondering if this now means that those two little girls are still in the country. What on earth do we tell the parents? I mean, they will be devastated, and it's a huge world out there," said the policeman.

A puzzled look came across Officer Milton's face. "Well, until we know what's what, young man, we will find out, at least if any prints on this pram match the prints from that awful house," he said to the crowd now around him.

"We can tell the parents once we know what's going on, but until we stay schtum, you hear, until we have further evidence, it does seem likely that it's a possibility and nothing should be ruled out," he said as he looked around at the group. He was nervous; maybe his police constable was right; maybe getting those girls back was a slim chance. *But a chance is a chance,* he thought to himself.

Chapter 7

"Where are we going? Back to the airport?" asked Kate.

"No, honey, we are going to the store to get you and Jess both some things; we didn't give Darlene a big enough list, but we wanted to see what you liked yourself!" replied Marnie.

They had both decided that once the girls woke up in the morning, they would take them shopping; it wasn't far to town; they wanted to get Kate some denims and some boots. Even though the weather was warmer than it was in England, they needed more weatherproof clothes. Robert parked the car, and they all got out. They had wanted to get a proper stroller for Jess; they left the other manky thing back at the airport in England. They wanted to get her an American one, so they were hoping to get that too. Robert held onto Kate, and Marnie was holding onto Jess. Marnie wanted to get the stroller first; that way, she could put Jess down and start pushing her everywhere, rather than that flimsy thing that Darlene had brought around.

They went into the baby shop. Marnie saw a couple she liked; they were Chicco and Graco; one was blue-check, the other was deep purple. "Well, that looks a little more girly, rather than the blue one; what do you think, Robert?" she asked him.

"Yes, I like that one; let's speak to someone," said Robert. Robert managed to get hold of a sales assistant, and they went out back to have a look; he came back with a brand new one, still in its protective cover.

Robert called Marnie over to have a look at it, and she nodded in approval, so Robert went to pay for it; the other assistant was putting it all together. "Look, Robert, it comes with a plastic rain cover; it looks comfy for Jess too," Marnie remarked.

Robert wasn't really taking any notice of what Marnie was saying; he just realised he hadn't seen Kate for a few minutes. "Marnie, have you seen Kate? She was just here, but I can't see her," said Robert, worried.

He left his change and receipt on the counter and darted around the store. He looked around every aisle and unit in the store. "Phew, found her!" shouted Robert. Kate was sitting on the floor in a corner.

She was sitting on a comfy seat, all curled up, with a book in her hand. "Kate, Kate, are you okay, honey?" asked Robert, trying not to scare her.

"Mmm," replied Kate; she looked half asleep.

"We got a stroller for your sister. Is there anything in this store that you like?" Robert asked, hoping she would choose something to take her interest rather than her nearly falling asleep.

"Oh, sorry, Robert, I didn't realise I was still tired," she replied.

She can't still have jetlag, he thought, *but maybe she did; she was only tiny.* "Would you like this book, honey?" Robert asked her.

"Oh yes, please; it's rather lovely; thank you," Kate replied.

Robert picked her up and the book, went back to the cash register and picked up his change and receipt.

"So you found her, then?" said Marnie.

"Yes, she was over by the books on a comfy chair; she was nearly asleep; we have to keep an eye on this little one when we go out; it seems that she likes to wander off!" suggested Robert.

He paid for the book, and then they left the store. Jess was happily asleep in her new stroller. Marnie preferred this one; it was very easy to push, and it had a great bag space underneath the stroller.

"Where to now, then, Robert?" asked Marnie.

"I think we should get some denims for Kate; we can wait for Jess for now; we have plenty of time for her to wear them," replied Robert.

They headed about halfway down the street, then turned into a shop that had denims, boots, flannel shirts, and just about everything you needed to live in the country. Robert picked up a couple of pairs; he put them up against her. The first pair were too big around the middle, but the second pair would have fit lovely. "Er, excuse me, is there somewhere we can try on these denims for our little girl, please?" asked Robert.

"Why, yes, we have changing rooms over here, if you would like to bring her over. Is there anything else you would like to get her before you go into the changing rooms? That way, honey, you won't be going back and forth a whole lot," said the lady, who had appeared from out back.

Marnie told Robert to sit down with Jess while she and Kate found what they wanted; they were in the store for a while. Marnie picked up some jeans, shirts, boots, cowboy and desert boots, and some braces because Kate had taken a liking to them. She even got her a cowboy hat, which she was delighted with.

Marnie took everything to the cash register. "Oh my, what beautiful bright blue eyes she has," commented the lady.

Marnie now wanted to pay and get out of the store; she knew she had brown eyes and Robert had green eyes; they didn't want to draw attention to themselves. "Thank you, ma'am," said the lady as she handed over Marnie's purchases.

Robert took hold of Kate. Marnie took over the stroller from him; she put some of the bags underneath the stroller, and Robert carried the rest. They got out of the store as quickly as they could.

"Why the panic, Marnie?" asked Robert.

"Because the lady noticed Kate's blue eyes. I have brown, and you have green," said Marnie.

"Marnie, these girls are adopted, so yes, their eye and hair colour may not be the same as ours; you do panic, you silly thang," replied Robert.

"If you want, we can take this stuff back to the car and carry on shopping; we have to still get a lot of stuff, and don't forget we have to get a school for Kate and soon; we don't want people asking too many questions, Marnie," Robert said to her.

There weren't too many stores in town; if they wanted to get a lot of stuff for the girls, they would have to go back to Denver, but for now they could get the few things needed. They went into another store to get some food. Jess had plenty of formula; she was too young to try anything else yet, but they wanted to get Kate into eating their food; it was very meat-based, like steak, lamb, ribs, and lots of chicken, so even though Darlene had again brought some food, they wanted to have a proper look around.

Once they walked in, Robert thought he heard someone call his name. "Robert? Robert," Darlene called; she was with her family, Mitch, their son Ethan and daughter Mary-Lou; they all rounded on Robert, Marnie, and the girls. Jess was fast asleep in the stroller, but Kate, she looked a bit scared of someone so full-on. "Well, aren't you the cutest little thing?" Darlene said.

Mitch nodded his head in agreement. Mary-Lou and Ethan walked up to Kate and said hello. Kate was standing behind Robert by this stage. "Hello," she just about whispered.

"How come you're down here shopping, Robert?" Darlene asked.

"Didn't I get you enough yesterday?" she added.

"Oh yes, Darlene, we just wanted to get some more stuff and some clothes for Kate; how are you?" Marnie asked her.

"We are just fine, waiting for our invitation to come over and meet your new girls, so can we come over this evening?" Darlene asked. Mary-Lou and Ethan nodded too.

"Yeah, okay, I suppose so," Robert replied.

"Bout six o'clock okay for y'all?" Robert asked.

"Yeah, we will be there. Dinner on you guys, then?" Darlene pushed.

"Yeah, okay, see you later; we have to get going. See you, Darlene, Mitch, Mary-Lou, Ethan!" Marnie said, and then she moved around the store to get what they needed.

Once they finished at the cash register, they made their way back to the car. "So now we have visitors this evening," Robert stated.

"I wanted us to get the girls settled before they came over, but at least we can get it out of the way now, then?" Robert told Marnie; it wasn't though she was really listening; she was sorting Jess out in the back, and Kate was holding onto her book in her car seat.

Robert drove back; it didn't take long, but they did have a lot of bags. "Steward Ranch." He drove down their huge drive then pulled up outside the garage double doors.

"Great to be home. Thank goodness, the town isn't too far away, and we don't have to go there very often," Robert said aloud.

He took Kate inside and some of the bags; Kate helped him; Marnie took hold of Jess. Now that she had a decent stroller, she was satisfied, because even though Darlene had good taste, she didn't think the stroller was good enough for Jess, who was now wide awake and wanting her lunch. Bang at six o'clock, the doorbell rang with Darlene, Mitch, and the children. Mary-Lou was seven years old, and Ethan was nine years old; they were good kids, not outspoken like their mother but quieter like their father. Robert opened the door to them; they all said their hellos again, and Robert invited them inside. Marnie hadn't really wanted the family over just yet because she wanted time to bond with Jess and Kate, but Darlene wasn't going to stay away for long; she had wanted her presence known pretty quickly.

Marnie had fed and changed Jess already; she was settled. Robert was cooking this evening: ribs, rice, salad, potato salad, coleslaw, and whatever else they felt like. "Oh, good food tonight," Mitch commented.

"Beer?" he added.

"Yes, Mitch, in the refrigerator over there," Robert told him, pointing to the fridge; it wasn't as if Mitch didn't know where it was; it's just that they didn't have them over very often for a meal.

Kate was doing really well. Mary-Lou wanted to sit and play with her. "Mama, Kate has the most perfect, bright blue eyes, come and have a look," Mary-Lou told her mother.

"My, she has beautiful blue eyes. I never noticed them yesterday," she said. *It's not like she could miss them*, thought Marnie.

Ethan was bored; he wanted to play with cowboys and Indians, but girls don't like playing with them; they want to play with dolls, and they have to be manly for cowboys and Indians. They had their food. Darlene didn't want to leave, but the children had school the next morning and needed to get some decent sleep. They said their goodnights. Robert took Kate upstairs, while Marnie had Jess in her arms. They were going to bathe the girls; well, Robert was going to wash Kate's hair; he wanted Marnie to wash both of them because they were, well, girls and little ones at that. Marnie took over with Kate once he finished her hair, then held Jess so once Kate was washed, Robert could scoop her in a big fluffy towel and pat her dry, but he was nervous about that too.

Marnie raised her eyebrows. "It looks like I will have to do most of this then," she told him.

"Go and get that book that Kate picked today; once she's in her nightwear, you can read her a story," Marnie said to Robert.

"Good idea, Marnie," he said, dashing off to fetch it.

Marnie told Robert to brush and dry Kate's hair before she gets into bed, then he can read her storybook to her. He towel-dried her hair, then brushed it out; it was lovely and soft, and she smelt so clean. "You okay, honey?" asked Robert.

"Yes, thank you, Robert, thank you for my book. Can I ask you something, Robert?" Kate asked.

"Of course, you can, Kate!" he replied.

"Who is Darlene?" Kate asked.

"Kate, Darlene is my sister, like Jess is your sister. Mitch is her husband, like I am Marnie's husband."

"And Mary-Lou and Ethan are their kids like me and Jess are to you, is that right?" Kate asked.

"Yes, that's right, honey. Me and Marnie are your mummy and daddy now, so you don't have to worry about a thing; you and Jess are both safe with us," Robert said.

He knew that Kate was grown up for a four-year-old; she was definitely clever for her age. Once he had read the story, he sat up. Kate had already fallen asleep; he left her nightlight on and kissed her gently on the forehead; he left the bedroom door ajar and went to find Marnie, who was in Jess's room, cradling her on the rocking chair; it seemed soothing for both of them.

"Is she asleep then, Robert?" asked Marnie.

"Oh yeah, she was asking me who Darlene and the others were, so I was explaining who was who and what their relationship was. I think she got it. How's little Jess doing, then?" Robert asked her.

"She's fine, wide awake and just looking at me. It's lovely, isn't it? Having children now?" she asked him with big wonder in her eyes.

"Yes, it's lovely, but Marnie, we have to get Kate into kindergarten or something soon. I know they have only been here a few days, but I don't want her to miss out on anything or withdraw by just being here with us and Jess; she needs routine. Shall we have a look at the local kindergarten or nursery school?" Robert asked her.

"Yes, I think we should, because we need to get some normality soon. Also, we don't want the authorities on our case either; don't forget these girls came from another country; as soon as we get them settled, they will both fit in. Jess won't know any different, but Kate may take some adjusting," said Marnie, looking down at her daughter, who had now fallen asleep.

Marnie moved off of the chair and put Jess into her crib. "Phew!" Robert said.

"Why the sigh?" Marnie asked him.

"This getting the girls to bed, getting them up, and routine is all new to us, Marnie, so it's just getting used to it, that's all," Robert told her.

***

The next day, Robert, Marnie, and the girls were heading over to look at the local kindergarten nursery, well, it was at least a mile away, so they went in the car. Once they got there, they bumped into a friend of theirs, Thomas, who was a Native American, who came over and said hello to them all. "Hello, Robert, Marnie. Who are these too little ones?" he asked them.

"Hello, Thomas. This is Kate and Baby Jess," said Robert. "Our new little girls," said Robert proudly. Kate stepped behind her father. Thomas was a rather big man in height, and Kate was a little nervous about him.

"Ah, Little Springs!" Thomas replied.

"Little Springs?" Robert looked puzzled.

"Yes, Robert, you have recently had a family in the spring, Little Springs!" Thomas said.

"Oh yes, I suppose so. How are you, Thomas?" Robert inquired.

"I am fine, just going down to the school to see my nephew; he has been acting up, do you say, yes, so I need to see what he has been up to, so I will be on my way, bye bye for now," Thomas said, waving as he went. Robert, Marnie, and the girls went over to the building and pressed the buzzer to be let in.

The receptionist let them in as they waited to be seen by Mrs Hodges, the manager of the kindergarten. She came out nearly straight away; she was a stout little lady; she had loose trousers and a shirt on; she seemed very personable to both of Robert and Marnie. "Shall we have a look around, then, Katie?" she said.

"It's Kate!" Marnie told her.

"Oh, sorry, Kate," Mrs Hodges replied. She took Kate by the hand, which Kate was happy to do, and they went along to the classrooms.

"It's recess at the moment, so we can have a good look around," she told them. They went in and out of classrooms, showed them the dining room, the library, the toilets, and the classroom that Kate will be in if she attends. There were a lot of paintings on the wall that the children had already done. There was a book corner, which Kate took herself over to; she liked books; she liked drawing too.

Once they had seen around the kindergarten, Mrs Hodges took them back to her office. "Now we do have a place for Kate, as Easter has just ended, so would you like her to start straight away? What we will do is have her in for a couple of hours to start with; once she settles down then she can come full time, Monday to Friday, 8 o'clock to 3 o'clock; the school bus can then bring her and take her home again. Would that be all right with you both?" she asked them both, looking at each of them in turn.

They both looked at each other and both nodded. "Now there is no school uniform, but if you could send a change of clothes, and is she in diapers or not?" Mrs Hodges asked.

"No, Kate is clean, completely potty trained, and she can use her cutlery," Marnie told her.

"Okay then, she can start on Thursday if you could bring her in for 9 o'clock and then collect her at 1 o'clock, so when the other children lie down for their nap, Kate won't disturb them?" Mrs Hodges added.

"Yes, that's great; thank you, Mrs Hodges," Robert said, standing up to shake her by the hand, and so did Marnie.

"Well, we will see you on Thursday then, Kate, bye," Mrs Hodges said as she stood up and opened the door for them both.

"Oh, lunch! Will that be dinner here, or do I send a packed lunch?" asked Marnie.

"On Monday, Mrs Steward, send her in with a packed lunch; we will try her with a cooked meal. As I gather, she's from England, she may have different food tastes; we can try and see what she likes to eat. I don't think the cuisine would be much different from what they eat in England, but she may have things she likes or prefers. Now before I let you go, do you know if she is allergic to anything?" Mrs Hodges asked her.

"Oh no, I don't think she is, but if there are any problems, please call me. I will leave all of the information with the reception," Marnie said.

"Actually, there are a couple of forms you can take with you to fill out and return them when you bring her in on Thursday," Mrs Hodges reminded Marnie.

"Yes, I will do; thank you, Mrs Hodges," Marnie said.

Mrs Hodges closed the door behind her. Robert and Marnie made their way to reception. "Hello, we were just with Mrs Hodges," Marnie said.

"Oh yeah, I have a couple of forms for you to fill out and return them when you bring in Kate," Sally said.

"I'm Sally, by the way; any problems, I will be the one calling you," Sally said, smiling.

"Thank you, Sally," Marnie said, taking the forms from her. Robert still had Kate's hand; she was holding on a little tight. They both said thank you and goodbye to Sally and made their way to the car.

"Well, that seems okay, don't you think, Marnie?" Robert asked.

"Yes. I think our Kate will be happy there, so let's get home and have some lunch," Marnie replied to Robert.

On the way home, Robert asked Marnie something. "Marnie, you know what Mrs Hodges asked about Kate or Jess having any allergies, well, that Mrs Carpenter never told us if the girls had allergies, so do you think we should contact her and ask? She should have some information," Robert said.

"Robert, don't you remember? Mrs Carpenter gave us a folder with all of the girls' medical stuff; maybe we need to read it when we get back home. I mean, we haven't stopped since the girls have been home, so maybe some light reading later on; what do you think?" she asked him.

"Good thinking, Marnie!" he replied.

"Well, nothing in here about allergies, so the girls must be okay?" Robert said.

"Hang on a minute, Marnie, this is really weird; it says something really odd here!" Robert told her.

"About what?" Marnie asked.

"I don't know, I can't make it out; it looks as though it's just been scratched out, I think. Let me just look up at the light; that might be better!" he told her.

He put the paperwork up to the light in the living room; that wasn't any good. He had a reading lamp in his study; he took it in there and shone it under the light, but he couldn't make it out.

"So, what does it say, then?" Marnie asked.

"I don't know; it looks like another name, but I can't quite make it out. Maybe I should ask Kate?" Robert asked.

"Don't you dare; you don't know what demons have been laid to rest; it could bring stuff up for her she has forgotten; don't forget what Mrs Carpenter had said, that the girls had had a traumatic time with their family, in a car crash or something; we don't want to go making Kate worse," Marnie said.

"What do you mean worse, Marnie? She's settling in beautifully," he told her; he was getting rather protective of Kate.

She was a little darling and, generally, a good kid. "I know, I didn't mean that, Robert. It's just that we don't really know why or how they came to us, and I don't want to start lightbulbs going off in her little head; she's happy here with us; I want it to stay like that," Marnie said, with a nod afterwards.

He knew she was right; she always was. It wasn't like she didn't like being there; she was settling in, and they didn't want to start asking awkward questions.

Thursday was already here. Robert wanted both of them to take her to kindergarten, but Marnie wanted to get Jess sorted out, so Robert took Kate. She was excited to go to kindergarten; she hadn't really been around other children since that last day she was at nursery before they were taken. She had a big smile on her face. Mrs Hodges was there to greet them both; she took Kate by the hand. Robert followed them; he wanted to see Kate's reaction when she got to the classroom. He handed her bag to the teacher, who took Kate over to her peg to put her coat and Wellington boots when it rained or snowed; where they lived, there was lots of snow.

Her teacher, Miss Wilson, showed her where the toilets were; she then took Kate over to a group of children.

"Kate, this is Jenifer and Alice; they are colouring in their books. We have one for you. Would you like to sit with them and colour in your book?" Miss Wilson asked.

"Yes, please," Kate said, pulling out her chair. She made a beeline for the pencils; she took out a yellow one first.

"That's for the sun," Kate said.

"Well, I think she will be okay!" said Mrs Hodges to Robert; she took his arm. "If you would like to wait outside for a little while, not that I think it will be necessary; she looks like she has already settled in!" Mrs Hodges told him.

"Yes, it kinda looks that way. Bye, Kate," Robert said. Kate looked around and said goodbye to Robert.

"If you want to sit here for a little while, Mr Steward, then have a look every once in a while, and then if you think Kate is okay, then you can go, yes? If there is any sort of problem, we will call you," Mrs Hodges told him, as she could see he was going to suggest.

Robert stayed about half an hour; he looked in on Kate a couple of times, but she was oblivious to him being there. He said goodbye to Mrs Hodges, who was on a telephone call and then to Sally; he remembered to hand the completed paperwork to Sally.

"Sorry, Sally, I nearly forgot it," Robert said. He waved as he left the building, then got into the car and drove home.

"Hi, Marnie, I'm home," Robert said.

"Shush!" she replied.

"I have just got Jess off to sleep. How did Kate get off?" Marnie asked.

"Oh, she was great, went in with no problems, was colouring with two other little girls, and she just slotted in, as if she had always been there, but I am sad she has to go so soon, but she needs to settle into life here. Marnie, I have had a thought," Robert said.

He had been going over it in his mind for the last twenty-four hours. "Yeah, what's that, Robert?" Marnie asked, slightly distracted.

"I was thinking about the ranch," Robert said.

"Yeah, what about it?" Marnie asked again.

"I was wondering if we should change its name?" Robert said out loud now.

"Pardon me?" Marnie responded.

"Robert, as far as I can remember, this ranch has always been called Steward Ranch; what would you change it to?" Marnie prompted him.

"I was thinking of changing it to 'Little Springs Ranch'; what do you think of it?" Robert finally said it.

"I was going over in my head what Thomas had said about our 'Little Springs' and thought, yes, we got the girls in the spring, it would be a great way to commemorate us getting the girls; what do you think?" Robert finally stopped talking so he could get a response from his wife.

"Yes, actually, I think it's a really good idea. Little Springs is a good name for a ranch, and it's positive, but it would mean changing the signage out front, plus what about Darlene? She's not going to be so happy about the name change. It's family property," Marnie told him.

"Well, she stopped being a Steward when she married Mitch and became a Carter, so, yes, I will inquire about the signage first thing on Monday morning. 'Little Springs Ranch' it is, then."

Chapter 8

Bang! Bang!

"ROBERT LINGARD STEWARD, YOU OPEN UP THIS DOOR!" screamed Darlene at the front door. Thump, thump, bang, bang, bang again.

"What the hell is wrong with you, Darlene? We have two kids asleep and you're banging on the door at this god-awful time. What time is it?" shouted Robert back at his sister.

"HOW DARE YOU CHANGE THE NAME OF THIS RANCH! OUR DADDY'S RANCH! HOW DARE YOU, ROBERT?" screamed Darlene again.

She pushed her way past him and went straight into the living room. Marnie came running down the stairs. "Darlene, please, can you keep it down? Kate and Jess are still asleep. Go and do your arguing outside, and please don't bring God into your argument; it's not right and not at this time of the morning!" shouted Marnie.

Robert turned to his sister. "First of all, Darlene, this is our ranch, and if you get your head on right then you would remember that this ranch wasn't our daddy's but our grandaddy's, you know, Phillimore Steward, who upped and left it to rot in the 1930s to live in California due to the sandstorms that were horrific; he took all of his and grandma's money and fled the house, and our daddy, you know, OUR DADDY, took it on later on in his life, but it was too much for him, so I took over, so now it's mine and Marnie's and our girls' ranch, our home. If I see fit to change the name of it, I will. Folks around here will always know it as Stewards Ranch, but as of now it will be known as Little Springs Ranch, which if you didn't have a cloth head on you now, you would understand that it's because of our girls. We wanted to make a fresh start, so why not change the name of our home to suit our new family? So if you don't like it, then it's tough, because it's staying that way. You don't have to like it, Darlene, but the name stays. Anything else you would like to say, hmmm?" said Robert rather quickly.

"Mitch, you tell him, tell him I'm right!" Darlene demanded.

"Well, you know, Darlene, I think it's kinda sweet, ya know; it's like Robert and Marnie wanted to tell the world they are proud they got their girls, so I agree with Robert, and I am sorry if you feel differently, but it's done now, so let's let it be and let them get on with their day; we have to get Mary-Lou and Ethan off to school now, so come on," Mitch called her, but also pulling at her arm to remove her from the situation.

Robert ushered them both out and closed the front door behind them. "Darlene, I knew it would be all right; you're making a big fuss about nothing; let's get our kids off to school and leave Robert and Marnie alone; he's right, and I know you don't like it, but it is his house, his home!" Mitch added, then thought they had better go before Darlene had a go at him.

He got into his truck, started up the engine, and then drove away with the kids in the back. Robert then went back upstairs; he was wide awake now; he wanted to be back in bed, but instead, he headed to the kitchen to put some coffee on. He went upstairs, checked in on Kate, and then on Jess. Marnie was in the rocking chair, feeding her.

"She started crying when she heard Darlene going off, but she has settled down now," she whispered.

"What on earth was she going on about, Robert?" she asked him.

"The name changes for the ranch, what else?" Robert replied.

He left the room, went back to check on Kate, who was still asleep, closed her door, and then went back to the kitchen to make his coffee. What a great start to the morning already! Trust Darlene; she was always getting into his and Marnie's business. *Why couldn't she just leave them alone?* he thought. The girls were settling in nicely; Jess was taking to her new surroundings, and Kate had adapted to her new routine. They had a couple of teething problems, but they were getting resolved slowly. He took his coffee back to bed; it was Saturday; he didn't have to go anywhere until later that day; Kate wasn't at kindergarten; Marnie liked to stay with Jess; she had gotten used to having a baby in the house; and Kate was starting to find her bearings.

Robert had taken them both down to the stables to see the horses, and Kate's eyes were huge. She had never been up close to horses, but she loved them. There were a couple of ponies that she may be able to ride later on, when she felt confident getting on one. He also wanted to take Kate fishing; he knew it was more of a boy thing, but there was no harm in teaching her. If they ever went up into the mountains, at least she would be able to fend for herself and wouldn't starve. As long as she stayed away from the bears and mountain lions, she would be okay, but that would be a long time in the future. It was nice that he and Marnie could think of a future with their two girls.

He drank his coffee and looked in on Marnie and Jess, who were both asleep. Marnie was in the rocking chair, and Jess snuggled up to her. He looked in again on Kate, who was sitting up in bed, rubbing the sleep from her eyes.

"Morning, Kate. How are you this morning? Did you sleep well?" he asked.

"Yes, Robert, I slept really well. I was dreaming of the horses that we saw in the week at the stables, then I remember running across the meadow, which turned into a street I don't remember, with a lady chasing me up the road, then I woke up. She looked familiar, but I don't know where from," Kate told him.

Hmmm, I wonder, thought Robert, *maybe Kate is having a memory retrieval.* Maybe this adoption wasn't exactly what he had been led to believe, but that didn't matter; he wasn't giving those girls back; they were with them now, their little family, and they had the papers to prove it. Robert had gotten himself a box, like a treasure chest; he was going to put all of the paperwork belonging to the girls into it and put it into the attic; that way, it was all together, but also out of the way. Also, when the girls get older, they won't go snooping and ask questions. He wanted to let them believe that they were his and Marnie's girls and that they had only lived with them; that was rather naive of him, but necessary at the moment. As time went on, it wouldn't be a problem.

Six months had passed, and Kate was having less and less bad dreams about ladies chasing her down the street. It was nearly Christmas; Thanksgiving had already been and gone. Kate didn't understand it, but there was still time. Robert was also called Robert Daddy now, and Marnie Mummy, both of whom liked it. Jess was thriving into a lovely little tot; she was coming up for her first birthday and was toddling along, not quite walking yet. Marnie and Robert had chosen some lovely cowboy boots for her once she was steady enough on her feet; they had soft bottoms for little tots and heavy ones. Kate was enjoying kindergarten and had her two friends, Jenifer and Alice, since the day she started. Robert and Marnie weren't really socialites as such, but they would like to start holding parties for the girls.

Even when Darlene came around to the idea of a name change, she realised how happy the girls had made her brother and his wife, so she backed down, which would be a first, but she knew when she was licked. Christmas was a big thing for the family. They had already given the girls as much as they could handle at that time but wanted to get them both horsey things; they had stables and about twenty horses, so, yes, they wanted them to get used to the horses, looking after them, tending to them, mucking out, making sure they had enough food, and popping down once in a while for a stroke and a brushing of them.

Since Edie had given the girls their adoption certificates and paperwork, it did have their dates of birth on them, so they knew that it was Kate's birthday in February, but Jess was in January, so they would have a party for both. Kate could have a party at kindergarten, but they would also have one at home for the family and a few friends, including Thomas and Thomas's niece Alice. So that was the plan once the holidays were over. Robert had seen a lovely soft rocking horse for Jess to have; she could sit on it, and it was safe as the seat went fully to a semi-circle, so she would be safe and not fall out, but he thought it was best for someone to be with her when she was riding it.

Jess had dark hair like her dad David, but her mother's green eyes, while Kate had Chrissy's fair hair and her dad David's bright blue eyes. Everyone commented on Kate's eyes; they were mind-blowing. On Christmas morning, they brought both girls down to see what Santa had brought them. The Christmas tree was huge; it was all sparkly; they had silver garlands on the branches that shone with the twinkly lights from the tree; it was beautiful, and as they always had a real Christmas tree, it smelt wonderful, like pine, but also Christmas. Darlene, Mitch, Mary-Lou, and Ethan were coming over for dinner, so they would exchange their gifts then, but for now, Robert and Marnie wanted to have that bit of time with the girls to themselves.

Both girls got tonnes of presents, and while Jess got her soft rocking horse, Kate's eyes were like saucers. Robert got up, took her by the hand, and took her over to the window.

"Look, Kate, do you see that pony, the one that is a chestnut, light brown colour? Well, she's your pony; she's just for you," Robert said.

"Wow, Daddy, is that big horse just for me? Does she have a name?" Kate asked.

"No, she doesn't have a name yet; would you like to name her, then?" Robert asked.

"Oh yes, please, Daddy, what about Chestnut?" Kate asked, looking up at her dad with the biggest eyes ever.

"You want to call her Chestnut?" Robert asked her, and she nodded in reply.

"Well, Chestnut it is, then. So it's a bit early, but would you like to get your wellies on, because it is rather wet, and we can go and see her?" Robert told her.

Kate was so excited; she rushed out the back to where her wellies were and put them on. "Well, let's put a coat on then, because you still have your pyjamas on, and it is cold out there," he added.

She ran out to the back and put her coat and hat on. Robert put his own boots on, and Marnie said she would stay inside with Jess in the warm. But Robert was as giddy as a kipper; he was like a little boy with his own presents on Christmas morning. He took Kate by the hand, and off they went to see Chestnut for the first time. Robert picked her up and let her pat her. Chestnut wasn't a very big horse, but a good-sized pony for Kate to learn to ride on. By the time Jess was Kate's age, she would be more experienced as a rider, as she would be on smaller ponies but with lots of assistance. Once they had seen and cuddled Chestnut, they went back inside to the warm. Gene, the stable hand, who would come in later on for his dinner with them, took Chestnut back to the stables to warm her up with her blanket and food. She already had a clean stall and lots of hay, so she would be lovely and cosy.

"Well, she loves Chestnut; she was so good with Kate, you know, Marnie. Gene has taken her back to the stables, and she will be back around twoish for dinner," Robert said to Marnie.

"Well, it's a good job I got that turkey in last night; it is all cooked and looks and smells delicious," she told him.

"What time are Darlene and everyone coming over then, Robert?" Marnie asked. "I think about 1.30 pm, so we had better get a move on, get the girls washed and dressed, and—" said Robert, but Marnie interrupted him.

"Don't you think we should have some breakfast first? Otherwise, it's a long time until lunch," suggested Marnie, looking at the clock; it was only 10.30 am.

"Yes, good idea!" replied Robert.

"So, what would you like, Robert, to eat?" asked Marnie.

"I think pancakes with maple syrup will do just fine, Marnie," Robert told her. Kate walked into the kitchen and said that she would like pancakes too.

Jess had already had her breakfast while they were looking at the horse; she had eaten porridge. Once they had eaten their food, Marnie took both girls up to get washed and dressed, while Robert took a look at the dinner; it was looking and smelling lovely. The doorbell went, and Robert went to answer it. "Well,

Merry Christmas, Robert. Where's Marnie and the girls, big brother?" asked Darlene.

"Oh, Marnie and the girls are getting ready; they will be down in a minute," said Robert.

"Merry Christmas, Darlene, Mitch, Mary-Lou, and Ethan," said Marnie, coming down the stairs with both of the girls.

Darlene had been bringing Mary-Lou over almost weekly, so the girls were becoming very close.

"Hiya, Mary-Lou!" said Kate, running over to give her a hug. "Hiya, Kate, did you get lots of nice presents?" asked Mary-Lou.

"Yes, Mary-Lou, lots of toys, dolls, what about you?" asked Kate.

"Yes, I did. Now, Mama, have you got Kate's presents? Can I give them to her, and Ethan can give Jess hers?" asked Mary-Lou.

Darlene went over to the big sack that she had for the girls and gave some to both of her children. Robert went over to the tree and took out some presents for his niece and nephew. "Come on over, you two; let's exchange these gifts nicely and comfortably, and nobody will fall over them," suggested Robert.

All of the children sat down on the floor. Mary-Lou handed Kate her gifts, and Ethan passed Jess's gifts to Marnie, who had Jess sitting on her lap. Jess didn't understand what was going on, but she did like the brightly coloured paper. Then she saw the gifts in the paper and squealed, clapping her hands together.

"Oh, thank you, Mary-Lou and Ethan," said Kate as she opened a doll and some clothes. There were some nightwear, pyjamas, and a dressing gown.

"It can get quite cold here in Colorado. Kate, Mary-Lou has the same one for Christmas also," Darlene told her. Kate got up and gave everyone hugs; she hugged Mary-Lou the tightest. They had become quite close over the last few months, and Darlene had made a point of bringing her children over to see them every week so they could get to know each other, as they were cousins.

Robert was Darlene's only sibling, and even though they got along most of the time, they had their moments. Everyone was enjoying their present exchange.

There were lots of ooohs and aaahhs. "Daddy, can Mary-Lou come and see Chestnut?" asked Kate rather excitedly.

"Yes, honey, but not until after dinner, because it's nearly ready, and Gene will be coming too, so later on, is that okay?" asked Robert.

"Oh yes, Daddy," Kate replied.

They had a great big dinner. Jess was sitting up in her highchair at the table. They had a houseful, and Robert and Marnie loved it. It's what they always wanted—a house full of children and laughter. They ate their food; they had dessert. Kate and Mary-Lou wanted to go and see Chestnut, but Robert told them to let their food go down before going outside in case they both got tummy aches, so they both sat down on the rug with the fire roaring; they got a fire guard when they got the girls. They both started playing with the toys they had got. Jess was crawling, so she found a piece of wrapping paper that didn't quite make it to the trash bag, and Marnie found it in her mouth.

It didn't taste nice, but she couldn't get it off of her tongue; thankfully, Marnie did. Then she pretended to scold Robert, but she started laughing. Jess looked confused, but then they all started laughing because the piece of paper was stuck to Marnie's finger. Once she went to the kitchen to remove the paper, she came back and asked if anyone wanted anything else to eat; nobody was hungry or even peckish. Marnie had made a huge dinner, and they were full.

"Well, maybe later on, then," Marnie said.

Gene had left; he wanted to check on the horses and ponies. Kate took the opportunity to ask if they could go and see Chestnut. Robert relented and said he would take them all over to the stables if they all wanted to go, but Darlene, Mary-Lou, and Kate wanted to go. When they were about to leave, Mitch said he would like to see the horses. Robert said it was ok, and they all put on their coats and wellies, as it may be a bit muddy. They hadn't had any snow yet, but it had been raining. It was getting a little dark, but they did have some outside lamp lights on. It was only really down the back of the house, a bit further down; thankfully, it wasn't very steep. Kate held onto Robert and Mary-Lou, while Darlene had hold of Mary-Lou. Mitch was walking with Robert.

"Here we are!" said Robert. Gene was there tending to one of the horses.

He was a little overexcited. Kate got a bit scared, but Robert reassured her that it would be okay; she could stand behind him if she wanted to, which she did, but she also held on tightly to Mary-Lou.

"This way, girls," said Gene.

They all followed him further down into the stables, and he stopped at a stall. When they peered inside, they could see Chestnut, who immediately came over to see her new audience. Kate put her hand out to pat her, and he brought her head down so she could reach her. He loved getting patted by Kate because she was little, she was gentle with her, and even though she had met her only early that day, she recognised her. She stroked the front of her face; she had a white stripe down the front, as if she had been licked by her mother, and it stayed white. Some of the other horses came to the openings of their stalls feeling a little left out, so Mary-Lou and Darlene went over to some of the other horses to pat them. Kate was still snuggling her face to Chestnut; she loved her already.

"Robert, can Kate come and pat some of the other horses?" asked Mary-Lou.

"Err, yes, I think so, but some of them are rather bigger and more boisterous than Chestnut, so we have to keep an eye on her, though Mary-Lou is rather small in comparison," he added.

Mary-Lou nodded her head. "But she is perfect," Mary-Lou said, and then she gave Kate a big smile, which Kate reciprocated.

They didn't stay too long; even though it was warm for the horses and ponies, they were getting a little chilly.

"Come on, everyone, let's get back up to the house. I could do with a hot drink, maybe hot chocolate?" Robert suggested.

Kate and Mary-Lou held hands as they went back home. Marnie had made some sandwiches; she had bathed Jess, who was in her nightgown. Robert looked at the time; it was already gone by 8 pm; Darlene didn't realise either.

"Once we have had hot drinks, we had better make a move, Mitch, Mary-Lou, and Ethan," Darlene commanded.

"Yes, Mama," replied both of her children, with hot chocolate around their mouths. Marnie had popped some small marshmallows in the hot chocolate, which everyone enjoyed.

Once they had finished their drinks, Robert went and got their coats; they put them on, said their goodbyes, and hugged one another. Mitch opened the front door and went and turned the engine on the truck so it would heat it up and it wouldn't be freezing.

They all jumped into the truck. "Thank you, Marnie, for a lovely dinner and a great day; we had an awesome time," said Ethan.

Mitch put his thumb up to agree, and Mary-Lou and Darlene waved back at them. "Thank you for the presents too!" shouted Ethan.

"Thank you for a great day," said Darlene.

Mitch put his arm out of the window and waved over the roof of the truck; it wasn't worth Robert doing the same back as their truck was nearly out of sight and Mitch wouldn't see him. He closed the door and rubbed his arms. "Marnie, it's damn cold out there tonight," he told her.

"Not so much of the damn if you don't mind," she replied, looking at the two girls.

"Oh, sorry," he said, reminding himself that Marnie didn't like swearing of any kind, especially if it was anything to God either. "Robert, I was thinking about something," she said, looking as if she wanted to continue.

"Hmmmm?" asked Robert.

"Robert, do you think we should get these girls christened, you know, to make it more official? What do you think?" she asked.

"What, Marnie? Christened? But they may have already been christened, you know, back in England," Robert added.

"No, I don't think Jess would have been; she was still only a little bubba. I don't think they christened them at that age. I think it's when they were little tots, so Kate maybe, but it wouldn't hurt, would it, really? We can have a word with the minister if you want," Marnie added, and Robert laughed to himself rather quietly. There is nothing that she doesn't want to do with these girls.

"Yes, Robert, we can see the minister in the New Year and ask; you know, it would be a great way for us to introduce the girls to church as well; yes, I think that would be a great idea." She was saying more to herself than him; she wasn't really seeking his approval but talking out loudly to herself.

Yes, she had made up her mind; that's what they were going to do. As they enjoyed the rest of the holiday, Jess needed a bit of support to get on her rocking horse. But she loved it; she was getting a bit more independent; her personality was also starting to come through; she was a happy little thing, but she was a bit feisty too; she wanted to do things for herself. Kate had been playing with all of her presents, but she loved going down to see Chestnut too; she would always be wrapped up, but Robert told her never to go down there on her own; she had to have grown up with her.

Once the Christmas holidays were over and they were in the new year, Marnie, true to her word, made an appointment for her and Robert to see the minister to get the girls christened. She told him about their situation that Kate might be christened, but they didn't know, but would it hurt to do it again. He saw nothing wrong with that, because they weren't aware if Kate had been. Better safe than sorry. If she had already been christened or baptised before, it wouldn't really make a difference. Marnie didn't want Kate to feel left out either; even though she had really taken with Jess, Kate was her daughter too, and she wanted the best for both of them.

The minister arranged for them to do it in the spring, as it would be a lot warmer, and even though it was January, it was still bitter cold. So, they arranged it for 12 May. It would also take around a year for the girls to live with them, so both Robert and Marnie were delighted. Until then, they had two birthday parties to sort out; their girls were going to be five and one, so Kate would have a party at kindergarten, and they both would have a party at home with the family, as Kate's friends would already have had a party at the kindergarten.

***

May 12 was here. Kate had a lovely white dress with pretty little roses around the neck and a waistband on top of the white sash around the middle of the dress, pretty white ankle socks, and white sandal shoes. Jess, on the other hand, wore a long dress, as she wasn't a little newborn anymore, but she was too little to wear what Kate was wearing. Both girls looked lovely, and Marnie did a good job with them; she added some floral clips to Kate's blonde hair and had a bow headband with little roses on It for Jess.

Marnie wanted Robert to take lots of photos with her and the girls, then him with the girls, and then Darlene to take photos of all four of them. Once they were at the church, some of their guests took photos of all of them: Robert, Marnie, the girls, Darlene, Mitch, and their children. Robert and Darlene's parents lived in California and couldn't fly as their dad wasn't very well, so that's why there were tonnes of photos so they could send them out to them. They were planning on going out to see them that summer, the first summer of the year, before they wanted the girls to themselves. Darlene and her family had seen them, but not their parents.

So that was going to happen once the summer holidays were here. They were going out. Gene would be able to look after the horses, and they had other ranch hands who were on hand as such to help so their livestock wouldn't be neglected. Once the ceremony was over, they all headed back to the ranch. They were having a celebration outside, so they had trellis tables, lots of food and drink, and a big cake. They didn't know if that was a thing, but they wanted to celebrate always with a cake, a tradition they wanted to start for their family parties. Some of their friends came. Thomas, the Native American, came with his niece Alice, who was in the same class as Kate. Kate was pleased to see her, especially as it was at her home.

Alice had been there only once or twice. Kate, with adult supervision, took Alice and Thomas to see and meet Chestnut. Alice loved him, and so did Thomas, who was a keen rider. Marnie and Robert had been perfect hosts; everyone got a moment or two from the day. Kate and Jess received a beautiful silver bangle from their parents. They both had three godparents, Darlene, Mitch, and Thomas, for Kate and Maggie, Thomas's wife, for Jess; they loved the girls; and Kate thought she and Alice were now sisters as well.

But that was okay; they were already like family. Everyone said their goodbyes. Robert and Marnie were exhausted. "Being the hosts of our parties is exhausting, Marnie. Good job; it doesn't happen too often!" exclaimed Robert. The girls were tired enough to go to bed. Kate was falling asleep, and Jess had already gone off. So, they took the girls up to bed, put their nightwear on, and they all fell into bed, all christened and now officially part of the family as far as Marnie was concerned.

Chapter 9

"Marnie, come on, honey, we need to get going. Kate and Jess are both in the car, all ready to go," shouted Robert.

Marnie was upstairs, trying to make sure she hadn't forgotten anything. She had Jess's teddy bear that she loved; it was a light brown one with the softest fur and had a red ribbon around its neck tied into a big bow. He still smelled fresh when Marnie put her nose to it.

"I'm coming now, Robert," she shouted back at him. She had a quick look around the girls' rooms, closed their doors, and made her way downstairs. Robert was standing in the doorway.

"Are you ready now?" He laughed at her.

"Yes, I am ready. I just grabbed Jess's bear; you know, she won't sleep without it. I don't want to have to get something else for her in town when we go to see your mama and daddy," Marnie added.

She got into the car. Both the girls were in their car seats, all strapped in. Robert got into the car and looked around at the three ladies in his life sitting on the back seat. "Are we ready to go now? I have locked up, but you know, just in case?" he said, looking at Marnie.

"No, we are all done; now can we make a move? I want us to get on the road; we still have to get to the airport, you know," Marnie replied.

They parked up in the parking lot of the airport. Robert was rather excited; he hadn't seen his parents in a couple of years, and this time he was bringing his family rather than just his wife. "Marnie, please make sure that you have everything; we won't be able to come back, you know, once we are on the plane," he joked, and she laughed at him.

"I have everything—the tickets, the passports, and some money because you know they do have banks in California," she joked, and then Robert laughed this time.

They had the girls, Jess in her stroller, and Kate holding tightly onto Robert's hand; she hadn't been on a plane before, as far as she was concerned, because the last time she was on a plane was the year before she had been dosed up with Calpol.

"Daddy, is it a long way to California?" she asked Robert.

"Yes, it is, honey, to walk, but we are going on an airplane, so it won't take too long," he told her. She held onto his hand a little tighter than before. "Daddy, who will look after Chestnut while we are away in California?" she asked.

"Well, Eddie and also Jed, who takes good care of our horses, but he will take extra care of Chestnut for you, so don't you worry about her; she will be just fine," he reassured Kate.

Kate breathed a sigh of relief. She had been worried about her pony for the last few days. She had gotten used to going down to see Chestnut after school and on the weekend. Even if it was to give her a carrot or two or an apple, Chestnut would come over to the stall entrance. When she would hear Kate coming down to the stables, she would let Kate nestle her head into the pony's face and neck while stroking her. Chestnut liked to be snuggled by Kate. Kate was brought back to now and was still walking, holding onto her daddy's hand as they walked through the airport. He had their luggage on the porter's trolley so he could keep hold of Kate, and Jess was being pushed by Marnie.

They found their way to check-in, and Marnie handed over the two passports as the girls had been added to Robert's. The girls didn't need their own passports at this time; that would happen a few years down the line. Robert put their luggage onto the scale so it could be weighed and to check they weren't over their weight; they were fine; they had some space still, but that would be taken up with what they brought in California. Marnie took their boarding passes from the airline steward, and as they made their way to passport control, Robert thought that if they went straight through, then they could wander into duty-free until they knew their gate number.

This was the first time they were travelling with the girls since they had moved to Colorado, and they were all excited. Robert couldn't wait to see his parents. Darlene had been to visit them two years before at Christmas, but Robert and Marnie couldn't make it. They had had another failed attempt at in vitro fertilisation, and Marnie didn't want to do it anymore. Her body had enough of all of the intrusion from the procedures she had endured. So, she told him that was it; they would have to adopt. So once Marnie had healed her body, she turned her mindset up for adoption. Surrogacy had been spoken about, but there weren't any guarantees, even though there was quite a good success rate of it in America. She didn't want to go down that road, so she and Robert put out the feelers for adoption.

Even though they were in their thirties, they thought it would be easy enough, but they looked into it, and it could take years because of all of the checks that had to be done and the courses they would have to take. By the time they would have done all of that, they could be nearly into their forties, and that could be frowned upon. How could they take on a baby at that stage of their lives? Would they be able to keep up? Robert had met a lady through Darlene; she had adopted her children, Mary-Lou and Ethan, from England. He thought maybe they could do the same thing. Darlene had given Robert the number, and he contacted her. She was really lovely—a lady called Deborah Hardy. She had worked at social services and knew how the system worked, but she didn't work in the department that dealt with adoption, but she knew the team that did.

She was talking to a friend out in the park one day, and she was telling her about how social services would be playing with these children's lives; they would foster kids around all the time, but some went into adoption. This one day, she didn't realise that she was overheard by Edie, who introduced herself as Elizabeth Carpenter, and she knew of two little girls, one just a baby, whose parents had died in a car accident, and she was looking after them, but it was too much for her, so she asked for Deborah's number. Deborah gave her a direct line, and Edie told her thank you and that she would get in touch.

***

They touched down in California with a smooth landing. Robert breathed a sigh of relief. The girls were both fine; their ears had popped a couple of times, but they both coped with flying. Jess was asleep most of the flight the last time. Robert and Marnie didn't tell Kate that she had flown before. Even though Kate felt it was slightly familiar, she couldn't think why. They disembarked off the plane, making sure they grabbed everything, including Jess's bear; they had dared not leave it behind. They made their way into the airport to claim a carousel to get their luggage. Marnie had grabbed a porter and his trolley so it would be easier on the family.

He made his way over to Robert, who was pulling the suitcases off the carousel. "Just one more, Marnie," he said as he grabbed the last one off. He handed it to the porter, who took it with such force that he nearly knocked Robert over.

"Sorry, sir!" the porter said.

"Not to worry; thank you for your help," Robert added. The porter pushed the trolley until they got to customs. Robert handed him something for his trouble.

They made their way to the arrivals; Robert was craning his neck and head, looking for his parents. Caroline and Deke were waiting a little away from the line and then pushed their way to the front.

"Hey, you guys! Oh my goodness, how are you, Robert? Marnie? And these two beautiful little girls must be Katie and Jessie?" said Caroline.

"Mama, Daddy, this is Kate and Jess, our girls, our family," Robert added.

"Oh, my Robert, Marnie, they are just beautiful; look at Kate's eyes; they are just beautiful like two bright blue sapphires," said Caroline.

When she said Kate, she looked straight at Marnie and Robert to check if she said her name right. She didn't know why they were stressing about not lengthening their name with lies. But she ignored it; she got it right; she didn't want to upset her son and daughter-in-law; they had waited a long time to have a baby, but now they had two real little sisters by blood; not that that mattered; as far as she and Deke were concerned, they were family.

"How was the flight, son? How did the girls do? Did they get upset at all?" asked Deke.

"No, Daddy, they were just fine," he said after they had both hugged.

"It's good to see y'all. C'mon, let's get you guys home and settled. Your mama has got you all some great things to do," said Deke, picking up Kate, who was as light as a feather. Deke put her on his shoulders. Kate liked being up that high.

"Daddy, am I going to fall?" asked Kate.

"No, honey, Gramps has you," Robert said.

"Gramps?" replied Deke, stunned.

"Gramps? Or would you rather be Granddaddy? I think it's a mouthful for Kate," he added.

"Gramps it is then, Kate, and you too little, Jess," Deke said, looking down at Jess, who in return looked up at him and smiled him a toothy grin.

Deke just laughed. "Come on, my family, let's go home."

They left the airport; thankfully, they had a huge car. Deke and Robert put the luggage in the trunk, and Robert got in the passenger seat as Caroline, Marnie, and the girls got in the back. "Daddy, where are your car seats for the girls?" asked Robert.

"If you girls can sit on your grandma and mama's laps for now, we need to get them today, but we don't know what size to get them. We can just do this to get home, unload your luggage, and then head off to the shops. There is a huge mall in town; I am sure we can get what you need there!" added Deke.

Marnie looked horrified, but Caroline patted her hand. "Honey, it will be fine; Deke is a great driver, and we can hold the girls tightly but not too firm to hurt them," said Caroline, backing up what her husband had just told them.

Marnie held onto Jess and hoped they would be there quickly. They were only in the car for about twenty minutes. As soon as it stopped, Deke opened Marnie's door so she and Jess could get out. Then he opened Caroline's door, and she slid out with Kate, who loved fast driving and thought it was fun. She got out and ran to her daddy, who gave her a bag; it was the luggage. Deke opened the door, and they took the luggage up to their rooms. Caroline and Deke had a huge house; you could fit the whole of Marnie and Robert's house, which was big enough in one wing of this house. It was spacious, had high ceilings, and was very modern.

The house had eight bedrooms, three ensuites, two other bathrooms, and a playroom for the girls and for when Darlene's family came over. Kate and Jess's eyes were like huge saucers; they hadn't been anywhere so big before. Kate thought the building was bigger than her school, but it was just designed differently, so it looked bigger in her eyes.

"C'mon, darling, let's show you where you and your sister are sleeping," said Deke, taking Kate's hand. Robert was quick to grab the other hand, while Marnie had hold of Jess, and Caroline followed up behind.

It was a very light and airy house and seemed to go on forever. They went down one hallway, turned left into another, and there on the right was a huge bedroom decorated especially for the girls. "Here we are!" said Caroline.

Deke opened the door, and inside was a beautifully decorated room in a shade of pale lilac, with butterflies, ladybugs, and stars painted on the ceiling, which they wouldn't see until it was dark.

There was a bed for Kate and a white cot for Jess to sleep in. "We know that Jess is already a big girl, Marnie, but we didn't want you to worry about her falling out, so we do have a bed for her when the cot is no longer useful," Caroline said.

"Oh, don't you worry none, Marnie. You and Robert are just here opposite," Deke told them both. He opened the door to a beautiful, soft shade of peach she had seen, also light and airy. They both had ensuite bathrooms, which Marnie was quite relieved about.

Robert left them and went to get their luggage. "Now, it's still early, would you like to go out or stay home for the rest of the evening? Then we can go out first thing tomorrow?" asked Caroline.

Robert and Marnie looked at each other and said, "Daddy, would you mind if we stayed home this evening, then, as you said, go out for the day tomorrow?" Robert told him, with Marnie nodding her head.

"Yes, that's fine. We can relax then. I will leave you to unpack, and Marnie, if you need a hand, I am sure Caroline will help too!" Deke added.

"Thank you, Deke. I am sure we will be fine. Robert can give me a hand," Marnie replied.

"Robert, those girls are just beautiful; Kate's eyes are just outstanding. Those girls are just the most beautiful little girls I have ever seen," said Deke.

"Wow, have you seen the size of this place, Marnie? It's huge," Robert said.

"Er, Robert, can you give me a hand, please?" Marnie suggested rather loudly.

"Oh, sorry, honey, yes, here, let me take that suitcase!" suggested Robert, taking hold of the biggest suitcase they had with them.

"Marnie, what did you pack? This is really heavy," said Robert.

"Oh, just clothes for me and the girls; your clothes are in the other suitcase!" Marnie replied.

Robert put both suitcases into the main bedroom, and then once Marnie had emptied her clothes, she took the case to the room next door, where the girls would be sleeping. She came back a little while later with an empty case that she had put into the closet at the bottom. When they had finished, Marnie took hold of Jess, Kate took Robert's hand, and they went downstairs.

"So, let's give you a guided tour, then, shall we?" asked Caroline.

"So, this is the entrance foyer where we came in; to the left is the kitchen." Marnie opened her eyes wide. This kitchen was huge; she thought her one at home was big, but it was nothing on this size. Then she walked into the living room, then into a big space.

"Mama, what is this room for?" asked Robert.

"Oh, that's the space we aren't sure what to do with it yet, but here are the stairs, which you know because you just used them, and then here on the right is your daddy's games room; it only has a snooker table in it at the moment, but he's hoping for some more toys," said Caroline.

"Outside here now is the garden, and yes, here is the pool. Do you all like swimming?" asked Caroline.

"Yes, we do, but we don't get much chance to go. Don't worry, Marnie, there is a shop in town that does all of those fancy, floaty things for the girls. We wanted to wait for you to come before we headed down there; we didn't want to get the wrong stuff for our girls," replied Caroline.

"Thank you, Caroline; we can go later, can't we, girls?" Marnie asked the girls. Kate nodded, and Jess followed her and nodded her little head too.

"Now, you have been upstairs, there are only bedrooms and restrooms up there, so there's no need to go up there again until you want to go to bed," said Caroline, and in this room, which is where me and your gramps sleep; he doesn't always like using the stairs, so we sleep down here.

"Oh, and this is our bathroom too; it matches our bedroom, like all of the ensuites do," she told them.

"Well, that's that now, so do you want to have some dinner? We were thinking of taking y'all out somewhere nice, maybe for steak or something. What do you think?" asked Deke, who came out to join in the conversation.

"Then, when we get back, we can all retire for the evening," he asked.

"Yeah, Daddy. I think that will be great, Marnie. Girls, do you want to wash up before we go out for dinner?" asked Robert. Marnie nodded. She took the girls both up to the bathroom upstairs to have a quick wash and brush up.

"Mama, why does Daddy call Deke Daddy all the time?" asked Kate.

"You know your daddy is daddy, but his daddy is also called daddy," she told Kate.

"But why do you call him Deke and not Daddy too?" she added this further question.

"Because he's not my daddy and it starts to get confusing, so I call him by his name, Deke, and Caroline by her name; does that make any sense, Kate?" Marnie asked her.

"Yes, I guess so, so what do we call Deke and Caroline, then? Daddy and Mummy then, that is gonna get confusing, Mama?" asked Kate, scratching her head.

"No, you can call Deke Gramps and Caroline, Grandma, or Coco," piped up Jess.

"Yes, as Jess said Gramps and Coco. I am sure they will like that, and Grandma is a big word for Jess," replied Marnie.

So, when they were done, Marnie came over to Deke and Caroline and asked, "Girls, can you say what you want to call them, if that's okay?" she asked, looking at the girls, and Kate went first.

"Can we call you Gramps and Coco?" Kate asked.

"That sounds lovely, Kate."

Jess repeated. "Gamps and Coco?" she said with a smile on her face.

"Yes, that sounds better, Gamps and Coco!" replied Caroline.

"I sound like I don't have any teeth," added Deke, laughing.

"Gamps, gamps, yeah, I think it will grow on me," said Deke.

"Gamps gamps," said Jess with her toothy grin.

They all had a chuckle. "Come on, let's get some food; I could eat a scabby horse!" said Deke.

Kate scrunched up her nose. "I don't want to eat a scabby horse; I want a steak!" she replied.

Deke just laughed. "Then steak you should have, little lady; come here," he said, picking her up.

He screwed up his nose, and Kate burst out laughing. They went to a local restaurant they used quite frequently, and they knew the staff very well. "Well, hiya, Missy, can we have a table for six, please? My family has just come to visit us for a couple weeks," said Deke to the hostess.

"Oh, and can we have one of those highchair things, please, Missy?" he added. Missy showed them to their table, which was near the window, so they could see outside. Marnie pulled Jess onto the corner in her highchair so she could feed Jess without her being in the way.

They ordered their food and drinks and enjoyed their first meal as a family with Robert's parents. Once they had eaten, Robert thought they should make a move back home. Kate looked like she was going to fall asleep, and Jess was asleep in her chair. Deke called over to their server and paid the check, and then they left. When they got back, both Kate and Jess had fallen asleep. Robert picked up Kate and Marnie Jess. They carried the girls inside and took them up to their bedrooms. They removed their sandals, took off their dresses, and put them in their night things. It was considerably hotter in San Francisco than in Colorado, so they wanted to take cotton nightwear as it would keep them both cool.

The girls were tucked up in bed, so Robert and Marnie went downstairs to speak with Deke and Caroline. "So, Daddy, you didn't mind us changing the name of the ranch?" asked Robert.

"Oh, shush, Robert, it's fine and was a long time ago now, and it suits you and your family, even though they are our family now too, but it's your ranch; you call it what you like. Yeah, I know Darlene wasn't too happy about it, but as I said, it's your ranch. Darlene has her own home and family; she should just accept it," said Deke.

"Well, she did in the end; thankfully, she saw how much it meant to me and us," replied Robert.

"Anyway, how are things going? How are the stables? Are the girls riding yet?" asked Caroline.

"Kate has her own horse, Chestnut; we go down to the stables every week so she can learn about the horses and ponies and how to look after them, as she has to realise they aren't just for riding," said Robert.

"That's it, my boy; it gives her a bit of responsibility, something else to think about. What about Jess?" he asked.

"We gave her a rocking horse for Christmas, but she goes on. You would have thought she was born in the saddle, but sometimes when we take Kate, we put Jess on the horse first, just so she can get the feel for it, you know," Robert said.

"That's it; get her in early and slow; that way, she can adjust, and it seems like she has," said Caroline.

"Mama, Daddy, we're going to go up to bed now; see you in the morning," said Robert, kissing his mother and hugging his father.

"Night, son. Night, Marnie," said Caroline, kissing Marnie on the cheek,

"Night," they both said as they made their way up the staircase. They both got into bed. Their heads hit the soft pillows, and they were out like a light.

***

Kate was running; she was running as fast as her legs could carry her; she was running over the meadow; she looked behind her; yes, she was still there running, but not as fast as Kate; she was running faster now; she didn't want to look this time; she just wanted to get away, but she continued running; she did take a glimpse back; there wasn't anyone there; she looked to her left and then to her right; no, she was on her own; she made her way to the stables; she saw Chestnut, and she came over to her. Kate was nearly out of breath; she had run for what seemed like ages; Chestnut snuggled her head into Kate's; she felt better; she felt warm and wet.

She moved her head; her pillow was both wet and warm at the same time. She shot up; she hadn't imagined it; she was only dreaming it, but it felt so real.

"Daddy, Daddy!" shouted Kate. Robert came running in.

"What is it, sweetheart? Did you have a bad dream?" he asked her.

"Yes, Daddy, that lady was chasing after me again. I ran and ran as fast as I could, and then I went to the stables, and Chestnut was waiting for me, which is why my pillow feels warm; it feels like Chestnut was with me," said Kate, not sure what she just felt or what had just happened.

"It's okay, sweetheart. You're here now with me and Mama, Jess, Gamps, and Coco. You must have forgotten you were on holiday. It's okay. Would you like to get up now and have some breakfast?" asked Robert.

"Yes, please, Daddy," she said, taking his hand. Robert didn't want her to have another nightmare if she went back to sleep.

"Morning, Marnie. Morning, Jess!" said Robert.

"Morning, Mama and Jess," repeated Kate.

"Would you like to come down for some breakfast?" asked Kate. Marnie looked at Robert. It was still early. Marnie was looking at Robert for some inclination to be up this early. He made a face to say, I will tell you later.

"Come on, get up!" encouraged Kate.

"Okay then, let's get up." Jess was already in with Marnie; she, like Kate, had woken up early but not to a bad dream but because she was in new surroundings.

They took the girls downstairs, and Caroline was in the kitchen. "I'm making waffles if you're hungry; there is maple syrup on the table as well as honey and jam if you want that," she suggested.

"Yes, please, Coco," said Kate, who looked happier now than she did a few minutes ago. Robert helped her up to the breakfast bar. They had already got a highchair for Jess the week before, so Marnie put her in it. Robert and Marnie didn't like talking about Kate's bad dreams or anything in front of her; it made it easier to try and work out what was bothering her. They did ask her in the beginning, but she would get upset, so they decided to talk about it when she was out of earshot.

"So did y'all have a good night's sleep?" asked Deke as he came into the kitchen.

"I had a lady chasing me, Gamps, but I ran faster and faster, and she couldn't catch me!" said Kate out loudly.

"Okay, well, that's good, Kate. You are a great runner, then; we will have to watch out for you in the Olympics!" said Deke, a little confused.

"What's the Olympics?" asked Kate.

"Oh, it's when athletes from around the world compete in various challenges, some running, some throwing things like javelins, and some like hurdles," said Deke.

Now, not sure why he said those things—maybe to throw Kate off her bad dream.

"It comes on the TV every four years, Kate, when it's held. I think it's just been on this last week. Well, finished this last week. I think we did quite well; you know, USA, followed by Romania and West Germany. We got lots of gold medals!" replied Deke, glad he could change the subject.

"Gramps, what's Romania and West Germany?" asked Kate.

"Well, little Katie-Kate—"

Marnie interrupted him, "Her name's Kate, Deke, not Katie."

"Oh, sorry, darlin. Kate, Romania, and West Germany are countries that are in Europe," said Deke.

"What's Europe, Gamps?" she quizzed.

"Well, we live in America, a fine country, but there are other countries in the world, and a lot of countries are bundled together, which are called continents, so there is Oceania, Europe, that's one, Antarctica, South America, North America, Asia, and Africa," said Deke.

"So, Gamps, what countries are in Europe?" asked Kate.

"Well, Germany, France, Italy, Spain, Portugal, England, and Poland," said Deke.

But Kate had stopped listening once she heard England.

"England, is that a long way from here?" asked Kate enquiringly.

"Oh yes, England is a long, long way away, Kate; you need to get on a plane to get there or a big boat called a ship," said Deke, rather proud of himself for being and feeling so knowledgeable.

"Come on, Kate, let's go and get washed and dressed now," called Marnie.

"Oh, Marnie, I was just getting into my flow there with my geography knowledge," replied Deke.

Marnie couldn't get Kate and Jess away as quickly as possible.

Deke looked confused. Had he done something wrong? He didn't think so. "Hey, Robert, Robert, come here in a minute, will ya?" called out Deke to his son.

"What happened there, son? I was talking to little Katie, and Marnie pulled both the girls away to the other room," he asked.

"Daddy, you were talking about countries, yeah?" he asked.

"Yeah, but what's that gotta do with anythin?" he asked, confused.

"Well, Daddy, Kate and Jess came from England; you know that, right?" Robert said, looking at his father.

"But Kate doesn't remember that because she came to us with Jess; they had to fly, but Kate wasn't well, so she was having some medicine called 'Calpol' to help her sleep that the lady had given us, but once we got home, we threw it in the bin. Anyway, I digress, so Kate and Jess were English, Daddy, but now we have adopted them, had them christened, and they belong to us now. I thought I told you this already," Robert said.

"Oh, I don't know, son; maybe you did; I can't remember. Anyway, so why don't you want me to talk to the girls about England?" asked Deke, now very confused.

"Daddy, the lady who brought us the two girls was an Elizabeth Carpenter. Yes. Yes," Deke replied.

"We tried contacting her once the girls were here a few days; they were a little testy; we thought that would be normal, but we did want to ask the lady whom we dealt with a couple of questions, but we couldn't get hold of her. The number she gave us was a phoney number. When we called it, it was a Chinese restaurant; then we got really stumped, so we don't really want to jog the girls', well, Kate's, memory. Jess was only a babe in arms when we got her, but Kate, who was called Katie, was already four years old. Even though they have been with us for a short time, it feels like they have always been in our lives. Anyway, please don't talk about England, if you don't mind. Also, when we got her, she kept having these nightmares about a lady chasing her, but they stopped until last night when she woke up after having another one, hence her talking about running," Robert said.

When Deke finally fell in, he understood why Marnie had removed the girls from the situation.

"I am so sorry, son. I didn't realise. I will tell your mama once you go home, so she doesn't slip up; we just have to make sure they have a great time," Deke said.

"Thanks, Daddy; it does help to talk about it. Me and Marnie were pulling our hair out when we got them, and Kate was having lots of these nightmares."

"Robert, are you coming up to get ready? The girls are all ready to go out," shouted Marnie.

"Just coming, love; be there in a second," Robert replied.

They had had a wild couple of weeks. They had been shopping at the mall, buying lots of new things for the girls to wear and some new things for Marnie and Robert. Kate had brand-new roller skates, which she wanted to try on at home; there wasn't the space at Gamps and Coco's. They had tonnes of new toys; at least they brought a spare suitcase to put their new things in. Deke and Caroline had taken them to the airport; they were with them when they checked in. They did leave some things behind for next time, but they were just under their allocated luggage allowance. Hugs were everywhere. Robert and his dad hugged tightly. Deke told them to call them once they got in so they knew they were back home safely.

Robert did just that when they got home, absolutely shattered. The girls were already asleep when they were put to bed. *On another good visit to my parents*, he thought when he pulled himself a brandy. Marnie opted for a cup of coffee.

Chapter 10

Two years had passed since the holiday to see Deke and Caroline. Darlene, Mitch, and the children went the following summer but stayed for over three weeks. Darlene always seemed to try and outdo her brother; sometimes it worked, sometimes not. Deke and Caroline were fully aware of their daughter's jealousy, but they didn't take any notice of her, and Mitch had got used to it and ignored her. But in those two years, Mary-Lou and Kate got especially close; they saw each other at Evergreen Middle School. Kate had not long started, but Mary-Lou only had a few years left there until she went onto high school, then onto college if she wanted that. Actually, most families wanted their children to go to college to give them a better education, which could lead to a better job, hopefully with good prospects.

They saw each other every day and sometimes on the weekends. Mary-Lou would do extra activities; she liked to dance. Kate wasn't too bothered. Ethan liked to come over to Kate and Jess's place because he liked the horses; he liked to muck out, groom the horses, and just be around them. They didn't live too far away, and Mitch would drop them off in the truck and collect them later on when it wasn't too dark. So, Jess and Kate saw lots of them throughout the year.

Mary-Lou was trying to encourage Kate to take up dancing, but Kate would rather be at the stables or read; she was an avid reader. Robert and Marnie brought the girls a lot of books, especially during the beginning of the girls living with them. At birthdays and Christmases, they would both get at least one each, so they had a good little library. Robert had turned a cupboard—well, it was more like a box room—into a library for the girls. So, when the latest books came out, they would go straight onto the shelves. They had the whole collection of books about a pioneer girl and her family, which would later be turned into a television programme a few years later.

Kate did like to go and see her pony, Chestnut; she had grown to really love her. She would groom her, give her carrots, and always brush her mane. She liked to ride her across the paddock. They had a meadow on the other side of the stables. She would ride her up there, but only when Eddie, the stables guy, was there. Kate was still young, but for Jess, it was like she was born on a saddle, as Deke and Caroline had mentioned when they came over in the summer before Jess started kindergarten and Kate started middle school.

"She looks right at home in the saddle, as does our Jess," said Deke.

Robert was rather proud of the fact, considering they were town children, not from the country whatsoever. So, at the weekends, Ethan would come over for the day. Robert and Marnie didn't mind. He was so enthusiastic about the horses, and he loved Jess and was always offering to help her. She would need his help to mount the ponies, but she had a harness that would steady her, but Robert and Marnie liked an adult to be with Jess when she was riding. So once she was up on a horse, Ethan would get one of the other ponies, but the rule was that if you were out riding them, when you came back, you helped cool them down, groom and brush them, muck them out if needed, and then feed them hay or, occasionally, give them a treat, like a carrot or two or a mint; they liked the little ones with holes in them.

But not too many; they didn't want them to ruin their teeth, just like the children; not too much candy, and as long as they brushed their teeth afterwards, that was okay. It was coming up to fall. Summer had been a bit quick that year, but fall didn't seem to last that long because winter always seemed to go on forever, especially when Christmas arrived. It hadn't snowed until just after Christmas, which they were all surprised about. Kate had only seen snow once in England, but Jess, being a baby, hadn't seen snow; even when she was a little tot before her first birthday, it had snowed quite heavily, and her eyes were like saucers.

So the leaves were already turning brown. Kate liked fall; apart from the fact that it wasn't far from Thanksgiving and then Christmas, it was a happy time. The harvest would already have been and gone, so it was a nice time to start getting cosy at home, with fires on and warm blankets, and until the snow comes, it's batten down the hatches, so to speak. Mary-Lou liked coming over when the weather was changing, so she and Kate would go fruit picking for berries, raspberries, and blackberries; if there weren't too early, they would find some wild strawberries; that was fun. Marnie would give them both a basket to fill with whatever they could, and then she would make a couple of pies and freeze them or make preserves to help over the cold months when they couldn't get anything like that in the shops, and Robert preferred the homemade stuff to bought if possible.

"Here, Mama, we have two full baskets. Can you empty those and we can get some more? There are tonnes more berries out there," said Kate.

Marnie nodded her head, took away the baskets, emptied them into a huge metal container, and handed back the girls their baskets. "Hold on a minute, girls, let me get you another one that you could carry between you and save you going back again once you get back." She chuckled to herself.

Mary-Lou and Kate used to collect a lot of blackberries and raspberries, but the blackberries seemed to last a little longer. At least she would have enough to last the whole winter. Once the girls left again, she went into her pantry to collect the big metal container; thankfully, it wasn't too heavy. She separated the raspberries and blackberries so she could sort them out later and clean them before she did anything with them. While she was waiting for the girls to return, she got out her ingredients and started to make her pastry.

"I do enjoy berry picking with you, Kate; it's a great time just for ourselves without my ma going off on one; she always tries to upstage your mama and daddy," said Mary-Lou.

"I know, but Mama and Daddy aren't too bothered; I think they are just used to it by now. You don't say anything to her at home, do you?" asked Kate.

"Oh no, me and Ethan and Daddy as well all know what she's like; we just let her get on with it, because while she is going off about it, she's leaving everyone else alone," replied Mary-Lou. Both girls laughed.

"Come on, let's get these other berries picked before the bears get to them," said Mary-Lou.

"Bears? What bears?" asked Kate.

"Oh, you know the ones who live up in the mountains and the forest," said Mary-Lou matter-of-factly, like Kate already knew this. Mary-Lou saw Kate's face; she was white as a ghost.

"Oh, don't worry none, Kate; they don't come down to town or to you at all, but we do have to be a bit wary," added Mary-Lou.

"Mary-Lou, I don't think I want to get berries anymore if there are bears here," said Kate.

"Oh, Katie, I didn't mean to frighten you, but we should get these done or your mama might not be happy," said Mary-Lou.

Mary-Lou always called Kate Katie when she was frightened; her parents never knew, and Kate never said anything, but it did come out a couple of weeks later. They were all sitting down having dinner, and the conversation turned to bears and berry picking. When Mary-Lou was reiterating her tale, she mentioned Katie, and Robert and Marnie's ears pricked up. "HER NAME IS KATE, MARY-LOU, NOT KATIE; PLEASE DO NOT CALL HER KATIE WHATSOEVER," demanded Marnie.

"All right, Marnie. There's no need to shout at my daughter, and what difference does it make to call her Kate or Katie? It's rather stupid if you ask me," quizzed Darlene.

"Well, I am sorry if you don't like her name, Darlene, but it's what we call her. Kate, not Katie, so please call her Kate or don't bother coming back to our home," commanded Marnie.

Darlene then looked at Robert, who also had flames in his eyes. "It's only a name, Robert!" exclaimed Darlene.

"Yes, but it's our little girl's name, so please, DARLENE and Mary-Lou, just call her Kate," demanded Robert, who then left the table to comfort his wife.

For the first time in her life, Darlene was dumbfounded by what to say. Mitch then got up from the table; they hadn't quite finished their dinner. He called the kids and his wife and left the house, slamming the door in the process, and got into their truck.

"Daddy, what did I do wrong?" asked Mary-Lou.

"Nothin, sweetheart, that brother of yours, Darlene, and his stuck-up wife—who do they think they are? Let's go home; we can get something to have as a dessert; maybe some ice cream," suggested Mitch. He didn't like his kids having too many sweet things because of their teeth, but this had left a sour taste in his mouth.

***

Bang bang bang on the front door.

"Who on earth is it at this time of the morning, Robert?" asked Marnie, looking at the alarm clock. It was four o'clock in the morning. "I'm coming. I'm coming, for goodness' sake," shouted Robert, hopefully, not waking up the whole household. He got to the front door, and the sheriff was there. "What's up, Sheriff Dodds? Do you know what time it is?" asked Robert, rather annoyed.

"Robert, I am sorry to wake you up so early, but there's been an accident, and I think you would want to know!" said the sheriff.

"Who's had an accident?" asked Robert with all sorts of things going around in his head.

"Darlene, Mitch, and the children; anyway, they are at the hospital in town. Would you mind coming with me?" the sheriff asked.

"Sheriff Dodds, you had better come in while I get some clothes on; I will be five minutes," he told him, and then he darted upstairs to put on some clothes.

He grabbed a shirt and jeans and was putting on his boots when Marnie came in and asked him what was wrong. He told her what the sheriff had told him. "You stay here with the girls. Are they awake?" he asked her.

"No, they are both asleep, thank goodness. You go; call me later and let me know what's happened," she told him. He grabbed his car keys, kissed her on the cheek, and then was out the door of their bedroom, and she heard the front door shut rather hard.

Robert followed the sheriff in his car so he could get home again afterwards. When they got to the hospital, Robert asked the sheriff rather nervously, "Do you know what happened, Sheriff Dodds?"

"What we can piece together is that they were driving along before the highway when a drunk driver in a bigger truck ran into them and off the road into a ditch; the left-hand side took the brunt of it," he told Robert.

"Was anyone hurt?" he asked.

"Well, it wasn't a pretty sight when we got there; we nearly missed them when we went past them. Even though it was dark, we couldn't really see because of the green-coloured truck with the trees, but we did see something reflected in the window when we passed, that's how we found them, that turned out to be the little girl's watch face with the moonlight." They went inside, and Sheriff Dodds took Robert up to the second floor. Mitch was outside a room with a huge window.

Robert ran up to him. "Oh, Mitch," he said. As he got closer, he could see it was Ethan in the room, with tonnes of tubes in him.

"He's only tiny, Robert, but he is strong; he has some fight in him," Mitch said, not looking at Robert but staring hard at the glass.

"Mitch, what happened?" asked Robert, as what the Sheriff had told him had gone right out of his head.

"Well, we left yours all angry, but I was driving good, Robert, not fast or nothing, as you know I hadn't had a drink in me at all. I don't drink and drive. I have my family to think of. Well, we were going down the road; we were nearly home, and then this huge truck came out of this road. His lights weren't on, and he came and smashed right into us. I still had the steering wheel; my hands never moved off it once, but he drove us off the road and into a ditch, but there were some trees there and our truck landed in a huge tree stump. I have driven past that thing for years, never did I think for one minute it would do so much damage to my truck but also to my boy. It landed with such force that we couldn't get Ethan out at first, but when the police came and the fire truck, they got him out, Robert, and now we wait, because my boy, he's such a fighter; he really is; he has to be all right," said Mitch, who then sighed a big sigh.

"How about Darlene and Mary-Lou, Mitch? How are they? Did they get out?" asked Robert nervously now.

"Yes, Darlene and me, we just got some cuts and bruises, but the kids took the most of it, because when that damn driver hit, the back of the truck took most of it. Robert, I don't know about Mary-Lou yet; they are working on her, but my buddy here couldn't move his bottom half; he was in so much pain that when they lifted him out, he screamed just like a coyote," cried Mitch.

"Mitch, did they get the driver?" he asked, a little less nervously this time.

"Yeah, they got him; he's in the cells at the sheriff's office. He was drunk and didn't know what he was doing. If I get my hands on him, I will strangle him," he added.

Robert didn't doubt that.

"Mitch, where is Darlene?" asked Robert.

"She's down the corridor and turned left; she's been up to see Ethan, but she's back outside the theatre waiting on news of Mary-Lou. Go on, go and see her; she will be pleased to see you!" he added.

Mitch continued looking at his son fighting for his life because he had no idea what was going on with him until he saw the doctor. Robert made his way down the corridor to see his sister.

"Darlene!" he shouted, and she came running over to him.

"Oh, Robert, my girl, my little girl is in there; they are working on her. She took most of the truck; she looked like a limp ragdoll. My Ethan, they couldn't get him out at first. What sort of monster would do this?" asked Darlene, searching Robert's eyes as if he had the answer.

"Darlene, Mitch told me this happened after you left our house last night. I am so sorry," he told her, starting to weep.

"Robert, this isn't your fault or Mitch's fault or his driving, but some awful man who decided to have a good amount of liquor then get into his truck and drive," said Darlene, who was, for the first time in her life, rational.

"But if me and Marnie hadn't gotten mad about you and Kate, this would never have happened," he told her.

"Now you listen to me, big brother, we didn't know how big a deal this name thing is; you should have told us, and we could have told the kids before now, but it's happened; we can't go back, but right now my kids, my beautiful kids, are fighting for their lives; that has to come first," she said, hugging her brother.

"Darlene, they will both be fine," he told her.

"The thing is, Kate's name was Katie and Jess, Jessie, but we didn't want to change them because it's what they knew—well, Kate more than Jess. We wanted to make them sound different but the same, if that makes any sense. We don't know what sort of life they had before they came to us, and if it was terrible, we didn't want it to remind them, so we just took off the 'ies' of their names and made them just a straightforward name. You do understand, don't you?" asked Robert pleadingly.

"Robert, they are your girls; you call them what you want to, but others have to know, not necessarily the reason why!" added Darlene.

For some reason, the chaos that followed Darlene made her chaotic, but when it was a crisis, it made her more reasonable than not on a normal day anyway.

"Mrs Carter?" called the surgeon, closing the theatre door shut. He shook his head. "I'm afraid there was nothing we could do; she passed on the operating table. I am really sorry. Would you like to go in and see her?" said the surgeon, who then returned to the theatre to make sure that Mary-Lou looked decent; there wasn't any blood except for around her mouth when she came in, but that had been cleaned up.

Darlene heard no more once he said they lost her; she wailed like a very wounded dog. Robert grabbed hold of her, and then flying down the corridor was Mitch. He had left Ethan on his machines once he heard his wife howling. He grabbed hold of her, and Robert, feeling like a spare part, didn't know what to do.

"Mr Carter," said the surgeon again a few minutes later.

"Mr and Mrs Carter, would you like to go in and see your daughter?" he asked. He didn't want to say, 'before she was taken away to the mortuary'. They both nodded and walked into the theatre. He held the door open for them, and they walked in. The staff, who nervously looked at the parents, were then ushered out to give them some privacy.

"Oh, look at her, Mitch; she looks like she's sleeping," whispered Darlene. "Yeah, yeah, she does, Darlene; she looks peaceful," he added. They stayed in the theatre for a good fifteen minutes. The surgeon returned and said that they wanted to take her downstairs to another room, but if they wanted, they could go to the chapel of rest for a while that was open all the time.

When they left the theatre, the staff had returned without them noticing; they then put a sheet over her to give her some dignity and privacy. Once Mary-Lou would be put in the mortuary, waiting for the undertakers to collect her, they could collect the death certificate in the next day or so, but they still had to go and see Ethan. Mitch and Darlene agreed that Mitch would stay with Ethan while she went with Robert to the chapel of rest, and then she would return to Ethan, and then they could swap over in a little while so she could sit with her son.

Once the nurses and staff had sorted him out, they were taking readings of his heart rate, blood pressure, etc. Before Robert took Darlene to the chapel of rest, Darlene and Mitch had a soft kiss and hugged briefly. They both knew they had to be strong. Darlene and Mitch were strong; they had had some tough times in their marriage. Mitch headed towards Ethan. The nurse let him go inside. There was a chair there for him and another in the corner of the room. There were so many machines that he needed, as Mitch thought, to keep him alive. He knew his son was strong, but this would be the fight of his life.

***

It was about 2 pm when Marnie heard the key go in the front door. "Robert, Robert, how are they? What happened?" asked Marnie, rushing to him when he walked in the door.

"Marnie, where are the girls?" asked Robert.

"Kate is upstairs reading, and Jess is playing with her toys in the sitting room," Marnie told him.

"Why?" she quizzed.

"I didn't want them to hear this yet," Robert reiterated the story to her.

Her mouth was wide open in shock, and then he told her that Mary-Lou didn't make it and that Ethan was attached to lots of machines. "Where are Darlene and Mitch now?" she asked.

"They are both at the hospital, sitting with Ethan. When I left, I told Darlene that I would call Mama and Daddy so they could come over and be with them; they were in shock, and they needed them," he told her.

"What about the driver, Robert? Did they get him?" she asked.

"Yes, they did; he was totally drunk and had no idea, and don't worry, they don't blame us for it happening. Even though they were angry when they left, that soon disappeared. No, Darlene and Mitch came away with cuts and bruises," he said as he could see.

"What about the girls?" asked Marnie.

"What girls?" asked Robert.

"Our girls, when should we tell them about Mary-Lou and Ethan?" asked Marnie.

"Nothing at the moment; let them play; they will know soon enough," Robert said.

"Yes, I agree. Now do you want something to eat or drink as you have been at the hospital most of the night?" Marnie asked.

"Er, yes, please, Marnie, pancakes or waffles if we have any, and a good, strong coffee."

***

A couple of weeks later, Deke and Caroline, Mary-Lou and Hank, Mitch's parents, came in from California and Arizona to spend time with their kids, even though they were parents, but also to be with Ethan, who was slowly on the mend. He had had numerous scans and an MRI. They had arranged the funeral for Mary-Lou. Her school friends came; they all wore light pink; the boys wore pink arm bands. Kate felt awful that she had lost her only cousin and that she was in some way to blame. They ordered some flowers in the shape of ballet slippers. Mary-Lou loved pink, so many of the floral arrangements were in pink.

Kate and Jess both wore pink, and on the day of the funeral, Kate wanted to hold Darlene's hand, which Darlene was grateful for. Ethan wasn't able to attend his sister's funeral as he was still pretty sick in the hospital, but both Mitch and Darlene told him they would take him to her grave when he was well enough. Kate felt a little strange; it felt familiar for some reason, but she couldn't put her finger on it. The funeral cars arrived to take them to the church. Mary-Lou was in the front car, a hearse, which was beautiful; she had a white coffin with lots of pink floral tributes.

Caroline brought her hankie to her face when she saw the coffin. Mary-Lou senior did the same. *How on earth were they going to get through this day?* thought Robert. They all lined up to get into the relevant cars; there were five for the family and close friends. Thomas, Robert's close friend, came with Alice, his niece, who was friends with Kate from kindergarten and got on well with Mary-Lou. She held Kate's hand for a moment and gave it a squeeze. Darlene was grateful to have Kate to hold onto. When she asked Robert and Marnie if Kate could sit with her in the car, they both nodded yes.

Everyone got into their cars and made their way to the church slowly. Darlene was silently crying. Kate held on tighter to her hand, and Darlene smiled at her. Kate had never noticed how much Darlene looked like her daddy, Robert. It took a little while to get to the church as there were so many cars. Darlene didn't realise how popular Mary-Lou was, but she was grateful that, at this time, her little girl was so loved.

The service was lovely; they had a couple of her friends read poems for Mary-Lou, and a few sang a couple of her favourite songs. When leaving the church, they had played some music that Mary-Lou enjoyed in her ballet class. Darlene started to cry openly as she held onto Kate's hand; she did squeeze it a bit tighter than she had thought. But Kate was worried that if she pulled it away, Darlene might fall apart. Even though she was only seven and a half, she was quite grown up when she needed to be. She looked around the cemetery; it felt familiar, but again, she couldn't put her finger on it. Once they left Mary-Lou there, Darlene couldn't be prised off of her coffin; she was in a terrible state, her only daughter lying in a cold coffin, even if it was lined with satin. That didn't bring Darlene any comfort.

When it was all over, they all went back to Darlene and Mitch's home for the wake. Robert, Marnie, Deke, Caroline, Mitch, Hank, and Mary-Lou senior were sorting out the food and drinks. A lot of people with children went home. Darlene started to have a meltdown, so her doctor gave her a sedative to help calm her down. Mitch knew it was a bit cheeky, but he wanted to leave and go back to the hospital to be with Ethan. He knew he needed him more. Now that Mary-Lou was no longer alive, they had to put all of their energies into getting him better, which was what got Mitch through this at this time.

Chapter 11

"Hi, buddy, how are you doing today?" asked Mitch.

"Okay, I guess," replied Ethan; he didn't seem to be interested in anything since the accident.

Mitch had brought him magazines, but as he had to lie flat on his back, he couldn't really read them properly. He was in pain, but he wouldn't have known it as he was on morphine, as he had been really in pain upon admittance to the hospital. He wasn't doped up on it, but he had enough not to notice the pain.

"Hey, Ethan, why don't I bring you that radio you have at home? At least you can listen to the music and stuff while you're lying here?" asked Mitch, now wishing he hadn't. He didn't know what to ask his boy now, and he seemed like he was always putting his foot in it.

"Dad, that sounds great, because then I won't feel like I am missing out on the outside world!" he replied.

He didn't want to sound ungrateful; his dad was trying more than his mama was, but that was another story he didn't want to think about right now. He felt quite angry that this had happened. It wasn't his dad's fault this had happened, and it wasn't his mama's fault either; he just felt angry with the world at this time. He had been lying on his back now for at least a month. He couldn't eat because if he did, he could choke, so he was being drip-fed, which wasn't much fun. He had a bag where he would normally be able to go to the toilet, and he didn't realise he was wearing a diaper, one for young people and not adults. One for people who had injuries, people who wouldn't be able to walk.

Hopefully, this would be a temporary measure, as the doctor had told them the first week. "Ethan has fractured his spine, which is why he has to lie on his back for the time being," he told his mama and daddy. Darlene couldn't deal with this new information, but Mitch, who never let on about his feelings, broke down. He sobbed like a baby, thinking that his boy wouldn't maybe walk again.

The doctor hadn't said that just yet, but that's the way it was looking. Mitch stood up, kissed his son on the forehead, and told him he would be back later that evening. Caroline and Deke had decided to stay with Marnie and Robert for the time being. They knew that Darlene and Mitch needed time together. The truth was, Darlene couldn't deal with any of this. She kept going up to the cemetery and sitting by Mary-Lou's grave, talking to her as if she were still alive. Mitch had gotten home; he needed to talk to Darlene about Ethan and what was happening to him. He thought Darlene would have wanted to be at the hospital more than not, especially as they had already lost their daughter.

"Darlene, hey, Darlene, are you home?" Mitch called out.

"Yes, Mitch, I am upstairs. I'll be down in a minute," she shouted back down to him. Mitch went to the kitchen and grabbed himself a cold soda. He didn't think he would ever drink alcohol again. Even though he wasn't the guilty one in this, it sure opened up his eyes to the dangers of drunken driving.

Darlene entered the kitchen. "How are you doing, Mitch?" asked Darlene.

"DON'T YOU MEAN, HOW'S OUR BOY, DARLENE?" screamed Mitch. "YOU HAVEN'T BEEN TO SEE HIM IN WEEKS. HE NEEDS HIS MAMA, DARLENE. WHERE HAVE YOU BEEN GOING ALL DAY INSTEAD OF SEEING OUR SON WHO IS IN SUCH A STATE? WHEN I LEFT HIM A LITTLE WHILE AGO, HE HAD TEARS STREAMING DOWN HIS EYES. NOW YOU'RE HIS MAMA AND YOU NEED TO GO AND SEE HIM!" Mitch screamed again; he couldn't take it anymore; it was like she had abandoned him, like he wasn't her son.

"Mitch, will you stop screaming at me? I'm getting a headache. I will go and see our boy, just not yet," she added.

"WHAT DO YOU MEAN, NOT YET?" he shouted at her again, then calmly asked her.

"Why won't you go and see our son, Darlene? He's lying in that hospital thinking his mama doesn't love him; he's fractured his spine, he can't sit up; he has to be fed; and you're sitting down here on your butt all day, doing what I might ask?" asked Mitch.

"I have not been sitting down on my butt all day, Mitch. I have been to see our girl, sitting with her, talking to her…"

"About what, may I ask, are you doing at the cemetery talking to our girl who is DEAD? Darlene, she's gone dead, but our son is in the hospital barely alive—well, alive, but he's in pain. Darlene, he needs his mama; let me take you to the hospital," said Mitch after he interrupted Darlene mid-flow.

With that, she got up and fled the room, ran upstairs and into the bathroom, and locked the door. Mitch got up to pick up his keys for his car; he had a rental until he got a new truck. It wasn't a question of insurance, but the police were still looking into it because of the investigation, which could take months. He got in the car and drove; he didn't know where he was going; he ended up somewhere familiar; he got out of the car and knocked on the door; Robert opened it, and Mitch looked bereft. Mitch grabbed hold of Robert and hugged him tight; Robert didn't know what to do and hugged him back, but not as tight.

"Hey, Mitch, are you okay?" asked Robert, thinking that wasn't a good thing to say, but he didn't know what to say. Once Mitch finally let go of Robert, he noticed Marnie, Caroline, and Deke, who had already crowded around the entrance hall. "You okay, son?" asked Deke.

"No, no, I'm not, Deke. I'm falling apart, and Darlene, Darlene, she doesn't want to deal with this!" replied Mitch.

"I'm going to make some coffee. Mitch, would you like one? I can put something strong in it for you," said Marnie.

"NO, THANK YOU, Marnie! Sorry, I didn't mean to shout. I don't think I would ever drink liquor ever again after what that bastard did to my family; he's ripped us apart. First, we lose Mary-Lou and my boy is in the hospital and they don't know if he will ever walk again, and Darlene doesn't want to know. DO YOU KNOW WHERE SHE GOES EVERYDAY, HUH? SHE GOES TO THE CEMETERY TO SIT WITH OUR DEAD DAUGHTER, TALKING TO HER LIKE THEY ARE SHARING MAKE-UP TIPS!" he screamed. He fell down into a big chair and balled like a baby again, but this time he had his family. Caroline jumped up and went and hugged him. Deke was right behind her. Marnie came up from behind him, and Robert hugged the best he could with all of the people there. When Mitch had calmed down and stopped crying, he realised where he was and who he was with.

"I'm sorry, y'all. I had to get it out," Mitch added.

"Mitch, you have nothing to be sorry about. So what can we do? We have been to the hospital a couple of times, but we don't know what to do for you or how to help you," said Marnie.

"Marnie, I know y'all mean well, but I don't know what you can do. Maybe you could talk to Darlene, try to get her to open up, maybe take the girls with you, and let her see what families are all about, because she seems to have forgotten. Deke and Caroline, I think the same. I know you have been to see Ethan, but I think we all, as a family, need to pull together. My folks are out of town; they are coming back over in a couple of weeks, but I need help right now," he said.

Marnie left to go to the kitchen; Caroline followed her, and they came back with coffee and homemade cookies. Mitch smelled the cookies; he loved homemade food made with love. That's what you do for your family; baking is the best way; it smells homely, familiar, and cosy.

"Mitch, how are you doing for money?" asked Deke.

"I don't know, actually, Deke; we haven't dealt with anything apart from Mary-Lou's funeral, and that wasn't much, not really; it's the last thing we could give our darling girl," Mitch said, then put his head down.

He hadn't really thought of Mary-Lou, not because he didn't want to or because he forgot about her, but because he knew she would be looking down on him from somewhere—heaven, he hoped—but his son needed him, needed them right now.

"Mitch, Mitch?" called Deke.

"What about day-to-day stuff?" asked Deke.

"Oh, that's all right, but we are expecting some big bills from the hospital, which I ain't looking forward to, but it has to be done," said Mitch.

"No, it won't, Mitch. You don't have to worry about Ethan's hospital bills; we are covering that," said Deke.

Mitch looked up at him. "What do you mean, Deke?" asked Mitch.

"Well, we have insurance out to cover all of your medical bills, so you don't have to worry about that; it's all been taken care of!" said Deke.

"What? Really?" asked Mitch. "You're covering Ethan's medical bills; why, Deke?" asked Mitch.

"Mitch, you're our family; your children are our family; we know what it's like when you need to have money for hospital bills; we know the worry; we don't want you to have that worry, which you look like you have at the moment—the world's problems on your shoulders," said Deke.

Caroline agreed. "Mitch, a long time ago, before we had Robert and Darlene, we had a baby boy, Taylor. He was such a lovely baby, but he had gotten pneumonia, and he was in the hospital for a long time for a little baby. He couldn't get better; he wasn't responding to any medication, and he died. My parents weren't in a position to help us, so we had to pay for his hospital bills. It took months. Me and Caroline both worked two jobs to pay for it and his little funeral. We promised we wouldn't ever be in this position again, so we made sure to put plenty of money aside to get started with insurance, and as our family got bigger, we would get insurance to cover it. We didn't want our family to suffer and struggle like we did. There is more than enough to cover Ethan's hospital bills," said Deke.

Mitch burst into tears again as he hugged Deke and Caroline, said a huge thank you to them, and then drank the remainder of his coffee. They all decided to have a rota of people going to see Ethan, so he was never really on his own; he always had company, and Marnie started to arrange to see Darlene with and without the girls. Having the girls would hopefully help, and when Marnie could see her on her own, hopefully she would open up.

"I didn't know your mama lost a baby before you, Robert?" she inquired.

"Neither did I, Marnie; there is no mention of Taylor whatsoever. Maybe they had been hurt enough, and as he died as an infant, they didn't want to keep reliving the pain of it and him not being there."

***

True to her word, Marnie had called Darlene and suggested taking over the girls for a visit. Darlene was delighted; she loved the girls visiting more so now, so Marnie drove over to theirs, and Darlene, who had been eagerly waiting for their arrival, opened the front door. "Hi, y'all, how are y'all doing?" shouted Darlene to the group as Marnie was taking the girls out of the car. Robert had stayed home with his mama and daddy.

"Hiya, Darlene, how are you today?" asked Marnie.

"I'm doin just fine, Marlene. Glad to see you and the girls," she replied as they entered the house.

Darlene picked up Kate for a hug. Kate looked a bit bewildered but let Darlene carry on. Then she put down Kate and picked up Jess. She hung onto Jess a bit longer, sniffing her, as if to make a memory that she didn't want to lose. Darlene finally put Jess down, then they all went into the kitchen. "Juice, girls, or would you rather like squash?" inquired Darlene.

"Squash is fine, Darlene," said Marnie. Darlene handed the girls their drinks, and Marnie reminded them both to say thank you. They went into the living room, and since they had been there, Darlene had put more photos of Mary-Lou, which Darlene noticed Marnie looking at. "I can't seem to stop looking at my girl, Marnie; I know that sounds really stupid, but it makes me feel closer to her somehow; does that make any sense?" asked Darlene as if like a child who had done something right.

"Darlene, you have as many photos of Mary-Lou out as you want; you can keep her memory alive, but you know she won't be coming back," said Marnie, feeling a little sorry now that she had said anything.

"I know that, Marnie, but I don't want to let go of her just yet. I know I should, but she's my girl; you would understand that, wouldn't you?" asked Darlene, looking at Kate and Jess.

Marnie totally understood that she wouldn't want to lose either of her girls. Even though she was closer to Jess, she loved Kate just as much.

"Hey, I tell you what, would you like to go for a picnic, Kate, Jess? That would be fun, wouldn't it?" suggested Darlene again, looking at Marnie.

"Yes, that would be great, Darlene. When would you like to go?" asked Marnie.

"What about today? We can go over by the river; there is a lovely spot that gets the sun all day; we can pick some flowers too if you want to," Darlene said, looking at Kate this time.

Marnie nodded to Kate. "Yes, that sounds like a great idea. Let me give you a hand getting some sandwiches ready, shall we, Darlene?" asked Marnie.

"Yes, I think we have some shopping in; I got some peanut butter and jelly, also some potato chips; these are Mary-Lou's favourites; also, we have some strawberries; that would be enough, and I can put in a couple of fruit juices," said Darlene, muttering to herself really, thinking aloud what they call it.

Darlene, Marnie, Kate, and Jess left the house and walked up to the river; it wasn't far away from their house. Marnie had thought that if she could get Darlene away from the house, she might be able to talk to her freely about going to see Ethan. Well, she had hoped to, but how Darlene would take it was another story. Ten minutes later, they were setting up their blanket for the picnic. Jess was trying to help straighten out the corners. "Here, Kate, you sit next to me then Jess can sit with your mama," suggested Darlene. Kate looked at her mama, who nodded in response.

"This is really nice; it's a beautiful day, Marnie; we have the girls with us, some lovely food, what more can we ask for?" Darlene said.

"Mmmmm…" replied Marnie. She wanted to wait to find a lull in the conversation to ask about Ethan, but Kate did it for her instead.

"Aunty Darlene?" asked Kate.

"Yes, honey," replied Darlene.

"When can Ethan come home?" Kate asked her.

Darlene was a bit shocked at the directness of the question. She stared into space. "Aunty Darlene?" Kate prompted, and Darlene seemed to come to her again.

"Sorry, honey, I don't know when Ethan can come home; he's very poorly, you see; it can take a long time for him to get better," explained Darlene. *How would she know?* thought Marnie. *She never goes to visit him.*

"Errm, Marnie, I wanted to ask you something," said Darlene.

"Yes, go on!" replied Marnie.

"Well, it's a bit delicate," said Darlene.

"Kate, will you take Jess just over there and pick those pretty wildflowers? But don't go near the water, just stay by the path," suggested Marnie. She didn't know what Darlene was going to ask her, but she didn't want the girls to hear her.

"Go ahead, Darlene; what did you want to ask me that's delicate?" prompted Marnie again.

"I was thinking, you know about adopting another little girl, like you did with Kate and Jess…" Darlene trailed off.

Marnie was glad she sent the girls over the way a little bit; she wouldn't have wanted them to hear this. "Darlene, I think you need to heal your heart first because of losing Mary-Lou, then you need to go and see the child that's in the hospital before you even think of adopting any more children. Your son is in the hospital, Darlene, and he needs you. Now I know you don't want to hear this, but you have to see your son."

Marnie was getting really cross now. "Kate, Jess, come on now, girls, we are going home!" shouted Marnie for them.

"Look, Mama, we picked you some flowers, and here, Aunty Darlene, there are some for you too!" Kate handed Darlene a bunch of flowers that were lots of different colours.

Jess handed her bunch to her mother, who kissed her on the forehead. Darlene kissed Kate on the forehead. "Come on, girls, we need to get back home to your daddy," Marnie said again.

"Oh, do you have to go now?" said Darlene, holding onto Kate's hand again.

"Yes, we have to get the dinner sorted out. You and Mitch are welcome to come over and have dinner with us, Darlene," Marnie encouraged.

"I will see what we are doing this evening. Can I call you later?" Darlene replied. Marnie grabbed the blanket and folded it up. She then held onto Jess; she didn't want her to wander off. Darlene had a hold of Kate's hand.

They walked back to Darlene's home, and Marnie handed her a blanket and bag of trash, then got the girls back into the car.

"Now you be good girls for your mama and daddy." She leant into the car and kissed Jess on the forehead and then Kate.

"Marnie, can Kate come over one night in the week and have her dinner?" asked Darlene, suddenly realising that would be a great idea.

"I'll have a word with Robert and see what we can sort out," Marnie said, as she did up her seatbelt, waved to Darlene, and then drove away, both girls in the back waving to Darlene.

"She said what?" asked Robert. Marnie was shushing him; she didn't want the girls to hear their conversation; Caroline was watching them; and Deke had followed the pair into the kitchen; he couldn't believe his ears.

"Did I hear right, Marnie?" asked Deke.

"What about Darlene wanting to adopt another little girl? Yes, you did. Robert, she also wants Kate to go for her dinner sometime this week!" she said it matter-of-factly.

"Oh, she does, does she?" Robert nearly shouted.

"Marnie, we cannot leave the girls with Darlene and can't let them out of our sight when she is in the room, and what about Ethan? Did you ask her about him?" quizzed Robert.

"Didn't need to; Kate did!" Marnie replied.

"Kate did? What did she say, or rather, ask?" asked Robert. Marnie reiterated what Kate had asked Darlene.

"So, she's evading the questions, but she is just saying that he isn't well, but she's making no attempt to see him; maybe me and your mama should have a word with her!" Deke offered.

Deke and Caroline went into their room to talk about this, away from the girls' ears. Kate and Jess were wondering what all of the whispering was about.

"Mama, why is Aunty Darlene so sad? I know Mary-Lou died, but she doesn't seem to be happy at all. Well, she was this afternoon when we went for a picnic," asked Kate.

"Aunty Darlene is a bit confused at the moment; she is grieving for Mary-Lou, which can take a long time to heal," said Marnie. Her girl was definitely growing up.

"Mama, I am seven years old. I can see that something isn't right with Aunty Darlene. Would it help if I stayed with her for a little bit of time?" asked Kate.

"No, honey, we can all help Aunty Darlene, but it's just going to take some time, that's all. Don't you worry, all right?" said Marnie. That was the last thing she wanted: her eldest girl staying with Darlene; she wouldn't want to let her come home, and this wasn't helping poor Ethan.

When the girls were in bed, Robert, Marnie, Caroline, and Deke had to talk; they needed to thrash this out. Maybe Marnie taking the girls to see Darlene wasn't a good idea; maybe they just needed to address the problem. They talked long into the night, with not much decided apart from going to see Mitch and continuing to see Ethan. He liked it when the girls visited him. The next day, Deke, Caroline, and Robert went to the hospital. Marnie took the girls to kindergarten, then headed over to the hospital to sit with Ethan so the other four could talk about this situation with Darlene.

***

Mitch was flabbergasted with what he was hearing. They had gone to the canteen, and he was trying to keep his cool as well as his temper. "I don't understand it, Deke. She has a live and kicking son upstairs in a room, and she's talking about adopting another one. I don't know where her head is, honestly," said Mitch in shock.

"This isn't my Darlene; she wouldn't want to do that again, not after last time; it was such a lot of hassle. Good hassle because we got the kids, but not now, not when one of them is lying in the hospital; I just don't understand it!" he said, scratching his head.

Robert and Marnie knew what it was like at that time; they had to jump through so many hoops; they couldn't adopt in the USA, and they went to England. Ethan was a toddler and Mary-Lou was a baby, just like Kate and Jess, really. Mitch had had some family problems, and they said no in America, but in

England they seemed to be fair better. They were lucky; they knew that, but Mitch never thought in a million years that Darlene would want to go through that again. That's why Robert and Marnie went to England, because they thought they would have also been turned down by the American authorities, so they didn't even try.

"Hey, sleepyhead over there, are you okay?" asked Marnie.

"Yes, Aunty Marnie, I am just resting. I have to go and have my physical therapy in a little while. Daddy normally comes with me for a little while; they like him to see my progress." Ethan smiled.

Marnie knew that physical therapy was good for him, but it wasn't going to get him better; it would stop his muscles from seizing up and massaging them. Ethan thought it would help, but they weren't going to burst his bubble. Mitch returned a little while later so he could go down with Ethan. Robert, Caroline, and Deke followed him to Ethan's room while they waited for the porter to collect him. The porter turned up. Ethan smiled at everyone, and he and Mitch left the room.

"So how did it go with Mitch?" asked Marnie.

"Not great; he thinks Darlene is losing her marbles. We suggested he talk to their doctor and see what he says; maybe she needs to see a psychiatrist or something," Deke suggested.

They all left the hospital. Marnie had to collect the girls, and she didn't like to be late. Robert, Caroline, and Deke returned home. Robert started to make dinner, which would take his mind off this for a little while. When Marnie and the girls returned, the phone rang, which Marnie picked up.

"Hello, oh yes, Darlene, yes, I am fine. How are you?" Marnie asked, not really wanting to know the answer. I don't know if that would be possible.

"You remember the last time. Look, I have just gotten in. Oh, hold on, your mama wants to say hello," said Marnie, gladly handing over the receiver.

"Hi, Darlene, yes, I'm fine, darlin. How are you? Yes, that's great. We just got back from the hospital to see Ethan; he's doing well. Oh, Darlene, you can't be serious, you need to go and see your son. Robert, take the girls upstairs for me, please," asked Marnie. Robert did as he was told and then came back downstairs again.

"Well?" asked Marnie.

"I think she has said the same to me and you?" asked Caroline.

"Yes, about going to England to get another little girl, as Kate isn't allowed over to hers anymore after last time?" suggested Caroline.

"Yes, that's exactly it!" replied Marnie.

"This can't continue, Robert, Deke," said Marnie, then the phone rang. Deke picked it up this time.

"Okay, Mitch, we are on our way; don't worry, he will be fine," Deke reassured him.

"Daddy, what's happened?" asked Robert.

"There's no time to tell, but we need to get to the hospital now. Come on, Marnie, I don't think you should come with the girls, but we will call you!" suggested Deke.

They left straight away. Robert drove, but not too fast. Deke had told them on the way to the hospital what had happened, and when they got there, Mitch was pacing the corridor.

"Mitch, how is Ethan?" asked Caroline.

"I don't know, Caroline; they haven't come back up yet, but they should be here soon." Then the double doors opened, and Ethan was on the bed, looking exhausted.

"I'm here, buddy. You're gonna be just fine," Mitch encouraged.

The doctor was right behind him. "Mitch, can I have a word with you?" asked the doctor. Caroline went to sit with Ethan. Mitch, Robert, and Deke spoke with the doctor.

"Mitch, when Ethan was having his physical therapy, his body went into spasm. As this hasn't happened before, we wanted to check, so we took him for an x-ray, and it showed us something we hadn't anticipated. Ethan has a fracture in his thoracic spinal area, causing damage to the spinal nerves. Unfortunately, he is paralysed from the waist down and will not be able to walk again. I am so sorry," the doctor told him.

"So, what does that mean, then?" asked Mitch, unable to take all of this in.

"It means, Mitch, that Ethan won't walk again and will be in a wheelchair for the rest of his life. Again, I am so sorry. He can continue to have physical therapy; it will help his legs with muscle tone and give them strength, but now he won't be able to walk," the doctor reiterated.

"Doc, does he know this yet? Have you told him?" asked Mitch.

"No, not yet; we thought it might be better coming from you," the doctor said sympathetically.

Mitch nodded. How on earth was he going to tell his son this information? Deke, Mitch, and Robert looked at each other, and they all burst into tears. This lad had been through enough already, and he was going to be on a long road and struggle for the rest of his life. Mitch decided not to tell him anything tonight but waited until he had told Darlene to try and make her understand that he needed her more now than ever. But he also knew that was going to be a tough call in itself, and with Darlene starting to go gaga, he definitely had his work cut out for him. He went to see Ethan, who had fallen asleep, and told Caroline and the others to go home; he would leave in a little while. He had to talk to Darlene that evening; he had to make her see sense.

Robert drove them back home, and Deke filled Caroline in with what the doctor had said. They pulled up outside Robert's home, and they all took a deep breath. They didn't want the girls to know just yet, but they also wanted to let Marnie know what was going on. Upon opening the door, Darlene was sitting there with Kate on her lap. Jess was with Marnie in the kitchen, who was mumbling to herself, and Jess was looking at her mother like she was trying to figure out her facial expressions. Robert said hello to his sister and then took Kate off of her and took her into the kitchen to see Marnie and Jess, closing the kitchen door behind him.

"What's going on, Robert?" asked Marnie.

"Not now, Marnie. I promise when the dust settles," he told her.

Because he knew sparks were going to fly in their living room any minute now. He was right, he could hear all of the shouting, and he wanted to shield his girls from it. Darlene was getting it from both of her parents. "I HAVE NEVER BEEN SO ASHAMED OF YOU, DARLENE, AS I AM RIGHT NOW. YOU CALL YOURSELF A MOTHER? A CARING WOMAN WHO CANNOT BE BOTHERED TO SEE THEIR VERY SICK CHILD IN THE HOSPITAL. WELL, I AM GONNA TELL YOU, LADY, THAT IF YOU DON'T GET YOUR BUTT DOWN THAT HOSPITAL TONIGHT, NOT TOMORROW, BUT TONIGHT, YOU ARE BEING DISOWNED. DO YOU HEAR ME, LADY?" screamed Deke.

"YOU DON'T DESERVE THAT BOY. HE'S BETTER OFF WITH HIS DADDY, WHO I NEVER REALLY CARED FOR, BUT HE HAS PROVED ME WRONG," Deke added. Caroline had never seen him so angry; it seemed to snap Darlene out of it and out of herself.

"Daddy, what's wrong with my boy, then? What has happened for you to turn on me like this?" she said in a whisper.

Deke and Caroline, both told her what happened and what the doctor had said. "Daddy, can you take me to him now, this very minute? Please?" she asked quietly. Deke nodded his head, grabbed the keys to Robert's car, and the two of them disappeared out of the door. Caroline followed Robert and Marnie into the kitchen. Marnie had taken over cooking dinner.

Caroline went to say something, but Robert put up his hand. "Mama, this was a long time coming; Mary-Lou has been gone for three months now, and she had to have a talking to, or rather, a screaming at, to get her to listen," said Robert. Caroline nodded.

"Can I help with anything?" she asked Marnie.

"No, it's already done; I have fed the girls, but I'm not really in the mood for anything. Coffee, Caroline?" Marnie asked. Caroline nodded, and Robert took the girls upstairs; they had already been bathed by their mother, who had them in their night things.

"Daddy, is Aunty Darlene going to be all right?" asked Kate.

"I don't want Gramps to shout at me like that!" said Kate.

"No, darlin, Gramps won't be shouting at you or your sister, but Darlene needed telling off, so Gramps did so; hopefully, it did the trick," Robert added.

***

Six months later, Ethan was able to be discharged from the hospital, but he would still be an outpatient for some time. He had his physical therapy on his legs but also learnt to sit up again. So, he could use his chair. He would need extra care at home, and adaptations had been done over the last few months, even a bedroom for the care staff that they had employed to take overlooking of him, which Darlene had been in charge of doing because she didn't want her son going into a home or rehab. It kept her mind busy, and she was back to her old self. She wanted to enjoy time with her nieces without worrying that she was going to want them to live with her and Mitch.

Ethan now had the whole downstairs for himself, but they kept the living room so they could all spend quality time together as a family, and when he got older, they would turn downstairs completely for him, like an adapted apartment.

"Wow, Ethan, you need some power put on the back of that thing, then you will need a driver's licence to be able to use it," said Gramps laughing.

Once Ethan and the family were settled back home and Darlene took charge, Mitch could take a small step back. He had never felt as responsible for his family as he had this year. Caroline and Deke had long overstayed their welcome, but now everyone was back on track. They went back to California to check that their insurance was up to date and that enough money was on them because Ethan was going to need all the help he could get.

"Darlene, we will never forget Mary-Lou, but Ethan is our priority now; he needs us more than ever!" said Mitch.

"I know, honey, and I am sorry about all of my craziness these last few months. Let's go and get our boy settled," said Darlene as they shut the door. They were home now.

Chapter 12

Seven years on from the tragedy of losing Mary-Lou, Kate and Jess have been with the Stewards at Little Springs Ranch for ten years now, so Kate is fourteen and Jess is ten. Kate has just started high school and Jess is in elementary school. At this stage, Kate is changing her mind every month on what to do once she has come to the decision of what college to go to and what to major in. Jess just wants to work on the ranch with Billy as Eddie left the ranch a couple of years ago. Robert and Marnie had both thought about talking to Jess about it; they loved the fact that she wanted to stay and work on the ranch, but they wanted a bit more for their second daughter. They still had lots of time to help guide her, but as Robert had said to Marnie the other evening, they couldn't believe how quickly the time had gone since they had gotten them both.

Ethan adapted very quickly to his disability with extra care and support, even though the doctors were surprised, but they did remind Ethan that he would never walk again. He had wanted to carry on with his studies once he was a bit more able to, where his head was clear, and also, he had also mastered his wheelchair. His school was very supportive from the beginning up to date, but he was now in college. He had gone to the local one so he could be taken there and brought back home afterwards each day because living there wasn't an option at this time. Maybe later on, but again, Ethan hadn't decided what he wanted to do; his major was computer science, which obviously he could do sitting down at a desk; he wanted to work on the IT side of things rather than fixing computers.

Darlene had suffered from depression for a little while once Ethan had come home; it was the reality kicking in. She was relying heavily on the carers; she would stay in bed sometimes; she knew that she should have been doing much more than she was. She started having nightmares about Mary-Lou too, like she was always out of reach, nearly with her, but Darlene couldn't ever get to her. The doctor had put her on tablets for a little while, but he didn't want her to get dependant on them. They did have enough going on with Ethan, but this was

Darlene's time to wallow. Mitch had had enough. She seemed to pick herself up when she knew Ethan was coming back and that Mary-Lou was not, but she had regressed back to that behaviour.

Robert and Marnie had tried with her, but they had their own lives, so Caroline and Deke returned to help sort her out; this time, they stayed with them so they could get her sorted out properly. She kept repeating to them, "I knew when the doctor opened the doors to the theatre that my little girl was gone, but I didn't want him to say it because then it may not be true." They only stayed for a month; by that time, Darlene had been given her meds and the doctor wanted to start weaning her off of them. Kate was enjoying her new school, which Alice and Jenifer went to as well. The three had become firm friends; Alice would come over with Thomas, so he could see Robert socially; they had built a bit of a man cave so that when the boys came over, it wasn't as if they didn't have the room.

Their house was huge. As the years rolled by, both girls had their bedrooms re-decorated. Kate was a girly girl, but Jess was rather a tomboy; she didn't want pinks and lilacs like Kate did, but rather bolder colours. Pink was definitely out of the question. She didn't mind deep purple or navy blue, so Marnie and Jess sorted out the bedroom with navy and cream; the cream would soften it rather than being so dark. Marnie had put up a dado rail; the skirting boards and doors were left wooden, but she also had her ceiling painted cream. Kate had chosen a soft lilac with cream accents in various parts of the bedroom. Their bathroom was a soft peach colour, and Jess wasn't too bothered about that; she never stayed in it long enough for it to impact her.

On the weekends, they would go down to the stables. Kate still had Chestnut, whom she had loved. Jess had a pony for her fifth birthday; she chose the name Blaze for him; she loved him; she loved grooming him, feeding him hay, and mucking out; it was as if she had grown up in the muck; she was no stranger to even that hard work. Jess was also more comfortable with her jeans and cowboy boots on, whereas Kate liked to wear a dress once in a while. She attended birthday parties of her classmates, and they had parties at home. Since both her and Jess's birthdays were in the winter, they would always have them at home, but now that the girls were getting older, Kate wanted to have her birthdays out with her friends in town.

Robert and Marnie didn't object, but they always wanted to have a birthday dinner for her at home rather than a party. Jess liked the parties but hated dressing up for them; she would be happy wearing jeans and a shirt rather than a dress; her mama would always tie up her hair for her, even if it was in a bun or just clipped up. Jess wore her hair in plaits when in the stables; then her hair was out of the way. Kate, on the other hand, liked her blonde locks put up in a lovely style. She had wondered whether she should be a hairdresser, but that would mean standing on her feet all day. She wasn't lazy in the slightest, but she had wanted to do something rather important; she just didn't know what that was yet.

With Kate's bright blue eyes and blonde hair, she was starting to get male attention at school. She hadn't done anything to warrant this; she was just growing from a little girl into a young lady, and the boys had started to notice. So had Robert. Kate looked stunning on a day-to-day basis, and he was concerned that it might attract the wrong attention, but Marnie reassured him that their girl was sensible, and if the other boys' parents had brought them up correctly, they would be sensible too. On the odd occasion, Alice and Jenifer would sleep over at Kate's. Jess wasn't too interested in having friends over; thankfully, in their growing library, she could read if she wasn't with the horses or doing her homework.

Robert and Marnie were heading for their twenty years' anniversary, and they wanted to have a party for their friends and family. Caroline and Deke would be coming, as well as Mitch's parents. Deke and Mitch had become real close friends since Ethan and Darlene and her shenanigans. He knew that his son-in-law had to step up to the plate, and he did so. They had also asked Thomas and Alice to come. They were going to do something out in the meadow over the back of the ranch; they were going to put up a marquee, have caterers, and wait for service because they wanted to have a fabulous time. Jess did get a nice outfit but not a dress, and Marnie was very careful about what she and Kate chose, as she had also noticed that she was filling out.

They had chosen a soft peach dress with a V-neck and loose, soft sleeves above the elbow; it fluted in at the waist and then out to flow, so when dancing, she would twirl it in a small circle rather than a big circle and everyone wouldn't see her undergarments. Marnie was also careful with her hair; she wanted her cascading curls down her blonde hair rather than an updo, which would make her look so much older.

***

On the day of the party, as they had caterers in, Deke and Caroline flew in the day before so the ladies could go shopping. They didn't go into town as there wasn't anything any of them had wanted, so Caroline took them into Denver itself. They found some lovely boutiques, and that's where they found Kate's dress and Jess's outfit of posh trousers, with a blouse and an oversized waistcoat. It had fine detail on it, which Marnie liked. Jess wasn't too keen, but she had already kicked up a fuss about something else that Marnie had her eye on.

So, on the day of the party, they had their nails done—not Jess, but Marnie had hers done to match her outfit—soft pink; Kate had a natural colour; and Caroline had hers done bright red. Marnie and Kate were quite shocked when they saw them.

"Why, honey, I always have red nails; they make me look powerful," replied Caroline, who then burst into laughter. Marnie had her curlers in, and while she was bossing the catering staff around, she had her shower. Marnie never really bossed anyone around, and this was fun. She wanted to make sure it was perfect. The cake was absolutely beautiful; it was in a heart shape with pink icing on the edges and the words, the same shade they had for her bridesmaid dresses. She had six in total; she kept in contact with some of them; a few had left town to discover their own dreams, but she knew a couple of them were coming.

She was delighted about that. She also wanted to have a couple of professional photos taken with Robert and with the girls, as they were getting so big now. Growing up, they were no longer little tots but big girls with big dreams, and she was delighted. Her and Robert had tried their hardest and did their best to give the girls a well-rounded life, in which both of them were thriving, so they had done their job. Even though the girls were still minors, they were on the right path each. So, with Marnie in her pink gown, Kate in her soft peach, and Jess in her outfit, they all walked down the stairs to Robert, who was waiting for them. He handed his wife a single pink rose and a white one each for his girls.

"Wait," said the photographer.

"If you could all back up onto the staircase, that would take a beautiful photo," he added.

They did as they were told. "You look beautiful, Marnie," said Robert, kissing his wife on the lips softly.

"Say cheese," said the photographer.

"No, we say sass," said Jess, laughing, so they all said sass.

The photographer scratched his head; he was not up to date on these new-fangled sayings anymore.

"Not to worry, sir," said Robert.

"If you want to take some of us when we cut the cake, please take photos of our guests too," Robert told him.

The photographer smiled at him as they made their way over to the marquee. Nobody had really turned up yet, but they had made sure the whole place was wheelchair accessible for Ethan with wooden flooring so that he could manoeuvre with the help of his carers. People started to arrive; it was a lovely summer's evening, so everyone wore short sleeves or sleeveless dresses. Marnie was pleased she found something with sleeves for Kate. She also noticed a couple of the young boys noticing Kate. Thankfully, Robert was in conversation with Thomas, but he had spotted them. He kept his eye on them because he didn't want to be a party pooper, but he was also aware that there may be minors there, and he didn't want any underage drinking.

So, the bar staff were told soft drinks were only for young people, even if they showed driver's licences, unless he knew them. Everyone was having a great time. Kate was dancing. Jess was sitting on the sidelines; she had already eaten; she was bored, so she went up to get herself a drink. Then two local lads, Noah and Mason, seemed to be checking out Kate, who was oblivious to it. She was talking to Alice and Jenifer, and when a song they liked was being played, they were up dancing.

"Trouble, isn't it?" prompted Thomas.

"What is?" asked Robert.

"Having girls. They are okay when they are little, but it's when they get to this age, Robert, that they can become a handful. Have you noticed those two boys looking at your Kate?" asked Thomas.

"Oh yes, I have seen them, Thomas; don't worry, I don't miss a trick." Robert smiled. He did have his beady eye on both boys, and he was watching the girls so that nobody messed with them.

It was time for them to cut the cake. Both girls went over to their parents to be part of the celebrations. The cake was beautiful; they didn't have candles on it, but they did have a countdown when they hit one. A huge balloon was popped, and they cut the cake. Everyone cheered. Robert kissed Marnie on the lips, then withdrew. He forgot he had an audience.

The music started up, and then Noah came over to talk to Kate. "Hi, Kate, would you like to dance?" he asked.

"Oh, yes," replied Kate.

Noah took her hand and guided her to the dancefloor. They had a shuffle around the floor; it was nothing too slow, but you know, tapping feet side to side, left to right, right to left, and so on. It was rather boring dancing, really, but what else were kids supposed to dance like? After that dance, they had another and another, then Mason came over and coughed a little to get their attention.

"I think it's my turn now, Noah. Kate, would you like to dance with me?" asked Mason.

Kate, not knowing what to do in this situation, said thank you to Mason and also to Noah for the last few dances. The music had a better beat to it now, so they could move a bit more than side to side. The party was in full swing. Robert and Marnie's friends and neighbours stayed quite late, but they all knew they had to be up in the morning if they had any animals, and some of them did. "I think we should wind it down a bit now, Robert?" asked Marnie.

"Why, well, I think some of the people have already left," said Robert, looking around the dancefloor. Jess was talking to Ethan; he was asking her about the horses, and she was telling him; she did also ask him if he wanted to pop along one day, then realised what she had said.

He wasn't too worried; he wasn't offended, but he was a little disappointed— not because of talking about it, but because he couldn't ride anymore or do anything else for the horses, except maybe feed them. Once the night was over, Mason and Noah both said goodnight to Kate; they both kissed her hand; she blushed; they said thank you to Robert and Marnie for their hospitality; then they went back to their families as they were leaving.

"Thank goodness we had the insight to get caterers, Marnie; no cleaning up," he joked as they were leaving. Caroline was just doing the rounds with the last of the guests and speaking with the caterers, giving them an extra tip that they had all worked hard that evening and night, and she wanted to show her gratitude.

They were grateful; they didn't always have a gig like this.

"I am so glad everyone enjoyed themselves, Marnie; we haven't had a party like that for some years now; we should have had a huge party when we got the girls," suggested Robert.

"Robert, we had a huge christening party for them both, remember?" Marnie said, trying to jog his memory.

"Oh yeah, I forgot about that," he added, as Marnie looked at him.

"What do you mean you forgot apart from our wedding day? That should have been a day you wouldn't ever forget—the time we got our girls. Oh yes, now I remember, then we went to see Mama and Daddy in California," he told Marnie.

"I am glad that you're not going senile in your—"

"Hey, I am only in my forties, Marnie." He laughed.

"Wow, time does fly," he added.

"Right off to bed now, girls; it's late. Now, I know you don't have school tomorrow, but you still need your beauty sleep, so night," he said. Kate came over, and her father kissed her on the forehead. Then so did Jess; both girls went to see their mama to say goodnight before they went up the stairs. Marnie was making coffee for the adults. Kate and Jess went into their bedrooms. Jess came back into Kate's bedroom.

"Kate, I was talking to Ethan earlier, and he seemed a bit upset that he couldn't go on the horses anymore because his legs don't work. Surely, he can still ride; the horses are very good with us people. Do you think I should ask Daddy about it tomorrow?" asked Jess.

"You could do; it won't hurt to try. Hang on, what do you want to ask Daddy tomorrow?" Kate asked; she was a bit preoccupied.

"I want to ask Daddy if we can arrange for Ethan to go on to the horses—not the big, fast ones, but a gentler horse. What do you think?" Jess said again.

"Jess, I think you're a genius; it's a great idea. I don't know why I didn't think of it!" replied Kate. Jess was scratching her head; she had no idea what Kate was talking about. But she was too tired now.

"Night, Kate," said Jess.

"Night, Jess," said Kate, who was already in her bed, snuggled down, and she wasn't ever going to wash her hands again.

***

"Morning, Gramps, morning, Mama and Daddy," said Jess, looking rather excited as she entered the kitchen.

"You okay, honey?" asked Marnie.

"Yeah, I have had a brilliant idea, and I wanted to talk to you all about it," said Jess.

"Go ahead, then, tell us this brilliant idea!" hurried Marnie.

"Well, I was thinking last night after talking to Ethan; he said he missed the horses, going down to the stables; he knew he couldn't feed them or muck out, but what if he could ride the horses?" suggested Jess.

"What? How?" asked Marnie.

"Well, it would take some thinking out, but maybe we can get a harness for him to strap him to the saddle, or if Gramps is good with his hands, we could make him a saddle with a support for his back, and he doesn't have to ride the horse on his own, but he could have someone guiding it, you know, like how they do with little kids, like you did with me before, when Eddie was holding onto it, and even if I didn't get strapped into it, there was always someone watching me. What do you think? It's not like we couldn't do it here at our stables, and maybe if he likes it, Ethan, that is, we could open it up for more children and even adults. I know Ethan isn't a child anymore, Daddy, but do you think it's something we could think about for now? It's such a shame he can't ride anymore," said Jess, finally taking a breath.

"Now breathe, young lady," said Caroline.

"We can think about it, Jess; it's not something we have thought about, but we can have a talk about it," said Marnie, pointing at the adults.

"Now, do you have any chores to do this morning before you go down to the stables and spend some time with Blaze?" asked Marnie.

"Do you know what, Marnie? That girl has a point; we have the stables and the room; I am sure we could at least look into it," said Robert.

"What a clever little girl she is and so thoughtful," said Gramps. "You know what? It's something that never entered our heads to even think about—a stable that can help disabled children and adults enjoy being on a horse," said Caroline.

"Yes, but it will mean a lot of work and a heck of a lot of money. Maybe look into it, Deke, but I don't know if it's plausible. We would need lots of help, and, to be honest, we have our own family member needing our help. That's going to cost enough without paying for more children and adults. Can you imagine how much the insurance would be, Robert? It's a great idea, but not for us. Our Jess is a clever girl, but it's not for us!" Marnie said it sternly.

"It's worth looking into it, Marnie," said Deke.

"No, Deke, once we start getting figures, getting ideas, Jess will think that we will be doing it, and I don't want her to think that we aren't taking her ideas seriously, but it's just not possible. I will tell her that. It's not possible, and do not, Robert, be going behind my back and doing just that, understand!" said Marnie, looking at Robert and wagging her finger. She was waiting for a response.

"Yes, my love," he said to her. She left the room. "Daddy, please, no," said Robert. He knew his father was going to say something but then thought better of it.

"I was going to just say, what if we try and do this for our Ethan? Surely, Marnie won't object, and it might be good for him as well as you guys," suggested Deke.

"I will have a word with Marnie and see what she thinks, but don't forget that Jess will think that we will be going ahead with this. Also, if we do it for Ethan, there is no argument not to do it for the other kids and adults," said Robert. "Let's forget it for now; I need to go and have a word with Marnie before we both talk to Jess about it. Please, Daddy," Robert said, getting up out of his chair and leaving the kitchen.

He went to find Marnie; they needed to talk about this and nip it in the bud before they all got carried away. Even though he thought it was a great idea, it wasn't feasible to do; it would cost a huge amount of money. Yes, they had lots of money, but they couldn't put everything they had into a project that might do well. What would they do if it didn't, or if they didn't earn enough out of it? He found Marnie upstairs in their bedroom, putting some clean laundry away.

"Please, Robert, don't be trying to get me to change my mind," she said, looking him squarely in the eyes.

"I wasn't, Marnie; I do think it's a great idea, and our girl is very clever in thinking about it and Ethan and his well-being, but it would cost a whole lot of money," he said, telling her everything he was thinking about.

He was glad they were on the same page, but now they had to tell Jess.

"But, Daddy, it wouldn't cost a lot of money; we already have the stables and the horses. Please, Daddy, it would be great," cried Jess.

"Jess honey, it's a great idea, but even though we are comfortably off, it would need a huge amount of money that we really don't have," Robert told her, but Jess wasn't budging, and neither was Robert or Marnie, who then jumped in.

"Jess, we have a good living; we have enough to do on a day-to-day basis. Yes, this would be a great idea, and you are a clever girl in thinking about it for Ethan, but this isn't just possible. I love you and the kindness that you have for others, but now we drop it; we don't think about it anymore. Because it's not happening, understand," said Marnie in a little stronger and more controlled voice.

Jess knew not to push it. Her parents rarely told her or Kate off. They were good kids. Robert and Marnie knew they were very lucky with the girls, but they were not going to be bullied into something because one of them wanted to do something for other people. Marnie had agreed it was a good idea, but maybe somebody else would do it instead. There were also a few people who had stables. She knew Ethan loved to ride and that Darlene and Mitch would have loved that too, but since the accident, they knew they had to be realistic, so for now it wouldn't happen at their stables. She asked Jess where her dirty laundry was, and she told her mama that she had put it down the chute to the utility room to be washed.

When Robert and Marnie left her bedroom, she laid down on her bed. Kate had heard the conversation, so she joined Jess on the bed. "It's not fair, Kate; I thought they would all go for it, you know, for Ethan," Jess said.

"It was a great idea, but, Jess, don't forget, these things cost lots of money. It's costing the family a lot of money to care for Ethan. What if they run out of money? Ethan is going to be in that chair for the rest of his life," said Kate.

"I know, Kate, that's why I wanted to help," Jess replied.

"Yes, well, you had better forget it; they won't change their minds," Kate added.

"Yeah, I know, so I had better go and do my chores; what about you?" asked Jess.

"I have some homework to do with the shopping, and I haven't had a chance to do it."

A couple of weeks later, a package was delivered. "Hey, you guys, come down here!" called Robert, and both of the girls came running down the stairs.

"Hey, Daddy, what do you have there?" asked Kate.

"If it's what I think it is, I will be very happy," said Robert, opening up the package. There was a lot of brown tape on it.

"Come on, Daddy, hurry up!" said Jess. Robert had gotten most of the brown paper off now, and then he lifted it up.

"Oh, Robert, it's beautiful," said Marnie.

"It's us, but not on paper," said Jess.

"Yes, I had the photos taken at the party; this is the one to go over the fireplace," said Robert, and Marnie nodded in agreement.

It was a lovely close-up of the four of them in their finery. "It's a shame Mama and Daddy have already gone back home; they would have loved this," said Robert.

"Yes, they would have," said Marnie, hugging her husband. Jess and Kate came up to them both to admire the picture; it was a beautiful, ornate wooden frame.

"I looked at the silver and gold frames, but they didn't look as nice as the wood," said Robert.

"So, you wanted to buy silver and gold frames for this picture, but you don't want to pay for Ethan to go on a horse with a special saddle," shouted Jess.

"ENOUGH, young lady," shouted Marnie.

"Your daddy wanted to get a special photo of us because you have both grown up so beautifully. Now, I will not tolerate this from you, Jess, so now you can go to your room and think about your words and actions. UNDERSTAND? I said, do you understand?" demanded Marnie.

"Yes, Mama," she said, and Jess left the room and went to her bedroom.

Kate was not going to get involved with this argument. She knew that Jess wasn't going to win. Marnie never told Jess off; she was her baby; she had been attached to Jess since they got there, or so she thought. Kate can't remember when they came to Robert and Marnie; even though Robert and Marnie had said that they had them for ten years, Kate didn't remember much before that, except a horrible lady chasing her all over the place. Thankfully, she stopped having those nightmares a little while ago. Kate went back upstairs; she had some things to do, and she had been sent a card from Noah asking her if she wanted to go to the movies at the weekend, but after what had happened downstairs, she didn't fancy her chances, so she thought she was asking in the next couple of days, when things had cooled down and tempers had disappeared.

Chapter 13

"Mama, Mama, he's here; I'm not quite ready," said Kate. Marnie went upstairs.

"What was that, Kate?" asked Marnie.

"I said, I'm not ready. Has Daddy let him in?" asked Kate nervously.

"Of course, your daddy let him in; now he is grilling him, giving him all the rules; make sure he drops you home; time limits—"

"What?" interrupted Kate.

Marnie started to laugh.

"Oh, Mama, how can you laugh at a time like this?" asked Kate.

"Kate, I am only joking; come here, let me help you. You look beautiful, by the way," said Marnie, rather proud of her eldest daughter.

"I am ready!" said Kate.

"You sure, honey, double-check in the mirror first," Marnie told her.

Yes, good job she did, thought Marnie. Her little bit of make-up wasn't quite finished; she had done one side but not quite finished the other half.

"Dummy!" Jess laughed.

"Oh, Mama, tell Jess to leave; I'm nervous enough," Kate added.

"Come on now, Jess, don't tease your sister; she's nervous enough," Marnie scolded.

Jess left the doorway laughing; she came back a few minutes later. "Hey, Kate, he has big-checked trousers and big stripes on his shirt. He only needs a big red wig and he will look like he escaped from the circus." Jess started laughing again.

"Enough, young lady. Leave your sister alone. Go into your own bedroom, please," Marnie said sternly.

Lately, Jess had been really winding up with her family, getting into arguments. This wasn't like Jess at all; something must have been troubling her, but she didn't let on.

"There, now you're ready. Give me a twirl," said Marnie.

"A what?" asked Kate; maybe she wasn't ready for this dating lark.

"Turn around, Kate. Let me see what it looks like from the back. Hence, give me a twirl," said Marnie.

"Oh, right!" said Kate, doing as she was told.

"You look beautiful, and you will knock his socks off, even if he has a size 16 shoe." Marnie laughed, thinking of what Jess had said. Kate took her handkerchief and grabbed her bag; she had money in it, her keys, and her lipstick to reapply when necessary.

She left the room and made her way downstairs. Noah looked lovely in his suit; he didn't have checked trousers or stripes on his shirt. She was going to kill Jess.

"Wow, Kate, you look beautiful," said Noah, his eyes as wide as saucers. Robert had to look twice; he thought the same: wow.

"Kate, you look lovely. Now don't be late home; Noah is going to bring you home afterwards," said Robert, looking in Noah's direction. Robert coughed lightly.

"Oh, sorry, Kate, this is for you; it's a corsage for your wrist. Here, let me help you," Noah said, taking it out of the box.

"Wow, an orchid; that's beautiful, Noah; Kate is a lucky girl," Marnie told him. Noah blushed lightly.

"Are we ready to go, then?" asked Kate. She wanted to get out of there as quickly as she could, so she grabbed her wrap over for coming home in case it was cold. She opened the front door, said bye to everyone, and then got in the car Noah drove. Kate didn't know much about cars, but it was a nice, stylish one. He opened the door for her and then got in the driver's seat.

Off they went. "That's them gone now, Robert," Marnie said.

"Marnie, you know, when we got the girls, I thought, yes, girls, pretty, you could dress them both up in lovely dresses. I had forgotten they grow up and then have boyfriends and such. Do you think we will cope with this?" he asked her.

"It's too late now to take them back because they are grown up, and when, may I ask, have you seen Jess in a pretty little dress apart from when she was a baby? It's jeans and shirts for her. Look at our anniversary celebrations; she wore trousers, a shirt, and a top over it. Her hair is short; she doesn't want to grow it. You could never get more different girls than we have," Marnie said.

Robert nodded his head; he knew what she meant, though. It was more stressful than he had thought it would be. Jess came down.

"Have they gone, then?" she asked.

"Yes, they have; they both looked rather nice, really," said Marnie.

"I suppose if you like that sort of thing. What's on TV, and can we get takeout this evening? I am starving," Jess added.

Noah pulled up at their school; this was the summer dance before they packed up for the summer holidays. He opened the door for Kate, took her hand, and made their way to the entrance.

Everyone was dressed up, and they all looked lovely. "It's amazing how good people scrub up when they want to," said Noah.

They went into the main hall. Mason was there with another girl from Kate's class, Madison. Kate liked her but thought she was too good for Mason, who at that time saw Kate and Noah arrive. He wasn't too pleased as Kate looked breathtaking, and even though Madison had made a huge effort, it was Kate he wanted to take that evening.

"Kate, Kate," called Alice and Jenifer.

"Hi, Alice, Jenifer, where are your dates?" asked Kate.

"Oh, they are getting fruit punch from the bar with the staff serving; nobody will be able to get alcohol, but that's not a bad thing," said Alice.

"Would you like something to drink, Kate; fruit punch or something else maybe?" asked Noah; he was the perfect gentleman.

"Yes, please; whatever you think will be nice is fine with me. Thank you," replied Kate.

"Kate, you look beautiful; I love your dress," said Jenifer.

"Thank you, Jen; my grandma, or rather, Coco, took me shopping to get a dress for something like this," she told her.

Jenifer was wearing a lovely pale blue dress, and Alice wore deep pink, as she didn't like the pale colours on her skin tone. Thomas came a little later to make sure she was behaving herself and to make sure her date hadn't left her to go home on her own. Noah and the other guys returned with the girls' drinks.

There was lively music on. "Kate, would you like to dance?" asked Noah. She said she wanted to have a sip of her drink first. Then she and the others all got on the dance floor and had a great time.

They were doing all sorts of dancing, and the staff were watching to make sure there was no hanky-panky going on. There wasn't anything inside, but the young people—some of them—went outside to have a kiss and cuddle, but nothing more. Noah kept his hands to himself; otherwise, Kate wouldn't have been as ladylike as she normally is. But there wasn't anything for Robert and Marnie to worry about; Noah was a good boy, which is why they didn't mind her going out with him to the dance. They weren't too keen on Mason, though. He looked a bit rough for Kate. Before they knew it, the evening was over. Alice and Jenifer said goodbye to Kate and Noah, who both replied with the same goodnight.

Then Noah took Kate by the hand and walked her over to the car. She could see Thomas, and she waved at him, and he waved back.

"Who is that, Kate?" asked Noah.

"That's Thomas, my daddy's friend; why?" she asked.

"I just wondered; I have seen him lots of times but didn't know who he was; he seems friendly enough," Noah added.

"Yes, he is. Alice is his niece," Kate added.

Noah put on his seatbelt and started up the car. He checked his mirror and pulled away. Soon they were at Kate's home. As the gentleman he had been all evening, he opened the door for her and walked her up to her front door. Robert inside had heard the car pull up and wanted to open the door to them, but Marnie pulled him back down onto the sofa so they could say goodnight, which was what Robert was afraid of.

"Noah, thank you for a lovely evening. I really enjoyed myself," she said.

"I did too, Kate; maybe we can do it again. I mean, go out for a burger or a movie if you want in a couple of weeks. We have the holidays in a week, so maybe we can hang out?" Noah suggested.

"Yes, that would be lovely. Well, thank you again, Noah," she said.

He leant in to give her a quick kiss; she just stood there waiting for it to happen. His lips were as soft as hers as he brushed them against hers. He pulled away, then said goodnight. Thankfully, Robert was looking out of the window behind the net curtains. Marnie again pulled him away, and they both darted to the sofa as they heard Kate put her key in the door and open it. Both Marnie and Robert had tried to look like they hadn't moved.

"Good time, honey? How was it?" asked Marnie.

"It was lovely, Mama; we had a good time. Oh, on the way back, Daddy, as we were leaving, I saw Thomas and I waved over; he waved back," she said.

"I didn't know he was going to be there this evening?" asked Robert.

"No, I think it was to make sure that Alice's date was still there to take her home and not leave her behind, but they left, the same time as us," she told him.

"If you don't mind, I'm going to bed. I am so tired all of a sudden. It's rather warm this evening," she told them both. Marnie smiled, and Robert looked more concerned than anything else.

Kate continued to see Noah; they had been dating for a few months now; Noah was already sixteen; Kate was coming up to fifteen. Thanksgiving had been and gone, and now it was only a few weeks until Christmas. Kate had been busy with her studies and had only just managed to get to the shops for her presents. She had gotten her mama a bottle of her favourite perfume, her daddy a scarf and some slippers, and for Jess, she had gotten her some new boots, which she had her eye on. She wasn't sure what to get Noah. Even though he was still at school, he had a part-time job at the local mall in town; he worked for an independent pizza place. He was also saving up for Christmas; he had two brothers and a sister, so he had already brought their Christmas gifts, and he was getting Kate a delicate gold chain he had seen with the initial 'K' to go onto it. Kate thought about getting him a new watch, but she was still only fourteen, and even though she and Jess had pocket money, they earned it by doing extra jobs as well as their chores.

Noah had let slip that he was into R.E.M. for a few years now. Daddy also liked their music, so she knew he already had their *Murmur* album, but she wanted to get him something to add to his collection. When she went out shopping, she had been lucky enough to see their latest album, *Monster*, so she got him that. They were starting to do more merchandise, so she was on the lookout for a t-shirt or something. She hoped he would like the album if she couldn't get him anything else.

They were having the whole family over; they had made their home more wheelchair accessible for Ethan because they didn't want him to feel like he was being left out or that it was too much trouble for them. They also brought his carers; he now had two. Darlene would help, but Mitch and she had decided they were better equipped to let the carers do their job, but Darlene was always on hand if they needed an extra pair of hands.

So, they had a bit of Christmas, and as the family was all there, they lent a hand too, giving the carers a bit of a relaxed day. They had their own families they would go to, but they both wanted to be with Ethan for the day. Darlene and Mitch had another set of carers to call on if one of them was sick or on their time off or holidays. Darlene and Mitch were quite relaxed with them; they did a great job of looking after Ethan, but they didn't want to end up stuck for help with him. Marnie was going to be cooking for at least thirteen people, but she didn't mind, and Robert liked to entertain, and Christmas was no different.

Kate would see Noah for a little time on Christmas Eve and then the day after Christmas, so that he could spend time with his family, which was definitely precious because they were hard at work with school and then his part-time job. His parents thought he was a lodger, as they hardly saw him anymore. They had met Kate and liked her a lot, but family came first, and Kate understood that. Robert and Marnie had a bit of trouble looking for gifts for the girls this year. Jess never really asked for anything apart from clothes, jeans, and boots, maybe a waistcoat, which she got a new one each year if she wanted one.

She had been given Blaze, and she loved him. When she wasn't at school or doing her homework, she was down at the stables with Billy and the other ranch hands. Even though she was only ten, she was as tough as old boots. She would get stuck in, just like one of the boys. Robert was a little concerned that she spent most of her time there, but he knew she enjoyed being around the horses.

***

Christmas came and went. Everyone enjoyed themselves. Kate loved the necklace. Marnie thought it might be too much, not in the monetary sense, but maybe a bit too serious too early, and she was still only fourteen. Robert reassured her that wasn't the case, and Noah was a good boy and wasn't expecting anything like that yet, even though he was trying to say it to convince himself. Noah was delighted with the album; he didn't realise how much Kate was listening to when he was talking about himself and his likes and dislikes. The new year came, and so did Kate and Jess's birthdays. Jess was going to be leaving her elementary school and going to middle school, where Kate had left the year before. Kate was still in high school, where she still had four more years to do after this one, but she didn't mind; she liked school and learning.

Noah still had two years until he could go to college; he hadn't chosen where he wanted to go; he wanted to stay local; he didn't want to end up slicing and dishing up pizza for a living. Those sorts of jobs helped you get by in the workplace, but he didn't want a career in it. When the girls went out to town for their birthdays, Caroline and Deke spent so much time with the family at Little Springs Ranch that they were starting to think about moving back to the area they loved California, but they wanted to be nearer to their family since having the girls, and now only Ethan, they knew they were needed more now than ever.

So, when they were back for the girl's birthday bash, they started to look around at houses in the area. Once they had found one in between both Robert and Darlene that they liked, they put in an offer, and it was accepted. Robert, Marnie, and the girls were home, watching TV together for a change, when Caroline and Deke knocked on the door. Marnie opened it and invited them both in. They had a huge bottle of champagne, and Darlene, Mitch, and Ethan were on their way over.

"Hey, Daddy, what's the champagne for?" asked Robert.

"You will see, son, once Darlene, Mitch, and Ethan get here," said Deke.

About twenty minutes after they all arrived, Mitch had brought a van that he had adapted to hold Ethan's wheelchair; he would be completely strapped in for safety reasons. Mitch also got a new truck, a smaller one with only two seats; he didn't want Ethan in that whatsoever.

"Come on in, everyone," said Marnie.

She had moved out of the way for Ethan, and he was starting to pull himself along in his chair. "Wow, Ethan, your muscles on your arm are huge now," Kate said, noticing how strong he was looking.

Ethan gave her a smile back. He had been working out with some more intense physical therapy, not to hurt him but to build up his muscle tone, and it was definitely working. Marnie had gone to the kitchen to get glasses for the champagne, and she came back with them on a tray. "Here you are," said Marnie.

She laid the tray down on the dining table. Deke opened the champagne with a huge pop. He filled up the glasses, even two smaller ones for the girls; he knew none of them were old enough, but this was only a little bit of a celebration.

"Come on now, Daddy, what is it?" asked Darlene.

"Well, me and your mama have found a house in Evergreen, which we have put in an offer for, which has been accepted, so we are moving back home, yeeehhhaa," Deke told them rather excitedly.

"But, Daddy, you and Mama can move back to Little Springs Ranch with me, Marnie, and the girls," said Robert, a little upset they didn't ask them to stay with them.

"Robert, Marnie, Darlene, and Mitch, we know how busy your lives are; we want to be on hand to help in any way that we can, but that doesn't mean us living in your pockets; you both have your families; we couldn't ask for more, but we don't want to impose; you need your space, and basically, we need ours. Anyway, none of you want to hear your mama snoring." He laughed.

She clipped him around the shoulders. "You cheeky so and so, I don't snore, you do." Caroline laughed.

"Well, congratulations to Mama and Daddy," said Darlene.

"On your new home!" she added. They all raised their glasses and clinked them, then all took a sip of the champagne. Both Kate and Jess winced.

They didn't like it, which Robert was pleased with. He didn't really want them to be drinkers; too many of his daddy's relatives drank in their later years. "So, Daddy, where is the house, then?" asked Robert.

"It's about half a mile up the road, the old Jenson home; do you remember it?" asked Deke.

"Yes, that's a lovely house, Daddy." Darlene jumped in very quickly.

"So, have you put the Californian home on the market yet then, Daddy?" Darlene asked.

"Yes, Darlene, we have done that; we had the realtor around before we came back as we knew we wanted to sell up and come back, so, yes, we have a buyer paying exactly what we wanted, which doesn't always happen, as you know. So hopefully, we can be back here in the spring—maybe May? June? But in time for the summer, you know how much I love the summer in Evergreen," said Deke.

"That's fantastic news, Daddy. We can help you at this end; what about in California?" asked Robert.

"Oh, we have found a moving company that will help us pack up too; we can do most of it, but there will be stuff we can't do, like all of the wrapping of those old books and stuff like that, which will take forever to pack. But don't worry, we will get it sorted out, and once we have the date, we can get the keys to the new house, and y'all can come and give us a hand," said Deke, smiling.

"Of course, Daddy," said Darlene. They drained their drinks, and Deke filled the adults' glasses and looked at Ethan.

"Are you allowed to drink when in charge of a vehicle, young man?" asked Deke, laughing.

"No, it's all right, Gramps. I don't want any more, but thank you for asking about my chair!" Ethan laughed, knowing his granddad was joking with him.

He liked that; he didn't want people to feel sorry for him. Ethan was also watching his father and mother drink; he didn't want them to drink. Mitch then looked at Ethan and could tell what he was thinking. "Don't worry, son. I'm not having any more either. Marnie, do you have a large glass of lemonade for me and Ethan?" Mitch said, looking at Ethan, who nodded and said he would like a glass too.

This accident changed Mitch's outlook on alcohol and driving. He didn't ever do it himself, but because somebody did, his son ended up in a wheelchair and his sister died. The guy got done for it. The sheriff was very good at getting his man, especially as these were people he had known all of his life. The guy got ten years on the charge of manslaughter. Mitch and Darlene thought he should have gotten murder, but it wasn't intentional, or so the judge said. *At least he won't hurt anyone else,* thought Mitch. He didn't realise Marnie was standing there holding out his full glass of lemonade.

Spring was soon here, and everyone was excited that Gramps and Coco were coming back to Evergreen to be with them. Even though it was down the road as such, they wouldn't have to get on a plane to see them. They had all of their furniture brought over by air on one of those huge airplanes not just for them; it was more cargo than passengers apart from the pilot. That came a day or two after they had moved in, which gave them a chance to get the house decorated to their desired colours throughout, and they had gone for a completely different look to what they had in California; they wanted more earthy tones and more Native American accents in their home.

Thomas came around with some items for them to get started. Caroline and Deke stayed with Robert and Marnie for a few days while they got everything unloaded. Once they moved in, it was great that the girls and Ethan would see them nearly every weekend, and Deke had decided to help out more at the stables. Robert had taken on a couple of new staff to help out; they were starting to give riding lessons. Ethan had found a stable nearer to where they lived, which he was happy about; he knew his family meant well, but he wanted to do this on his own without feeling like it was charity.

Jess still felt bad about it, but Robert and Marnie were not hearing it at all, which surprised Jess. They were so fond of Ethan, but her parents had wanted to use their money for something for the girls later on. They loved Ethan, but this was for their girls. The one thing that Robert did was get Ethan a handmade supportive saddle, which was referred to by the specialists. He didn't tell Jess; he wanted it to be a surprise, not for Christmas or his birthday, but when he was going to start with the lessons.

He had chosen it himself; he wasn't worried about what it would cost him; he just wanted the best for his nephew. The girls were both doing well in school. Jess liked to help out at the stables if she didn't have any homework, which at the moment was a lot; she didn't have exams or anything, but she would in a year or so, well, maybe tests, just to see how she was coming along. Kate was doing really well; she was very clever and bright. When her report came in a few weeks later, Marnie and Robert were over the moon; she had gotten the highest grade for her subjects.

"Now, what are you girls going to do over the summer?" asked Robert.

"Well, I would like to be down at the stables if that's okay, Daddy?" asked Jess; she wanted to ride Blaze as much as she could.

"Now, what about you, Kate? Do you have any plans for the holidays?" asked Robert.

"Not really, Daddy. Noah will be working as much as he can; he wants to get some money together; he wants to get a new car. He has enough for his college fund for the moment, and he still has a little while before he leaves high school. But I don't know yet," replied Kate.

"Why, Daddy?" asked the girls together.

"We thought we might go to Aspen or Martha's Vineyard for a couple of weeks. Gramps and Coco are still settling in, and we thought they might get more done and settle in if we weren't here. What do you think? Would you like a holiday?" he asked them.

Marnie was looking in close too. "Yes, it would be fun, but Martha's Vineyard might be better, as isn't Aspen better for skiing in the winter?" said Kate matter-of-factly.

"Yes, I think that might be better. So in a couple of weeks, do you both need to get any new summer clothes?" asked Robert.

"I will check, Robert, and then we can take a shopping trip into town," said Marnie.

"Oh, do we have to?" Jess sighed. Marnie laughed to herself; her younger daughter doesn't like getting new clothes, let alone trying them on.

Marnie asked Caroline if she would like to come with them to town; that way, Robert and Deke can get on with whatever they get on with when the women aren't there.

"Robert, how are those new stable hands getting on?" asked Deke.

"Who, Randy and Elijah? They seem to be working out well so far, Daddy. They seem to know what they are doing!" said Robert.

Actually, he was really pleased with how the new guys were doing.

"Daddy, they are really good with Jess. I mean, what that girl doesn't know about horses, but they let her just get on with it. She's no trouble, really—well, not with the horses. Actually, Daddy, a few months ago, Jess was really playing up; we have no idea why, but it stopped as soon as it started," Robert told him.

"She wasn't having any problems at school; was she being bullied or anything?" asked Deke; he was very fond of both of his granddaughters.

He had lost one, and he didn't want anything to happen to the other two he had. It was a terrible shame what had happened to Ethan, but he was getting the best care he could.

"Anyway, things seem to be looking up for all of us, Daddy. It's great you and Mama decided to come back; you know, I don't think you realise how much it lifted everyone's spirits," Robert said. He had felt like he was the head of the family when his parents moved away, and that was a lot of responsibility he had inherited but not really wanted.

So, when they both said they were returning, he knew that his part in looking after everyone was now over, at least for hopefully many years to come.

Chapter 14

Kate and Noah had been together for a few years now. He was now in college as a sophomore, which he loved. He wanted to be a lawyer. A few of his friends, who were good boys, sometimes got into a bit of trouble, but his father wanted him to be an accountant so he could work for him for free. But Noah carried on with what he wanted to do, unless his father would become unbearable about it. So far, he was okay; his dad wanted to be an accountant, but he changed his major at the last minute.

Kate, on the other hand, was still in school as a 12th grade senior; she still wasn't sure what she wanted to do. Robert and Marnie had told her to do what she felt she wanted to do; they didn't want to pressure her at all. Robert's father had also adopted that attitude, as his father had tried to push him into something he wanted to do, but Deke was having none of it. He made his own way and made sure his children would do the same, just as long as they weren't going to be bums doing nothing. Robert wasn't sure what he wanted, but he did go to college and study business, which Deke was delighted with because he knew that someday Robert would inherit the ranch and stables.

Darlene had no idea what she wanted to do; she chose to be a beautician so that way, she could always look beautiful. Caroline was pleased that she could always have her hair and nails done. Once Darlene had children, she concentrated her energies on them. Once things had changed with their family, their dynamics had changed, and she was going to return to her beauty, especially once Ethan had carers and Deke and Caroline had returned from California. Caroline started to encourage Darlene. Her and Deke had seen a shop in town that was now up for sale, so the three of them went into town to have a look at the building to see if it had enough sinks or room for enough sinks, hairdryers, and nail stations.

Darlene liked looking around the shop; it was very spacious. Mitch had popped along; he was very good with his hands and decided he wanted to help her get it up and running. So, he had a wander. Looking out back, they had a bit of a room where they could have a cuppa if there weren't any clients at all, room to have a unit for their towels, yes, room for mirrors, as well as the little sections for the hairdressing department.

Darlene's face lit up. "Yes, Daddy, I think this will do for us. Mama, will you come and help out until we get up and running? Yes, and you, Mitch, will you help with the fixtures and fittings?" asked Darlene, hoping they would all lend a hand.

"Of course we will, Darlene; just think we can fix it up real nice," said Mitch, glad that at last Darlene had something else to focus on and not just Ethan, and even though she went to the cemetery quite a lot, she had calmed down her frequent visits that she had become accustomed to making to Mary-Lou.

So, Deke spoke with the realtor, and he gave them the price for everything. Deke told Darlene, and she nodded. Yes, she wanted it; it was something they could all do with, and Darlene thought that Marnie, Kate, and Jess might want to pop along—well, not Jess, as she was more of a tomboy, but she wasn't going to not invite her niece; that was the most important thing. It was Darlene and Mitch who took care of it. Ethan was going to college and was loving it. Jess was in middle school, in her final year. The following year, she was going into high school, and she couldn't wait for school to be over. She didn't want to go to college.

She wanted to work on the ranch with her father and grandfather, who loved the horses so much. Marnie wasn't too bothered, as long as her girls were happy and not just lying about the house all day. Marnie was excited about Darlene's new project so she could go to the beauticians once in a while.

"You know, Mama, I don't know what to call the new beauty salon. Do you have any ideas?" asked Darlene.

"Well, instead of giving it a weird name to draw people in, honey, why not just call it 'Darlene's Beauty'? What do you think? Because that can cover everything. If you put 'Curl Up' or something like that, people will think you're only doing hair and you're doing hair and nails and anything else that becomes new," suggested Caroline.

"Mama, you're a genius; yes, Darlene's Beauty. I can look for signwriters now and a nice font—something colourful to get everyone's attention," Darlene replied.

"What colour do you think? Red and white?" asked Darlene.

"Oh, no, honey, something a little more subtle than that; it will look like a baseball team or football. What about something along the lines of bright pink with light pink, you know, kind of girly?" suggested Caroline.

"Yes, that sounds better, and you can tell it's for ladies. So that's what I am going to go with—two shades of pink!" she said matter-of-factly. Marnie wanted to help get things done. Mitch was glad to get started; he ordered the timber he would need; he put a lot of it in his truck. Deke went with him to help out. Mitch was glad of the company; he was someone to talk to about this new project and venture for Darlene.

"It's a great idea, Deke. Keep Darlene from going crazy. Once we get this nearly finished, she had better start advertising for staff. She will have some customers, but she will need staff to help her achieve this."

"I agree, son, and at last you may get some peace!" Deke said, and they both laughed.

Work on the salon had started, and Darlene was clucking around like a mother hen trying to get it all sorted. It only took about ten weeks to get all of the construction work completed. Everyone gave a hand, even the girls. Jess loved it. "She should have been a boy that one," said Deke, laughing.

Robert knew what he said was true. Jess was definitely a tomboy; she loved doing anything with her hands—picking up a hammer to whack some nails into the wall, screwing in the screws with the screwdriver—she loved getting stuck in with stuff. Kate, on the other hand, didn't want to do anything that would break her nails, but she did love going down to the stables and riding Chestnut still once in a while. Chestnut had grown into a beautiful horse, and Kate loved her. But the stables were Jess's forte; she loved it down there with the horses, feeding them and mucking them out, and they loved her; they got excited when she would go down there to see them. Elijah and Randy were good workers there, but they absolutely loved her. Elijah was a quiet soul; he would do his work, but he liked poetry and would read some to Jess, not to impress her or anything, just to share it with her.

Randy, on the other hand, was a bit more of a handful, but neither of the young men ever slacked on their work, which Robert was pleased with. Billy was in charge of them; he never tolerated any rubbish with the ranch hands, but these two were okay and dependable. As long as they didn't give Billy any trouble and the work got done, he was fine with them.

"Hey, Caroline, you won't believe this, honey. Do you remember Tom Wyatt? Used to live up on the hill. Yeah, of course, you do. Well, his whole family—the son, his wife, their three children—were going out in the car. Tom was supposed to go with them, but he wasn't well enough, he got a call. They have all been killed, wiped out in a road traffic accident. Snap went his fingers just like that; he has no family left, all on his own, gone in a second," said Deke. Darlene burst into tears. Mitch started to shake, and Deke took one look at them both.

"Oh, I am so sorry, Darlene, Mitch, I didn't think; I am so so sorry," he said again, hoping that those words could be retracted. Caroline went to her daughter and held her tight, and Deke did the same to Mitch. They all had a good cry, all four adults sobbing.

"Daddy!" Darlene said when she stopped and composed herself.

"Daddy, things are going to happen; we can't stop it. It was just hard to hear about Tom's family. How is he doing?" asked Darlene.

"He's in shock, Darlene. I told him to come and stay with us for a few days, but he wants to be alone; he now has to sort out their funerals. Don't forget, he lost his daughter Suzie a few years ago; talk about having so much bad luck, that poor man. I did offer help if he needed it; he said he would get back to me about that," Deke added.

Mitch pulled away from his father-in-law. "Deke, it's life, I'm afraid. Some have it worse than others. As long as Tom knows he's not on his own, he still has his friends," Mitch said.

Deke smiled at him. "Yes, you're right, son. I think I will give him a couple of days and see if he needs anything," Deke added.

"Now come on, or we will never get this beauty spot up and running," he said.

They carried on with their work. Robert and Marnie came in later on with the girls to get an update on the building work. Darlene had put a sign in the window advertising the positions: hair stylist, junior, nail technician.

"Wow, I have never heard of a nail technician, Darlene; does that mean you leave with no nails at all?" asked Robert.

"It's not funny, Robert; it's what they are called nowadays—not a manicurist anymore!" she retorted as they all laughed.

Within two weeks, they opened up the new beauty salon, but they delayed it so they could go to Tom Wyatt's family's funerals. All of the family turned up because they wanted Tom to know he wasn't on his own.

"Actually, Daddy, I don't know if this is a good idea, you know," said Robert.

"Why, son?" asked Deke.

"Daddy, he has just lost all of his family, and you're turning up with all of yours; isn't this a bit insensitive?" asked Robert.

"Oh, I hadn't thought of that; I thought we were showing him that he has us; that's all, Robert," added Deke.

Tom, thankfully, didn't seem to notice; he was just glad that his old-time friend was there. It was like everything else had faded away. Kate stood with Jess, looking at the white coffins of the children; they weren't very old, and their coffins looked lovely and angelic-like. Darlene, though, held onto Mitch's arm tightly the whole time they were there. One of the coffins was tiny; it looked like it held a toddler inside it. Kate started reeling; she had a very familiar feeling but couldn't think of what it was; she didn't have it when Mary-Lou had died or even saw her coffin.

But she kept getting weird feelings; she couldn't fathom them out. She sat on a bench, and Robert headed towards her. "You okay, Kate?" asked her dad.

"Er, yes, I think so!" replied Kate.

"You sure, you don't look it; you look like you have seen a ghost; are you sure you're okay?" asked Robert, pressing to see if something else was worrying her.

"No, Daddy, I am fine; I will be with you in a few minutes," she added, and Robert left her to her thoughts and returned to the little group. Darlene looked over at her, and she could see that Kate's eyes were very focused on the smallest coffin; they were all ready to be carried into the church.

There were now more people, and everyone wanted to help Tom.

Robert had taken the smallest one in for Tom; Deke took the next size; Mitch had a couple of deep breaths and carried the biggest of the children's coffins into the church with Tom's other friends; it was his son. Deke, Robert, and Mitch followed the two adult coffins; Mitch had tears in his eyes; Darlene was sobbing; they didn't take Ethan to the funeral; they didn't think it would be fair; Marnie and the girls followed behind Tom and his few friends; Kate still couldn't take her eyes off the small coffin.

The priest told everyone to sit down on this solemn occasion. He then started the service. He started saying the family members' names: Trent, Abigail, Louisa, Issac, and Kim. *Kim*, Kate thought, shuddering at the mention of the name. Why did that name and not any of the others make her feel like that? It wasn't like she was a little girl anymore; she was seventeen. Why would a child's name make her shudder? Kate had blocked out the priest's voice until he said Kim again; she got up out of her seat and ran out of the church. Robert was sharp on her heels.

Kate had to take deep breaths. "Kate, Kate, what's wrong, honey?" he asked her, a bit out of breath.

"Did you know Kim or the other children at all?" asked Robert.

"No, Daddy, I didn't, but when the priest said Kim's name, I got a shudder, and then he did it again and I felt funny all over, but no idea why!" she exclaimed.

Robert looked at his eldest daughter. He had already wondered if there was more to Kate and Jess's story before him and Marnie had got them, but as Jess was a babe in arms and Kate just out of the toddler age, he didn't think there were any real problems, even though that lady said their parents had died in a car crash. But maybe now was the time to ask questions. He also just remembered that when Kate had moved with them, she kept having nightmares about a lady chasing her. Maybe there was more to these two girls, or maybe these two girls were three girls, and Kate had suppressed a lot of these memories.

Robert stayed outside with Kate; he had wanted to return but felt he needed to stay with his daughter. Deke would understand, and Tom, well, he was just pleased that he had some support. When everyone came out, they all headed into the cemetery. Darlene held onto Mitch still. Jess was walking with Marnie, who looked at Robert, and he nodded his head. They had to follow the congregation to where they were going to be buried. Once they got to the plot, Tom lost it; he couldn't control his tears any longer; they flowed, and he just let them. Deke held on to him. Darlene looked at the coffins, then looked over in the direction where her little girl was. She had been gone for ten years. Her brother had blossomed into a handsome young man, who was enjoying life as much as he could. Even though he was in a wheelchair, he was determined to live his best life the best way he could.

Once the service had finished, one of the group members handed Tom some soil to put on top of the coffins; they were all going to be in one burial plot. Tom had told Deke that he wanted to go to one place, so they were all together, so he bought a double-sized plot; they could all fit inside it. He placed a single red rose on top of each coffin; he loved his family and was shattered that they had all now gone. He had no surviving family; his siblings had died years before; there was only him. Tom was being held up by Deke; they went over to sit on the bench where Kate was sitting previously. Darlene, Mitch, Robert, Marnie, and the girls went over to Mary-Lou and stayed there for a little while; none of them had brought flowers, but they knew she wouldn't have minded.

Darlene started to weep silently. Mitch did the same; the others in the group tried to hold it together. Even though they were there for Tom, this was their family who had already passed; they didn't want to forget her.

"Now everyone," Tom said, waving his hands over to everyone.

"I have set up a little bit of a wake for them in town—you know, that new restaurant—I have booked the whole place for a few hours. Will you all join me in saying a proper farewell to my family?" he asked, pleadingly with his eyes.

"Of course, we will," said Deke, looking at his family for reassurance that they would attend. They nodded in agreement.

"Come on then, we still have the funeral cars; we can go in them," said Tom, delighted that his friends who have rallied around to support him wanted to celebrate his family's lives rather than their deaths.

He knew that people, humans, had hearts, good hearts; he felt like he was ten feet tall with friends like these. When they got there, Marnie collared Robert, wanting to know what was wrong with Kate, but he told her they couldn't talk there, but they would later that evening. He had wanted to talk to Kate again, but without the whole town present. He also knew his dad had his best intentions, but this was something that only the four of them could try and work out, well, three; Jess wasn't up to knowing much of what happened before they had gotten them. They stayed for a couple of hours. Robert and Marnie thanked Tom for his hospitality, and they left Caroline and Deke to stay with him for a while.

They got home. Kate had been quiet all afternoon, and Jess had no idea what was going on; she felt like she had been forgotten out of the invitation to the party for the three of them.

"Daddy, what's up with Kate?" she asked in the car. Kate was staring out of the car window, not engaging in anything.

"I don't know, honey," he replied.

When they got home, Kate got out of the car straight away, opened the front door, and went straight up to her bedroom, took off her coat, and fell down onto her bed. "How come I can't remember who Kim is or why I got so upset earlier?" she said to herself.

She didn't hear the door open; she had closed it. She looked around to see her father in the doorway. "Can I come in, Kate?" asked Robert.

"Okay, Daddy, I know what you're going to say, so please don't," she told him.

"Why, honey?" inquired Robert.

"Because I have no idea why I felt the way I did earlier today!" she told him.

"Kate, do you have any memories at all of before you came to me and your mama?" he asked her. Kate had wished he hadn't asked her that.

She did keep getting memories but had no idea why and didn't want to hurt her father's feelings.

"No, Daddy, I don't," she replied.

"Kate, are you sure? You haven't acted up in a long while. Today obviously was some sort of trigger. Who is Kim, or who was Kim?" he asked, looking into her eyes.

"Daddy, I have no idea, I promise, and I am sorry for running out of the church today; please, can you tell Tom I am sorry?" she said, and then she put her head down on her pillow.

Robert didn't want to push it. Even though she was a teenager, she wasn't a little girl. Maybe she didn't remember anything—not because of trauma of some sort but because she was so young.

"Okay, honey, will you come down later for some dinner?" he asked.

"Yes, later on," she said, putting her head back on her pillow.

Robert shut the door and went back downstairs. Jess looked over the handrail to check if he had left and then knocked softly on Kate's door. "Go away!" she exclaimed.

"Kate, it's only me, Jess," she told her. "Please, can I come in?" she asked her bigger sister.

"Oh, all right then, but only for a minute," Kate said.

Jess opened the door and then closed it behind her; whatever was going on, she didn't want her parents to hear her.

"Kate, what is going on? Why did you run out of the church, and what does the name Kim mean?" asked Jess.

"That's a whole lot of questions, Jess," said Kate, turning over to face her sister.

She leant on her arm and had her head in hand at the back.

"To answer your questions, Jess, I don't know," replied Kate.

"You don't know what?" asked Jess, a bit confused.

"That's just it, I don't know. I don't know why the name Kim upset me or why I shuddered at hearing the name, but I just felt weird, strange. I have been thinking about it all day, and I have racked my brains, and I still can't remember why that name haunts me," said Kate.

"It haunts you; you have never said that before," Jess said.

"Well, it's not a name I have heard in a long time, so I don't know why it affects me, Jess, but I don't want to talk about it anymore, so please, can you shut the door on the way out?" said Kate.

"Why do you always shut me out, Kate? We are sisters, but you don't want to talk to me about it, about Kim," said Jess, a bit louder than she had realised.

"Jess, I have no idea who Kim is either. I can't think with you shouting at me, so please can you leave while I try to work this out in my head?" she told her younger sister.

Jess had the hump now, so she left Kate on her bed and slammed her door shut. Kate put her head back down on her pillow again. She closed her eyes and tried to remember something, anything about her life before living with her mama and daddy, but she just drew a blank; there was nothing. Later on, that evening, Robert and Marnie were sitting all alone; the TV was on, but neither of them was watching it. Both girls were up in their bedrooms; they had heard Jess shout at Kate but left them to it. Robert took a deep breath and started a conversation with Marnie.

"Marnie, do you remember when we got the girls, we got a lot of paperwork that we put in the trunk up in the attic? Do you think we should go through it and see if it says anything at all about the girls and their life before? There may even be something about this Kim girl that we may have missed, you know. What do you think? Huh, should we have a look? Maybe find some answers to this. We haven't really looked at it once the girls got here, and that was nearly fourteen years ago, eh?" suggested Robert.

But Marnie was having none of it. "Robert, I don't think it's a good idea. I mean, they are both settled. Jess was only a baby when they came to us. I don't think we should upset our applecart," said Marnie.

"But, Marnie?" interrupted Robert.

"NO, Robert, we leave it as it is; we can always put Kate in therapy if it becomes a problem. At the moment, something has rattled Kate; we can sort it out, but I refuse to open that chest, and anyway, I think we lost the key to it, so please leave it," she said rather sternly.

"Do you want a cup of coffee, and that's the end of this, please?" asked Marnie.

"Er, yes, please, and okay," he replied. *For now,* he thought, though he would tackle this at a later date.

Chapter 15

Kate had a few nightmares following the funeral. She kept seeing a little girl who looked just like her but was smaller, chasing her through the meadow over the back, calling her Katie. Then she had this miserable-looking old woman chasing after her. She would wake up in a cold sweat. She felt they were both familiar but still had no idea who they were or why they were haunting her dreams. Noah had decided to take her out for a few nights when he was back from school. They would go into town. There were a few films on at the local theatre, but he checked them out first. Nothing scary, nothing about dead people or funerals, so he just looked for chick flicks and hoped that helped, which it did.

Robert didn't mind Kate going out. Even though she had school and exams coming up, he had wanted something to take her mind off the past few months. Thankfully, it did the trick. Noah never brought up what happened. Robert had told him on the quiet; he also swore him to secrecy to Kate. Noah had no intention of telling her. Kate was still trying to decide what she wanted to do. She knew she didn't want to work in an office, but she did want to be able to help in the community. So, she started to research becoming a social worker; she hadn't told her family of this yet, as she wanted to be a hundred percent sure first.

She needed to know what courses she would need to take, but first, research. Kate found out that she could do a BSW bachelor's in social work course; they did the course in Arizona, Seattle, and Washington. She applied to all three colleges to see what came back. If all three did, then she would really need to think about it. Meanwhile, Jess was doing well in school; she wasn't really bothered as she just wanted to work on the ranch, but she didn't want to disappoint her parents, who had always been supportive of everything she wanted to do. She and Kate had their moments every once in a while, even though Jess didn't have any recollections of her time in England. She knew that

Kate had struggled in the past, but nobody wanted to address it if they could help it.

So as far as she was concerned, if she got good enough grades, they would leave her alone. She knew enough about horses; she had even helped when Chestnut had her accident; she was okay, but thankfully, she only ever rode on the ranch and not out on the public highway. Robert had suggested she become a veterinarian because of her love of animals, but it wasn't all animals; she wanted to just work with horses.

Would she need a degree in that? Probably not. She has asked her grandpa, and he said they only got one if the horse was in dire straits, so she didn't want to know. Noah was doing well in college, but he had a long way to go until he could become a lawyer. Marnie had done a few courses; she had worked with Darlene for a couple of years as a nail technician; she loved it. Darlene had about five members in staff, and her mama came in weekly to have something or other done, her hair, nails, and bikini wax, which Caroline refused to point blank when Darlene had suggested it.

Robert was dealing with the ranch, and his father was on hand if he needed him, which Robert rather liked. So, everyone was doing rather well. Ethan had already finished his education, and he worked in town for one of the major companies that were expanding. He was loving his job, and he wasn't too far away from his family. Yes, he still had carers, but he had become more independent, and he would need help from time to time, which he was grateful for.

Kate had all three replies from the colleges in the same week. Robert and Marnie were shocked that she kept that information to herself, but as she had told them, she wanted to make sure it was what she wanted. She had seen Jenifer and Alice; they were both going to do what they had decided they wanted for themselves—a gap year of travelling before they went to college. Robert had asked Kate if she had wanted to do that, but she said no, she wanted to go for her career, so that would mean more education for her first. Robert and Marnie both sighed a sigh of relief; a few of their friends' children had done that and ended up not going back to education.

Robert was concerned that Thomas had allowed Alice to do that, but she had taken a different path. She was going to stay with family in different states, and Jenifer was going with her brother, travelling all over the place, working if she had to so they could further their travel, sing for their supper, so to speak. Alice didn't want to do that; she wanted to find out more about her heritage, and sometimes experiencing it firsthand is better than being told.

Alice was excited about it, and Jenifer too; they both had been leaving parties a week apart. Jenifer was going off first, so her friends and family turned up to wish her well. Then Alice was next. Thomas was sad to see her go, but he knew she had to open her wings and fly.

"Daddy, how did you and Thomas meet?" asked Jess.

"At school, I was being bullied by some other boys, and Thomas was a bit bigger than me, so he saved me; the other boys stayed away, and we became firm friends; we have called on each other when we have needed to in the past and not always just at school." He laughed as he told Jess.

Jess was glad her daddy had a friend he could call on; she had a couple of friends at school, but she was happier around horses. Kate had decided on a college in Arizona that wasn't too far from home if she wanted to come back more regularly. They went one weekend to have a look at it—all four of them. Jess liked it, but she wasn't going. Kate liked it, and Robert and Marnie were both impressed with it. Robert was really glad it was down the road really; he never liked his girls to be too far away. But it was Kate's decision, not his or Marnie's.

When they returned home, Robert asked Kate if she wanted to look at the other two colleges.

"No, Daddy, I think I would rather the Arizona one. It's nearer home, you, Mama, and Jess, so I will contact them and accept and let the other two know. Thank you, but I will go nearer to home," she told him, searching his face for his approval, which he gave his daughter.

He was relieved, and so was Marnie. "Oh my goodness, Kate, what are they going to do about your room? Mama, can I have it?" Jess teased.

"Oh, I don't know, maybe!" suggested Marnie.

"Well, if you're only bothered about my room and not me going, maybe I should go to Washington instead," said Kate.

Robert looked horrified by that revelation. On seeing his face, Kate teased, "Daddy, I am only joking."

Kate was getting ready to go to college. Robert and Marnie were very proud of her. Jess wasn't too bothered.

She was glad she had that part of the house to herself. Well, Robert and Marnie's room was now at the other end; they had moved a year or so ago. "So,

Daddy, when you and Mama go and visit Kate, I can have a party?" asked Jess rather coyly.

"No chance, Jess, not without us in the house. Sorry, you could end up getting gate crashed. What if some people got down to the stables and let all of the horses out? No, sorry. Even if Gramps and Coco were here, we can't take that chance. I'm sorry," he added.

Robert had always been wary of having parties that were contained in the barn or outside under a marquee. "People have no consideration for other people's things, especially their property," Robert said to himself, shaking his head.

"We can have a celebration for Kate when she comes back. Jess, other than that, no parties, understood," Robert said, looking at her sternly, waiting for an answer.

"No, Daddy, I won't. I'm sorry, I was just asking!" added Jess.

"I know, sweetheart, but we can't take any chances," he added. Jess left the room; she didn't want her father to go on and on as he sometimes did when he got a bee in his bonnet. Kate was eighteen now, and Jess was fourteen and in her first year of high school, so by the time Kate finished her degree as a social worker or welfare worker, depending on where she would be working, different places use different names for the same thing.

***

Kate enjoyed her education, her courses; she came home on major holidays like Thanksgiving, Christmas, and Halloween. They used to do fun stuff on campus. She got a part-time job as did everyone else; it's not that she didn't want to be left out, but she wanted to learn how to budget her money. She was good with money, and Robert and Marnie never let them go without anything, but Kate and Jess weren't greedy girls like some of them at school. They were happy with their lot, and Kate thought that she and Jess were lucky to have horses. When the girls were younger, Robert and Marnie would have a party at the house with their friends—well, the stables really—so they could all ride the horses.

A few of their friends wanted to learn about horses, how to tend to them, look after them, and what they can and cannot eat. Robert had held a couple of workshops. Ethan never held it against them for not having his horse riding lessons there; he had found another place.

Robert was worried about insurance; he once told Marnie, "You know, Marnie, it's a great responsibility to have your own children but other people's children, especially if they are disabled." He wasn't worried about himself, but he wanted to make sure that the staff would be able to cope, and he didn't really have staff who were trained to look after disabled children and adults.

Something he did, though, was put his money into where Ethan went so he could access the service, and they were more geared up for it. He never told Darlene and Mitch; he had told his daddy on the quiet, but not his mama. He didn't want to get a mouthful from her. Unbeknownst to him, Deke had told Caroline, but not to ever mention it to Robert, which she never did. Robert was very proud of how Ethan had turned out, and with all of the physical therapy he had had over the years, the ride was the icing on the cake. He did really well but didn't want to proceed with it. He liked riding as he always had, but he found it wasn't the same.

He just wanted to work with and, in the end, create video games for children via a computer, which he did really well; he had a great imagination. Jess was enjoying school, and on the weekends she was down in the stables unless Kate was home. They had been close when they were younger, but Jess had started to act up, but now that Kate wasn't home very often, they seemed to get close again, which Marnie was delighted about. They were full sisters and should get along well, but that wasn't always the case in other families. A friend of Marnie's from school had two girls two years apart, and they couldn't stand each other since they were little, and they were older than her two girls.

So, Marnie was relieved when Jess settled down again. Kate was coming up to twenty-one, and Jess was nearly seventeen. Kate had come over for Thanksgiving, and then again at Christmas; she and Noah were still together, but they were now in different circles. He had finished his college education but still had further learning to do. Now it was the practical stuff. He was working at a law firm in Washington as an article clerk, so he would be supervised by a lawyer. Noah had to sign an articles of clerkship contract, which commits him to a fixed period of employment, which he was delighted with, and in the field of work that Kate was going into, it would be handy to have a lawyer in the family. Kate celebrated her birthday and made sure to return for Jess's birthday, which was only a month before hers. They got mainly money now as they were getting older; there was always a couple of things under the tree, like a gift set or two. Robert used to like going down to the stables with Jess when he was there, spending some quality time together. She would muck out the horses, taking care of them. She still had Blaze, and Kate had Chestnut. Her foal was a lighter colour, so they called her Honey.

Kate didn't ride Chestnut very often now, but she always went down with Jess to see her and give him the odd apple, carrot, or, on the odd occasion, a couple of mints; Chestnut didn't have them very often.

"Daddy, I will be home for spring break. It's only for a couple of weeks, so we can do lots of stuff together, all of us. It will be great to see you all again," said Kate.

"Honey, you have only been back a few weeks!" Robert told her.

"Yeah, I know, but it goes so quickly. Tell Mama I said hi, and to Jess too," she added.

Robert finished the conversation and then put the receiver back down. He went to find Marnie and let her know what Kate had told him.

"She does worry so much," said Marnie.

"I know; I told her it would be fine, but we will see her soon enough," Robert said.

He left Marnie in the kitchen while he went outside to the garage. "Hello there, Robert," said Deke.

"Hi, Daddy, how are you today?" asked Robert.

"Yeah, I am good, great, even. I am just going to see Marnie. Your mama is on her way. I think they are going into town; I am just the messenger," said Deke, laughing.

Caroline started going out with Marnie a bit more often; they liked going to town shopping, having a bite to eat in the middle of the day to look at their purchases that morning, and then they would go to Darlene's to get their nails done. Deke liked it because it gave Caroline something to do and she wasn't driving him crazy at home when he was home. Since they were hardly home, Robert and Darlene liked that, as did Caroline on the quiet.

On their return, Marnie and Caroline came back laden down with bags. "Did you two women leave anything else in the shops for other folk?" asked Deke.

"Now, Deke, we didn't go that mad, but it's nice for a girl to have some new clothes and new shoes; you know the whole enchilada!" said Caroline with a beautiful smile.

Deke shook his head. He knew his wife was dangerous around the shops, but sometimes it was the right time. When Darlene finally got herself sorted out, Caroline and Marnie took her out shopping. It did her the power of good.

"Hey, Robert, this retail therapy lark, is it just lost on the women?" asked Deke.

"No idea, Daddy. I hate shopping for myself; thankfully, I don't have to do it. Marnie gets everything for me; she has great taste, which I might add my girls both have!" he added.

"Including Jess?" Deke said, raising his eyebrows. Robert laughed.

Spring break had been and gone. Caroline had gone shopping in town with Marnie; they always popped into Darlene's; sometimes she goes with them if she had enough staff and not too many customers. This Saturday, Robert had been tinkering in the garage, and Deke came over later on, wanting some time to himself for a change. Jess was working with the horses as always. Billy liked everything to be completed; nothing not finished, especially if he knew Deke was around, because he wasn't as relaxed as Robert. Elijah and Randy were getting on with their jobs, and Jess was mucking out Snowdrop, one of their newer horses. Snowdrop was a lovely horse.

He had quite a sensitive nature; he wasn't very old, but he loved Jess. She would snuggle into his face like she did with the horses. Blaze was at the far end of the stables, and she hadn't gotten to him just yet. Chestnut and Honey were in the stall opposite. Elijah was at the other end of the stables, doing his work, where Randy had been, but there wasn't really anyone about to tell him what to do, so he had a wander down the middle of the stables.

When Jess was raking the new hay on Snowdrop's bedding, "Hiya there, Jess, do you need any help at all?" asked Randy.

"No, thank you, Randy. I'm doing okay. Don't you have your own work to do with Elijah?"

"Nah, Elijah is nearly finished, and I have finished all of my work today, so I thought I would just walk on down and watch you work; you're a great little worker, Jess, and always have been from what I heard," added Randy.

"So, what have you heard then, Randy? I like working with the horses. Yes, of course I do, that's why I spend so much time here. So can I get on now, or are you going to stand there all day?" asked Jess.

Jess didn't like Randy; he made her skin crawl. "Nah, I'm just gonna stand here and watch you!" he said.

"I like the view," he added, looking at her butt.

"Well, I wish you wouldn't, Randy. I have work to do, and so do you, or do you want me to tell my daddy that he doesn't have enough work for two ranch hands but just one?" she told him as she picked up some more hay.

"Right, little tattletale, aren't ya? Always here, looking like butter wouldn't melt," replied Randy.

"What are you talking about, Randy? Just go and get on with some work; I have enough to do here," Jess told him.

Jess was standing up with her back to Randy, who seemed to pounce. He grabbed her from behind. "Now, Jess, isn't that better?" He had a hold of her and was fondling her breasts, and he looked like he was enjoying it.

"Randy, stop! Randy, Randy, pleaaasseee stopppp!" cried out Jess.

He then let go and grabbed a hold of her, pushing her down on the ground. The horses were getting very antsy. Chestnut started to make lots of noise, and Blaze at the other end could pick up on something wrong with Jess. He was stomping in his stall, raising up his legs, and banging on his stall. Elijah had left the stables, so he was unaware of what was going on, but he could hear the horses and bolted back to the stables, but he didn't know what had set them off. Chestnut was going crazy, and Snowdrop didn't do anything because he didn't understand what was happening, even if it was going under his nose.

By now, Randy had Jess under him, and her jeans were already down her ankles. She had started to scream, but Randy put his hand over her mouth to stop her, but she bit him on the web part of his hand between the index finger and thumb. Next thing Randy knew, there were a pair of hands on his shoulders, pulling him off of Jess. Who had screamed out eventually?

"How dare you do that to my granddaughter? You worthless piece of shit! I should string you up right now." Deke was so angry that he straight-up punched Randy in the face. "I should let those horses loose on you," he told Randy.

Even though Deke had punched him, he refused to let him go. Robert, Marnie, and Caroline had all come running. "Elijah?" called Deke. Elijah was trying to calm Blaze down.

He knew something was wrong with his owner, as animals can sense it. "Deke, I will be there in a minute," Elijah said.

"Daddy? What the hell?" shouted Robert. Marnie and Caroline saw Jess move in the stall; she was shaking from head to toe.

"Oh, my goodness, Jess! What happened?"

"Darlin' take Jess inside the house, and can you call the sheriff," shouted Deke.

"Caroline, do not let her take a shower or bath, for goodness' sake," whispered Deke. Caroline knew her husband meant business when he was in this mood, but this time it was for the right reasons.

Once Jess was out of earshot and the ladies had taken her, Deke called Elijah over. Deke still had a hold of Randy. "Elijah, I want you to go and call the sheriff. Tell him Deke needs him to come out to Little Springs Ranch urgently, you hear?" asked Deke.

Elijah, in shock, nodded his head. He ran to the office at the other end of the stables. He came back to let Deke know that the sheriff was on his way, and he then asked if he could go back to Blaze to check on him, which Deke said he could do. Elijah had worked for Robert for years with Randy and had never seen Randy like this; he couldn't even look at him. Jess was like one of the boys, and they always looked out for her, but Randy, this was definitely a no-no. He went back to work, shaking his head, not sure what to do.

The sheriff came shortly after Elijah had called him. Deke had a hold of Randy because he knew if he let him go, Robert would have probably killed him, so Robert was told to go back to the house and also check that Jess was okay. He did as he was told by his father; he knew that his father respected him for his position at the ranch, but this was in his territory. He had been doing this for a lot more years than Robert had. Deke spoke with the sheriff who took away Randy, who had a bloodied nose and his eyes had puffed up. Robert was fuming, but he didn't want his daughter to see him like that.

"Jess, honey, are you all right?" asked Robert; he was devastated that his beautiful daughter, who had just turned seventeen a few months before, looked like she had at the age of five when she got told off for something a little trivial.

"Daddy, has he gone?" she asked rather nervously.

"Yes, Jess, the sheriff has taken him away. I don't want to ask you what happened because you have already been through enough, but you will need to tell the sheriff or his deputy. I don't know how it works with these things. But we will get it sorted, and that man will not work in this town again; once we press charges, nobody will want that man near their daughters," Robert said seemingly out loud rather than to anyone in particular.

Deke came back inside. "Darlin, how are you?" asked Deke, a little nervous.

"Oh, Gramps, thank you so much. I have no idea what would have happened if you hadn't caught him in time," she said, hugging her grandpa.

"Now, this isn't something I would ask, but you know about the birds and the bees? I take it that, of course, you do; you are around horses. I know this is a little bit personal, darlin, but did he actually, you know?" asked Deke, going red in the face.

"No, Gramps, my underwear was just still in place, but he did try to get his fingers on the edge to pull them down just before you grabbed him, so, no, he didn't penetrate me, thank goodness," said Jess, relieved.

"Thank goodness," said Deke.

"Honey, I am so glad; that is for when you have a husband, you know when you want one," said Deke, now a little embarrassed.

"No, Gramps, I don't think I want one, not after this. Oh, don't worry, it didn't put me off men; I wasn't too bothered by them anyway," Jess added.

Deke was definitely red in the face now.

"Er, well, anyway, they are going to send someone over. Now that nothing you know, penetrated, did you scratch him?" asked Deke.

"No, Gramps, I bit him instead," she told him, showing him where on her hand.

"Well, that is really going to hurt," Deke said.

"So, they will have your DNA in his hand. Let's hope he needs stitches." Deke laughed. Robert and Marnie didn't think it was funny, but they knew he was trying to make light of the situation.

A few hours later, from a different county, the sheriff came over to speak to Jess, with Marnie and Caroline, with Deke and Robert not wanting to be in the room listening to every word of the encounter that had taken place. They both went down to the stables to see how the horses were and check on Elijah.

On entering the stables, Elijah walked up to both men. He held his head low. "I am so sorry, Mr Steward. I never knew that Randy was like that. I would never have recommended you to him, sir. I am very, very sorry! Sir, how is Jess doing? Is she all right? I wanted to keep an eye on Blaze, sir, because he was very agitated in his stall, and now we know why," added Elijah.

"Jess is okay. She's on the mend, Elijah, thank you. She's resilient, our Jess, but this has shaken her up some. So, are you done here, Elijah?" asked Robert.

"I have a few more things to do, and then I will be on my way, sir. Sir, I am so very sorry for not stepping in to help Jess before," said Elijah, finally looking up and giving Robert eye contact for the first time.

"Thank you, Elijah, and see you in the morning," said Robert.

"Robert, don't give him a hard time; a similar thing actually happened to his sister a few years ago, it must have brought it all back to him," Deke told him.

"How do you know that, Daddy?" asked Robert.

"There was nothing I didn't hear back in California; people were sometimes worried about you and Darlene, then when you got the girls, anyway. Let's lock up and go inside. Billy isn't going to be so happy tomorrow; he's down a pair of hands," said Deke.

"No, but he will wish he was here to give Randy a go-over," said Robert.

"Now what is done is done, so as long as young Jess is okay, we can deal with the rest of it later on," said Deke. He was always wise, like an old owl.

***

"What do you mean attempted rape? Daddy I'm coming home; I'm not worried about my course; Jess is more important; I will be there in a few hours. Tell Jess I love her, and I will see her and the rest of you in a little while. Please, Daddy, it's okay; I'm going to where my family needs me," said Kate, putting down the phone. She ran to the office to let them know that she had to go home due to an emergency.

She flew back upstairs and threw things into a bag, left a brief note for her roommates, and made her way to the airport as quickly as she could. True to her word, she was back within a couple of hours; it didn't take long to get home.

She put her key in the door. "Daddy, Mama, Jess, where are you guys?" shouted Kate.

"Honey, we are up here, down in a minute!" Robert shouted over the stairs.

She dumped her bag onto the sofa, took off her jacket, and made her way to the kitchen. Robert, Marnie, and Jess came down the stairs.

Kate ran over to her little sister and grabbed a hold of her; she didn't want to let go. "Jess, are you okay? Are you all right?" she asked nervously, but she had to ask anyway.

"Kate, I am okay, honestly. Gramps and Coco have left but will be back. A lady has just left. She took my statement, and so did Gramps," said Jess.

Kate looked bewildered. "Gramps?" she reiterated.

"Yes, Gramps, he was the one who caught and stopped."

She couldn't say anymore. She had just relayed it to the lady who was taking notes very quickly, but read back to Jess what she had just said to make sure she didn't really make a mistake.

"She was very brave," said Marnie.

"Mama, Jess isn't five; she's seventeen going on a hundred, I think?" She laughed as she said it to Jess, who, in turn, laughed.

"This isn't a laughing matter, you know, girls?" instructed Marnie.

"We do know that, Mama, but I just wanted to break; I shouldn't have bothered. Anyway, Jess, how are you really?" asked Kate more seriously now.

"I am okay; going over it again was a bit difficult as it now seems a bit of a blur. I am just so grateful that Gramps turned up when he did," said Jess, thinking.

"Now, girls, can we change the subject? So, Kate, what did you say to your tutor?" asked Marnie.

"You didn't tell them, did you?" Marnie asked.

"No, Mama, I just said there was a family emergency; they won't ask. But I wanted to be home with you all," she said, hugging Jess again.

Jess wasn't as emotional as Kate, but this had hit her hard.

"You don't mind if I go and have a bath, do you? I have seen the lady, and the police department said they have finished with me. I need some time on my own for a little while; this has been overwhelming, to say the least," Jess added.

"Are you sure you want to be on your own, honey?" suggested Marnie.

"Yes, Mama, I will be on my own when I go to bed tonight. I will be fine, honestly," Jess said, reassuring her mother.

"Okay, then, Jess, but shout if you need me, won't you?" Marnie added.

"I will, Mama; see you in a little while," Jess said, going up the stairs.

"This has hit her hard, you know, Kate; do you think I should follow her up there?" asked Marnie.

"No, Mama, Jess wants some privacy; she's nearly had that taken away today, thankfully not. She needs some time, Mama. Shall we make some coffee, just to while away some time?" asked Kate.

"Yes, honey, come and help me, Robert; are you okay?" asked Marnie.

"What? Yes, yes, I'm fine. Can I have a cup of coffee too, Marnie?" replied Robert.

"Why sure? Be a few minutes, and I will make a fresh pot," Marnie told him.

Robert sat back down on the sofa. It was going around and around in his head; he couldn't get over it. He had known Randy for years; what on earth would make him do that to Jess, his girl? He couldn't get his head around it. Elijah hadn't done anything like that, so why would Randy do it to his sweet girl, Jess, who never did anything to anyone? She hadn't shown an interest in boys, especially Randy or Elijah; she only loved being at the stables for the horses, and they had sensed something wasn't right; horses were clever animals.

He hoped Snowdrop would be okay; he seemed nervous when Jess was being attacked. Blaze, on the other hand, and Chestnut were going bananas. They must have known Randy was wrong; animals can sense it. Robert was going over and over in his head, and his head was starting to hurt; he was getting quite a pain right on the top. He called out to Marnie to get him some painkillers. He moved off the sofa, then lost his balance and fell on the floor; his arm was hurting him. He was getting pain up his arm; he held onto it with his right arm. He didn't like this feeling; it was strange. He closed his eyes. Marnie came into the lounge talking to Kate, who was holding two hot cups of coffee. Marnie looked in his direction, dropped her cup, and screamed. Kate looked in the same direction, and she did the same.

Marnie ran over to Robert, who seemed to be struggling to speak. Kate grabbed the phone and rang for an ambulance, who, on the other end, said they would be there as quickly as possible. Jess shouted out to see what was going on. Five minutes later, she was at the top of the stairs with a towel around her and soap suds on the top of her back, where the bubbles were. She ran downstairs. Kate had already called Gramps and Coco, but there wasn't any answer.

"Mama, I can't get through; they must be on their way here!" said Kate.

"Robert, Robert, can you hear me? I am going to put you in the recovery position, make some noise if I hurt you, and actually scream if you can." But Robert wasn't making any noise at all. Jess was by her father's side.

"Mama, you need to give him some space so he has air," said Jess.

Kate knelt by the other side of him.

"You too, Kate; he needs air. Hold his hand, so he knows you're there," said Marnie.

Kate didn't want to leave her father's side, but the doorbell went off. Kate got up and opened it to see the ambulance and two paramedics with their equipment. They got down on the floor, asked Marnie some questions, and laid him flat on his back so they could perform CPR on him.

Kate heard a car pull up outside; it tooted behind the ambulance. Whoever it was slammed their car door and then entered Gramps and Coco. "Oh my goodness, my boy, what has happened?" asked Deke.

Caroline was as white as a sheet. "Robert, oh, Robert!" screamed Caroline.

"Please, ladies and sir, could you go in the other room while we do our jobs? Thank you; we can't concentrate on what we are doing with this shouting," said the lady.

"Come on, everyone, out into the kitchen; let these good people get on with their work," said Deke.

"But I'm his mama," said Caroline.

"And I'm his wife," added Marnie.

"Yes, we know who you both are, but I am sorry we need to do this, and every second counts," shouted the lady.

The guy paramedic was pushing on Robert's chest and blowing air into his mouth. They worked on him for over half an hour, but they both knew it was too late. Robert had gone, but they had to take him to the hospital. They couldn't leave him in the middle of the lounge, and they had to get the necessary paperwork sorted out. He would need an autopsy anyway. That way, they can sort it all out at once.

The guy went into the kitchen. Jess had a coat over her towel, and they were all sitting down at the breakfast bar. "Yes, how is he?" asked Deke.

"I'm afraid he didn't make it; we tried everything we could." All of the women burst into tears. Kate and Marnie were rather loud. Caroline wasn't crying; she looked rather blank, as if she had been hit by a brick wall.

"No, my Robert is in the sitting room, watching TV with Thomas; we saw him," Caroline told them.

Deke walked over to her, put his arm around her, and hugged her. He was their only son, and they had already lost Taylor years ago, but they didn't expect to lose another boy so early.

"Oh my goodness, what are we going to do now?" screamed Marnie. She had been with Robert for over twenty-five years; they had been childhood sweethearts, but now she was on her own. Thankfully, the girls weren't babies anymore, but how would she cope without him? He was her rock.

Suddenly, out of nowhere, Marnie howled. The three women all jumped out of their skins. Marnie couldn't stop. Caroline went over to her and hugged her so tightly, and she told Marnie to let it all out.

Both of the women started to cry. Deke left them in the kitchen. "Er, excuse me, but what happens now? Is Robert able to stay here?" asked Deke.

"I'm sorry, sir, but no, he needs to go to the hospital—" Deke held up his hand to stop the guy.

"But he's dead, not sick; why would he need to go to the hospital?" asked Deke. Like the women, he was also in shock.

"Sir, he has to go to the hospital because he will need to go to the mortuary. He died at home, he will need an autopsy, which will be carried out at the hospital; once that is done, he will need a death certificate; then you will need to contact the funeral home and make arrangements for his funeral. Do you and the ladies want to come and say goodbye before we leave, or do you think it's too soon?" asked the guy now, not sure if he said the right thing or not.

"I will get the women and see what they want to do; I won't be a minute," he told him. Deke ran into the kitchen. "Caroline, Marnie, girls, I know this is real quick, but do you want to go and see Robert before they take him away?" asked Deke.

All of the women nodded their heads. "Well, we have to be quick," he said as he ushered them out of the kitchen.

They all went over to see him; he was on a stretcher but still on the floor. The paramedics didn't want to cover his face in front of his family, so they all kissed him on the head. Marnie and Caroline kissed him on the forehead, Kate on the cheek, and Jess on the other cheek. They all told Robert that they loved him and then turned back and went into the kitchen. Deke stayed with the paramedics; they then covered Robert's face and lifted up the stretcher, giving him his dignity. They didn't want to put him in the body bag at home but would do it when they got to the hospital.

"Mama, can we go to the hospital with Daddy?" asked Jess.

"No, darling, that's it until we see him at the funeral home," said Marnie.

"But why the hospital? If he's dead, doesn't he go straight to the funeral home?" asked Jess.

"No, darlin, he has to go to the hospital to go to the mortuary; he needs an autopsy—" Caroline popped her hand up.

"Too much information, Deke. He will go to the funeral home once all of the necessary paperwork is done. We have to wait until the hospital can release his death certificate, then start to arrange his funeral. But for now, we need a hot drink and a hug each," said Caroline.

"Coco?" said Kate.

"Yes, honey," replied Caroline.

"We need to tell Darlene and Mitch," said Kate.

"Oh no, I forgot about Darlene, Deke. Can you do it? She will be at the salon now. I will get tongue-tied and start crying, please, honey," pleaded Caroline.

"I will do it, but I will go now." Deke left the house with the women crying; the ambulance had already left.

How on earth was he going to tell his only living child that her big brother had just died, probably from a heart attack due to the stress of the day's events?

Chapter 16

It was a sad few days following Robert's death; nobody knew what to do with themselves. Marnie was beside herself, and Kate wasn't too far behind. It was like they were functioning on autopilot; the adrenaline had really kicked in; they weren't dealing with anything important at all. Marnie couldn't deal with arranging his funeral; Deke and Caroline had to take over the arrangements. All Marnie could think of was what flowers to have made for her and the girls. Kate had already told the college that she was going home for an emergency, which had now turned into a terrible tragedy.

She was walking around as if in a dream state; it didn't seem real. Her daddy, whom she loved more than anything, was gone forever. What was she going to do without her daddy, who had been there for as long as she could remember? The funeral was arranged for two weeks later. Caroline and Deke had wanted to have the wake at the ranch. Marnie had agreed to everything, and Jess was out in the stables with Elijah and Billy trying to make sense of it all.

"If Randy hadn't done this, Billy, my daddy would still be alive; he wouldn't have had a heart attack. I feel so guilty," Jess said.

"Now listen to me, young Jess; your daddy was a sensitive but honourable man; he was so upset about what happened to you that he couldn't take it; not many men could. Randy was out of order. It was great your gramps was here to take care of him and give him to the sheriff, but that doesn't mean it didn't hurt your gramps and daddy; they both loved you. Your daddy's body couldn't take that sort of stress, so his heart gave out. But don't you worry, none; your gramps will make sure that Randy gets his just desserts. Now if you want to stay here with Blaze or the other horses, you can; we know you will be fine here, and nobody is going to interfere with you while we are both here, me and Elijah," Billy told her.

Elijah put his head up and nodded with Billy, then put it down again. "I think I'm going to go back to the house and see if I am needed for anything, Billy."

"Thank you, you too, Elijah," Jess replied. She gave Blaze a stroke on his face before she left.

She took a slow walk up to her home. Thomas was waiting outside the house. "Hi, Thomas, are you okay?" asked Jess.

"Hello, young Jess, er, I think so. I am still in shock about your father; he was a wonderful man. You're going to miss him, I bet?" said Thomas, who looked like he had aged ten years.

"Yes, yes, I will; we all will. He was a big personality, and everyone loved him, which is why I suppose this is such a shock. I'm going in; are you coming in?" asked Jess.

"I will in a little while." He smiled at her, then walked away from the house and went to sit on a huge log that was a little further away from the house. As Jess watched Thomas, it was as though he was reminiscing about happier times as his facial expressions changed, as if he were talking to Robert himself. Marnie still didn't seem to know what day of the week it was; she was definitely not in the mood for entertaining, even though the household was always full now. Kate did what she could to be hospitable, but she would have rather stayed on her bed and cried her eyes out for the father she was never going to see again. Darlene came into her own; she helped out with everything and everyone. Caroline and Deke would never have been able to manage all of this without her help. Mitch lent a hand too; they were both very practical.

I suppose losing their daughter and their son in a wheelchair for the rest of his life was enough of a wake-up call to get on with life.

***

On the day of the funeral, everyone close to Robert came early. Caroline and Darlene had been up since dawn, getting stuff ready for Marnie and the girls. The place had been cleaned from top to bottom in the last few days. Kate had come to realise that housework and cleaning were great for trying to forget your problems. Also, if you were angry, getting on with the cleaning was great because you got stuck in and took your anger out on it. It was very exhilarating at this time. The cars turned up outside with Robert in the hearse; there was a huge coffin, with tonnes and tonnes of flowers. Marnie had a HUSBAND; Kate and Jess got DADDY, Caroline and Deke got ROBERT; Darlene and Mitch had a BROTHER. There were floral sprays and arrangements. Caroline and Deke were surprised by the amount of flowers for Robert. Marnie, Kate, and Jess were in the main car, and Caroline, Deke, Darlene, and Mitch got right in the back. It was a huge car. Ethan was going with his carers; they were making their own way to the cemetery. He had an adapted car, but the carers could get in the back.

They had been with the family for years and got to know Robert quite well; he was well respected in the community. Kate wore a black suit with a white blouse, and Jess wore a black trouser suit with a white shirt. Marnie wore a black dress with a veil over her face. The last time she wore one of those, she was getting married to her love, Robert, and now she was going to his funeral at his untimely death. Caroline and Darlene both wore black dresses, and the men wore dark grey suits with black ties and arm bands.

When the cars pulled up outside the church, Marnie was impressed with the amount of people waiting outside—people they had known for years, old farmhands and ranch hands from other stables and ranches. She took a moment, then walked inside the church with her two daughters behind her. Caroline and Deke, then Darlene, Mitch, and Ethan, his carers, Thomas, and then the rest of the congregation. They had a few hymns. Thomas did a reading, and one of the old ranch hands, who had since retired, said a few words. Marnie and Kate had both lost it by now; they couldn't stop crying. Mitch grabbed hold of Kate while Deke took hold of Marnie while holding onto his wife, who was just as upset; this was her second son she had lost, and she was devastated, as were the rest of the people in Robert's life.

It was a sad and solemn occasion. Once the minister had finished his sermon, Robert was picked up by his father, brother-in-law, best friend from school, and his ranch hands, Billy, Elijah, and Sam, from way back. Caroline and Marnie held onto each other; Kate and Jess were holding each other too. Kate was still crying; she was so upset that her daddy was in this box in this cold building, but he was going into the ground next to where Mary-Lou was now residing. Kate and Jess held hands as they left the church. They turned right towards the cemetery, the men still holding onto Robert. They went along behind the minister, then he stopped. This was the place; this was where their daddy was going to be for the rest of his days and nights. Caroline handed Marnie and the girls, Darlene, Mitch, Ethan, and Deke a white rose each.

Once Robert was lowered into the ground, even though there was a beautiful arrangement on his coffin, they all placed their roses respectfully. Then they all left. Kate and Marnie didn't want to leave. Caroline took Jess's arm. Darlene came over from Mary-Lou's grave, she had put fresh flowers on it for her. She also asked her daughter to look after her brother now.

Darlene put her arms between Marnie and Kate's arms. "Come on, you two, we can't stay here forever; you can always come back later or tomorrow," she told the women.

"Come on, Kate, your aunty Darlene is right; we can come back later or tomorrow; we have to go home now," Marnie added.

Kate left reluctantly; she didn't want to go home; she wanted to stay with her daddy, who she had always known, had dried her tears, comforted her when she was sad or scared, and was gone. She sniffed the air, and to hold back the tears mainly, she nodded her head and left with her mama and aunty. They got back home, and they had people everywhere. She really didn't know how much her father was loved by everyone and the things he had done for people, like helping them when they were sick, making sure their families had food on the table, and having their utilities paid when they couldn't work so they would have heat in their home.

Helping down at the welfare place once in a while, especially at Christmas. "Your daddy always knew how to help everyone, and he did all the time!" said a gentleman that Kate didn't know.

Some of these people no longer lived in the area, but they knew her daddy. She felt proud that he had done so much for the community. Caroline came over with a hot cup of coffee for them. It was cold outside, but they hadn't really noticed it. Kate took hers into the kitchen. Robert was everywhere—the décor, the handiwork—he was so good with his hands; she had to look away. She went back into the living room. Caroline had seen Kate look a bit discombobulated as she went over to her; she told her to take some food and go upstairs to her room for a little while; it might make her feel a bit better for her to reflect on her daddy without the prying eyes of everyone else. Kate nodded. That was a good idea. She grabbed a plate and put some food on it. She wasn't bothered; she just wanted to appease her grandma and get out of that place.

She went upstairs with her plate, put it in her bedroom on her bedside cabinet, and went to see if Jess had the same idea. She looked in her bedroom, and no, she wasn't there. So, she took herself back to her bedroom, laid on her bed face down on her tummy, and was just staring at the walls, not taking any notice of anything. Slowly, she closed her eyes, and she fell silently asleep.

She was running, looking back; he was behind her. Now they were neck and neck, her and her daddy, and they were running across the meadow. She was about ten. "Daddy, I am faster than you," she said, out of breath.

"Yes, you are, Kate; I must be getting old." Robert laughed.

Kate had the biggest smile on her face. She felt someone knock on her door. "Kate, Kate," said Jess, who had brought Kate a drink.

"Kate," she repeated.

"Yes, I am awake," Kate replied.

She then opened her eyes. "Jess, what time is it?" asked Kate.

"It's just gone nine," she told her.

"In the morning?" asked Kate, a bit confused.

"No, nighttime. Everyone has gone home except Coco and Gramps," Jess said.

"Oh, I didn't realise," said Kate.

"Don't worry, Mama told everyone you were tired and didn't sleep well last night," said Jess.

"Is Mama okay now?" asked Kate.

"No, she went to bed as soon as everyone left. Coco and Gramps are clearing up downstairs; do you want to come down now, then?" asked Jess.

Kate looked at the plate of uneaten food and thought she had better get something fresh to eat. She took her glass of water with her; she had left her coffee downstairs when she got some food.

"Hi, honey, are you all right?" asked Caroline.

"Yes, now, Coco. I fell asleep, but I am hungry now," replied Kate.

"Okay, I take it you didn't eat that food earlier," she said, looking at the plate.

"There is a big black bag in the kitchen; dump your plate in there, honey, and grab yourself something else to eat; there are tonnes in the fridge and on the side as there isn't enough room in the fridge," she told her.

"Didn't it all get eaten, then?" asked Kate.

"Oh yes, lots of it went, but we had ordered far too much. Some of the ranch hands took it down to the stables; they felt once they had paid their respects to Robert; they didn't feel right being here in the house, but quite a lot old and new went down there to celebrate his life rather than his death, Billy told us," Deke said.

"That's just like Billy." Kate laughed.

Laughing, her daddy was lying in the cold ground, and she was laughing. She wanted to scold herself, but Gramps cut her off first. "Listen, Kate, your daddy was a great man. I didn't realise until today how well liked and respected he was in the community, but he wouldn't want you to be sad to see you upset like this, and yes, you have to laugh; life has to go on, okay?" he told her.

She smiled back at her grandfather.

"Oh, Gramps," she replied.

She went to the fridge and grabbed a couple of chicken drumsticks, potato salad, and whatever she felt like, as she thought her stomach had never had food in it. She was ravenous. She filled her plate high; Jess came into the kitchen; she did the same. Coco made some coffee, and Deke joined the ladies at the breakfast bar, stuffing their faces. "This eating lark on a rough day does make a lot of sense," said Deke.

"It's called comfort eating, Gramps," said Jess, laughing.

They all tucked into their food and had mouthfuls of their hot drinks in between. Marnie didn't join them; she was on her bed, which she had shared with Robert, holding onto one of the pillows that still had his scent on them. She held it tight to her chest while the tears started streaming down her face. She didn't care; she just felt wretched. He had gone, the love of her life. What was she going to do now? How was she going to carry on without him?

***

Life was slowly getting back to normality. Marnie had taken to wearing black every day; Kate wore dark clothes but more navy blue; Jess didn't have many dark clothes, but she had lots of jeans. She was worried her mother may not like the fact that she wore jeans all of the time, but Jess was spending a lot of time at the stables, which Deke and Caroline were pleased with; they had thought that what had happened with Randy may have frightened her off the stables altogether. But no, like a boomerang, she came back. Billy and the others told Deke that he would have nothing to worry about and that he and the others would watch her like a hawk, especially when the young men were around.

But they had already been warned off by Billy and then again by Deke, and that put Deke and Caroline's minds at rest. Randy had gotten what was coming to him; he got done for attempted rape, so he got generally charged as a Class 1 misdemeanour with 'extraordinary risk', which meant one penalty for this charge is six months—two years in jail and $500–$5,000 in fines. However, as with rape, aggravating factors can increase the penalties. Randy, however, got two years and a four thousand dollar fine. His family had to pay the monies as he didn't have any, and even though his father disowned him, his mother couldn't do that to her only son.

Deke couldn't care less; he had hurt his girl, so he was glad about the outcome of the trial. Jess had been in another room and was shown by video link, which had only been tried out a few times before, but Caroline and Deke had confidence in Jess; she was very confident in court, the judge could see she had been hurt but was trying to get her life back. Considering what had happened to her father because of the stress of this situation; the judge felt he needed to be taught a lesson about life and the consequences of your actions. Once he had been done and was finished, Deke wanted Jess to get on with her life the best that she could. A few months later, Marnie had decided that they had to start sorting out Robert's things; she couldn't do it, so she asked Kate.

Kate was having to go through his desk to study. Marnie had told her to put what she could up in the attic; that way, it was still to hand, but out of the way; she couldn't bear going into the study anymore. Caroline and Deke had suggested that Marnie and the girls do it, as it would be therapeutic for all of them, and they didn't really want to look through his personal stuff. So, once they had a look at the study, Kate had found a big box where she could put his papers; there were bills neatly stacked for the household, and then another pile of papers from the bank was all organised. In other paperwork, Kate took the box up to the attic, where she felt like she had never been up there before, even as a little girl. It was huge, and as big as the rest of the house; her and Jess loved to play dress-up up there; it was like a huge playground.

Kate started to look around; she found huge mirrors that had sheets over them and a rocking horse that was huge but very old; it may have been Robert's and Darlene's when they were younger. There were fishing rods and all of that equipment that also looked rather old—again, Robert's or even Deke's. There were tonnes of dusty books, and when Kate blew off the dust, she started coughing. She should have known better not to do that. She carried on wandering through the attic. She opened a huge chest and found wrapped in tissue paper her and Jess's christening dresses they had made when they were brought. There, she opened them both up carefully, took a look at them both, and put them back the best she could. Then she found a box that was quite flat in shape but thick, big enough to keep or large enough to store information.

There was a little clip on the side to lock it with; she had never seen this before, so she thought, why not? She tried the clip; it was stuck at first, as if it had rusted a bit. She loosened it in with her finger with a bit of force, and it opened. She lifted the lid, and she found a folder. She hadn't seen this before. "What secrets are you hiding?" she said aloud to herself.

She started to peel away the paper; an envelope fell out with a couple of photos and a letter. She put the folder down and took out the photographs; one was of a bride and groom on their wedding day, and another was of two little girls, one with the brightest blue eyes and blonde hair and one with brown eyes and a dark tuft of hair. Kate let out a small scream; she put her hands to her mouth. Her mama called out if she was okay; she said she was, then it was silent again. She took the photos into each hand and poured her eyes over both of them. She looked again at the couple and saw herself looking back at her from the bride, but then noticed the groom's bright blue eyes.

What did this mean? Who were these people? She put the photos back into the envelope, but next to her, they were not back in the file. She then took out the paperwork; there was tonnes of it—adoption certificates, paperwork from social services, letters from the police—what on earth did it mean? Kate's head started to spin; she felt dizzy and hot all of a sudden. When she found her bearings with her body, she steadied herself and went and closed the attic door. Her mama knew where she was, but she wanted to look properly at this stuff, and she didn't want to be disturbed while doing so. She couldn't lock the door from inside, but she knew they thought she would be doing just that, looking at her dad's stuff.

She sat back down; this time on a wooden chair. She gathered the paperwork and left the file on the floor. This would take some real reading. Kate knew she had a lot to go through, and she wanted to be thorough. So, she put it in a pile on her lap and started perusing through it; there were only two photos. Once she had read through all of the paperwork, she knew she would have to try and piece this all together. So she then sat back on the floor. She found a rug in the trunk, put that on the floor, and sat on it. She spread everything around her so she could put it all in order and try to make some sense of all of this new information. What on earth would she have on it once she had deciphered it? After a few hours, Kate came out of the attic with the file and paperwork inside it.

She had locked the attic; she was done with that for now. All she could think about was the precious information she had in her hands. She knew she would have to tackle her mama about it, but now was not the time to do that. Kate went down to her bedroom, locked the door, and sat on the bed. She took out a pad and pen and started to make some notes. There was little information about the bride and groom, except a letter that her birth mother had written to them both and some more information from the social services dealing with the case of Katie and Jessie, or rather, Jessica. She now knows her full name, Katie Crawford; her sister, Jessica Crawford, is not Steward, as she had thought all of this time.

For the first time, Kate had thought about another lady who was her real mama. What she must have thought when her and Jess were taken from their mother in England and how devastated she must have been. She found all the information about her and Jess, and she felt like she was in a whirlwind. Would she let on to her mama? Would she tell Jess? Should she tell them? But she couldn't leave it like it was; she now knew that she was adopted by Robert and Marnie, but she had started life as a big sister in England and not the USA. This was a huge shock to her, and it would be to Jess too. How was she going to tell Jess that she has another mama and daddy in another country halfway around the world?

It was going around and around in her head; she had already had one shock in the attic, then another one in her room. There was a knock on the door, it was Jess. She didn't want Jess to know about this just yet, because she couldn't get her head around it, let alone explain it to someone else without it sounding weird.

"Kate, Kate, can you let me in?" asked Jess.

Kate had grabbed all of the paperwork, stuffed it into the file, and threw it under her bed.

She opened the door. "You okay, Kate?" asked Jess.

"Yes, sorry, Jess. I had fallen asleep on the bed; you okay?" asked Kate.

"Yes, I'm fine. Did you want something to eat? It's nearly dinner time. Mama said that Thomas was popping over to check on us. Is it supposed to make sure we are doing all right?" Jess added.

"Thomas?" Kate said.

"Yes, Thomas, Daddy's oldest friend," said Jess, looking rather puzzled at Kate.

"Okay, I will be down in a minute. Yes, I am rather hungry," said Kate. Jess turned on her heels and left Kate.

She made sure the file was completely out of sight, and she closed the door behind her.

She went downstairs to find Coco, Gramps, and Thomas at the table; Marnie was dishing up dinner for them. Jess sat at the table, and Kate went into the kitchen to help her mama.

"Do you need some help, Mama?" asked Kate.

"Oh yes, Kate, please, can you grab those two plates for Coco and Gramps? I have Thomas and Jess's in my hand; then the other two are for us!" Marnie told her.

Kate returned to the kitchen once she had placed the plates down. She grabbed the other plates; Marnie had grabbed the drinks; the glasses were on the table already. Marnie set down the jug of lemonade, and everyone poured their own drinks out. Everyone was starting to eat steak, chips, tomatoes, mushrooms, and onion rings, Jess's favourites.

"It's a shame Darlene, Mitch, and Ethan couldn't make it this evening," said Coco.

"Yes, never mind, Coco; there is always next time," said Kate.

She gulped down her food, to which everyone started looking at her. "You all right, Kate?" asked Marnie.

"Oh yes, Mama, just hungry," Kate replied.

She carried on eating her dinner with gusto; everyone just got on with their dinner. The conversation at dinner was quite strained; you could see that Deke and Caroline were trying not to talk about Robert, but with Thomas there, it was quite difficult. "Thomas, Caroline, Deke, we need to keep talking about Robert; he was in our lives for a very long time. I don't want him forgotten. I don't mean I am going to lay a place at our table, but we need to talk about him. He was important in our lives, all of our lives," said Marnie. Caroline nodded in agreement.

Kate just sat there; he was her daddy, and she had loved him, but she had just found out that she has another mother and father somewhere else in the world. Once everyone had finished eating and they had chocolate cream pie for dessert, Thomas went outside to smoke his cigar. Jess had gone to help her mama in the kitchen, but Kate, watching her grandparents as they got cosy on the sofa, followed Thomas outside.

"Hello, Kate, you okay?" asked Thomas.

"Oh yes, I am fine, but I wanted to talk to you about something, Thomas. Is that okay?" she asked him.

"Yes, of course, fire away," he replied.

Kate cleared her throat; if anyone knew anything, it would be Thomas. "Thomas, you have known Daddy and Mama for a long time?" asked Kate; she knew he had, but she was trying to find out rather craftily, but she didn't know if it would come across like that.

Thomas was waiting for Kate to continue. "Yes, and?" asked Thomas.

She couldn't skirt around this; there was no logical way of asking, so she just cleared her throat again, and then she started.

"Thomas, do you know if Mama and Daddy had any children before me and Jess came along?" she finally asked.

"Er, no, I don't think so. I do know that they waited a long time for both of you, and when you both came along, they were delighted; your daddy told me so," Thomas added.

"What do you mean when we both came along, Thomas? There are four years between me and Jess; wouldn't they have had me first, then Jess come along years later? It sounds as if we came along together at the same time, which is impossible," Kate said, boring her eyes into Thomas, who in turn had no idea what to tell Kate. Biologically, she was right, but he met both the girls at the same time. He had no idea where this was going, but he was rather nervous being alone with Kate while she was talking like this.

"Er, Kate, don't you think we should join the rest?" he told her.

He couldn't wait to get some space between them and some more company. He also made a note not to be with Kate on her own again, as he didn't know what this was about, but he didn't want to party to it. Kate nodded and followed him back inside.

Marnie was now bringing coffee in for everyone. "Oh, there you are, Kate. I wondered where you had gone to. Thomas, would you like a coffee?" asked Marnie.

"Oh, yes, please." Marnie and Thomas went and sat beside Deke and Caroline. Marnie handed a coffee to Kate, who looked intensely at Thomas and then shifted her gaze. She knew she had rattled him, but she thought that he may have known, but by the way he was acting, she had a hunch he had no clue.

Kate made her excuses and left the sitting room. She went upstairs to her room, saying she was tired, and turned in for the night. Everyone said goodnight to her, and she went up to her bedroom. Once Kate was out of sight, Thomas had a quick, quiet word with Marnie, who in turn frowned. Maybe Kate had found the paperwork and knew what had happened, Marnie thought. She thanked Thomas for this new information and continued her conversation with Caroline. They were going out the next day to shop, but now she had an idea why Kate's behaviour had changed.

Kate got into bed; she had remembered to lock her door; she wanted to have another read of the paperwork; she wanted to ask her mama about it, but she couldn't just yet, not with company in the house; Coco and Gramps were staying the night. They had said goodnight to her through the door, and she did the same. She had hunkered down on her bed, with the covers up to her chest and the paperwork on top of them, and she was looking at the photo of her mother and father on their wedding day. Then look at the photos of the two little girls. She fell asleep with the paperwork on her still; she had been dreaming; she was running, not from someone for a change, but running towards the lady and man in the photo. Jess was right by her side, holding her hand; they were both running.

They were so happy, and so were the lady and the man. This was when she nearly reached her. Then she heard her name being called. "Kate, Kate?" said the voice downstairs. She had woken up in the same position as when she had gone to sleep.

Who on earth was calling her? She was called again, and she knew it—her mama was calling her. But she felt alien now. The lady she was dreaming about was her mama; she wanted to see her, not the lady downstairs making her pancakes for breakfast. Kate had to get up; they still had visitors over, and she didn't want to talk about it in front of Coco and Gramps. She pulled away the file and made her way downstairs.

"Yeah, I was saying that too; you know that would be great..." Caroline trailed off; Kate had no idea what they were talking about; she wasn't bothered anymore.

"Morning, Kate, sleep well?" asked Coco.

"Yes, Coco, just great. I was having a lovely dream; I was younger and running with Jess, holding my hand; we were running towards this lady, and we were really happy," she said, not looking at anyone in particular. She took her breakfast and went to sit down.

Jess looked at her as if she had three heads. "Kate, what is wrong with you? You have been acting really weird since last night," said Jess.

"Oh, I am okay, just thinking, that's all," she replied, putting pancakes and maple syrup into her mouth.

"Marnie, what's wrong with Kate? She is the more responsible one; she sounds more like Jess than I have ever heard her," said Caroline.

"No idea, Coco," said Marnie, looking daggers at Kate. Kate just ignored her; this was definitely not Kate's normal behaviour.

Once breakfast was over, Caroline and Deke were going over to see Darlene and Mitch for the day, so Kate was going to tackle Marnie, but Marnie was going to get in first; she didn't want tension in her home, especially as Robert was no longer there to keep a lid on things and have the home harmonious. Once Caroline and Deke had gone, Jess went down to the stables, and Marnie collared Kate in the sitting room.

"Now, young miss, what is this all about? Your behaviour is disgusting: talking to Thomas on the sly, asking about your daddy and me, asking about Jess and your birth, and you both coming together, which isn't possible. Well, I think you have found some paperwork giving you all of the information you have now acquired. So let me tell you, miss young lady, you now know about you and Jess being adopted; we never made it a secret; you know yourself that you can't have two girls, not twins, born at different times, so yes, you are sisters, you are the elder, there are four years between you and Jess, and your birth parents died in a car accident when you were children, Jess a babe in arms. So now that you know, what are you going to do? Tell Jess, are you upsetting her apple cart? Don't you think she had been through enough without knowing this information? I will leave it up to you, Kate. But let me tell you this: me and your daddy have loved you since you were a little girl, since we got you both. Yes, I was sorry you didn't come from my body, but that's the way it is. We have never hurt you; you have both had a good life and benefited from having money and great holidays. If you continue with this behaviour, I will have to send you back to college. You have already been home a lot longer than we had anticipated; yes, we didn't know your daddy was going to die. So just think about this before you make up your mind; if your daddy was still alive, we wouldn't be having this conversation," Marnie said.

Kate didn't think she had ever spoken to her as much as she had done with this speech. Kate was never one to play up, but this information unsettled her; she wanted to know where she came from. She was going to tell Jess because she thought it was unfair of her not to. Once she had sorted that out in her head, she would take it a step at a time. Kate found Jess at the stables; Marnie was busy in the kitchen, so she wasn't privy to this conversation; Jess was mucking out Blaze. Whenever Jess was in the stalls, you had to make yourself known; otherwise, she may have attacked you; she nearly did to Elijah; he wasn't even going to see Jess, but this attack from Randy made her jumpy still. So Kate called out her name. Jess sighed to herself, but she said where she was. Kate asked her to come outside, she wanted to talk to her.

"Okay, but I can't be too long, Kate; I still have a lot to do," said Jess.

Jess followed Kate outside; they were just outside the stables. Kate made sure nobody was there listening to what she was going to say. She took a deep breath, then reiterated to Jess all of her findings and what had happened to them. She didn't stop for air, and when she had finished, she took another deep breath.

"So, what do you think, Jess? Would you come with me to find out what happened to our family? To our birth parents? Maybe they have relatives alive who can help us fill in the gaps," suggested Kate.

"Why, Kate? Why do you want to do this? We have our family; we have Mama, Gramps, Coco, Darlene, Mitch, and Ethan; they are our family; let's just stay here and let sleeping dogs lie," added Jess.

"But, Jess, they are our family, our birth family," added Kate.

"No, Kate. No, they aren't our family; they are here; these people gave us away. I don't want to know about them; I have Mama, you, and our family. I don't want to talk about it, and I won't be going anywhere except here, our home, and our family, so if you want to go on this wild goose chase, then you go ahead. Me? I am staying right here, so if you have finished, I have work to do," Jess said as she left Kate and went to carry on with her work.

"Will you come with me? I have nowhere to go; I am staying right here," Jess said to herself.

Right then, thought Kate, *I know what I have to do.* She went inside, grabbed her things, packed a suitcase, put the paperwork in the file at the bottom, and she had her notes with names and addresses on them; she had done that the day before. She had her money; Marnie was right; they did live comfortably, so she knew she would be okay financially for a while. She would call the college once she got where she needed to be. But for now, she wasn't going back; she needed to do this for herself and her well-being.

There was a knock at the door; it was her mama. "Jess has just told me that she now knows, but she's not bothered about it. She wants to stay here, but you already know that, so what are you going to do about it?" asked Marnie, but she looked at Kate's bed and saw the packed suitcase.

"Mama, I love you, and I have always done so, but I need to do this. I need to find out who I am and where I come from," said Kate.

"You know where you come from, Evergreen, Colorado," said Marnie.

"No, Mama, I need to know…" She put her hand up to stop Marnie from interrupting her. "I need to find out who this lady is, who kept chasing me whenever I was sad or somewhere different. She has haunted my dreams, and I think the answer is in this paperwork. So yes, I love you, and I will be back, but I need to do this. I know if he were here, Daddy would let me do this, to find out the answers for myself, because you don't know who she is either, do you?" asked Kate.

Marnie shook her head; she didn't realise Kate had so many nightmares about this woman, but Robert did, and Robert would have let Kate do this for herself.

"Okay, Kate, you do this, but please be safe and take care, and please let me know when you get there," said Marnie, holding onto her elder daughter, not knowing if she would really come back once she found the answers she was looking for. Kate held her mama for a little longer, then pulled away.

"I will call you Mama and let you know what happens. Tell Jess I understand her reasons, and I hope she will understand mine."

She picked up her suitcase and made her way downstairs. Thomas was downstairs, waiting for Kate to give her a lift. He smiled at her and took her suitcase and put it in the trunk.

Marnie hugged her daughter again, and she left the house. "Kate, Kate, wait, please wait!" screamed Jess.

"I'm sorry, Kate; you have always been there for me. I want you to feel the same as I do. You are my big sister, and I love you. You have to do what is best for you. Mama told me you have been having nightmares. You need to do this for you, but please let us know when you get there, and please take care and stay safe," said Jess, hugging her older sister.

Both girls pulled away, and Kate got into the back of Thomas's car, and she waved to both of them until they were out of sight.

"Where to, Kate?" asked Thomas.

"The airport, please, Thomas," she replied, excited at the prospect of an adventure halfway around the world.

Chapter 17

Kate was on the plane; they were going to be landing soon. She was so excited, but she hadn't thought of what she was going to do when she got out of the airport; she couldn't just go to the address she had. She had a thought about the flight into the UK; she would go to the area or roughly that area and find a hotel and check-in depending on the time; she didn't want to go knocking on doors as soon as she had landed; it could be dark or late, and they may not open the door. So, she had a look online and found a cheap hotel. Well, it seemed cheap enough for her. She would have to get a train from Heathrow into Paddington, which she was happy enough with. Even though she hadn't met her biological family, she was delighted she was that nearer to them, especially being in the UK.

Once she had something to eat, a shower, and some sleep, she would make her way to the area. She had never heard of it before, but that was okay.

"If you could please return to your seats and put on your safety belts, we will start descending shortly. Airline crew, if you could please check that everything is present, correct, and put away your trolleys, then if you could be seated and then put on your safety belts, thank you," said the captain.

Kate was getting really excited now; this adventure was really living up to her expectations, and she hoped it would continue. Kate had never carried a diary, but she had brought one to the airport so she could make notes and document everything she felt was important. They were descending, and the plane was lowering slowly. She could see past the clouds now and see greenery and fields—lots of them—but they still had a little way to go. Then she could see houses; she could hardly contain herself. She was never this excitable in her life, but somehow this felt right. Then, a few minutes later, they touched down onto the runway. *There, home now,* thought Kate. *That's it, I'm home.*

"If you could all refrain from getting up from your seats until we are stationery, as we don't want any accidents, again, my airline crew, please could you make sure the overhead storage is all closed until we disembark? Thank you," said the captain again.

The plane came to a complete stop, with the engines slowing completely down; the plane was still on the runway.

Hurry up, hurry up, thought Kate; she was so impatient. "Calm down, lovey, we will be getting off soon," said the lady sitting next to her, an extremely English-speaking lady. Kate laughed to herself silently. She was English too; she should be more reserved, which is what she saw on TV about the English or British, however they referred to themselves. Once the plane came to a complete stop, Kate got up from her seat, looked in the overhead storage, and grabbed her bag.

"Bye bye, lovey, have a lovely time in England," said the lady who had been sitting next to her.

"Yes, bye, and thank you for a lovely flight," said Kate.

She had been a bit jittery when she got on the plane in Denver, but the lady sitting next to her was calm, so that helped Kate. For some reason, she felt a bit anxious. Maybe this was a crazy idea, but she had to find out. Kate left the plane, thanking the crew on the way out.

Wow, they work so hard, trolley dollies, she always thought when she was younger, going on holidays with her family.

She had only known her family when she was a little girl, whom she left behind in America to find her English family. She shrugged her shoulders and then thought, no, this is what she wanted; at least it would hopefully put the pieces of the puzzle of her life into place. What would she do after that, she had no idea. But for now, she was happy just to go to her hotel and sleep; it was starting to catch up with her. Once Kate managed to find her way out of the airport to the train station, she grabbed a ticket at the ticket office and made her way down to the platform. She only had one suitcase and her handbag, so she didn't have to wait long for her train to arrive. There were people getting off with their luggage and others waiting to get on the train to get to their destination.

She was so excited; she was the one with the strong head on her shoulders; even Jess, in normal circumstances, would have been the same. It was a shame that Jess didn't want to come; at least she could find out about their roots and how on earth they had ended up living on another continent, let alone another country. They were pulling into Paddington. She waited a little while for others to get off the train; she was in the right place, and rushing would only put her head in a spin. Once the other passengers got off, the cleaning staff were getting on the train so they could clean it, ready for the next lot of passengers going to Heathrow.

"Are you okay, dear?" asked the cleaner.

"Are you a bit lost?" she added.

"Oh no, well, no, not yet; I just wanted to take my time. Is that okay?" asked Kate.

"Yes, that's fine, but you don't want to end up going back to Heathrow when it leaves in a few minutes," the cleaner added.

Kate didn't realise how long they had been on the station.

"Thank you," Kate said as she got up and grabbed her luggage and her handbag. She didn't want to leave that behind; otherwise, she wouldn't know where she was going. She had a quick look around to make sure she hadn't left anything behind. She stepped off the train; the platform was deserted. She made her way to the front of the train; she found an information desk; and she waited to be seen by the operative there. Once she had spoken to the member of staff, she found her hotel wasn't that far away; the lady gave her a map of where to go, which was only really around the corner. Kate thanked her and made her way up the big slope, then turned right. She waited at the traffic lights, and then, when it was safe to go, she walked straight down the road.

Just before the corner, she had reached her hotel, 'The Railway Lines Hotel'. Kate laughed at the name.

You couldn't make it up; the hotel must have named it because of where it was situated near the railway station. She carried her luggage up the stairs and found reception straight ahead.

The receptionist gave Kate her key and told her that her room was on the third floor. "If you take the lift to the third floor rather than walking up the stairs," the receptionist told her.

"The lift?" asked Kate. "Oh, sorry, you mean the elevator?" corrected Kate.

"No, in England, we call it the lift; it won't take you long to get to your floor; don't worry, miss, you will soon pick it up. Elevator? Lift? It's the same thing, just different names for it. Anyway, have a lovely evening," said the receptionist, who said her name was Carol.

"Thank you, Carol; you have a lovely evening too," added Kate.

Kate found her room; it was nice enough—a single bed, a closet, a small bathroom with a shower—it seemed cosy enough. For now, all Kate wanted to do was have a shower and sleep, but with all of the travelling, she hadn't really eaten that much. She called down to reception, and Carol answered. "Carol, it's Kate from Room 9. Do you serve room service?"

"No, sorry, Miss Kate, we don't, but we have some lovely fish and chip shops or Chinese or curry houses around here if you would like to try some. Actually, I am going off in a little while. I could pick you some up and you could eat it in your room. We don't really recommend food eaten in the rooms, but you're new in town and won't know where to go. Just open the window once you have eaten, but if you could take your rubbish out with you, there are plenty of bins outside on the pavement," said Carol.

"Pavement?" asked Kate.

"Oh, I think you would call it sidewalk?" asked Carol, not sure if she got the terminology right.

"Oh yes, sidewalk, thank you, Carol. That would be great. What would I like? I don't know what is there—cod and chips—is that nice? Yes, I will have that. Thank you. Can I give you the money when you bring the food? I am about to jump in the shower. Thank you, Carol," added Kate, grateful she had met someone who was willing to help her.

Kate jumped in the shower, and she felt the force of the water, which she was chuffed to have; it was quite powerful, and she was getting very tired all of a sudden, so it helped to wake her up a bit, enough for her to have her food and at least towel-dry her hair. Once she finished, there was steam all over the windows and in the bathroom. She opened the door; she had a towel around her, and she had already put her money on the dresser to pay Carol when she turned up with her food. A few minutes later, Kate had opened her door a little. She was a bit wary of people in a country she didn't know.

She thanked Carol and gave her the money. "Oh, Kate, that is far too much. Do you have a change of ten? Fifty is far too much, and I don't have that much on me to give as change," said Carol.

"Oh, sorry, Carol," Kate replied. She went over to get her purse, and she did have a ten.

"Here, Carol, and please keep the change, and thank you for doing this for me. I do appreciate it," added Kate.

"That's okay, Kate. Have a nice night. I am back on in the morning, about eleven, if you need help with directions or anything or if you want to know what's going on locally, but thank you for this. Night," said Carol.

Carol had already handed Kate her dinner. Kate went over to the dresser, took out a towel from the bathroom, and put her food down on the paper. There was a wooden fork in the package, and she opened it up fully to see a big piece of fish in batter and a huge pile of chips. She had forgotten to ask Carol if it needed anything with it. But she thought, *You know what? I am so hungry and tired, I will just have this, then get my nightly things on the bed.* When she put the fish on her fork, it fell off at first. When she managed to stab it with the fork and put it in her mouth, it tasted familiar, but it was also very scrummy. She soon finished her food; she loved the chips too, and that also tasted familiar.

She put her rubbish into a carrier bag she found, dried her hair the best she could, and then put on something; she didn't fancy opening the door in the middle of the night if someone knocked with nothing on. She got into bed and closed her eyes. She fell asleep straight away. She was with Jess at home, and they were running, holding hands over the meadow, to their daddy, who had his arms out to hug them both. When Kate woke up, she had tears streaming down her face. She didn't realise how much she still missed her daddy; even though he had only been gone a few months, it still felt like yesterday. She looked at her watch; it was 2 am, and there was no way she was getting up, so she turned over and went back to sleep. This time, she didn't dream but rested the best she could.

She did wake up at about 9 am; she had booked to have breakfast, but with the dinner the night before, she wasn't really that hungry. She got up, threw back the covers, and went to the window to have a proper look at where she was. She had already heard cars tooting and people swearing. Even though it was still early, people were going about their daily business. Kate didn't want to take another shower; her hair just needed brushing and styling. She had a quick wash and then got herself ready. She had already pulled out the paperwork she needed. But before anything else, she wanted to photocopy all of the paperwork, so if she did lose any of it, she had a backup.

She asked reception if there were printers in the area; the day receptionist gave her directions, and she followed them to a tee. She found the shop, and they said that she could do it herself if she wanted if the paperwork was confidential, which she was pleased with. She didn't want the whole world to know why she was in England. She copied everything; there was so much information; she had written down a lot of it in her journal, which she wanted to leave at the hotel in her luggage. Once she was going to her destination, she wanted to take as much of the original paperwork with handwriting as possible, in case somebody recognised it.

She was going to leave the journal and copies at the hotel, just to be on the safe side; she didn't know what sort of reception she was going to get. When she was finished, she paid the guy who seemed to be in charge and made her way back to the hotel. She sorted out the copies and put them away. She checked her bag to make sure she hadn't left anything important behind. She checked her luggage, put her dirty stuff in a bag, and put it at the bottom of her case. She took a deep breath and then locked her room, putting the key in her bag. She saw Carol at the reception, who looked up and said hello.

"Carol, I need to go to this address, but I'm not sure how to get there," Kate said.

"Oh, that's easy enough; once you come out of the hotel, turn left, walk back up towards the station, but cross the road, so you're opposite and you need to get a number seven bus, ask to be put off at St Marks Road, and it's not far from there. There is also a huge park, so you can always go there and have a bit of a sit-down to collect yourself. You know if you need a few minutes before you go there," Carol told her; she could see Kate looked a bit nervous. "Kate, you will be fine; just count to ten if you're unsure and take a deep breath or two," said Carol reassuringly.

"Thank you, Carol; see you later," Kate added. She was nervous now; it was one thing to arrange this out in your head in America, but now that she was back in England, the nerves had really started to kick in. She made her way to the station, but as Carol had told her, she crossed the road. She could see all sorts of people coming and going to and from the station. She looked at the bus stop, and yes, she could get her bus here, so she waited. Her bus came a little later on; she paid at the front. She was watching everyone else. Once she paid, she took a seat; she did ask the driver first if he could let her know when they got to St Marks Road, which he said he would. She thanked him and took a seat at the back of the bus.

The driver pulled away. She was a little startled at first, but she relaxed a bit. She was enjoying watching the streets, roads, cars, and people. She doesn't live in the city in the States, but on the outskirts. Where they live, there is so much greenery. But here, it was very different. Had she been here before? No, it didn't feel familiar. She carried on looking out of the window. She was still in town; there was lots of traffic, but she knew she wouldn't be too far from where she needed to be. The bus went straight through the market; it ran across the road they were going down. Hopefully not too far away now; it turned right; there was a bridge. Had she been here before? No, this definitely didn't feel familiar.

The bus carried on and stopped at a station for the tube. What was the tube? thought Kate. Then it started up again and turned left. There were very leafy trees, and then there were some traffic lights. The bus had its indicator on for turning right, and the lights went green.

The bus continued on its journey to St Marks Road. The driver shouted, "Oh, hang on, there are three bus stops at St Marks Road; take the next one in the middle, and you should find where you need to be. If you get stuck, ask someone; everyone is friendly around here," said the lady across on the other side of the bus.

"Thank you," replied Kate.

When the bus pulled up, Kate got up from her seat and made her way off the bus. She looked down the road; there were just houses—lots and lots of houses. She made her way in the direction the bus continued. She was sure she was on the right path. She carried on and saw a park. She went inside, and there were benches every so often. She sat down on one. She gathered her thoughts; this was totally nuts, but she had to continue now; she couldn't turn back; well, she could, but she would still have unanswered questions. She wanted to sort this out. Otherwise, it was a wasted journey. This, Kate had hoped, was the piece of the puzzle she had no clue about; she wanted it sorted out in her own head.

Why was she adopted, and why were she and Jess taken away? She knew her parents had died in a car crash, but they may have left siblings for her and Jess. She just wanted to know, so she would feel whole at last. She got up to go the way she came, but she saw people coming and going in from a different entrance or exit; she didn't know, but she thought she would follow them. She may have to turn back if she went the wrong way, but she just went with it. She was looking around as she was walking, not in a suspicious way but trying to find her bearings.

She reached the end of the road; she was literally in the middle of a road, with smaller houses that were where she had just come from, but she saw a man and asked him which way to go for the address on the paper she had.

"Oh, you go down this road; if you go right down to the bottom and then turn right, that brings you out onto a big side road; either end is a main road. I hope that helps," the man said.

"Oh, thank you, sir. Have a nice day now," she said, wishing she hadn't because it sounded so corny and she didn't sound like a tourist, even though that's not what she wanted to sound like.

She knew she wasn't really a local; she had been. She walked to the end of the road, and there she found the road, and yes, for the first time, it looked familiar. She recognised the road, and the houses looked smaller somehow, but when she was there last, she was only a small child. Kate carried on down the road; she looked at the numbers; yes, she was going the right way. Then she saw it. She saw the house she had grown up in. The front door was a different colour: the net curtains had changed, but it was still spotless.

She walked up to the gate, took a breath, and counted to ten, as Carol had suggested. Yes, that felt better. She opened the gate inwards towards the path; it also seemed much bigger and taller. She took a huge, deep breath. She knocked on the door. She wasn't sure if anyone was in; it was lunchtime, so hopefully somebody was in. Then she heard footsteps. The front door opened, and a young girl of about fifteen opened it.

"Yes, can I help you?" she asked. Kate heard a voice from inside.

"Kim, who's at the door, darling?" said the lady's voice. Kate didn't get a chance to say a word. The lady was at the door, and she said, "Hello, can I…" She didn't finish her sentence. She took one look at Kate, and she fainted.

Chapter 18

"Kim, where am I?" asked the lady.

"Mum, you are on the settee," replied Kim.

"Oh yes, oh bloody hell, yes. Did I dream it? Did she come, or was it my imagination? I have been rather busy lately, Kim," said Chrissy. She looked around the room, and yes, she was standing there all grown up; there was no mistaking this was her Katie.

"Katie?" asked Chrissy, standing to take in this beautiful, young woman standing in front of her.

"Katie, my Katie?" asked Chrissy, trying to take it all in.

"Well, yes, my name is Kate. I wanted to know if you could tell me if you knew my mum, Chrissy? You see, I have lots of information, and I don't know who you are, but I had hoped you could tell me about my mum Chrissy?" asked Kate. Kim laughed a silent laugh. *Who was this nutter?* she thought.

"Kate, you say your name is. I think you had better sit down," she said. Chrissy offered her a seat at the table, which Kate gratefully took. Chrissy took a deep breath, which Kate understood because she had done the same thing before she had knocked on the door.

"Kate, I think you're going to need a drink because what I am about to say is going to floor you, like it has me," Chrissy told her.

Kate was confused. She didn't know what this lady was going to tell her, but she knew she wouldn't need a drink; she didn't touch alcohol.

"Kate, I am Chrissy; I am your mum," said Chrissy.

"No, you can't be my mum; my mum Chrissy died in a car accident when I was four years old. Me and Jess went to live in America—" Chrissy interrupted Kate.

"America? You mean Jessie was with you? You were kept together? Oh, I am glad!" said Chrissy. Kate looked more confused than when she started.

"Excuse me!" said Kim.

"Look, Mum, I think one of you needs to talk, the other listen, and then hopefully you can get this story because you're not going to get anywhere and end up going around and around in circles," said Kim.

"Yeah, you're right, Kim, so do you want to go first, because I know the first part of the story and you know the second," said Chrissy.

"Hold on a second, who is Kim?" asked Kate. "Because I remember Kim, and I am sorry, it's not this young lady here," said Kate, getting more and more confused.

"Kate, I want you to sit down over here. I want to explain everything until I don't know the rest. Then, can you please fill me in on what happened when you went to America? Is that the best?" asked Chrissy, finally trying to make a bit of sense of what was going on in her sitting room, more than Kate and Kim did, but they would eventually get there.

"Okay, so when I was pregnant with you, I was also pregnant with another little girl called Kim. Katie and Kim, but Kim died at birth. So, you were on your own, but we kept little Kim's memory alive. We took you to her grave. She had a white coffin." Kate's head was spinning.

Kim, who was her twin, whom she kept dreaming of, kept thinking of, but never knew who she was. Kate started to cry. Chrissy had stopped in her tracks and could see that it was starting to dawn on Kate what had happened to her sister, her twin sister. She couldn't stop crying. Chrissy grabbed a hold of her; she held her tight as she did as a little girl. Kate felt it; she felt right. All the time she had lived with her other mother in America, it never felt right, which is why she geared up for Robert rather than Marnie.

When Kate stopped crying, Kim had already given her a tissue; she also made Kate a cup of tea. "Always good in a crisis!" said Kim.

She blew her nose, took her cup, and told Chrissy to continue, which she did. The phone went; Kim answered it in the hall, and she put the receiver down. Next thing, a man opened the front door. He was tall, dark-haired, and had the bright blue eyes that Kate had. He looked at her and couldn't stop staring at her.

Kate, in return, knew this man was her father; he looked just like Jess, but for the eyes. "Katie!" he said. Kate stood up, and this man, David, pulled her in for a hug.

"My Katie has come home," David said.

Kate was so overwhelmed with this situation; this wasn't what she had expected to happen. Yes, she had hoped to find family, but not her biological parents. She started to cry again, but so did David.

"David, we are never going to get to the end of this story if we keep crying, so let's all sit down together and talk this through," said Chrissy.

David nodded his head in agreement and just watched Kate. Chrissy continued her story, and Kate was listening, hanging on to her every word. When Chrissy got nearly to the end of her story, the door went again; this time it was Pam and Phil. Pam dropped her bag in shock. Phil didn't know what to do, and Kim went out to greet them and asked them to come in and just listen, not to say anything for the time being, because they wanted this story to come out, and they were getting interrupted all the time. Pam and Phil agreed; they sat down at the dining table and just waited, listened, and stared at Kate. When Chrissy had finally finished, Pam went into the kitchen. She grabbed some tissues, put the kettle on, made more drinks, and then brought them in.

Now, it was Kate's turn to tell them what happened when they left. But before she said anything, she told them about the nightmares she had when she had gotten to America—the lady chasing her and her sister Kim—that she knew about and always knew of a Kim, but as time went on, she had forgotten who she was. Chrissy and David waited with bated breath for Kate to tell her part of the story, which she did. Chrissy went to interrupt her, but David stopped her, gave her a pen and pad, and told her to write it down and ask once Katie was finished. Pam nodded, thinking that was a good idea, and Kate wouldn't lose her train of thought. She carried on with what she remembered because a lot of it had become blurry and fuzzy, but she knew she had paperwork that she could show them once she had told her story.

There were lots of ooohhsss and aahhhs in this part of the story for them because they had no idea of the lady chasing Kate. Once she had finished her part of the story, she explained about her parents, how she had come to know about them, and Jess being adopted.

"So, Jessie was with you too?" asked David.

"Yes, we were together and are together," said Kate.

"So, where is Jessie, then?" asked Kim.

"Well, she couldn't deal with all of this. I am sorry; she will do so once she knows more about it, but she was still upset with an upsetting thing, then our daddy died," said Kate, looking at her real father.

"I am sorry; I didn't mean to say it like that," said Kate, apologising to David.

"Kate, it's not your fault. Honestly, you and your sister are still alive and thriving, as we can see. It will take time, but once you get used to it, I am just grateful that you had good adoptive parents who loved you like you were their own, and to them, I will be eternally grateful," said David with a tear in his eye.

Pam and Phil were still trying to take this all in when the front door opened again. This time it was a younger girl who was the double of Jess, and she was called Kelly.

"Kate, this is Kelly, your youngest sister," said David.

Kelly looked at him as if to say, 'What the hell?'

"Kelly, we will fill you in later. Do you have any homework?" asked Chrissy.

"Yes, I have some; can I do it in my room and come down when I have finished?" asked Kelly.

She smiled at Kate the same way Jess did. "Hi, Kelly, it's nice to meet you!" said Kate. Kelly went upstairs to her room.

Pam came over; she stood up next to Kate and hugged her. Phil did the same. "We are your grandparents; I'm Pam, your grandma, and this is your granddad, Phil," said Pam.

"Kate, how on earth did you know how or where to find us?" asked Phil.

Kate told them all, whose attention she had grabbed as soon as she started to speak. She looked at David and said, "Something happened at home, which caused my father to have a heart attack and die, which threw us all already, but with Daddy's death, it was just impossible," Kate told them.

She had already explained about Jess being Marnie's golden girl as a baby and Robert taking charge of Kate. Even though she was Marnie's daughter, she had felt that Jess belonged to Marnie and Kate belonged to Robert. Even if belonged wasn't the right word, Kate was getting a bit stuck with it all; it was very overwhelming for her. Anyway, she continued and said that when she looked in the old trunks, putting stuff away, she came across a box, so being nosey, she looked through it, and as she looked at both of her parents, she knew this was her family. She produced their wedding photo and showed it to them. Chrissy burst into tears, and so did Pam; the men in their lives had to hold it together.

"Kate, do you have any more photos? Or paperwork?" asked her dad.

"Yes, I have another photo and a letter you wrote Mum to the social services, who then forwarded them onto my mum in the USA," said Kate.

With the realisation of what she had just said, "So social services in England knew you were in America, when?" asked Pam.

"I don't know; I think it was a couple of years after we got there, but it wasn't straight away. Honest," replied Kate.

Pam, Phil, Chrissy, and David all looked crestfallen.

Kate was confused. "I don't understand?" asked Kate.

"That means the social services knew you were there. How? We didn't know where you were; we had no idea. We had social services involved—the police, the local press—it was a big story. But they found out, and they didn't tell us a thing, not a word," said Chrissy.

"We were going out of our minds, Kate; we had no idea what happened. Who took you?" said Pam.

"Took us?" Kate stated.

"We were told you died in a car accident; nobody said anything about being taken!" Kate added.

"Hold on, so you thought we were dead, but we knew you were taken. Someone has played one deadly joke on all of us. I wonder who on earth hates us that much and would do this to us. Mum, how can someone do this to us? We were a young family; we had already lost one daughter, but someone wanted us to suffer. Who would have done that?" asked Chrissy.

"You can't think of anyone, Chrissy, not one person, because I can, and so can you, Pam!" said Phil.

"Kate, did you say that you have paperwork? Do you have it with you, or is it in America?" asked Pam.

"I brought it with me; otherwise, I wouldn't know where to go. What do you want, the letter Mum sent my mum in the USA?" asked Kate.

"No, do you have other paperwork besides that? Letters? Paperwork? Birth certificates?" asked Phil. Kate put her hand in the file, pulled out everything, and laid it all out on the dining table.

She spread it out. "That's our adoption certificate; that's our medical stuff; that's the paperwork that Mrs Carpenter gave my mum and daddy when they got us," said Kate.

Pam grabbed the adoption paperwork. "Mrs Carpenter, Kate?" asked Pam.

"Yes, Mrs Elizabeth Carpenter; I don't remember her, but she was the lady that Mama and Daddy dealt with," said Kate.

Pam was scouring the paperwork. "Mrs Elizabeth Carpenter, Chrissy, do you remember dealing with Mrs Elizabeth Carpenter?" Pam asked, looking directly at Chrissy.

"No, Mum, there were those two ladies; oh, I can't remember their names, but when we went to social services, they had the same names as the women who turned up here, but it wasn't them," replied Chrissy.

"I knew it, Phil. Do you recognise that handwriting?" asked Pam.

"Take a good look, Phil," added Pam.

"OH MY GOD!" screamed Phil.

"Kate, do you know of a lady called Edie, Edie Carter?" asked Pam.

"No, I don't, sorry," replied Kate.

"Oh, but you did as a little girl; you sussed Aunty Edie out long before we did. I will explain later on, but for now we need to get to the bottom of this, agreed?" asked Pam.

"Agreed!" they all said in unison.

"Pam, do you think she orchestrated all of this?" asked Phil.

"Yes, I do; when I think back, Phil, all the signs were there; just we weren't looking for them, until now!" commanded Pam.

"So, what do we do now, then? I mean, with all of this information?" asked Phil.

"We get the truth from her," demanded Pam. "She has screwed with this family for too long, now she's going to get it, taking our beautiful girls from us, where none of us knew what had happened to them, not knowing if they were alive or not," said Pam. She was looking at Kate the whole time she was saying this.

"That woman has ruined this family, our mental health, and our sanity, but now it stops," said Pam.

"Do you know where she is, then?" asked Kate.

"Oh yes, we do; we put her there. Her poor husband died a few years ago, and none of us wanted to look after her, and now, well, you will see, because I can assure you, Kate, when she sees you, she will know," said Pam.

"Are we going today, now?" asked Kate.

"No, we can't go today, but we can go tomorrow; I will call and arrange it," said Pam.

"Kate, where are you staying?" asked Phil.

"I have a room in a hotel in Paddington, is it?" Kate told him.

"How long have you booked it for?" asked David.

"I only booked for a few days. I didn't know if I would have any luck in finding any of you or relatives of yours, which is what I expected to find. If you didn't still live here, I was hoping for a forwarding address," said Kate.

"Good thing we didn't move then, eh?" said Phil, with a cheeky wink.

"Dave, I don't want to talk out of turn, but it's up to you," said Phil, nudging him towards Kate.

"Oh yes, you don't mind?" asked Phil, looking in his direction, then changing to Kate's.

"Kate, would you like to stay here with us? We have room; we had to extend. We were supposed to extend so Edie could live here, but we changed our minds, so we have a room at the back if you want to stay. We can go and get your things from your hotel and pay the bill; that won't be a problem, that is if you want to stay, of course," said David hesitantly.

"I would love to stay. Are you sure you have enough room for me?" Kate asked.

"Absolutely!" said David and Phil at the same time.

"Right, that's arranged; we are going tomorrow afternoon, after she has had her lunch," Pam told them.

"Shame that!" said Chrissy.

"Why?" asked Pam.

"Because I think the sight of Kate will make her choke on her lunch," said Chrissy, who then burst out laughing. They all did.

"We shouldn't really, you know; I mean, be this nasty," said David.

"Oh yes, it is, David. You have no idea what she has done. Honestly, once this episode is over, you will be thanking me," said Pam.

"Oh, I have just thought, Joanie, Cherry, Diane, they don't know," said Pam.

"Not today, Pam; maybe tomorrow or the day after, but let us have this time with Kate, please?" pleaded David.

"Okay, once this is sorted out with Edie," said Pam.

Chrissy and David went over to their daughter and hugged her. "We are so sorry, Katie; we didn't know this was going to happen, but boy, are we grateful for you being nosey and coming to find us, even if you didn't know we were still alive. Now that you have been here, you haven't spoken to Jessie since you got here, so do you want to call her?" asked Pam.

"Coco, sorry, Grandma, it's America; it will cost a fortune at this time of day; she won't be home; she will be at the stables. But I will get one of those money card things that I can use; I think I can use them at a call box or something," said Kate.

"Stables?" piped up Kim. "Does she work at the stables, Kate?" asked Kim.

"Oh no, we own stables; she loves horses; she has been on one since she was about three. It took a little while to adjust to it, but she took to it like a duck to water!" exclaimed Kate.

Her own stables? WOW, Kim thought. Kate saw her face. "We were very fortunate to have a family with money, lots of it, so we were indulged in quite a lot, had a lot of chances that some kids may not have had. But don't worry, we can do some fun stuff like that if you want to, Kim," said Kate. Kim was warming up to having a bigger older sister.

"So, Kim, how old are you? And Kelly?" asked Kate.

"I am fifteen; Kelly is twelve going on twenty-five," said Kim, laughing.

"Oh, don't be like that, Kim," said David.

"Can I ask something?" asked Kate.

"Yes, of course," said Chrissy.

"Well, if my twin named Kim died, how come you called another daughter after Kim?" asked Kate.

"Good question, Kate. I have always wondered," added Kim.

"Well, the way we looked at it, Katie was here; we had four years with you, but sadly, Kim didn't last five minutes. By the way, we didn't know we were having twins until Kim popped out. Anyway, we did say if we had any more children, especially girls, we wouldn't call them either Katie or Kim. Because, as far as we were concerned, we were never going to see you again, you or Jessie, but we did really like the name Kim. So, when we did fall pregnant and she was a little girl, we both chose Kim," said Chrissy.

"I am sorry, Kim; you should have had your own name!" said Chrissy, and then David.

"Yes, you should have, but we felt you were a replacement for Kim, and that wasn't fair to you," he added.

"It doesn't matter, really; I'm just glad you didn't call me Edie!" said Kim, and everybody laughed.

"Right then, who's going with Kate to collect her things and pay her bill?" asked Pam.

"I will. Kim, do you want to come with us?" asked David.

"No, Dad, you go with Kate on your own; you have a lot of catching up to do. I will stay with Mum, Nan, and Grandad, honest," said Kim.

She may have been only fifteen, but she was definitely growing up. So, David and Kate went over to Paddington to collect her things. When they walked in the door, Carol was at reception. "Hi, Kate, So I see you found them, then?" said Carol, taking one look at David and realising straight away that she was his double.

"Your brother?" inquired Carol.

"No Carol, how long have I booked my room for? With so much going on today, I can't actually remember," said Kate.

"You were booked in for three nights, with the chance to extend it if need be, but I take it you want to check out?" asked Carol.

"Er, yes, please, if I can get my things first?" she asked.

"Of course, I will charge you for today, but not tomorrow; that's okay, it's just that the cleaners can't go in until tomorrow now," said Carol.

"That's okay; I won't be long, Dad," she said, and he nodded.

Kate went up in the lift, and Carol spoke to David. "She is a lovely girl; I only met her yesterday, but she was obviously on a mission to find someone, and she has found her?" asked Carol.

"Father; she's my daughter. Oh, Carol, she said something about a money card for the public telephone; do you sell them here at all?" asked David.

"Yes, we do; they are over there. If you want to get one, I can charge it up here for you, and then you can add to it at any newsagents," said Carol, taking it off David to put the money on it for him.

Kate returned with her things and her suitcase; she had checked to see if she had everything before she left the room. She had already removed her rubbish from the fish and chips the night before.

"Got everything?" asked David.

"Yeah, I guess so. I did a clean sweep of the room, Carol. I had already made my bed, so that's it. I have my paperwork in my case, copies, just in case, you know?" said Kate.

"So, Carol, what do I owe you, then?" asked Kate.

"Oh, nothing; I sorted it out; you have paid in full," said Carol.

"But how come?" asked Kate.

"Well, you're the first client we have had who has made their own bed. I can get housekeeping in a little while and one of the staff owes me a favour. Anyway, have a great trip in London, and hopefully we may bump into each other again, you never know," said Carol.

"Bye bye, and take care of yourself, Kate, and your newfound family," said Carol. Kate thanked her, and she and her dad left the hotel.

When they got back home, Pam had already sorted out Kate's room; they had an extension on the ground floor, which they had turned into a chill-out room, and above that, they had converted into a spare room, which they used when Phil's family stayed. David took her suitcase upstairs. Kate followed and put her stuff away. When she came back downstairs, Pam had made tea for everyone.

Kate was already feeling like part of the family. "Is there a call box that I can use? I need to call Jess and my American mum to let them know that I got here and that I have found you all. Is that okay? They would have been worried; I was so concerned about finding any of you that I had forgotten to call them to let them know I was safe, which sounds ridiculous to whom I am talking to," said Kate.

"No, Kate. It's okay, really. We want them to know that you are safe here with us. Talk to Jess and your mum. Put their minds at rest," said Chrissy.

"Would you like me to take you to the phone box, Kate?" asked Kim.

"If you don't mind, Kim?" asked Kate.

"Not at all; I offered," replied Kim.

"We can go after dinner, if you like," Kim suggested.

"Yes, please," said Kate.

Chrissy had made a chicken casserole, and Kate told them she had fish and chips for the first time in a long time, because Chrissy and David knew they had it quite a lot when Kate was small. Kim and Kate went up the road to the phone box. Kim stayed outside because she didn't want Kate to think she was listening.

"Hi, Jess. Jess, it's me, Kate, yes. Yes, I got here safely. Yes, I did go on my mission, which is turning into an adventure. Jess, I found them—our parents, our biological parents—well, family, really. I know, but we also have two more sisters, and the youngest one, Kelly, is your double. Even when she smiles, no, I am not trying to make you feel bad; I just wanted to let you know. How is Mama? Yes, she is all right. Oh, she's sleeping. Will you tell her that I am sorry? I missed her, and yes, you will always be my sister. We just have two more, but that's fine. How's Coco and Gramps? Oh, okay, give them my love, won't you? Love you, Jess. Yes, I will take care. Oh, how is Chestnut? Oh, good. Yes, take care too, love you!" said Kate, ending the phone call.

Kate put the phone down and came out of the telephone box. "Everything okay, Kate?" asked Kim.

"Yes, she's okay. She was upset when I was coming and also angry because she felt I had lost one father, and then I was on the hunt for a second one, which isn't the case. I had no idea I would find you all. I am just grateful I have it. Come on, let's go home," said Kate.

When they got in, the family was aware that Kate was still on American time, so they suggested that she go to bed early. They had a big day the following day. They had talked about what they were going to do when Kate and Kim went to the telephone box, not to be talking behind her back, but they wanted to get some sort of strategy for the following day, which they had; they would tell Kate in the morning, once she had a decent night's sleep. The following day, they all got up early. Kate wasn't used to a house full of people on a daily basis, so they all had a cup of tea to get started, then they filled her in on what was going to happen. They had a fry-up, and Kate had some toast. She still had to get used to the English cooking.

She had a lovely soaking bath when everyone was up. David had arranged a couple of days off with Mark, who was very understanding. As David worked in the market, it got around like wildfire about Kate's return, but Mark told everyone to back off for a few days. Also, Chrissy wanted to contact the police and social services, but first she wanted to deal with Edie, which was about what it was. She had gotten out of the bath, sorted herself out, and got ready. They were leaving for about 1.30; lunch was at 12.00. They had two cars, so Chrissy, David, Kate, and Kim went in one car, and Pam and Phil went in the other. Joan popped in the night before Kate had gone to bed, and they had filled her in on all of the goings on and what they were going to do.

She was all for it, but she wasn't well enough to go with them, but she would wait patiently for their return with the news, good or bad. Joan knew that Edie had what was coming to her. They pulled up outside a huge building; it was about four floors up; it had huge windows; there were lifts and stairs; the bedrooms were on the ground floor for the residents; the staff had rooms upstairs, but there was also a day room where they were going to be. Pam walked to the door, pulled it open, and scanned the room. There she was, sitting in the bay window at the side. She was looking out of the window, oblivious to what was going to unfold. Pam walked in with Chrissy, David, Kate, and Kim. Phil was at the back. Pam walked up to Edie, looked straight at her, then turned her head, looked at Chrissy, Kim, David, and Phil, and then she looked straight at her and said, "Hello, Katie!"

Chapter 19

"You, Aunty Edie, it's you; oh my goodness, it was you all along!" stated Kate.

"Yes, it was me, and I am not sorry. Where were you living? America, I suppose? Considering your dad to be a Yank!" shouted Edie.

"I think you had better start at the beginning, Edie," said Pam.

Instead of being ashamed of what she had done, she was revelling in it; she told them all how she orchestrated it, what she had done, all of the planning, but also: "The times you tried to keep Jessica away from me when she was born, I would never forgive you, Pamela. You were supposed to be suckered in, but you started to get suspicious; you checked about the scan photo, yes, I took it. I took them both. I didn't want you to have them; you see, they were what I needed to give to that American couple; that's why I needed to go to the hospital. I needed a photo of Jessica, but they wouldn't let me in. Then, when they brought her home, you changed your net curtains so I couldn't see in, couldn't get a photo of her, so you were starting to suss me out, but you weren't clever enough. You were never clever, not even at school. The wool could be pulled over your eyes so easily. But, Chrissy, you weren't as dumb as your mother; you cottoned on," Edie said, looking squarely at Chrissy, who had her mouth wide open.

"Why, Aunty Edie, why did you do it?" asked Chrissy. Edie ignored her; this was her moment—her moment to shine, to get it all out, to gloat about something she had done to all of them.

"It was so easy. Those three idiots nearly got caught because of their stupidity; they weren't very clever with their prints. The police went over that place like a fine toothcomb, but nowadays, I would have been caught a lot earlier, but that stupid lot, they hadn't a clue."

"Aunty Edie, who were the people pretending to be the social workers and the policemen?" asked Chrissy finally.

"Oh, those are the three idiots I told you about just now. That was the cleaner who worked in the council offices, her and the boyfriend and her mate. Anything to make a few extra quid, they took the identities of the social workers but put them back the next day. Katie bit one of them on the arm; she wanted to hit her once they got her to that house, but I told her not to lay a hand on those girls," she admitted, looking at Katie.

"You had a good grip. Years later, I bumped into her, and she still had a scar on her arm," she told them. *Good*, thought Chrissy. "They were easy to fool in those days, the police," Edie continued, as if none of the people were standing and sitting in front of her.

They didn't matter, but they didn't as far as she was concerned. Edie told them everything she had done, and she went into great detail about how she did it.

"Pam and Phil walking around like they owned the place, their two perfect little girls, well, their time would come, and yes, I would strike; I did. They would be so proud of me to have upset their little applecart, their happy family," Edie scoffed.

"Who would have been proud, Edie?" asked Phil.

"Oh, you wouldn't understand, Arnold; you never understood me; you always thought I was jealous of our Pam and Phil, but I wasn't. I wanted a life with my own baby, but that didn't happen; Mother and Father took care of that, didn't they, Arnold!" Edie said.

She didn't seem to know who she was talking to. Pam bent down to be on her level. "What did Mother and Father do, Edie? What did they take care of?" asked Pam, absolutely dumbstruck by what she was hearing and what her parents took care of for Edie.

"They took him, didn't they? My boy. They took him away when he was a few days old, my boy Charlie; my beautiful boy Charlie had blonde, curly, fine hair; he had blue eyes, bright blue eyes that sparkled. They did; they hurt me; they didn't care; they said that fifteen was too young, that I was too young, but I wasn't. I could have looked after him. I know I could, Mum," Edie said.

There were tears in her eyes, full of tears. For the first time in her life, Pam saw her big sister alive—really alive; she had never seen such emotion from her. "Mum, I would have made a good mum, wouldn't I?" she asked, looking at Pam fully in the face.

"Yes, you would have made a great mum, Edie, so is that why you arranged all of this to upset Pam and Phil?" asked Pam.

"Yes, them with their perfect lives, their perfect girls, oh, and Katie's eyes, Mum, they were just like Charlie's; he had beautiful eyes that glistened," Edie replied.

"Edie, what happened to Charlie once Mother and Father sorted it out?" asked Pam.

Edie looked at her again, as though she were Pam. "He found me, Pam, just before Arnold died five years ago, before I ended up in this place; he's happy, and I am a granny; he has two children; he has a daughter called Edie, his little boy, Ernest, Ernie, really. Oh, she showed me a photo of them; they are beautiful. But Arnold didn't know who he was, but he left us alone to talk for hours. I miss him; he has been to see me here a couple of times because I had to tell him where I was going to be. He's coming to see me at Christmas; he wants me to spend Christmas with his family for the first time, so that's what I am going to do," she added.

She looked around the room again and looked past everyone; she had no idea who they were. "Pam, I am tired now; can I go and rest?" asked Edie.

"Oh, and can you tell all of these people they have to leave now? I'm not dying yet, they can come and get me when the time is right, but I'm fine just now, to have Christmas with my family first," said Edie.

Pam called one of the staff and said that Edie wanted to go to her room now, and if she could speak with the manager of the home. She just wanted to ask her a few things. The member of staff took Edie back to her room and let the manager know that Pam wanted a word.

"Mrs—"

"Er, call me Pam!" interrupted Pam.

"What can I do for you?" she asked Pam.

"I need to clear a few things up. Now, I know Edie has Alzheimer's, but what does she remember? Is it the past or recently?" asked Pam.

"Edie remembers as much as possible about the past and nothing of now; she does have her moments, but lately, she has been remembering stuff from a few years ago—someone called Chrissy, her daughter Kim, another little baby that she wasn't allowed to see, and also someone called Katie," she told Pam.

"How long has she been like this, because she never used to remember me?" asked Pam.

"Pam, she has been steadily getting worse for the last six months or so, but sometimes she talks about Charlie. Do you know who Charlie is?" asked the manager.

"Well, yes, she gave that little story, shall we say, a little while ago, which is part of this problem. Edie has just confessed to a crime she arranged seventeen years ago, which has broken my family apart, so even though we had the police and social services involved—"

The manager interrupted her by putting up her hand. "There is no way at all whatsoever that Edie could face the police, the courts. Pam, she is not stable enough to do so; what she has told you here today, she may not remember tomorrow," said the manager.

"Well, she sung like a canary today, revelling in all of the details, but as you say tomorrow, she may not remember, so where do we go from here, then?" asked Pam.

"Well, you can't really inform the police now as she will not be a good or reliable witness for any of this, and anyway, by the time this goes to trial, she may have died, Pam. I am afraid we will end this here. Now before I go, is there anything else?" asked the manager.

"Yes, she mentioned Charlie; she said he was her son, and he came here to see her. Is this true? Has Charlie been here to see his birth mother?" asked Pam.

"I am afraid I have no idea, and if I did, Pam, I couldn't tell you due to patient confidentiality. If you weren't here when he arrived or visited her, we cannot tell you. I am sorry, but that is company policy," said the manager, getting up to move Pam out of her office.

"So, my sister can arrange for my granddaughters to be abducted and taken halfway across the world, and there is nothing we can do because she has Alzheimer's and she's in a home?" asked Pam, totally bewildered.

"Mrs Pam, I am sorry this conversation has ended, and there is no more that can be done about this, so if you would be so kind and leave my office, and as Edie has gone to bed, if you and your party could leave, that would be great," she added, pushing Pam slowly out of her office.

When Pam left, she beckoned for the others to come and follow her. "So, what happens now, Pam?" asked Phil.

Pam looked so angry. "You're not going to believe this; because she has Alzheimer's, even if she gets prosecuted for it, she can't be touched; she can't go to court because of her not being a reliable witness. Can you believe this?

She's got away with it; even if we go to the police, they can't do anything. Let's go home. We can't talk about this here; I am too mad here; I might end up doing something I will regret!" Pam was nearly shouting now.

Phil held onto her; they all left the building; they went into the two cars and made their way home. As they pulled up, Pam got out of the car. "Phil, go in, take the others in, and put the kettle in. I think we need to get someone else to hear all of this!" said Pam, walking away from the car.

"Come on, everyone, we need to all have a stiff drink!" said Phil.

"Granddad, I don't think I can; I'm not old enough; I'm twenty-one," said Kate.

"Yes, but you're in England; our age limit for alcohol consumption is eighteen; you will need either a scotch or brandy. Here you are," said Phil, pouring a large brandy for Kate.

Chrissy and David joined her on the sofa, and Pam returned with Joan. "So you must be Katie; you are just beautiful, the same as the last time I saw you being run up the road; you have just gotten older," said Joan, giving her a kiss on the cheek.

"I thought Joan needed to hear this. Kate, your grandaunt Joan was there when it all happened. I just filled her in on a little bit of it," said Pam.

"I still can't believe that Edie would do this," said Joan.

"Can't you really, Joan? Because we can. If you heard her, she was gloating at what she had done, how she did it, and then why she had done it. Have you ever heard your parents talking about Edie having a baby boy when she was fifteen?" asked Phil.

"No, I remember hearing snippets of conversations, but in those days, Phil, you didn't ask questions, you just got on with your life; let the adults speak. Children were seen and not heard in those days; they couldn't join in with conversations like we do with the girls. It just wasn't the done thing. Now can you go to the police?" asked Joan.

"We can do it, but it won't do any good. Because she's in a home and has Alzheimer's, she won't be a reliable witness in court. She has well and truly gotten away with it!" said Pam.

"But what about the authorities? Can't they be prosecuted or something? You know, if they had this happen all under their noses, it would make them look kinda stupid," said Kate.

"It's worth a try, you know, Phil?" she asked, looking around the room for some support.

"Pam's right; if you take on the police or social services, you may not get the result you want, or you could end up being watched by them, you know, looking at everything you do," said Phil.

"But someone has to be accountable, Grandma," said Kate.

"Yes, they do, Kate, but this is England; the justice system is so different from the USA law," said Phil.

"Chrissy, David, you have both been awfully quiet. Is there anything you wanted to say about all of this, because it was all of you who went through this?" said Pam, looking at Kate.

"Do you know what, Mum, is the audacity of her. She just admitted it all as if it were a joke. It was our family, our daughters; she had them taken away, then handed them over to some people, without a thought for us or our feelings," said Chrissy.

"She didn't care about them or us; she was jealous; she is now and always been a bitter, twisted old woman; now I understand why she did it; she didn't want us to be happy because she had lost her happiness years ago, but that still doesn't excuse what she did; I hate her, and I hope she has a terrible, painful death; and no, I won't be going to her funeral when she dies; she's not worth it; she's a horrible person. No wonder Arnold died when he did; he must have had enough of her for years; probably glad for some peace wherever he is," Chrissy told them.

Everyone downed their drinks. Kate wasn't used to brandy; she had only really had wine, but she thought she could get used to it. David picked up his jacket and left the house. "David, where are you going?" asked Chrissy, following him.

"Chrissy, go back inside; it's cold out; I need some air!" he told her.

She closed the door again, sat down next to Kate, and held onto her hand. "I am so sorry, Kate. This must be awful for you. Hearing all of this, we knew between us what happened, but I didn't expect her to just spill it all out like that, but sensitivity was never her strong point," said Chrissy.

"At least I now know who has been haunting my dreams for years; it was Aunty Edie chasing me all over the place. I would wake up in a cold sweat, and Daddy would always come and comfort me; he had no idea either," said Kate.

"So, she caused you grief even once you left here—a nightmare woman," said Phil.

"Do you mind if I get some air? I won't be long," she told them.

She got her handbag and went out the front door. "Do you think she's coming back, Mum?" asked Chrissy.

"Chrissy, she has just heard what her grandaunt had done to her and her sister. Can you really blame her sister for not wanting to come back here? She doesn't know us or any of this, and I think, for now, that's the best way, honestly, love," added Pam.

***

"Can I speak to Chief Inspector Prince, please?" said David. The desk sergeant left reception and returned.

"She will be with you in a moment, David!" he said.

"Thank you!" David replied.

The chief inspector came through the door and called David into a side room. "Hello, David, how are you, and what is important for you to have to call for me?" she asked him.

"Well, you said if anything happened regarding our situation, get in contact. Now I know Officer Milton has retired—"

She interrupted him. "He died a couple of years ago, stress of the job, I suppose," she added.

"Oh, sorry, I didn't realise, anyway." David explained everything that happened in the last couple of days, about Kate, Edie, and what they were told at the care home.

"Is there anything that can be done? Even though Edie is cuckoo, she won't be able to take the stand if she goes to court with this; I mean, will she even be arrested?" asked David.

The CI cleared her throat. "Now, David, I am really sorry, but the care manager is correct; if we can arrest Edie, at her age and with her condition, there will be nothing that we can do; it won't stand up in court; the care home will not help you with that because Edie is their patient and they are being paid for her being there; they are not going to help you put her in prison. Plus, as they said, she could die before that; it will leave you nothing but solicitor's fees and a hell of a lot of stress for all parties involved. Even the social workers. The girls are adults now; there won't be a thing any of you can do. But what would I suggest?" she added.

"You get to know your daughters again, even though they lived in another country and time has passed; they are both still alive. Make some new memories with them. You all have to heal. Once you lost them, which you did, you added to your numbers, now you have them back again, you may need to move house. As far as Edie is concerned, there is nothing that can be done. I am sorry. But thank you for letting me know what happened. We can close the case on this," she said, as she stood up and shook him by the hand.

"Enjoy your life, David, and make lots and lots of memories; it will help you all to heal," she suggested.

David thanked her and made his way out of the station. He took a slow walk home; he didn't know what to do now, apart from going home and telling his family what he was just told. He walked silently past a telephone box with someone in it; he didn't look up; he just carried on his way home.

***

"What do you mean Coco is acting up, Jess?" said Kate.

"She wasn't too happy none, with you leaving for England to meet your English family, that's all," replied Jess.

"So, is she angry with me, then?" asked Kate.

"Yes, she is; she thinks it's ungrateful for what Mama and Daddy have done for you, but Gramps understands; he says that you need to work it out for yourself," Jess added.

"I found out today, Jess, what happened to us; we were abducted…" Her voice trailed off into the phone, and she explained everything that she had heard today from the horse's mouth. Jess, for once, was dumbstruck. She couldn't believe it. Now, she was starting to wonder if she should go to England as well and see what this family was like, especially this Aunty Edie, as she said. Before they ended their call, Kate gave Jess the home phone number so she could call her back, because it was easier than running out to the phone box every time she wanted to speak to Jess or the other way around. Kate went back home. David was explaining the situation to the family; Kim and Kelly had just gotten home too, and they were being filled in with everything.

Pam made some tea, and the phone rang. "I'll get it. Hello, who? Oh, sorry, I will just get her. Kate, phone for you," said Pam, not realising she had just spoken to her other granddaughter for the first time.

"Hello, Jess," said Kate. Chrissy's ears pricked up.

"Yes, okay, yes, that would be great, everyone. Okay, yes, that's fine. Hold on a second. I have it here. 'The Railway Lines Hotel', okay, then I will see you then. Say hello to Coco and Gramps for me and Mama," said Kate, realising who she said that in front of.

She put the phone down. "I'm sorry, Mum, but—" said Kate.

"Kate, you have two mothers, one who gave birth to you, one who raised you. I am just grateful that you had a lovely family and weren't sold as slaves to another country. You both had great lives. For that, I am truly grateful. Now who's coming and when?" asked Chrissy.

"Jess, Mama, Coco, and Gramps," said Kate.

"Who is Coco?" asked Phil.

"Oh, she's my other grandmother, but she doesn't like the word granny; she said it makes her feel old," Kate replied.

"Kate, when are they coming?" asked Chrissy.

"They have booked flights for the day after tomorrow, but they are booking a hotel because there are four of them; they didn't want to impose, but I will meet them at Heathrow, if that's okay with you guys?" she asked.

"Of course. You can; we all can if you want. Actually, that might be a bit much at first; take them to the hotel, and then we can pick you up from there; they can come as well if you want; see how the land lies," added Pam.

Pam looked at Chrissy for her approval. Chrissy nodded, then looked at David and said, yes, whatever they wanted to do. They had dinner; they chilled out the best they could, and once the girls were upstairs, Joan, who had stayed for dinner, was talking to Pam in the kitchen, asking how on earth Edie thought she had gotten away with it. "She has got away with it, Joanie; there is nothing anyone can do; my girl has only now got her daughter back, and thankfully, the other one is coming too, but she may not stay; she may want to go back, but saying that, Kate hasn't said if she's staying or going back; we just have to see what pans out over the next few days, weeks, or months, but I know one thing, I don't think our Chrissy will survive if they don't want her or David in their lives," Pam told Joan. Kate had no idea what she wanted; she was just finding the pieces of her puzzle of a life to make it fit somehow. She was looking forward to seeing Jess, Mama, Coco, and Gramps, but also hoping they wouldn't be too mad at her for doing this.

The family were already on the flight to come to England, and they were very nervous: Jess because she was meeting the family she hadn't remembered; Marnie, if it weren't for this family, she wouldn't have had her two girls; Coco and Gramps were worried that their girls wouldn't want to come back to the States with them, but they were also anxious to meet this family who had lost their daughters and Robert and Marnie to have many precious years. At first, Coco was pretty angry with Kate, but once Jess had told them some of the information Kate had told her, they wanted to see this family. She had lost Taylor as a baby, so she totally understood where this mama was coming from, her son died, and hers had been taken to another country across the world.

They soon touched down at Heathrow, and once they had gotten their luggage, they made their way to the arrivals, where Kate was waiting for them with her English mother and father. "Hiya, Jess, Mama," said Kate.

Marnie and Jess grabbed hold of Kate; even though she had only been gone for a few days, they had missed her. Then Coco and Gramps hugged Kate, while Marnie and Jess shook hands with Chrissy and David.

"Jess, Mama, Coco, and Gramps, this is Chrissy, our birth mum, Jess, and David, our birth daddy," said Kate. Jess and Marnie both hugged Chrissy, while Coco and Gramps hugged David, who in turn hugged them back.

Once everyone had hugged, Chrissy hugged Jess again, and Jess didn't seem to mind, nor did Marnie. She hadn't realised this day would come, but now she knew that she loved her girls and wanted them to be happy, but this other lady knew nothing about their lives, even when they were alive.

"Come on, let's get you back home," said Chrissy as she walked with Kate on one side and Jess on the other.

Marnie could see that this lady did not want to let them both go, and for the first time, she totally understood. David had hired a huge car; there were going to be four extra people and their luggage. He also got a driver so they could all talk on the way back. "We know you have booked a hotel; we would have made room, but we know that you would want some privacy and time for yourselves; we are nearly bulging at the seams," said David, laughing rather nervously.

"Don't worry, y'all; it's great that we could all come and meet y'all," said Gramps, not sure if he said the right thing.

"Coco, Gramps, how are Darlene, Mitch, and Ethan?" asked Kate.

"They are all just fine, a little surprised at our quick trip, but you know Darlene, she likes to be in the thick of it, but thankfully, she's busy with that salon of hers!" Gramps added.

Everyone was nervous; small talk was made, and none of them wanted to tackle any of the big stuff this early on. Once Kate's other family was settled, Chrissy and David waited for Kate to check them in and see them for a little while.

"They seem really nice, Chrissy," said David.

"Yes, they do. I am glad they have given the girls a great life, David, but I am worried that once they go back, we won't see them again," said Chrissy nervously.

"I am sure it will all be fine," said David.

Kate got back into the car. "They will come over later on. Can we come back and collect them, David?" asked Kate.

"Of course, Kate, I have hired the car for the week. I have no idea how long they will stay, but at least we can drive them around if they want to," said David.

Kate was really chuffed at how her English family was welcoming to her American family. The next day, Kate met her family at the hotel; thankfully, Carol remembered Kate when she came in. She met her family, and they were collected by David, who drove the car. They all sat down in the back and were conversing about going back home. Kate had only been in England for just under a week, and she had already felt like part of the family. David pulled up outside the house; there was plenty of room for the car. He had moved his car down by Joan's house.

"Welcome, welcome, everyone," said Chrissy, who was standing at the front door. David opened the door for Marnie and Coco, and Jess was standing behind her mother. When they got to the door, Chrissy hugged each of them and showed them inside. Kate followed at the back. Kim and Kelly were at school. They all met Pam and Phil, who were just as welcoming to them.

They also hugged everyone; they were staring at Jess, who looked a little uncomfortable, but Kate seemed to put her mind at rest. Pam had made tea; they all took a cup and sat down in their chairs. The living room was a good size, but it was nearly at full capacity with all of these extra guests. Jess sat next to her mama; Coco and Gramps sat on the sofa, and Pam, Phil, and Joan sat up at the dining room table. Once the niceties had finished, Gramps wanted to get down to business, so Pam looked at Chrissy, and Chrissy started to tell them what happened from their end before the girls were handed over to Robert and Marnie. Coco, Gramps, Marnie, and Jess sat there wide-eyed. Nobody wanted to interrupt Chrissy while she was in mid-flow. She cried a couple of times explaining, especially when Jess was a baby. Jess started to cry, and Kate held on to her.

Coco and Gramps made ooh and ahh noises in the right places. Then, once Chrissy stopped, Marnie took over and told them what happened once they got the girls. Kate knew a lot, but Marnie had filled in the gaps. Still, Coco and Gramps were astounded at what happened to these two little girls, who were now adults—well, nearly adults in their own right. A key was put in the door, and it was Kim and Kelly, who both stopped in their tracks, and so did everyone else. Kelly looked at Jess, and Jess looked at Kelly. Jess got up from the sofa and went over to Kelly and hugged her, then she turned to Kim and hugged her too.

Coco and Marnie burst into tears; they hadn't realised the impact these four girls had on each other's lives, and if Jess had any doubts about being here, they had disappeared.

Once everyone had dried their eyes, Kim and Kelly removed themselves from the sitting room. "We will be back down in a little while; you all need to hear all of this, Mum. We will be down for dinner!" said Kim.

"Chrissy, you have raised your daughters beautifully. I am so sorry this has happened to you and your family. We just need to sort out where we go from here," said Marnie.

"Marnie, I had Kate for four years and Jess for three months; you have had them the rest of their lives until now, so I don't know a solution; just there is one, and we have to find it," said Chrissy.

"Why does there have to be a compromise?" asked Kate.

"Why can't we just be one huge dysfunctional family like everyone else has?" added Jess. Coco and Gramps laughed.

"Wow, Jess, you would say that!" said Gramps. "But she does have a point," he added.

"I mean, you have your life here, we have ours in the USA, but that doesn't mean it can't work," Gramps said.

"It could do with some fine tweaking, but it could work, you know?" said Marnie.

"Let's have a think about it and see what we come up with," added Coco.

The phone rang, and Pam went to answer it. "Hello, oh yes, I remember you. Yes, okay, oh, thank you for letting me know, and you will call me in the next couple of days to confirm. Yes, okay, thank you. Bye," said Pam.

Pam looked at Joan and said, "I'm afraid Edie passed away a little while ago; she died in her sleep, so it was peaceful," said Pam, leaving the room and going upstairs.

Phil rushed after her. Kim and Kelly came down and sat with Joan. "You know what, girls, she was my biggest sister, and I hated her, especially when I saw how she was around you two; she didn't get much chance to be around these girls; there was always something, but how she had ripped this family apart, I can never forgive her," she scolded.

Marnie went over to her and said, "I know she was your sister, Joan; nothing sadly will ever change that, but I am sure she was hurting; otherwise, she wouldn't have done this, but she did. Sadly, your niece had lost her girls temporarily, but now, even though it's a few years down the line, she didn't win; she has brought two families together, who share a huge bond and always will do. I am just sorry it's taken so long for us all to get together," said Marnie.

"Chrissy, she is right; it's not good at all what she did, but look at the other end of it, we have our girls back. If they want to stay, then that's up to them. If they want to go back to America, that's up to them, but as Jess has suggested, we can all be one dysfunctional family. Edie was never a happy person, and if she thought she had won, she's wrong, because now we have a bigger family. If they all want to be part of us, then we have won like the lottery; our big family is now a huge family, and I think that is to be celebrated," said David.

"I agree with you there, David. We are here for a while, we can sort it all out, and then we can arrange for you guys to come out to us. Do you have your passports? We have horses, stables, and our daughter Darlene has a salon, for, you know, girls and women's things, what they like doing to nails and hair, and that," said Gramps.

"Also, Kate, are you going to continue with your education? You wanted to be a social worker, didn't you, or do you want to do something else instead?" asked Gramps.

"Gramps, at the moment, I think we all need to spend some time with our family and take it from there and see where we go," Kate told her grandfather.

For the first time in her life, Kate had all of her family under one roof, except her daddy, whom she really loved and lost; nobody would ever take his place.

But this was hers and Jess's second chance at being with her birth family, and she didn't want to let that go. As Jess had already said, "Why not just have a big dysfunctional family like some people do?" And for Kate, that was just fine with her; no matter how weird it would look, they were there for her and Jess.

The End